Alexei Petriv. Crown Prince of the Tsarist Consortium—though "crime lord" and "thug" would also be accurate descriptors.

Robin Hood, too, in some circles. Thorn in the side of One Gov. Pirate of the tri-system. In my office. Wanting a reading. The need to faint grew stronger. So did the feeling in my gut.

I had a terrible suspicion I was about to be made an offer I could not refuse.

PRAISE FOR THE FELICIA SEVIGNY NOVELS

"Imaginative. Fans of romance in science fiction are going to love this!"

—Kim Harrison, #1 *New York Times* bestselling author

"Cerveny's debut blends steamy sci-fi with breathless intrigue and action, all set on a far-future Earth that's equal parts fascinating and terrifying."

—Beth Cato, author of *The Clockwork Dagger* and *Breath of Earth*

"A compelling and intriguing read built on a fascinating premise. Cerveny's future world is richly drawn, and Felicia and Alexei's adventure is definitely an edge-of-your-seat ride."

—Linnea Sinclair, award-winning author of the
Dock Five Universe series

"Terrific world building and hot science fiction romance. What's not to love?"

—Sharon Lee, author of the Liaden Universe novels
with Steve Miller

"A fresh heroine pairs with a dangerous hero to confront nuanced and compelling ethical dilemmas…fast-paced, tightly plotted."

—*RT Book Reviews*

"A novel with depth…a terrific story."   —*The Qwillery*

"The perfect blend of futuristic intrigue, engrossing action, and passionate romance in a riveting adventure that will leave you hungry for more. Intensely absorbing. Emotionally satisfying."

—Amanda Bouchet, author of the Kingmaker Chronicles

By Catherine Cerveny

The Felicia Sevigny Novels
The Rule of Luck
The Chaos of Luck

THE
RULE
OF
LUCK

A FELICIA SEVIGNY NOVEL: BOOK 1

CATHERINE CERVENY

www.orbitbooks.net

Copyright © 2016 by Catherine Cerveny
Excerpt from *The Chaos of Luck* copyright © 2016 by Catherine Cerveny
Excerpt from *Six Wakes* copyright © 2017 by Mary Lafferty

Author photograph by Ash Nayler Photography
Cover design by Lisa Marie Pompilio
Cover photos by Trevillion, Shutterstock
Cover copyright © 2017 by Hachette Book Group, Inc.

Orbit
Hachette Book Group
1290 Avenue of the Americas
New York, NY 10104
orbitbooks.net

Originally published in ebook by Redhook in January 2016
First Trade Paperback Edition: November 2017

Orbit is an imprint of Hachette Book Group.
The Orbit name and logo are trademarks of Little, Brown Book Group Limited.

The publisher is not responsible for websites (or their content) that are not owned by the publisher.

The Hachette Speakers Bureau provides a wide range of authors for speaking events. To find out more, go to www.hachettespeakersbureau.com or call (866) 376-6591.

Library of Congress Control Number: 2017948500

ISBNs: 978-0-316-51056-1 (trade paperback), 978-0-316-35550-6 (ebook)

Printed in the United States of America

LSC-C

10 9 8 7 6 5 4 3 2 1

To Lily and Ellee, with all the love in the world.

I

I've always been a big fan of eyeliner. The darker, the better. Growing up, I'd heard the expression "Pretty is as pretty does" almost every day of my life—but I believe that sometimes pretty needs help. Since I've decided against tattooing my way to beauty or using gene modification, I do things the old-fashioned way. And as one of the only Tarot card readers in Nairobi, I've cultivated a certain look that is as much personal choice as mysterious mask. So the fact that I stood in the tiny bathroom of my card reading shop and scrubbed my face clean, opting for tasteful over flashy, made me feel like I'd sold out.

"All for the greater good," I mumbled, examining my nearly naked face. "I can look straitlaced and respectable for an hour. Two, tops."

A quick time check showed it was nearly seven in the morning. It made me glad I'd decided to close up shop early at two and catch some sleep on the reception room couch. At least I didn't look like complete garbage, even if my sleep was more tossing and turning than actual shut-eye.

I hightailed it to the front door. I needed to be on the other side of the city by nine sharp. To do that in an hour using the unreliable Y-Line would take all the prayers and karmic brownie points I had to spare. Maybe if I lit some incense sticks and offered a prayer for guidance... but no, no time for that.

Then I had to stop, my hand frozen in mid-reach on the way to the doorknob. Standing in the entranceway of my shop was the most beautiful man I'd ever seen. I know it's shallow to focus on looks since they are so easily bought and modified, and yet...

"I'd like a Tarot card reading, please," he said, his voice so deep, I was certain the windows rattled.

"I'm sorry, but we're closed. I can take your information and schedule an appointment for later this week." I infused my voice with as much formality as I could muster. Anything to prevent stammering like a drooling idiot in front of such a good-looking man. Even though "good-looking" barely covered it.

"This won't take long and I'm prepared to pay generously," he said, as if he'd already dropped gold notes into my account. Wonderful—arrogant enough to assume money buys everything and he thinks his time is more valuable than mine. Well, that was exactly the shot of ice water I needed to break the spell.

"I appreciate your offer, but I'm afraid you'll have to book an appointment." *Like everybody else.*

"Unfortunately, I'm leaving Nairobi today. This is my last stop before my flight. I've heard of your reputation as a card reader. My research says you're quite accurate."

And just like that, he pierced the proverbial chink in my armor. When people said they'd heard of me, I felt honor-bound to accept. If word got back to the source that I was ungracious or unobliging, I could lose business. Damn it, why had I let my receptionist, Natty, leave early? She could have dealt with this situation. Oh right, it was so I could sleep and get ready in private with no one the wiser. But why had I forgotten to lock up? I did not have time for this.

I studied him. He wore reflective sunshades that prevented me from getting the full picture, but there were still plenty of other clues to give me a sense of what I was dealing with. A well-cut carbon-gray suit and scuff-free shoes screamed gold notes and good taste. He was tall, very tall. His fashionably scruffy thick black hair brushed his suit collar and nearly met his very nicely broad shoulders. He was clean-shaven, with chiseled cheekbones and a slight tan that had to be Tru-Tan since no one exposed themselves to the sun anymore. Good tans cost a fortune. But his accent was the real giveaway. His deep voice carried a lilt that made it clear he was from the Russian Federation of Islands. In a word—money. Lots and lots of money.

But I wouldn't reschedule my appointment for all the money, contacts, or goodwill in the tri-system. I gestured toward the door, intending to walk him out. "I'm sorry, but perhaps next time you're in town."

He looked as if he hadn't the slightest intention of leaving. "If you're concerned about the time, my people can ensure you arrive at the fertility clinic before nine this morning."

I froze. "Excuse me, but that information is classified."

"And so it will remain. It would be a shame for One Gov to learn the true nature of your appointment, after all."

3

My eyes narrowed. "It's just a routine fertility consultation."

"Of course," he agreed. "I ask only for a brief reading. Surely you can spare a moment?"

I should have been both angry and terrified that he knew my plans. Hell, I hadn't even told my boyfriend, Roy! His words stopped just short of blackmail. And yet . . . I found myself intrigued, damn it. What would this Tarot reading show me? I had that odd feeling again—the one that hit deep in my gut and paid no attention to what I had lined up for the rest of the day, let alone my life. It demanded I follow through on whatever happened next. Over the years I'd learned never, and I mean *never*, to ignore that feeling no matter how pesky it might be.

He removed his sunshades and I was snared by blue eyes so intense I wondered if he had to hide them or risk turning people to stone—or women to mush. I peered closer, considering the whole package. The looks. The play of his muscles beneath his clothes when he moved. The symmetry. I wasn't sure why I hadn't caught it earlier: His MH Factor—Modified Human— was turned up high enough to scorch.

Out of my mouth came: "I can fit you in now with a short reading."

"Wonderful." He offered a smile that had no doubt removed numerous panties. Nice to know one of us was having a good time.

"I don't see many advanced-stage Modified Humans in my shop. Are you fifth generation?" My question was beyond rude. Asking about genetic modifications was worse than asking how much money someone made. But if he knew my business, I didn't see why I couldn't know his. "I heard it's less invasive to upgrade technological modifications later in life rather than opting for full pre-birth gene manipulation. The t-mods are supposed to be less expensive too."

"Perhaps it depends on how many gold notes exchange hands and how natural you want it to look," he said, noncommittally.

So there was some genetic manipulation involved. I knew it! But how much? Some people went overboard with their upgrades and the results weren't always as advertised.

I waited for more follow-up from him. Instead, the silence stretched. Okay, then. "Is there a particular aspect of your life you want to know about? Or an issue that's troubling you?"

"I'm concerned about a meeting and its success. Should I continue on my current path, or cut my losses and run? You no doubt receive many similar requests."

He was right; I'd built my business on less. I had a steady clientele including a few minor celebrities, but nothing had really launched my career. Not that I wanted to be a card reader to the stars, but I definitely wanted to ensure I never had to worry about money.

"Follow me," I said, and with those words went my last lick of common sense.

I removed the c-tex bracelet I'd put on—so that no one could accuse me of skimming the Cerebral Neural Net and faking a reading—then led him through the shop. Gentle lighting flicked on as we entered the back room. Soft music began, the automatic soundtrack set to a Mars chill funk vibe. The room was decorated with thick Venusian carpets, decadent pillows on velvet chaise lounges, and paintings of exotic Old Earth terrain and new-world Martian landscapes. Rich colors that begged to be touched—a tactile experience for the senses. Customers had certain expectations as to how a Tarot card shop on Night Alley, the most exclusive and decadent street in Nairobi, should appear. If my Russian stranger had been there the night before when business was in full swing, he would have seen my designer silk print dress and makeup just this side of too much, instead of the prim beige knee-length skirt and sky-blue blouse I now wore. I looked overdressed, conservative, and slightly out of style.

Oddly, the idea that he'd caught me this way made me feel vulnerable, like I'd allowed him to see the real me instead of the persona I wore when I cast a reading. That woman didn't care what her clients thought because she knew they were all in awe of her. In those silk dresses she was untouchable. She held their future in her hands. This stripped-down me was too exposed, too likely to get caught up in things that didn't concern her. Well, too bad. I wasn't letting a hot guy and an off-the-chart gut feeling get the best of me. What I wore now was just another disguise. After all, how could I convince the Shared Hope program's fertility Arbiter I should be allowed to have a baby if I didn't look like a respectable member of society?

"Have a seat." I directed him to one of the chaise lounges with an ornate gold-leaf table beside it. A chandelier that appeared to drip with gemstones, but were really artfully colored glass, hung overhead.

"Interesting décor," he said.

"Would you be as impressed with a rickety table and some collapsible benches?" I asked as I took the chaise across from him.

He laughed. "I suppose not. I understand the need for showmanship. At times, it can be as important as the act itself."

"Hence the décor." I gestured around us.

I smiled, so did he, and suddenly the table between us seemed ridiculously small. The feeling in my gut grew, paired now with a growing sense that this man, whoever the hell he was, held some significance for me. It hung in the air.

I took a breath to center myself and refocused on the box in the middle of the table. Whatever designs were once painted on its black lacquered wood surface had long since faded. What it contained was easily the most valuable thing I owned.

I opened the box and removed the Tarot cards. They'd been in my family for generations, dating back to a time before the Earth's axis shifted thanks to a series of massive global quakes, polar melts, and then the two wars of succession that followed. Family lore claimed they came from the Old World—an all but forgotten place that existed only in history books and on the bottom of the ocean floor.

"Since we're pressed for time, I'll do a five-card spread using only the Major Arcana," I explained. "They are the heart of the Tarot. Each card represents a different state of being. I'm forgoing a Significator since you're asking about yourself, but I want you to select five cards from the deck which represent what may or may not happen, what will prevent it from happening, why you're in this situation, what you can do to either encourage or change it, and finally, depending on the steps you take, what will happen."

As I shuffled, I fell into my usual banter where I reassured the client they were in capable hands. Its familiarity made me feel more secure. I could do this. No need to panic because I was looking into the bluest eyes I'd ever seen. Once done shuffling, I fanned out the cards, let him pick his five, then arranged and flipped them over.

I'd been doing this too long to gasp, but that was what I wanted to do. I had a bizarre affinity with this set of cards—more so than anyone in the family according to my dearly departed Granny G. In fact, the cards had bypassed two disgruntled and pissed off generations of Romani to come directly to me, per her wishes. So when I examined the cards, I never lost my smile, even though I'd cast this identical reading for myself only an hour earlier.

I've always believed that things happen for a reason, and when the universe taps you on the shoulder, you pay attention. This was the equivalent of the universe punching me in the face.

He leaned forward. "What does it mean?"

"This is the Emperor, reversed." I pointed to the first card. "You have goals, but waste energy on pointless things that get in the way. You have the will and strength to fight, but aren't using those gifts properly. Next, the Moon. You want to shape events, not be shaped by them. You need to learn to read what's happening around you and act accordingly. However, you also need caution. You have hidden enemies who've yet to reveal themselves. The third card is the Falling Tower. It's the destruction of everything you've built because of your own misunderstanding and lack of judgment. Your bad choices may have put you in a situation where you could lose everything."

The man laughed. It didn't sound forced nor did he look worried, but at the same time, I could tell something was going on in his head. "So far it appears I shouldn't have gotten out of bed this morning."

"It's not all bad," I said consolingly. "Fourth is the Lovers.

It could mean attraction or love, but given the other cards, it appears to be a partnership and mutual commitment. This connection will help you overcome your difficulties and further your control of the events. Lastly, the Judgment. It represents the end of an old life, and the beginning of a new one. It's a radical change, but one you will need if you are to overcome your situation."

When I looked up, he was gazing at me with such an intent expression that I worried I'd offended him. Well, I didn't have time to couch the reading in the prettiest of terms; he got what he got. He had to smarten up or he'd lose everything. Sadly, the same applied to me as well. Quickly, I swept the cards back into their box.

"I hope you found it useful."

"Very. I appreciate you making the time to see me."

He was still looking at me. I mean, *really* looking. Looking at me the way a man did when he wondered how a woman looked naked or was considering ways to get her naked. I wondered if he was thinking about the Lovers. Or maybe I was the one thinking that? My throat went dry. I hadn't been studied like that in a long time and it felt better than it should. Even if I didn't have an active MH Factor, I was no slouch. My almost-black hair reached mid-back, my olive skin held tones of Old World ancestry, and I could make my green eyes pop by dressing in shades of blue-green. My figure and height also fit One Gov's genetic specification guidelines, hence putting me in the Goldilocks zone: just right.

No, enough of this. What was I thinking? I had a boyfriend. I had plans for the future. In an hour, my whole world could change. And yet...

I stood. He stood with me. Even in my metal-clad high-heeled boots, my eyes were barely level with his shoulder. I felt feminine in ways I hadn't in years. The air felt charged with potential. My gut jerked again, reminding me to act before the moment disappeared. What the hell did it want me to do? Jump him? Rip his clothes off?

He held out his hand. I shook it. It swallowed mine. "Thank you, Felicia. I know how I need to conduct my future affairs now."

I froze when he said my name. Not that him knowing it was a surprise; it was how he'd said it. If I tried to describe it I'd sound crazy. He said it like he knew me. Or, had made it his business to know me. Or, planned on knowing me so well, I would some-day learn what his body pressed against mine would actually feel like.

I flushed and released his hand as if it burned. "Feel free to leave your payment on the way out."

He laughed and a bolt of heat shot through me. "As I said earlier, my people can ensure you make your appointment at the clinic if you're concerned about time."

Again, I should have been terrified. If he contacted One Gov, getting arrested would be the least of my problems. Yet I had the oddest feeling that whatever this stranger knew, he'd keep it to himself. Still, I had to make some sort of a token protest, didn't I? "My private schedule is just that—private. I understand your investigating my flat-file avatar on the CN-net. Many clients do and access is always open. However, any personal information I've logged is off-limits. I would appreci-ate it if you left my shop now."

He seemed amused instead of angry. "My apologies. I'm glad

to have made your acquaintance. Hopefully, we will have other dealings in the future."

Gut feeling be damned, I sincerely hoped not. However, I must not have managed to school my expression well enough since he added, "Despite what you may believe, the future isn't decided yet. There are always gray areas left to explore."

He turned on his heel to leave. Bemused, I followed. Outside, I found two personal bodyguards—all muscle and matching suits. They fell into step behind him as he continued down the sidewalk to the street. I saw four more musclemen at either end of the block, and a helicon hovering overhead in the dull gray sky. Street-side were two flight-limos ready for takeoff, one with its windows down. I could see the pilot in front while in back sat a gorgeous redhead. My mouth fell open. I know it did—just open and flapping in the breeze.

He paused before he climbed inside the first flight-limo. "Ms. Sevigny, you'll find my payment inside, as well as my halo should you need to get in touch. Your reputation is well deserved. Feel free to use me as a reference."

With that, he got into the flight-limo. I saw the redhead attempt to climb onto his lap and watched him push her away before the windows rolled up. The security detail ducked into the second flight-limo as the helicon zipped away. In a few seconds, the street was empty.

I ran back inside. On the reception desk was a blue chip wafer used to transfer funds between locked CN-net accounts. It was old tech, the kind used by people who didn't have direct CN-net t-mods. People like me. I tapped its face and the readout displayed an obscene amount of money. I charged seventy gold notes a reading. The readout said ten thousand—very near to the amount that had been in the savings account I'd recently decimated. I almost fainted. Beside the chip was the promised halo. Like the blue chip, it was also old tech. I touched it and watched the name unfurl in bold script.

So I'd been right about the accent. I knew the name. Who didn't? I'd just never seen his face. He rarely surfaced in public, and when he did, he came and went like smoke.

Alexei Petriv. Crown Prince of the Tsarist Consortium—though "crime lord" and "thug" would also be accurate descriptors. Robin Hood too, in some circles. Thorn in the side of One Gov. Pirate of the tri-system. In my office. Wanting a reading. The need to faint grew stronger. So did the feeling in my gut.

I had a terrible suspicion I was about to be made an offer I could not refuse.

2

'm not sure how long I stood in the doorway to my shop feeling slightly unhinged while the c-tex bracelet shimmered and vibrated on the reception desk. No doubt it was Roy, checking in. I picked it up, tapped the screen, and the holo popped up.

Sure enough, Roy's image appeared. His sandy-blond hair was in desperate need of trimming, as usual. Conventionally cute, his appearance fell within One Gov specs—tallish, broad-shouldered, decent build, nice brown eyes. He always seemed worried and concerned about me, a trait I'd once thought adorable. Lately it made me wonder why he never loosened up. Then again, working undercover for the MPLE (Mars Planetary Law Enforcement), or on the Earth-to-Mars drug trafficking cases he took on, would give anyone reason to worry. Today he looked annoyed, which was also, unfortunately, normal. He hated that a face-chat shim with me meant using an antiquated charm-tex bracelet rather than a direct synapse hookup to the Cerebral Neural net. He claimed I was the only person he knew who wasn't chipped. He was probably right; my family had severe tech phobia. But even if I wanted One Gov–sponsored free tech modifications, or t-mods as they were known, it was too late. The first implants had to be done before puberty. And if I was bitter about missing out on the advantages that came with the upgrades...well, there was no point crying over what I couldn't change.

"Hey, babe. Still at the shop at this hour? You're usually finishing up when the rest of the city is just starting. Thought you'd be home by now." He made the last part a question.

"Just leaving. I had a last-minute walk-in I couldn't ignore."

He snorted. "Figures. You work too hard." In the background I saw various buildings, but not enough to pinpoint his location. Somewhere in the city center.

"I have to if I want this shop to succeed. You know my family will be the first to say 'I told you so' if there's even a whiff of failure."

He cracked a wide grin. "True. I've experienced the Sevigny clan's displeasure firsthand. Not something I'd care to repeat."

My family loathed Roy. Never mind their inherent suspicion of anything law-enforcement related; they also felt he wasn't good enough for me. Sometimes, I agreed. Other times, being with him felt safer than throwing my heart out there for anyone to stomp on. Mine had already been stomped on once. I didn't need a repeat performance. "I have a couple errands to run, so don't worry if you can't reach me. After that, I'm crashing for the rest of the day. I should be home by noon."

"I hope your idiot business partner hasn't gotten you into something sketchy."

"If Charlie Zero needs me to do something that benefits the shop, I'll do it."

He made a dismissive grunt. "Hey, I'm not shimming to fight. I'm just reminding you about date night. It's your turn to pick the place."

I almost swore out loud. Roy and I had aligned our schedules so we'd have a night off together every two weeks. That was tonight, and I'd completely forgotten. "Already picked," I lied. "Just sit back and be surprised."

"Looking forward to it, babe. Sorry, gotta go. Just got a ping from headquarters. I'll shim when I'm free. Love you."

"Love you back." I broke the link without waiting for a reply. Now I had to worry about date night on top of everything else! Fuck. It was almost funny—Alexei Petriv, a complete stranger, knew my plans better than Roy did. It didn't say much for my current state of affairs.

I slapped the bracelet back on my arm. Immediately, it fluttered. Gods, now what? No face-chat shim this time—only a voice and a cloudy screen. Apparently my appointment had just decided to reach out to me. A tingle of fear raced up my spine.

"Have you hailed the Y-Line?" I was asked without preamble.

I swallowed. I couldn't tell if the voice was male or female. "Yes, I'm leaving now."

"Location code?"

I scrambled to find the information for the pod I'd booked. "Launchpad 16. Pod 2176."

I could hear a beep in the background. "Location confirmed. Courtyard Office Center. Mayfair Fertility Clinic. Meeting time, nine hundred hours. Payment transfer received."

I said nothing. The payment had dissolved my savings. Then I recalled the gold notes from Alexei Petriv. If my gut had feet, it would have kicked me.

"Worried?" the voice asked.

"Of course not. I do stuff like this every day before breakfast." Well, truthfully, with the shop hours I kept, my breakfast tended to be everyone else's dinner time, but that was no one's business but my own.

"I assure you nothing will go wrong."

"So you've said, but none of this guarantees the blacklisted status will be wiped from my fertility record."

"Now seems a little late for doubt, don't you think?"

The voice was right, and I wasn't naïve. I might be scared, but my future with Roy depended on the next few hours. "I know, but I've never broken the law before. Well, not like this anyway."

"Trust me: all will go according to plan." The voice cut out.

I sighed, letting the air out slowly so I wouldn't hyperventilate. I had the basics of the plan, but none of its specifics. What I knew included making an appointment at the local One Gov–controlled fertility clinic to speak with an Arbiter—standard practice for anyone with a fertility dispute. However, how I'd alter the record to remove my blacklisted status was beyond me. It was risky, but if I wanted to participate in the Shared Hope program, this was my only choice.

When One Gov came to power during the Dark Times, they followed through on their promise of prosperity and equality for all. Unfortunately, some felt their legislation turned humanity into a flock of sheep. Maybe four hundred years ago we'd needed that direction. But now, One Gov took issue with those they felt weren't well-behaved citizens, and it often meant losing out on things like career choice, housing selection, or calorie-consumption allocation. Or in my case—for reasons I didn't know—access to the Shared Hope program.

The Shared Hope program meant one child per couple, with One Gov providing subsidies until the child turned eighteen, then guaranteed living space and full citizenship rights until death. And nowadays, death was further away than ever, thanks to the Renew treatments. Unfortunately, long life put a strain on resources. So did the fact that once the last of the ice caps had melted and water covered many of the most populated cities on Earth, humanity had been left scrambling for what space remained. And based on the history I'd read, that scrambling hadn't been pretty once countries begun closing their borders to refugees fleeing the rising waters. My family was damn lucky to end up in Nairobi thanks to my great-grandparents' foresight and Granny G's Tarot cards. They'd moved to high-altitude, cash-strapped Kenya before the mass exodus happened throughout the world. Many others lost everything, including the ability to keep going in the face of such disaster.

The Shared Hope program was the only thing keeping the world in balance. It was open to everyone and ensured valuable genetic material wasn't lost, while keeping population growth in check. If you didn't like it, then you were welcome to try your luck elsewhere in the tri-system. If you were rich enough, moving to Mars was a viable option. And if you were desperate enough, you could try life on Venus. Full colonization of Venus had begun only in the last hundred years, and there were many who felt a trip to hell might be more fun.

It all made perfect, rational sense, except why should I be blacklisted without explanation? What happened to One Gov's stance on equality for all? I should be eligible to have a baby just like any other woman. And after today, I would be. The Tarot had said as much, and the cards never lied. Alexei Petriv might believe the future still had gray areas, but the feeling in my gut said otherwise. This was my last chance and I had to take it.

Ah, hell. The day I took advice from Russian gangsters was no doubt the day my world ended. Hurriedly I grabbed my belongings, locked the shop, and rushed out to meet my future.

———◆———

The Y-Line was Nairobi's answer to mass transit. Unfortunately, "A brilliant design with poor execution" was the most complimentary thing anyone could say. Whatever the case, the grids were always clogged, the pods never arrived on time, and you rarely got exactly what you ordered. I'd ordered my pod twenty minutes ago and there was still no sign of it.

I waited on the crowded launch platform, tapping an anxious toe and peering up at a gritty-looking sky that promised rain. The first wet season of the year loomed around the corner, so we'd be inundated for the next month. Luckily, my shop on Night Alley lay outside the city's flood plain. It was also one of the nicer streets in the city. Though today, the city cleaners had yet to hose away the latest gang signs inked on the cracked gray tile around me. Hopefully my pod would be in better condition. Sometimes pods came filled with garbage, vomit, excrement, or worse. The auto-cleaners handled that, but the system existed in a constant state of breakdown. Even if I got a half-decent pod, it might be double-booked—which was how I'd met Roy. It wasn't immediate attraction, but he made me laugh and wore me down until I agreed to see him again. At that point in my life, funny and sweet overrode passionate. I'd already lived through a relationship with all the passion I could handle—the kind where you don't think you can even breathe if he's not with you. So when it ended and I realized I had to keep on breathing regardless, I decided I didn't want more of that in my future.

My toe tapping increased. I couldn't seem to calm myself. Worse, I couldn't pinpoint the reason for my anxiety. Was it the man I'd just left, the situation I was about to hurl myself into, or the man waiting at home? Maybe all three.

I tried analyzing my reaction to Alexei Petriv. It wasn't entirely sexual, more like a feeling that being with him, or at least following where he led, was the right thing to do. Others in my family had similar experiences—moments where we stood at a crossroads and instinct told us which way to choose. We talked about them whenever we got together at family functions, rare events now as we became more scattered throughout the tri-system. We found the instinct varied in strength and regularity, depending on the situation or person. To us, the gut feeling was just another sense letting us see the world a little more clearly when making decisions. You never knew how it would turn out, but it always felt like the most appropriate action at the time. But with Petriv...the feeling had been extreme. Then, the identical card reading...I'd done what I could to appease my gut feeling, yet somehow it felt like I'd made the wrong decision. Maybe I should have confronted him instead of letting him walk away. Well, what did it matter now? I'd probably never see him again.

A few more minutes of toe tapping before a swarm of pods arrived at the open-air receiving bay. I always thought the pods looked like gigantic gray sperm, tails cocked in the air to connect with the magnetic slide overhead. The fact that I traveled to and from work each day inside a giant sperm pod while I had no control over my own fertility issues was the sort of irony that could make a girl tear her hair out. Somewhere in the tri-system, I bet a team of design engineers secretly giggled up their sleeves.

I caught my name flashing across the scroll above the door of the last pod, and my c-tex bracelet fluttered. People around me groaned—a tired-looking mother with a squalling two-year-old; a businessman who seemed frazzled and out of time; a couple of Net spacers no doubt late for the next space elevator launch, their matching One Gov uniforms giving them away. I sympathized; I'd experienced more than my fair share of late pods.

I skittered across the slippery tiles to the pod and settled into one of the four seats. The door closed with a gentle sucking sound and I turned to set my belongings on the empty seat beside me. Except, it wasn't empty.

I jumped, swore, and barely missed cracking my head on the low ceiling. "What the hell...? I didn't even see you!"

The occupant looked at me. "Perhaps you should pay more attention to your surroundings."

Wonderful. I'd been up to my neck in cocky attitudes for hours. No reason the trend shouldn't continue. "You're my contact?"

"So it would seem."

I regarded my traveling companion while I fought for calm. Male. Or, possibly female. Sometimes they appeared so gender neutral I honestly couldn't tell. Fair-skinned with graying black hair cut in an unflattering bowl shape, weak and unremarkable facial features—odd, given that beauty was commonplace, preferred, and available at any price. Yet, this face was also forgettable. Combine the bland face with a green-gray pantsuit that could be either business or casual depending on the light and you wouldn't be able to describe this person ten minutes after meeting them.

"Ms. Sevigny, I presume? You may call me Mr. Pennyworth."

Well, that settled that. Maybe. "Hopefully it will be nice to have met you, Mr. Pennyworth." *Depending how the day goes*, I added silently.

"I've taken the liberty of putting the pod recording system on an infinity loop so we may discuss our business privately. With you not being directly linked to the CN-net, relaying information is challenging."

I shrugged. "My family doesn't trust t-mods. My great-grandmother called them bad juju. Besides, they're a liability in my line of work. If I can sift all the net-dump into my head with an e-blink, who's going to believe anything I tell them when I do a reading?"

"But you must concede it comes in handy. Otherwise, you wouldn't rely on that antiquated tech." His eyes drifted to the silver charm-tex bracelet clipped around my left wrist. Once it had been the height of technology. Now my tech-med struggled to keep it operational.

"I'll give you that one. A girl's got to keep up somehow." I frowned, not sure I could continue making small talk with a thief and con man who held my entire future in his hands. "So when do I get the details on this secret plan that's cost me a small fortune?"

Mr. Pennyworth held up an empty glass cylinder the size of my thumb, secured with a gray screw-on cap, and smiled. His teeth were feral looking, and I revised my earlier opinion—you might forget most of Mr. Pennyworth, but you would never forget his teeth.

"Of course," he said. "Here it is."

I could only imagine the look on my face. "Must be one hell of a tube."

"If I thought you were an idiot, I would never have agreed to this shell game. It's smart-matter in an inert gaseous state. It reacts when exposed to air."

My eyes widened. "How? I want to fix my blacklisted status, not kill the Arbiter."

Mr. Pennyworth merely blinked. "This will induce an effect similar to mild intoxication, without impairing mental or physical faculties. Anyone exposed becomes susceptible to suggestion. The effect will last twenty minutes, which should be long enough to convince the Arbiter to modify your status."

"Can't you just snipe in and change my status? Isn't that what you do?"

Again, the long blink. "I do all manner of things. And yes, I could snipe in if I had enough time and you enough gold notes. Unfortunately, that isn't the case. One Gov's echo-wall is virtually impenetrable. If I did snipe in, I'd have to nullify their AI queenmind. One wrong move would have a drone army replicating the data and laying so many false trails, we'd both be en route to a Phobos penal cell before I found my way back. This way, the changes will be legitimate in the database, made by the one responsible for them—the Arbiter."

I had to admit it was elegant, but my gut wasn't reassuring me of success one way or the other. "We're breathing the same air. Won't I be infected too?"

"Yes. It will enable you to make your points all the more

convincing. I suspect it will be a veritable Isis Falls of tears and sob stories from all parties by the time we're done."

I refused to rise to the sarcastic bait. Isis Falls is the highest and most dramatic waterfall on Venus's Ishtar Terra. It was even said that its crushing power could produce diamonds. Impressive, but nobody needed that kind of grief.

"What about you? If we all lose our minds, how does that help me?"

Mr. Pennyworth did the blink thing again; the man was a wealth of physical tics. It made me wonder what sort of t-mods he had. No doubt my tech-hating family would lose their minds if they met him—*not that they ever would*, I reflected.

"I won't be affected."

"It's nice you're so confident."

"I am," he said, and left it at that.

"What if we don't get a human Arbiter? I requested one, but I've put in so many petitions in the past, we may only get AI access. How—?"

"Ms. Sevigny, nothing is foolproof. What we're doing today is a criminal act. Its very nature lends itself to complications. I can't provide the guarantees you want. However, I find it disconcerting you're calling my professionalism into question. I predict a high degree of success, provided you follow my instructions."

"I know. I just need this to work. If it doesn't..." My voice trailed. I couldn't think about failure. "It has to work."

Sometimes I wondered about the convoluted road that had brought me to this moment. Normal people didn't consort with criminals. Desperation was the usual mode of transport. And thanks to my family's seedier connections, Mr. Pennyworth had dropped into my life. I shouldn't have needed him if things had taken their regular course. If I hadn't fallen desperately in love five years ago with a man I thought held my future in his hands, I'd never have applied for a reproduction approval permit—the gut feeling again, prodding me to act on impulses I normally wouldn't consider. Without that push, I wouldn't have learned about my blacklisted fertility status. I also wouldn't have lost the man I thought loved me unconditionally.

"You and the father-elect must be very desperate to have a child."

I almost laughed, but bitterness and despair wouldn't let me. "The father-elect doesn't know I'm here."

"Ah, I see. He wants a child and you're afraid he'll leave you if he knows you're blacklisted."

At that, I did laugh since it was better than crying. Were the problems I thought so secret and painful as common as dirt? "Actually, that's already happened once. I'm just trying to keep history from repeating itself."

"I'm not sure I understand."

Gods, did I have to explain everything? "I was with someone before. We were young and in love, and I thought he was *the one*. I had this feeling he might propose so I checked on my fertility status, just to see what I needed to do to get the fertility inhibitor removed. Kids are important in my family and I wanted to be ready. That's when I found out about my blacklisted status. I told him because I didn't think it would matter. After all, we loved each other. I assumed we'd figure it out together. Instead, he left me. End of story."

"What happened to him?" came the relentless follow-up question.

"He found someone less complicated than me. They moved overseas, to Bolivia I think. They had a baby. A boy. He's two now." I surreptitiously swiped at my eyes. Only one tear. That had to be some kind of world record.

A beat of silence, then: "So you're lying to your current partner?"

I glared at Mr. Pennyworth. "Not that it's any of your damn business, but I don't even know if he likes kids. I just feel like I have this sword hanging over my head and I want it gone. I don't want to be that lost, pathetic woman who gets left all over again because she isn't good enough. I want control over my own life. Maybe I don't want a baby right this second, but I want the option there if I choose it. Right now, for reasons I don't understand, I'm blacklisted. So if he brings up the subject, do I say, 'Sorry, I forgot to mention I can't apply for the permit to have the fertility inhibitor removed because some official somewhere decided I'm ineligible to reproduce'? I already know that won't go over well."

"So you're doing this for the potential in the relationship."

"I don't think I need to answer any more questions, unless it's somehow going to help you do a better job," I said pointedly.

That earned me another long blink. "Forgive me for asking."

What I refused to say, and he had no right to know, was I also had unresolved parental issues. Everyone thinks they can do a better job than their own parents. Yet what happens when your mother dies, and your father disappears because you look too much like your mother and that resemblance upsets him and makes him insane? How does that twist a person's insides, stirring up a murky soup of resentment but also determination to fix the past?

We fell into an uncomfortable silence and I spent the remainder of the ride watching the cityscape drift by out the tinted window, taking in the lush greenery mixed carefully with urban sprawl. Seeing the city like this, it was easy to appreciate why Nairobi was considered the Star of the East and the gateway to Africa. Thanks to its altitude the city had managed to flourish in spite of itself. Somehow Nairobi had been spared the worst of the chaos and magically came out ahead of the disasters that rocked the rest of the planet.

As if sensing my discomfort, the Y-Line stalled only twice, for a total delay time of ten minutes. Thank the gods for small mercies. The pod soon docked on the other side of the city and we disembarked onto the gray-tiled receiving platform in Karen. It was noticeably dirtier than the launch platform in my division. Ironically, Karen wasn't far from the largest slum in the country, if not the entire continent. Reclamation projects for the Kibera slum came and went every time it was an election year. Local One Gov representatives always promised to clean it up, threw gold notes at the problem, and then gave up when the residents resisted change. We could build a space port on the Moon, put a sunshade around Venus, alter its rotation and give it a moon, anchor two space elevators to the Earth, and even terraform Mars, but we couldn't touch a thousand-year-old slum in the heart of Africa. I wasn't sure if that was something to be proud of or not.

The Mayfair Fertility Clinic lay on the slum's outskirts, not far from the Y-Line platform. Mr. Pennyworth and I waded through people going about their business, drooping a little in the humidity. Well, I drooped. Mr. Pennyworth soldiered on as if the weather was a nonissue. This man was a creepy enigma I didn't want to unravel.

Along the pedestrian walkway the storefronts grew shabbier. Not shabby-chic or whatever trendy look the CN-net target ads told us were popular, but downright shabby. People loitered with nothing better to do than stand with their hands in their pockets. Refuse piles grew, their stink perfuming the air. We passed the occasional gang sign, and anyone with business in the area hurried about it at a brisk clip, except Mr. Pennyworth. If he rushed, it was only to keep pace with me.

The clinic stood out from a row of decrepit office buildings. It was oddly cathedral-like, loaded with Gothic spires and stained-glass windows. It might have looked ethereal and beautiful if it wasn't so out of place. Bars on the windows, armed guards, and the electrified barbed-wire fence around the perimeter didn't help. Ridiculous One Gov spending at its all-time best—put one of the most significant government facilities near one of the seediest areas of the city, pretty it up, then watch the fireworks. It was a miracle the place still stood.

We approached the first checkpoint at the outer gate of barbed wire and mesh. I felt a trickle of nervous sweat roll down my back. I needn't have worried, as Mr. Pennyworth rested his left hand on the graphic interface and One Gov's citizen chip at the base of his thumb gave up his basic statistics and the nature of the appointment. The interface beeped, and he walked through the gate. I followed, relieved I didn't have to do the same. I wasn't chipped, not physically at any rate. I could blame my family for that mess too. My citizen chip was in my c-tex bracelet. It made life damned inconvenient whenever I ran the c-tex over the reader and the thing refused to scan. I probably wasted more time trying to get my wrist to beep than I did sleeping and eating put together.

We continued along the sidewalk and up the clinic's front steps. The breeze picked up, bringing Kibera's stench with it. I fought not to gag at the odor of raw sewage while my eyes started watering.

"You're doing well, Ms. Sevigny," Mr. Pennyworth murmured. "Only two more checkpoints, then the Arbiter."

I nodded, swiping my eyes. I looked back to those still outside the gate. The crowd appeared to be gathering steam. I could hear singing and saw a few e-thought posters waving. Hardly a surprise. Someone was always protesting in front of these facilities. The Shared Hope program was so significant and vital to the survival of the human race, the only way anyone got real media attention was to protest at a fertility clinic somewhere in the tri-system. Even if it was something trivial like a problem with sanitation pickups or a street name being changed, fertility clinics were always the protesters' target. It didn't make sense, but it got you attention.

"Think they'll close the clinic for the day?" I nodded in the protesters' direction. "I'd prefer we didn't have to do this more than once. My nerves couldn't handle it."

"You also couldn't afford it. I anticipate everything will go according to plan."

I took what reassurance I could from his vague answer and we passed the next two checkpoints with ease. Pennyworth's chip was scanned again, and we waded through a weapons detector that checked for organic compounds and tech assaults. I worried about the smart-matter, but when no alarms sounded I offered up a silent prayer of thanks to any god paying attention.

Finally, we were met by a human who escorted us to the

Arbiter's office. Arbiter Black was the name we were given. It meant nothing, merely a pseudonym. I'd been through this process enough to know the drill.

Our guide was a tall young woman, reed-thin with ebony skin and luxurious black hair that bounced around her shoulders. Strong white teeth and blue eyes gave her a startling beauty you didn't often see even in this age of genetic modifications. She seemed wasted in such a worthless One Gov outpost. Mr. Pennyworth watched her ass sway as she walked.

"Third generation MH Factor, Mars model," he commented to me. "Good work, but better exists. The center of gravity is off. It will be corrected in the next batch."

Okay, so there was more to his gaze than I thought. At least it gave me something else to think about besides my own predicament.

We followed Miss Third Generation with Gravitational Problems down the dull gray hall. It was as if only the cathedral shell remained. The rest of the building had been gutted and filled with ugliness. Not even the stained-glass windows brightened the hall.

She led us to an office and told us to wait. It was empty except for a long table, a data portal, and a handful of mismatched chairs. I sat in the first chair, which was hard, lumpy, and the color of faded rust. I turned to Mr. Pennyworth, but he held up a finger and shook his head. No, the gesture said. Not yet.

So I sat in helpless suspension, hands in my lap, not sure what to do and afraid to talk. Mr. Pennyworth did the same, although he looked more at ease.

An immeasurable amount of time later, the door opened.

My eyes slid from Mr. Pennyworth to Arbiter Black. Male. Caucasian. Still looked like he had true youth. My spirits drooped. Damn. Why couldn't I have gotten a woman? A man wouldn't feel the same emotional tug of my sob story. I glanced at Mr. Pennyworth and saw the glass cylinder in his left hand. When I looked again, the cylinder had vanished. How long would it take until I felt the smart-matter's effects? How would I behave?

"Sorry to keep you waiting," the Arbiter said as he shook the hand Mr. Pennyworth extended, then reached out to me. I stood to meet him halfway. His voice was pleasant, and he smiled at us. That had to be a good sign. He seemed nice. Maybe this would work. If I spun my story right, with the extra push from the drug...maybe...

I'm not sure what should have happened next. One moment, I reached for Arbiter Black's hand. The next, I felt a sharp twinge in my gut telling me to forget the hand and move away. So I did. And after that...

The wall exploded. Not just the office. The whole building. Through a haze of dust and smoke, I could see clear to the outside.

Arbiter Black was gone.

Well, not gone, given the red smear on the far wall and the scattering of bricks and mortar. Just not among the living anymore.

I backed away, hand shaking, my whole body shaking, in fact, and a scream locked in my throat. I tripped on an overturned chair and came to rest on the edge of the conference table, which had been blown clean across the room. I couldn't hear anything except the ringing in my ears. I covered and uncovered them with my hands, as if that would help. There were people rushing through the hole in the wall. Some looked like they were screaming, but I couldn't hear them. Then I noticed security outside, subduing the crowd. Oh gods, the crowd...the protesters...It took a moment for my brain to piece it together in a way that made sense. The protesters must have decided to do more than voice their displeasure. They bombed the clinic.

Movement caught my attention. Mr. Pennyworth rose from where he'd crouched on the floor. Aside from a dusting of rubble, he looked unscathed. He hesitated. Looked at me. Looked at the hole. And proceeded to make his way toward it. He was *leaving* me?

"Where the hell are you going?" I could barely hear myself though I was probably screaming. I saw his lips move, but couldn't make out the words. "What? I can't hear you!" Dust coated my throat when I breathed, and I fought to keep from coughing.

He took the handful of steps in my direction and stopped so close his lips brushed my left ear. "One Gov hooahs are on their way, and only one of us needs to take the fall. My advice is to cover your eyes and shut your mouth when they spray the gas."

Then he moved in a burst of speed, using the dust and confusion for cover as he slipped through the hole in the wall. Panicked, I shuffled after him, but my rubbery legs failed and I hit the debris-littered floor. I tried crawling, pulling myself with desperate arms when my legs wouldn't work. Beneath me, I felt the ground thundering, and when I reached the shattered office wall, I understood why.

A squad of hooahs charged down the corridor, dressed in

full riot gear—face shields, gas masks, and body armor. They looked like shiny black beetles walking on their hind legs, ready to crush anything in their path. But the only thing in their path was me.

When I saw the gas cannon pointed in my direction, I screamed. It fired, I ducked, and it hit the wall over my right shoulder. A cloud of smoke later, I did the only thing I could—took Mr. Pennyworth's advice and prayed to all the gods in the pantheon that I lived long enough to explain everything to Roy so he could arrest that freak's androgynous ass.

I caught a whiff of the sickly sweet gas. Immediately, my body seized. My thoughts just sort of…stopped. Panic doubled. Tripled. I wasn't even sure I knew my own name.

"What do we do with this one?" I heard someone say. Couldn't tell if they were male or female, but they must have been leaning right over me if I could hear them. "She's not with the scum outside."

"Filters detected a foreign substance while in the Arbiter's presence. That makes her garbage too. Let's see how much she likes twenty years in a Soweto East holding pen shoveling out shit pockets."

That was when they did…something. Rolled me over. Pressed the base of my skull. And darkness descended in a smothering wave.

3

It's never pleasant to wake up somewhere and not know where you are. It's doubly unpleasant to realize you're exactly where you thought you'd be—jail.

I sat up on a lumpy cot, wincing at the kinks in my neck and back. I tried stretching, but the pinching sensation I felt made it impossible. I'd never been someone who suffered from muscle cramps, so this was a horrible first. At least it seemed like my hearing had returned, so I thanked the gods for that tiny blessing. As I massaged my aches, I studied my cell.

Overhead, dim halogen bulbs struggled to illuminate the gloom. The walls were a dingy gray concrete covered with stains and scuffmarks, the air chill and dank. There were no windows, not even in the solid metal door. Eight cots were attached to the walls. Mine contained a mattress zipped into a white plastic case that crinkled when I moved.

I lay on a bottom cot, close to the door. Across from me, a dented metal bowl jutted from the wall—the toilet. In two of the ceiling's corners hung cameras, meaning should I use the bowl, it would be a fine show for anyone watching. It was also antiquated tech. Cameras were essentially obsolete given how easily images could be manipulated. I shifted uncomfortably, bladder straining, and sighed. Someone would be getting a show today.

I scurried to the bowl on shaky legs. I won't bother describing the treasure I found inside as I made my own deposit. When I reached for the handle with my bare foot—gods, not my hand—horror filled me when the thing wouldn't flush. Shake, rattle the handle…Nothing. I swore and hurried back to my cot, away from the offending bowl.

That's when I felt eyes on me. On the cot above mine was my cellmate.

The woman smirked. "Nice floor act. Can't wait for the encore."

She looked older than me by several years, meaning for some reason she hadn't kept up her basic Renew treatments. Dirty brown hair pulled into a messy topknot, thin to the point of unhealthy, dark skin turned sickly green under the harsh florescent lights—she had a hardness to her face that came from years of anger, drugs, and general neglect. I'd seen that look before—I'm a Tarot card reader; I've witnessed plenty of desperation.

"I'm not here for your entertainment." I hovered in the center of the cell. I didn't want to go back to my cot; it would put me too close to the woman. Then again, I didn't want to spend any more time near the bowl. "You going to keep watching?"

"No point. Show's over." She cackled with laughter. "First time in the pit? You was out so long, I thought the guards'd tag you DNR."

"DNR?"

"'Do Not Resuscitate.' Then again, the dead don't pee." She laughed again before offering an appraising look. "They let you shim anyone yet? If not, better think long and hard, sweetie. Whoever you shim's gonna need magic up his sleeve to get you outta the pit."

I looked at my wrist. No c-tex bracelet. Fear gripped me as the woman's words sank in. I was in prison gods only knew where, in a situation I might never escape. My shady, tech-adverse family could do nothing. Hell, half of them would be arrested themselves if they so much as sent helpful thoughts in my direction. I took a breath. I'd have to shim Roy. He had MPLE contacts he could use. Yet even if he bailed me out, how could I explain the magnitude of what I'd done? I'd been caught in the presence of an Arbiter with a foreign substance. Damn that Mr. Pennyworth. How could I have known others had tried the same gambit before and that sensors existed to scan for it? Never mind that I hadn't even had a chance to do anything—One Gov's justice system would automatically consider me guilty.

"Funny, you being in here," the woman continued, oblivious to my dilemma. "You seem the type who could afford decent t-mods."

That made me pause. "I don't understand."

She made a vague gesture with her thin arm. "Only regulars get the pit. One Gov doesn't have to worry we'll go all chain-breaker with some jumped up MH Factor for strength and smash our way out. They got a special hate on for our particular kinda rat—spooks. Can't read 'em. Can't control 'em. And we all know One Gov loves control."

"Except for spooks," I echoed.

"Grifters outside the CN-net," she clarified.

"I know what they are," I snapped, then crossed to the other side of the cell away from the woman. She was right; I was a spook. Hell, I came from a long line of spooks. The Romani were a rare breed who patently refused to enroll in the free technological modifications and genetic enhancement birthing programs One Gov sponsored. Private sector adjustments were frowned on as well. My family was determined to remain pure human, whatever the hell that meant anymore. Still, that's what made my card reading abilities so unique. No gimmicks or cheats; the talent I had to predict future events was real. My family had always been proud they hadn't gone tech. Now I wondered if we were all suspected criminals on a watch list somewhere.

I looked up at her. "You're a spook too?"

"Only one in the group."

"What group is that?"

"At the clinic. Who you think arranged that mess? Every group needs a mix of tech and spook, depending on the job. Funny you're in here though, given who I seen you with. Always thought he had more finesse."

"Saw me with?"

"When you walked into the clinic, I seen you at the first checkpoint. You and your friend."

That brought me up short. She knew Mr. Pennyworth? That seemed unlikely. Then again, what did I know about the world of organized crime? I knew enough to land my ass in jail and not much else. I wanted to curse my own stupidity. Yet my gut said something was going on and I needed to figure it out in a hurry.

"How exactly do you know my...friend?"

"Nairobi's a small town. Your friend's got lots of aliases. Not sure who he really is, but I know who he's linked with and it goes way up the food chain. That's a chain I'd like a piece of."

I looked at the camera, then back to the woman. She returned the stare, unblinking yet somehow anxious. Her body language spoke nonchalance as she reclined on her cot, but the way her eyes darted to the cameras said something else.

"You're a plant, aren't you?" I guessed. "They want him, I'm the most obvious connection, and you're here to figure out what I know. They're probably feeding you enough information to draw me in and get me to confide in you, thinking I'll be so concerned with protecting my own neck, I'll give them anything they want." I looked up at the camera, addressing my comments to the unseen viewer. "Considering how I've just been screwed over, I'd like to help, but I have no idea who he is. Until this morning, or yesterday, or whatever day this is, I'd never seen him before. I can't even tell you the chain of connection between us because I don't know how anyone got in touch with him either. Further, I'm guessing you've seized my client list, my business partner's name, and are looking up my family members to decide who to arrest next. Have fun with that. It'll be like beating your head against a brick wall. Now, do I get my shim or not?"

Even though I didn't have a clue what I was talking about, I sounded incredibly savvy to my own ears—like I breezed through these types of situations every day.

The woman's head cocked to the side as if listening to something I couldn't hear. Then she leaped up from her cot, padded barefoot across the cell, and pounded on the door.

"Spook don't got the goods. Let me out!" she yelled as she pounded.

Nothing happened. She pounded harder, but the door didn't open. She pounded a good five minutes to no avail. At first I thought it was a show for my benefit, designed to manipulate me. But as I watched, I revised my opinion. Her frustration grew and her pounding became more desperate. She tore out an earpiece and hurled it to the floor.

"Let me out!" she screeched until she was in tears, wild with rage. She whirled on me. "Tell 'em what they want! Tell 'em about the hopped-up t-mod git. I gotta get out! I can't take more time in here! Do it, or... or I'll hurt you real good!"

She looked like she could too, but what could I offer when I didn't know anything? She advanced. I stood my ground and held up a hand as if that might stop her. "If you touch me, any confession I make will be suspect. No one will believe what I say if it's under duress. Beating me up may make you feel better, but you won't get out any quicker and you'll have another charge against you. Besides—if you really were one of the protesters—we were at the clinic for the same reason."

"What reason's that?" she asked suspiciously, voice hoarse.

"We're both women denied a basic right for reasons we don't understand, and we want that to stop." I wasn't sure on that last part, but it couldn't hurt to appeal to some sort of sisterhood if it kept her from punching my lights out. Besides, I felt sorry for her. "You picked your way to protest. I picked mine."

"Give 'em the name," she said, but sounded less certain. "I got people waiting on me. I can't spend time in here again. The hooahs got no problem forgetting you're here. Don't care much about basic human rights either. No such thing as that in here."

38

"I don't have anything to tell," I lied. Maybe I'd feel different if left in the pit a few more days, but right now, all I had were my convictions, and I'd stand by them.

The woman went back to her cot. She looked defeated, but I still wondered if it was an act. I sat on one of the vacant cots, tucked my legs against my chest again, and rested my chin on my knees. The woman lay down and sighed, rubbing a hand over her forehead, then her belly. The plastic mattress cover crinkled under her.

"My baby died," she said softly. "Real good boy. Always did what he was told. Giving everybody kisses. So happy and smiling. Knew he'd grow up to be somebody. Just knew it. Then one day... there was an accident. He died. I held him, bleeding all over me... I wanted to die too." She stopped and I heard a sniff followed by a rattling cough and the ever-present mattress crinkle. "I applied to have another baby, but they wouldn't let me. Said I'd used my start-up allocation on my boy. Not enough resources left. Not enough calories. Shared Hope's only one baby for every two people. Wasn't allowed to have another. Then, they stopped my Renew treatments 'cuz they said I was becoming a problem. Figured I may as well give 'em what they expected."

Another sniff and cough. No more words came after that. Nothing but the sound of her muffled cries. Maybe she was playing me, but no one could manufacture that kind of grief—the kind that wore a person right down to the bone until nothing remained.

"I'm blacklisted," I said after she'd settled a little. "I'm not allowed to have a baby and I don't know why. I've appealed a dozen times and haven't gotten anywhere, so I thought I could get around the system, but... guess not."

"Then I'm sorry I tried to make you give up a name."

"And I'm sorry they tried to use your pain in this way."

"You're the Night Alley card reader, ain't ya? Bet you didn't see this coming." She laughed humorlessly. "My name's Bahati. Means 'luck' in Swahili. Guess I didn't see it either."

I thought of my last card reading and the identical reading I'd gotten for Petriv. I shivered. "I think I did. I just didn't know it until it was too late."

"If we ever get out of here, I'll get you to tell my fortune. Maybe it'll help me figure what to do next."

"It'll be on the house," I agreed lavishly. To be honest, I doubted we'd see each other again, but to say those words and give voice to the implications would be too terrible.

I crept back to my original cot under hers and we each huddled on our mattresses in the chilly cell. I hated to be so callous, but I didn't have time to dwell on Bahati's plight. Her story was sad and I raged at the injustice, but I couldn't help but circle back to my own problem.

At some point, I fell back asleep. It was a restless sleep, full of awful dreams I couldn't remember. I woke up huddled in a fetal position, my arms tucked against my chest for warmth. It took me a moment to realize I was alone. While I slept, Bahati had been removed. I hated to think her story was a lie used to manipulate me, but I'd probably never know.

I sat up with slow, aching movements. There was no way to know how much time had passed, but I was dizzy, I had to pee again, and my stomach cramped with hunger. Worse, I was so thirsty, my tongue felt swollen in my mouth. I leaned forward and let my legs dangle over the cot's edge, in no hurry to use that disgusting toilet a second time.

Then the cell door opened. My eyes burned at the sudden brightness. I flinched and covered my face.

"You are free to go," said a heavily accented male voice I didn't recognize. "The charges have been dropped."

I paused, face still covered, thinking. Charges dropped? But I was guilty! I couldn't imagine any court in the tri-system would find me otherwise and yet…Roy must have pulled off a miracle. It was the only logical explanation. Maybe when he realized I was missing he'd put out feelers and tracked me down. That didn't quite make sense, but I didn't care. I just wanted the hell out in case someone realized they'd made a clerical error and changed their mind.

I slipped from the cot, one hand shielding my eyes as I hobbled barefoot out the door. It closed behind me with the click of an electronic lock. We progressed down a long corridor. The harsh overhead light showed a collection of gray doors, identical to the one I'd just left. I heard faint shouts from behind each. It made me curious, but now wasn't the time.

As my eyes adjusted, I glanced up at the One Gov officer, or "hooah," was the derogatory term. Young male, dark skinned, dressed in the standard One Gov uniform of gray pants and shirt, insignia crest featuring a yellow sun and three white dots to represent the tri-system of Mars, Earth, and Venus over his left breast, a black beret on his head. Around his waist hung a regulation sidearm, a Sudanese mind spring that could stun the tech quiet in any t-mod, and a decorative dagger that was more for local custom than practical use.

We eventually reached the end of the hall and another door. Outside was probably a prisoner-processing center I'd have to deal with before my release. Gods, I could only imagine the questions they'd ask, and I was fresh out of lies.

I heard another lock click and the door swung open. The hooah pushed me inside when I hesitated, and I found myself in a large white room filled with rows of desk terminals. Each was occupied by a waxy-skinned and glassy-eyed search jockey. Their desks were empty save for their gracefully folded hands. Their minds were wired into the AI queenmind, processing data. They spoke rapidly in gibberish, as if giving voice to the queenmind's internal processes. This couldn't be right. Why was I being paraded through such secretive, high-scale tech? Why not take me out front?

At the end of the room was a door that led into a tiny antechamber. Inside was a low table where my personal effects lay in a heap. With little fanfare, the hooah directed me to pick them up: my c-tex bracelet, a pair of sapphire earrings I'd bought when I first opened my shop on Night Alley, my belt and velvet boots with their metal-clad heels, and a handbag whose contents seemed intact. I rushed to put myself back together, not even taking the time to check my bracelet. When I finished, the hooah opened another door and shoved me out into the waiting sunlight. The door thudded closed behind me.

I stood blinking owlishly in the warm, slightly muggy— I checked my c-tex for the timewatch—mid-morning haze. What the hell? I'd been thrust outside without being questioned, processed, or interrogated. The whole situation was so incongruous that I couldn't figure out what to do with myself next. I'd expected to see Roy, or have a guard sit with me...or something. Instead, I found myself in a deserted back alley, surrounded by garbage bins and shanties with rusted metal roofs. Shit. I'd be rolled in no time.

Then I saw a flight-limo parked not far from where I stood.

The windows were tinted, but it didn't take a genius to figure it out. It wasn't like Nairobi was overflowing with flight-limos.

I watched as a burly bodyguard climbed from the cockpit, stepped around the limo, and pushed the door release. He stood to the side in traditional guard pose—bulging arms folded across his chest, impassive face, wraparound shades. He was tall, fair-skinned with a blond crew cut, and his shoulders alone were so massive they appeared to be wrestling his black suit jacket for dominance. He probably had a boosted MH Factor for strength and could have smashed out of the pit without a moment's hesitation. In Bahati's words: a true chain-breaker.

In a seamless gliding motion, the limo door folded back into itself. Although it seemed the stupidest thing in the world, I stepped forward to get a better look inside.

Alexei Petriv. Surprise, surprise.

"Please get in, Ms. Sevigny. I suspect you've had a trying day and we have much to discuss." He gestured to the seat beside him.

"You arranged for my release?"

"I'm also your ride. You were very expensive. A planet's ransom in bribes."

He'd bribed the prison hooahs? Was that even possible? Now was clearly not the best time to ask, and to be honest, my mind was refusing to process any more information, but I couldn't help myself.

"Not that I'm ungrateful, but why are you here? How did you even know?"

"I've had my eye on a few dodgy connections. I believe you were entangled with one of them. I felt I owed you a bit of help."

Mr. Pennyworth! It made an odd kind of sense. Bad guys all know each other, right? Petriv must have learned what had happened and bailed me out because of the Tarot card reading. It was the only thing connecting us.

"You were lucky you weren't killed during the bomb blast. Others were. It made the tri-system news. One Gov wants someone to pin this on," he continued, blue eyes meeting mine.

I blanched and felt the world swim around me. I had to reach out and grab the side of the flight-limo to keep from fainting.

"I convinced them you weren't the party they were looking for."

"I had nothing to do with it," I whispered.

"I know, although it took some persuasive negotiation to convince them to overlook the smart-matter."

Again I cursed Pennyworth. Had he known it would give us away? I filed the thought to puzzle over later.

"I appreciate that," I said with all the sincerity I could muster. "I'll pay you back somehow. I . . . I can return your payment for the card reading. It was too much anyway."

"Keep it." He waved a hand dismissively. "Your services were worth every gold note. I'd be willing to pay that and more for future readings. But if you would kindly step inside, I'd like to get out of here and discuss another arrangement with you."

My gut twisted. I'm surprised I didn't throw up. The feelings I'd had at my shop were nothing compared to this. My gut wanted me to jump into the limo, his lap, whatever he wanted.

"What kind of arrangement?"

"I have a business proposition concerning someone in whom we share a mutual interest."

I swore under my breath, though I'm sure he heard. Was this the slippery slope to organized crime? I owed him now.

"Who is it?"

"Monique Vaillancourt."

I blinked first, thrown. "She's dead."

"You're certain of that?"

"I have documentation proving it."

"All forgeries. Ms. Vaillancourt is very much alive. Get in. We'll discuss it over lunch."

The way he said it made me shiver, and not in a good way. "But she can't be alive. If she was, she would never...You're lying."

"Hardly. I rarely lie to beautiful women."

That jolted me. I rolled my eyes. He may have bribed me out of jail, but he could shove flattery up his ass. "I call bullshit on that one. I look like crap right now."

He laughed. "Get in, Ms. Sevigny. This is business—nothing more. I've helped you out of your situation. Now I would like your help in exchange. Should you say no after hearing my proposal, our paths will never cross again."

"Monique Vaillancourt is dead. No one can help you."

He merely looked at me, serious now. Under the weight of that gaze, I faltered, afraid. Afraid of what he knew, what I didn't, and what it all meant.

"Please get in, Ms. Sevigny. Time is passing."

So I got in the flight-limo. What else could I do? After all, Monique Vaillancourt was my mother.

4

Having never been in a flight-limo before, I wasn't sure what to expect. Queasiness—yes. Maybe some vertigo. But they had to be safe, considering the rich and famous zoomed everywhere in them. Those same rich and famous were also the only ones who could afford them—the lunar refined HE-3 jet fuel that powered flight-limos cost a small fortune. I slid in and took the cool leather seat facing Petriv rather than the one beside him. A moment later, we were off and I felt all the discomfort I could have wished for. However, it had little to do with seeing the streets rush by through the tinted windows. No, the nervousness, anxiety, and queasiness I felt were all thanks to the man sitting across from me.

"You must be anxious to check your c-tex." He flicked a casual hand to my bracelet. "Your friends and family are no doubt worried about you. It's been over twenty-four hours since your arrest."

A whole day? I felt sick at the thought. My fingers itched with the desire to tap the bracelet, but I didn't want him spying on my personal interactions. He knew enough about me; I wasn't going to give him more fuel. "I'll tell them later I had a new client who wanted complete privacy. It will annoy them, but they'll get over it." Except maybe Roy. He was going to be pissed. I wasn't sure I could even lie creatively enough to save myself from that fight. "I want to discuss what you mentioned outside. I assume that's why you tracked me down in the first place."

Another smile, another view of those perfect white teeth. "I'm not saying the reading wasn't accurate, but you are correct: your card reading skills weren't my primary reason."

"What proof do you have she's alive? Where is she? What's your proposal? I doubt your end goal is a touching family reunion."

"That's more questions than a simple limo ride will allow for—comfort and the cost of HE-3 notwithstanding. As I said, let's discuss this over lunch."

"I can't afford the extra calorie consumption points," I said, hedging. "I'm almost at One Gov's allocation limit. I'd hate to cut back on milk next month."

He waved it away as if it was nothing. "Lunch will be off the record."

Wow. He bailed me out of the pit *and* could get around calorie restrictions? I knew more than a few people who would kill for the luxury of being able to eat whatever they wanted, when they wanted, without worrying about point deductions the following month. I fought to look unimpressed.

"You'll need to do better than a free lunch."

"You're not the least bit curious about your mother's whereabouts?"

"I didn't say that, but I also don't know if you're telling the truth. I may read the Tarot and look for answers in the cards, but some questions are better left unanswered. If she wants to be dead, she has her reasons. I'll listen to your proposal and take the lunch, but I'm not promising anything more." Not what I wanted to say, but I refused to give him the upper hand.

"Something to drink?" He pushed a button on the console on his left. A compartment opened in the seat beside him, sliding up to reveal numerous crystal decanters. "Would you care for some water?"

"No, thank you."

"Are you sure?" He poured himself a drink from one of the many decanters. The liquid sloshing into the glass was slow torture for my bladder and parched throat.

Ah, hell. "I need to use the bathroom. Can you stop somewhere so I can pee?"

Petriv's chuckle turned into a full-blown laugh. It made me want to both slap him and run my fingers through his thick, black hair. I pressed my hands into my lap instead.

"Glad you find me so amusing," I said, sounding grumpier than I'd intended. "I assume you'd have pulled through a night in a holding cell like a champ?"

"Ah, Ms. Sevigny, I've done my own stint of time and I know it's unpleasant." He pressed the button beside him again and the minibar disappeared. Another button press and a speaker buzzed to life. A flurry of Russian followed. I frowned. Learning Russian had never been a priority. My Swahili was passable, I knew most of the Old World languages, such as French, Spanish, and Italian since they helped in my Tarot studies, and I was working on conquering Mandarin since I had many Chinese clients. But I'd never bothered with Russian. Now I regretted the lapse.

"What did you say?" I asked. A second later, I felt the flight-limo change course. "Where are we going?"

"It's a restaurant I frequent whenever I'm in Nairobi. It's out of our way, but I enjoy it. It's called the Kremlin. Maybe you've heard of it?"

I had, and always thought the name pretentious. The Kremlin was located in Little Russia, in the city's northeast section, a part of Nairobi I rarely visited. After the Big One in 2459 that shook apart much of southern Asia and the devastating North American quakes in '61 and '65, along with the rising waters from the polar melt, anyone who could fled to cities in the world's highest elevations before countries closed their borders. Nairobi was one of them, along with Lhasa in Tibet, La Paz in Bolivia, Santa Fe in what was once the United States of America, and several others. But what was once Russia had been almost completely destroyed. That was the beginning of the Earth's infamous Dark Times. Billions died in the two global conflicts that followed. Entire swaths of land vanished from the map. Living space and arable land came at a premium, until One Gov eventually came to power out of the chaos. Kenya's population exploded as refugees flooded its borders. Many of those refugees came from northern Russia, which had long since disappeared under the rising waters. In fact, outside of what was left of the Motherland, Nairobi boasted one of the highest concentrations of Russians in the world. I didn't have anything against Little Russia in general, but they did things their own way. Most of those ways tended to be violent, scary, and made the CN-net news flashes on a regular basis.

I frowned. "No chance of going somewhere closer to my part of town?"

He smiled. "Where's the fun in that, *dorogaya moya*?"

My frown grew. "No Russian. I want to understand every word spoken to me."

"Of course. I apologize."

"I enjoy learning new languages. Just not in the back of a flight-limo." Shit, that sounded like flirting.

"It means 'my dear.'"

"Thanks. I'll file that away for future reference." Gods, I wanted to smack myself. Time to refocus on the most important thing. "You said you have proof my mother is alive. Show me."

"Check your bracelet." He waved in the direction of my hand. I edged away from him. While the flight-limo was roomy, our knees brushed as we sat facing each other. Every move he made brought him into my personal space, the same way it had at my shop. I also remembered the rush of heat I'd felt then, so I made sure to keep my legs as far away from his as I could.

I tapped my bracelet and scrolled through my messages. More than two dozen filled the holo pop-up. Lots from work and friends wondering, then *demanding* to know where I was. Each shim sounded more desperate. I also counted eight from Roy. I groaned, imagining the fight we'd have.

"Something wrong?" Petriv asked, watching me.

"I'll sort it out later," I muttered, rubbing my free hand over my eyes. He had no business asking about my personal life, even if he seemed to know more about it than I did.

I jumped to Petriv's message, the last on the screen. A picture opened. Its date stamp showed two months ago, although that could be altered. Anything could be changed if you knew how.

Again, as if he had a hardwire right to my brain, Petriv said,

"That is a true image. I will have it certified by a pixel-wizard of your choosing if you like."

A face dominated the shot; the background was blurry. Thanks to the Renew treatments everyone started at age twenty-five, aging slowed significantly. With enough money, you could upgrade beyond the basic One Gov programs and in theory remain perpetually young. I'd promptly started the program when I turned twenty-five six months ago, and as a present to myself, splurged for whatever I could afford. Still, no one lived forever, and time eventually made an appearance somewhere, such as a weary look around the eyes. Seen too much, lived too hard...whatever. It sounded clichéd, but it was true. This woman had that look. There was a directness in those green eyes that came only with time and experience. Pale blond hair was piled atop her head. Full lips. Smooth, creamy skin. High cheekbones. She was gorgeous, and you would never know her true age. Most significantly, however, if not for my darker coloring from my father's side, we looked so much alike we could have been sisters.

My wrist dropped. The image disappeared. My other hand pressed against my mouth and I gasped softy through my fingers. I had seen pictures of my mother before, back when she'd been with my father. She'd been smiling and happy, not the determined woman Petriv presented. Who was this woman? Why had she hidden all these years? Why had she let me believe she was dead?

"I think I'd like that drink you offered earlier," I said moments later in a voice that almost sounded normal. "Do you have anything in your cart stronger than water?"

I caught a ghost of a smile. "I always do."

The rest of the ride was silent. Petriv said nothing and I gazed out the tinted window. Once over the initial shock, I didn't know what bothered me most. I couldn't bear thinking she was out there in the world, doing her own thing and not caring about me. Had my father's family known and kept the truth from me? No, I couldn't imagine they'd be so deliberately cruel. I wished I could talk with my father to see what he might know—if I could even locate him. Grandmother might know something if she deigned to talk with me. We weren't on the friendliest terms ever since Granny G had bequeathed the family Tarot cards to me. I think it galled her that I, a mere great-granddaughter among many, should somehow rate higher than an actual daughter. It was a family drama involving years of heartache.

But now, Petriv wanted me to contact my mother as if we'd just chatted yesterday. Or worse, looked to exploit a connection by dredging up unresolved family issues. That made me angry. Angry enough to take on a Tsarist kingpin? Well, we'd see.

I swirled the glass of whiskey I held, my second, and the ice clinked. Three fingers of Jack straight from the protected reserves of Tennessee—real stuff, not synth, which meant it cost a small fortune. I was impressed. I was also getting the warm feeling that came with too much alcohol and not enough food. A feeling that could make a girl do stupid things.

"Where is she now?"

"Curitiba, Brazil. She's resided there for the past few years."

I took another sip of whiskey, then put it down before it clouded my thoughts further. "You must know I've never been in touch with her. As curious as I am about her, I can't help you."

Petriv looked amused, which annoyed me. I wanted to throw my king's ransom in whiskey all over his expensive suit. Maybe ruin his perfectly groomed dark hair as well, which looked way too touchable. Right now, he had all the cards. But strangely, the feeling in my gut didn't care and wanted to agree with whatever he had planned.

"It's what we can each do for the other, Ms. Sevigny."

Maybe it was me or maybe just the whiskey, but I felt that heat again. I fought not to squirm. He leaned forward a little. I refused to edge back.

"Your mother holds the key to something very valuable to me. With your help, I believe I can persuade her to give it to me. And with my help, you will achieve your greatest desire."

"And you know what that is, I presume?"

He shook his head as if I was being deliberately obtuse. "I bailed you out of prison for trying to influence a government official at a fertility clinic. Unless that's an everyday occurrence for you, I believe we understand each other."

"You can remove my blacklisted status." My eyes narrowed. "What would I have to do?"

"It's complicated. As I said, we'll discuss it over lunch."

That sounded ominous. In fact, everything about the situation was ominous. I stared into my nearly empty glass, thinking hard. Though he may deny it, Alexei Petriv was organized crime. The Tsarist Consortium claimed to offer another option to One Gov's rule, but many said they weren't much better than thugs. They'd even tried running in the last global free election two years ago, but lost—though not by much, if I recalled.

They ran on a platform of change and wanting to ease some of One Gov's more restrictive mandates. They asked questions like: Why should we continue to live as if we were still in the Dark Times, with the end of days upon us? Did One Gov really need to regulate our lives so carefully now that we had Renew treatments, space travel, and two nearly empty planets open for colonization? Many people agreed and started wondering the same things themselves. Whatever Petriv ultimately wanted, I suspected I wouldn't be comfortable with it.

When I looked up, Petriv was watching me. A half smile played on his lips. Gods only knew what the man was thinking. His leg shifted, touching mine as if in personal challenge. My eyes narrowed while I kept my leg where it was. No way was I backing down or making it seem like I was afraid of him.

"You have one hour to convince me." I crossed my arms over my chest and meant business, gut feeling be damned. I didn't get into bed with gangsters. "If I decide I want no part of this, I'd still like the information you gathered on my mother. I appreciate the measures you took to get me out of yesterday's situation, but I need to make up my own mind on what I want to do about her. I promise I won't say how I got the information."

"Done. I will provide whatever assistance you need."

He agreed so readily to something I thought he'd scoff at, I suspected I set my price too low. "No offense, but I'm not in a hurry to jump down the rabbit hole just yet."

"None taken. However, allow me to point out that once you made Mr. Pennyworth's acquaintance, you'd already started your descent."

"One hour," I said instead.

"All right. One hour."

As if on cue, the flight-limo descended much like a helicon—hovering and landing with a gentle thud as it connected with the ground. I risked a look through the tinted window. We'd landed curbside in a premium parking space. Not that the pilot had much traffic to fight given the widespread use of the Y-Line. I suspected Petriv never had problems getting anything he wanted, parking included.

I reached for the door and found that it slid open before I touched it. A blond chain-breaker stood there, along with another man I hadn't seen before, made from the same mold except with sandy brown hair. Petriv slid out first, brushing by in a wave of musky cologne that went straight to my head. I fought not to gasp at how good he smelled. After the smart-matter incident with Mr. Pennyworth, I knew how easily people could be manipulated with scent.

Petriv murmured something in Russian to the chain-breaker, then held out a hand to me. "Come along, Ms. Sevigny. If we only have an hour, let's make it count."

I wanted to slap aside his hand, but I'd look childish. Instead, I smiled and placed my hand in his. He pulled me to my feet with unsurprising strength. Worse, I couldn't stop myself from reacting to him, regardless of how loaded he might be with t-mods or what his MH Factor was. I knew what was happening. I'd lived this before, five years ago, driven by what I believed was love and that feeling in my gut. Dante had been good-looking, charming, and had swept me off my feet. He'd also had a wide enough rebellious streak that even my unconventional family raised an eyebrow. Alexei Petriv was all that and more, amped up to a level I couldn't even begin to calculate. I hadn't resisted Dante then and didn't know if I could resist Petriv now, even with Roy in my life. But at least I could be smarter about it—maybe.

"This way, Ms. Sevigny," he said, tucking my arm in his.

The bodyguards fell into step around us, my boots with their metal heels making the only sounds on the gray concrete. I felt overwhelmed, and the Jack Daniels I'd consumed wasn't helping. I concentrated on my need to pee. That, at least, was real.

The Kremlin loomed ahead, a replica of the famous building that existed centuries ago in the former heart of Russia. Its colorful spires were a glorious finishing touch. The buildings around it emulated a similar style, copying its onion-shaped domes and multicolored spires. Street signs flashed in both English and Russian, pulsing in a hypnotic rhythm, following some internal music only the machines could hear. I caught whiffs of delicious odors I couldn't identify. Some made my stomach rumble, and at least one left me lightheaded. People wove along the sidewalks swathed in colorful, lightweight suits and fabrics in a curious fusion of Kenyan and Russian. Everything had an ornate, overdone feeling, like I'd stepped into a Venusian-inspired opium den. Russians, if nothing else, transformed whatever they could into a reminder of former Mother Russia—with love and reverence.

While I was considering how comfortable I was with Petriv's world, I heard a muted explosion a few blocks away, followed by shouts and alarms. One of the chain-breakers spoke a flurry of Russian and Petriv nodded. His hand went to the small of my back, sweeping me into the restaurant. I saw little more than faux redwood paneling and elaborate golden scrolled handles as the doors slid open at our approach.

"Worried it was meant for you?" I couldn't help asking.

That earned me a grin. "It doesn't hurt to be cautious."

Once inside, we stood in a regal antechamber. The floor was rich red marble shot through with veins of white, and the walls were covered with large portraits and mirrors framed in gold leaf. Gaudy as all hell, yet it somehow managed to look elegant. My mouth started to water. Maybe lunch wouldn't be so bad.

A waiter approached. I was the grubbiest person in the room. He bowed, then launched into a stream of Russian. Petriv answered and the waiter bowed again.

"Ah, forgive me," he said in English. "I didn't realize."

I shot a look at Petriv from the corner of my eye. He'd asked the waiter to speak English for my benefit. Part of me couldn't help but be a little pleased. The other part wanted to berate myself for enjoying the feeling.

"Sir. Madam. The Kremlin is pleased to welcome you," the waiter continued, a slight trace of Russian accent in his words. Then, it was all Petriv. "Sir, it's always a pleasure to see you when you're in Nairobi. Your usual table is waiting for you."

"Excellent." To me, "I always feel like I've had a little piece of home when I'm here."

"I need to hit the ladies' room," I reminded him before I could be swirled away into this ridiculous fantasy.

The young waiter smiled and nodded. "Follow me," he said.

I cocked an eyebrow at Petriv. "You don't think I'll bolt?"

"I think you'll consider it, but I'm holding cards far too interesting."

I shook my head. Damn it. He was right. I was ushered down a hallway and to the door at the end. Once inside the bathroom, I let out the breath I'd been holding. Finally, a second to myself! I locked the door, took care of my immediate business, and proceeded to wash my hands under the gold-plated waterspout. I stopped short at seeing my reflection in the gold-leaf mirror. Saying I looked like shit would have been kind. No makeup. Matted hair no brush could save. Not even rats would feel comfortable spending a night on my head.

I scrubbed at my face, brushed my hair as best I could, and rinsed out my mouth. I had lipstick and powder in my purse so I slapped both on liberally even as I chastised myself. Once again Petriv was seeing me at a complete disadvantage. I'd always prided myself on at least being able to *look* like I was ready for any situation with the right outfit and the right makeup. Even wearing the right color was often enough to move things in my favor. (The intuitive kicks I got in my gut didn't hurt either.) While some people could use tech to make temporary modifications to their appearance for things like eye color, skin tone, or even hair texture, I had to compensate the old-fashioned way. It was hard work, but I was good at it thanks to years of practice. Except now; *damn it*, I couldn't even do that right! I groaned aloud. Gods, what did it even matter? I wasn't supposed to care what Petriv thought about how I looked.

I unlocked the door and stepped out into the hall. The blond chain-breaker was waiting. Despite his bravado, Petriv hadn't trusted me after all. I almost laughed out loud, then caught myself. I shouldn't be getting such a charge from this. Yet there I was, following my familiar patterns—allowing my gut to lead the way and letting what felt right dictate the situation. It felt right to go with Petriv. Forget Roy, my friends, my business partner, even my mother. Right now, being with Petriv was what I most wanted to do. Sometimes, I hated this side of myself, where logic

fell by the wayside. I didn't want to be that person; she got me
into trouble. And yet...I could feel myself getting lost in the
moment in a way I hadn't in ages. Being with Alexei Petriv was
scary and exhilarating. Everything else in my life felt drab and
colorless, and even though I knew it was a horrible thing to do,
I couldn't help but measure Roy against Petriv. How could I not?
And Roy, gods help me, was starting to pale in comparison.

I gestured extravagantly down the hall. "Lead the way."

The move seemed to irritate the giant, and with a jerk of his
head indicating I should follow, he marched us back the way
we'd come. A few turns later I found myself in a room at the
end of a long hallway. I noticed other doors—all closed—and
heard muted voices, but hadn't seen other patrons. Presumably
they wanted privacy too.

Petriv and the waiter were there, making idle chitchat in
Russian about gods knew what. When they saw me enter, the
waiter bowed and backed away.

"I'll return in a few moments," he said, then ducked out
through the set of sliding doors, which closed behind him.

Unsurprised, I found Petriv and I were the only ones in a
small dining room that was about the size of my bedroom.
There was an intimate table set for two with wall-mounted can-
dles providing soft lighting. There were no windows and no
door other than the one through which our waiter disappeared.

"Well, this is cozy," I said, voice throatier than I'd intended.

He smiled at me and somehow managed to look innocent
and wolfish at the same time. "They know what I like," he
said, and stepped to the sideboard to pour a drink. The liquid
was clear. Given all I'd seen so far, I guessed vodka over water.
"Something to drink?"

"No, thank you. I'm still feeling the whiskey. No need to add to the mix."

"Very prudent." Somehow he made it seem like a tease. That rankled.

"Look, this is all fascinating, but let's get to the point. If I can do whatever it is you want, I will. And if you see fit to do something about my blacklisted status, even better."

He walked toward me, stopping a few steps away. I held my ground, refusing to back down. "Not everything needs to be a personal challenge, Ms. Sevigny. There's no reason why we shouldn't enjoy ourselves while we work."

I swallowed, nerves kicking in. "I think it's best if we just stick to why I'm here."

Another step closer. "Is it always business with you?"

The heat was back in my belly and nudging lower. I wanted to slap myself, if only to snap out of it. I had a boyfriend. Roy. Crime lords were not part of my world, no matter how good-looking, rich, or powerful they might be.

"Honestly, I'd like to forget the last few days ever happened," I said. He was so close. I could see a smooth expanse of chest through the open-collared shirt he wore, and the blue-black edges of a tattoo. It would be so easy to reach out and see for myself. Dangerous territory, and again I noted how wonderful he smelled. The thought brought me up short as I wondered how badly I stank thanks to my time in the One Gov holding cell. Considering my own disgustingness broke the spell, and I could think again. I glared up at him. "So are we going to eat, or what?"

"Of course." He stepped away, pulled out a chair, and motioned for me to sit. "By all means, let's begin. As you say, I only have one hour to convince you."

My stomach had been growling from the moment we'd entered the restaurant. Petriv arched an eyebrow as he took the chair across from me. He moved with a fluid grace I could probably achieve if I had a hundred years of practice.

"For the record, when I decide to seduce you, you'll know. I won't need all this to get the job done."

I paused in mid-reach for my water glass. "I didn't say this was a seduction."

"You were thinking it."

We were interrupted by our waiter bearing a tray with a soup tureen in its center. Wordlessly, he served up two bowls and set down a basket of warm rye bread. After refilling my water, he left.

"Listen, Mr. Petriv—"

"Please, call me Alexei."

I tested it out in my head. *Alexei.* He wanted to make this personal. How personal? Immediately, my imagination assaulted me with a series of hot, intimate thoughts about him that I had absolutely no business having. Hell no. I was not getting into this. "Mr. Petriv, let's keep this professional. I suspect you came to my shop because you wanted to test me and see if I could handle whatever task you had in mind. I assume I passed, or we wouldn't be here. I'd appreciate if you'd tell me what's going on, or I'm going to walk out that door and not look back. I don't like when people play games with me. After the last few days, I'm at the end of a very short rope."

He raised his glass to me in a silent toast, then took a sip before he spoke. "You may not be aware of this, but the contract for the Earth-to-Mars transit link has expired with the current carrier, and it will be re-awarded within the next few weeks. At present, two candidates remain in the running. The current carrier, TransWorld, is one. My organization is backing the other."

"So you want to get a foothold on Mars and Venus and spread the Consortium's influence?" I couldn't believe I'd just asked a crime lord to tell me his agenda, but I was in too far to stop now.

"I'm not certain what you've heard about me, Ms. Sevigny, but business is business. I acquire. I consolidate. I solve problems."

"That's not what the CN-net says."

His expression hardened and I stilled. I had the feeling whatever he said next would be absolutely deadly.

"The ultimate goals of the Tsarist Consortium are not for you to understand, nor are they up for discussion. I need help. You have the means to give it. Don't judge what you know nothing about. Have I made myself clear?"

"Yes. I'm sorry I implied otherwise." I refused to let him see how he'd shaken me. Instead, I ate my soup with all the unconcern I could muster. Better to concentrate on that than his irritation. The first taste just about killed me, the bitterness was so intense. "What is this?"

Bland face from Petriv. "It's called *shchi*. It's a Russian soup, typically served as the first course to any meal. Very good, although it may be an acquired taste."

I peered into the bowl, spooning its contents. "It tastes like cabbage." I hated cabbage.

"That and *smetana*—a heavy sour cream. The Kremlin's *shchi* is the best I've tasted."

"I think you and I have different ideas about what constitutes good food." I stirred the soup, dubious. Good thing I hadn't wasted precious calories on it. I looked back up at Petriv. His bland face looked like it could potentially become a scowl. Wonderful. First I insulted him personally, then I insulted his culture's food. Nothing for it but to keep plunging forward. "So, the Consortium wants the contract."

He took a long swallow from his glass, then gazed into it as if deciding what to say. "Yes, but it will be difficult. TransWorld has a flawless record: zero incidents for the entirety of their five-year contract. When shuttling human cargo between Mars and Earth, the slightest mishap can be catastrophic. For the organization in charge, the result is complete ruin. As admirable as TransWorld's record may be, our intel suggests their business model is not entirely ethical. If we can expose their methodology as the situation warrants, we win the contract."

"How does my mother factor into this?"

"She heads TransWorld's Research and Development department."

That brought me up short. I rested my spoon in the bowl. "My mother works for TransWorld? I always thought...I mean...This is confusing."

"In what way?"

I frowned, not sure where to start. "Families have stories and legends. In mine, my parents were the doomed fairy tale. Love at first sight, married within a few weeks of meeting. They applied to the Shared Hope program and had me nine months later. My mother went back to school to finish her geology degree. She received a grant to study the rock formations on Mars. We were all supposed to go. Instead, she supposedly died in a mining accident during a work placement in Chile. My father went crazy at the loss and was declared mentally unstable, and I was raised by my paternal great-grandmother and grandmother." I stopped there, feeling like I'd reopened a wound I'd believed was already healed. "Why would she lie?"

"I don't know, Ms. Sevigny." Petriv put down his glass and met my eyes across the table. "I don't know why parents do the things they do to their children."

I looked away, afraid I would cry—the last thing I wanted to do in front of him. I picked up my spoon again, promptly fumbled it, and then watched as it bounced across the table and onto the floor, splattering soup on the red linen tablecloth. Mortified, I leaned down to pick it up. Petriv caught my wrist, stopping me.

"Leave it. You don't approve of it anyway. It's no loss." He pushed the bread basket toward me.

His kindness unnerved me. Crime lords weren't supposed to be kind. Kindness might make me think he was a real human being. I took a slice of bread and tried to recover. "What does my mother do for TransWorld?"

"Monique is one of the world's leading geneticists and was once at the forefront of Modified Human research. I need to unravel how TransWorld applies her work to their transit program."

"Space travel and genetics don't seem like they go together."

"No? What if it were easier for humans to travel through the tri-system? Right now, our reach goes no farther than Jupiter. What if we were better able to survive the cold vacuum of space? Suppose we could enter self-sustained hibernation for weeks or months at a time? We could extend our grasp to the outer edge of the solar system. Her research looks into all these aspects and more, I suspect."

Shit, my mother was a genius. Could that explain why she'd left? I tried to imagine such a woman thriving in my tech-averse family and couldn't. But to fake an accident to get away?

"If her research saves lives, how is that a bad thing?"

He shook his head sadly. "I'm afraid I've made it sound nobler than it truly is. It's not the lives they're saving that concern me, but how they're achieving those ends. My priority is to expose TransWorld's actions and eliminate them as a contender for the contract. I believe you're the key. I just need to discover what door you unlock."

"You can't ask me to destroy everything she's worked for. I want to get to know her first, then decide."

"You may not like what you find."

I tilted my head and studied him, puzzled. "What aren't you telling me?"

He smiled ruefully and offered a shrug. "We Russians love our tragedies. We embrace our sorrows, then we fight our way free. My hope is you will feel the same." He sipped his drink and met my eyes.

I fought not to drown in his blue gaze. "Tell me."

"It's because of your mother that you're on the no-child list. Through her direct influence, you've been blacklisted from the Shared Hope program. And to change that, you may have to go to extreme lengths."

I opened my mouth. No sound came out. I tried again. "Extreme lengths?"

"Unfortunately, yes. When you learn the truth, you may have to kill her."

5

I sat in my chair for quite a while. Not moving. Not thinking. Just waiting for the punchline, or for the other shoe to drop. Yet when he merely looked at me over the rim of his glass, I knew there was no punchline to this particular joke.

"I'm sorry. I think I misheard you," was the safest thing I could think to say.

Petriv set down his drink. "No, you didn't. But that would be the worst possible scenario, and not my objective. Any move in that direction would jeopardize the award process and delay my future plans. We want to investigate TransWorld and we only have two weeks until the contract is awarded. After the two weeks, you and I will part ways. You will be paid for your time and your blacklisted status will be revoked. Once we come to terms, I will provide you with the documentation I have in my possession, which should answer any questions you have regarding your mother."

"Hold on! First you say my mother's responsible for my blacklisted status and now you want to talk business like it's not a huge issue? You can't lay this on me and not expect me to react."

"Agreed, but you've limited our lunch to an hour. I apologize if that has caused my powers of persuasion to include high drama and threats."

Fuck. He'd torn the ground out from beneath me once again. I took a breath and fought to get myself back on track. I could freak out later on my own time.

"I appreciate your candor. I still don't know what I can do for you. If she hasn't contacted me in over twenty years, I can't see why she'd take an interest now that I've been approached by the leader of the Tsarist Consortium."

"I'm flattered you think so, but I'm not entirely in charge. At least, not yet." His tone was light, but I heard an edge to his voice. All was not well in the Red Mafia. "At this juncture, what's important is your card reading skills. That will open doors to places I can't enter."

"I find that hard to believe."

He smiled. "Not everyone is as enamored of me as I wish they were."

"So you want to show me off at parties?"

"One particular party. It's hosted by a member of TransWorld's board of directors, which is the prime reason I can't get inside. Other key employees will also be in attendance—not your mother, but someone who reports to her. That employee needs to be discredited, which you will do with a reading. Without him, she'll lose control of her most valuable resource."

"I don't do fake readings. What the cards say, they say. My reputation is all I have and I've worked hard to build it."

"And how would the news you were arrested at the fertility clinic help your reputation? News that took an enormous amount of resources to scrub from the CN-net, I might add."

I scowled at him. "Don't twist the situation. Besides, you may not get your desired outcome. Anything I see in the cards could take months to occur. If you want fast results, this probably isn't the best way to get them."

"We'll play the situation by ear. What I have in mind may not need to be so dramatic."

"I thought you liked drama."

His lips quirked in a smile that let loose a storm of butterflies in my stomach. "Touché, Ms. Sevigny. Read your cards as you see fit."

"Already planned on it. If it's a private event, I'll need an invitation."

"You've already received one. My understanding is you turned it down."

It took at a moment to make the connection. Once I did, it took everything in me to avoid rolling my eyes. Would the man constantly be two steps ahead of me? "The fact that you're raking your fingers through my private life is not appreciated. In the future, please refrain from doing so. I don't have t-mods, so I don't share indiscriminately across the CN-net. If you want to know something, ask me. I'll either tell you or I won't, and you'll have to accept it."

"Duly noted. Now, your invitation. It's not too late to accept the trip to Denver."

"Yes, it is. It's in two days and my travel permits have expired. I'd never make it." I'd been asked to offer my services as one of the items up for bid at a charity auction for the developing rainforests on Mars. It was great PR and I wanted to go, but I couldn't afford the trip and didn't have the time—the fertility debacle had taken everything I had. I never would have guessed TransWorld was connected to the auction. Then again, I supposed it made sense.

"Nonissue," he said, waving a dismissive hand. "The Tsarist Consortium will cover all expenses and ensure you're outfitted with whatever you need. That includes any revenue lost due to closing your shop to perform at our behest."

I fought not to look impressed. "Aside from discrediting this employee of my mother's, what else will I have to do?"

"That is up to my discretion."

"What if you want something I can't agree to?"

"We won't kill you, if that's what you're wondering."

I hadn't been, but since he'd brought it up, now it was foremost in my mind.

"If the terms prove disagreeable, our partnership ends and all contact will be terminated." He sipped his drink and met my gaze across the table. "However, your blacklisted status won't be revoked."

I looked down at the untouched bread on my plate. I pushed it away, no longer hungry. I felt like I hovered on the edge of something impossible. I concentrated on the feeling in my gut that demanded I leap at Petriv's offer, consequences be damned. When I followed my gut, good things didn't always happen, but somehow, in the end, I came out on top. While giving Petriv the keys to the universe might help me in the short term, what I decided today would impact countless lives for years to come. Maybe I was being melodramatic, but the pressure felt so intense, I wanted to scream.

"What happens if you win the contract?"

"We begin running our star cruisers to Mars. Money will be made and everyone goes home happy," Petriv answered with a shrug.

I shook my head and leaned forward. "Not good enough. You said I have no right to ask this, but I need to know. If my agreeing to this gains the Tsarist Consortium the Earth-to-Mars transportation contract, what other plans does this put into motion?"

Petriv's expression grew serious, adding the weight of years to his face. Not age, but experience and perhaps a little exhaustion. It turned his attractiveness into something more compelling. "People have died to learn the information you're requesting so casually."

"I need to know."

"And your final decision rests on this? Not meeting your mother, resolving your blacklisted status, or the potential financial compensation?"

I nodded. "Yes, it does."

"If I learn that what I've said has gone beyond these walls and the source is traced to you, you will die. I will kill you myself. Do you understand?"

I held my breath, feeling like there was a dagger pressed against my chest. Like nothing before in my life, everything hinged on this moment. I nodded again.

"It is the Tsarist Consortium's ultimate goal to replace One Gov. This is the first step."

"And if you do replace One Gov, how will things be different from the way they are now? What's going to change?"

His eyes held mine and wouldn't let go. "Everything."

I let out the breath I'd been holding and felt the bubble inside me pop. Calmness returned. Not the answer I expected, yet I could see it was the truth. The fact that he'd told me spoke volumes. He had more invested in this than I could fully understand.

"I'll do it."

The meal wrapped up quickly. I picked at lunch—a sampling of Russian dishes I wasn't familiar with. Petriv mentioned the names, but I couldn't focus. My thoughts were on the damage control I needed to do to explain my twenty-four-hour disappearance.

Petriv grew silent. Maybe he regretted the bombshell he'd dropped. Though for all I knew, he could be zooming around the CN-net, having a million conversations with others. The thought irritated me. He'd gone through all this work to "get" me and now that he had my agreement, he'd lost interest in me.

I set down my cutlery with deliberate care. Any harder and I'd come across as angry. I surreptitiously checked my bracelet; the hour was up. "I think we're finished here. I'd like to go home and get things in order. You've probably started on the arrangements for Denver and can contact me with the details. I'll need a dress, by the way. Based on your research, I'm sure you'll pick whatever's most appropriate."

I stood. Petriv rose with me. "One of my people will escort you home."

"Don't bother. I'll order a pod and wait at the launchpad."

"I insist. This isn't the best neighborhood. Besides, we're on a schedule now."

"Fine," I relented.

I hurried to the door, wanting to reconnect with real life before whatever Petriv offered swallowed me whole. I hadn't walked more than a few feet when he was at my side, tucking my arm in his as he had earlier.

"At least allow me to walk you out. You're so determined to be independent. One would think you'd been alone most of your life."

"You've done your research. You should know."

"The unfortunate thing with research is you have no idea about the person behind the details. You can never know which assumptions are correct or where you may have gone wrong." Petriv turned to me. I found myself standing closer to him than necessary and gazing up into a look so intense, I shivered. "Hopefully in time, I'll see beyond the details."

Yup, definitely not something I should be hearing. "As I said before, this arrangement is strictly professional. That means this is inappropriate." I slipped my arm from his, though I admit it pained me a little to do so.

"Of course. I always honor my business relationships, Ms. Sevigny."

He took my hand and brought it to his lips, kissing my palm. Gods, was the man even listening to me? I felt myself blush and snatched my hand away. He straightened, and with a faint smile, stepped in so close, my nose almost brushed the hollow of his throat. Before I knew it, he reached over my shoulder to lock the door behind me. My heart thudded in my chest and I held myself still, hardly daring to breathe. A moment ago, it seemed he couldn't wait to be rid of me. Now he was too close and looking at me in a way that sent traitorous shocks of heat through my body.

"This doesn't seem very businesslike," I whispered.

"Perhaps"—his gaze went to my mouth and stayed there. He moved even closer until there was no more room between us— "it merely depends on the ground rules."

"There are no ground rules. I didn't realize we needed them," I said, my voice suddenly coming out breathier than I intended. I raised my hands, planning to push him away. Instead, they seemed to have a mind of their own as they ran down the hard muscles of his chest under his shirt. Every lustful thought I'd been suppressing suddenly jumped to the surface.

"One should always have rules, Ms. Sevigny. How would we conduct ourselves without them?" he chided softly, eyes still on my lips.

My throat went dry. "I have a boyfriend."

"I know." His tone seemed to say he didn't care in the least.

"That means this needs to stop."

"Does it?" His lips curved in a wicked smile that made my heart take off like a frightened rabbit. Then his hands were on my hips, pressing me against the locked door. He lifted me until I was up on my tiptoes. I gasped and my hands went to his broad shoulders for balance. "Or perhaps it means further negotiation is required."

His mouth descended on mine with bruising speed, as if he'd reached the end of his patience and could hold back no longer. His lips were soft, but his body was hard and demanding. He crushed my breasts against his chest. Helpless, my eyes shuddered closed against the onslaught. His tongue invaded my mouth, and I could taste the vodka he'd been drinking. That, and something else: desire. Hot enough to burn me alive. This man wanted me. It wasn't solely because of access to my mother. It was more than that. He wanted me in a way I hadn't felt from a man in a long time. Not even in those first days with Roy when everything was new and exciting had I felt like this. I was about to be devoured by a man who wouldn't stop until he'd taken everything he could from me.

My knees turned to water and his hands on me were the only things keeping me on my feet. Without intending to, I angled my head so the kiss could deepen. My tongue stroked his, meeting his wildness with my own. I shoved my fingers through his dark hair, pulling his mouth to mine and pressing my body back against his. I felt like I was on fire, my bones melting under my skin. His hands were on my hips, then lower, fingers digging into my thighs. I felt my skirt hiked upward, his leg slipped between mine. He ground his thigh into me with a pressure that made me moan into his mouth. Only his hands gripping the backs of my thighs, and the door behind me, kept me from falling.

That brought a sliver of reality back. What was I doing? Had I lost my mind? I needed to slow this down or stop it entirely before I did something I'd regret.

"Is this how you negotiate all your deals?" I gasped out, tearing my mouth from his and trying to push him away. Difficult, when my hands were tangled in his hair. "Why did we even bother with lunch?"

"Because I was hungry," he answered, lips now devouring my neck with sharp kisses. Then his tongue ran down its length, lingering in the hollow of my throat. For a few moments, he stilled and all I felt was his breath against my skin. I shivered. Then I felt him undo the first few buttons of my blouse. A heartbeat later, his mouth had found my right breast. "You've no idea what I could do with you right now."

I arched against his mouth, my back bowing deeply. His

tongue strokes turned my nipple into a tight, taut peak. He followed with his teeth, nipping with enough pressure to bring me within a hair's touch of pain. I didn't want him to stop.

He made a sound like a growl. It was so overtly sexual that my knees gave out completely. Not that it mattered. He had one hand fisted in my hair, holding me in place. His other hand cupped my backside, moving me against him in a way I was helpless to resist. My hands grasped at the solid muscle beneath his shirt, clinging to him. The fast, hard pace he set as he ground me against him coiled something deep inside me, twisting up a knot of desire so fierce it felt as necessary as breathing. Even if I wanted to stop him now, I couldn't. Instead, I found myself fighting down moans as heat burned through me. He rolled his hips against me, thudding me back into the door again and again. I felt his erection then, thrusting against my abdomen. What would it feel like to have him inside me? What would it be like to have this man naked between my thighs, poised over my body, pounding relentlessly into me?

The thought sent me over the edge and triggered an orgasm I hadn't even realized was building. I cried out loudly, indecently, shocked. Pleasure soared through me and my toes curled in my boots as he worked me over his muscled thigh, forcing every last bit of sensation through my body, drawing it out until I finally went limp in his arms.

It could have been an eternity later when he finally set me back on my feet. He chuckled softly when my legs refused to support my weight. I found my forehead against his shoulder and my arms loosely about his waist as I gradually caught my breath. Gods, what had I just done? Worse, what was I going to say to Roy?

As if he could read my thoughts, Petriv pulled away entirely and left me to stand on my own. With quick, efficient movements, he re-buttoned my blouse, tucked it back into my skirt, and smoothed my skirt down over my hips. As for him, aside from the hair I'd mussed and his straining erection, he looked utterly unfazed. I frowned. Had I imagined his desire? Had he *not* wanted me? Was he just shutting everything off now?

"You may want to brush your hair before your boyfriend sees you," he suggested. Then he ran his thumb along my bottom lip. It was slowly and carefully done, as if to make the sensation last. Even when he finished, it seemed I could still feel his touch on my lips. "Also, you'll want to reapply your makeup."

He then reached behind me and I heard the click of the door unlocking. It sounded like a gunshot, and I jumped. I felt a rush of cool air from the hall and shivered as it met my skin.

"Why did you do that to me?" I whispered, my cheeks still flushed with heat. "What was the point?"

His face was impassive. "Because I had to know if you were truly his. I needed to know how strong his hold was over you."

What? "And what did you find out?"

"That there is very little standing in my way."

Confused, I backed away through the open door. The blond chain-breaker was there, looking impassive and intimidating, still wearing wraparound shades.

Petriv looked down at me. "Until tomorrow, Ms. Sevigny." Then he turned away and closed the door behind him.

I blinked, stunned, and let out the breath I'd been holding. What the hell had just happened? I felt like Petriv had played my mind just as thoroughly as he had my body. Spooked, I went where the chain-breaker pointed—down the hallway, through the restaurant, and to the flight-limo. The chain-breaker tucked me inside before closing the door, which locked automatically. Immediately, we took flight. I hadn't seen the pilot. Was he another one of Petriv's ubiquitous and indistinguishable bodyguards? Maybe they were ordered from a genetics company specializing in crime lord muscle, packed to overflowing with whatever MH Factor they needed.

I spent the first five minutes of the ride trying to catch my breath and calm myself down. Then I pawed through my purse and pulled out my makeup bag. Yep, I looked like I'd been thoroughly fucked, though technically that wasn't the case. Still, it was close enough that guilt racked me. What would I tell Roy? Nothing, obviously. How could I when in those moments, Petriv's lips and hands on me were the only things in the world I'd ever wanted that much? I'd have to keep my mouth shut and live with the guilt. But how would I be able to face Petriv again? What was I supposed to do when I saw him next? How the fuck was I supposed to have a normal conversation with the man after this?

"Nothing," I said aloud, mostly just to hear myself talk. "I'm not going to do anything. I'm going to pretend it didn't happen and ignore the whole thing." And if that wasn't the smartest course of action, I'd come up with something else later. Right now, my brilliance had clearly short-circuited.

It didn't take me long to find the button that worked Petriv's little drink cart. A shot of Jack later, my nerves were calm enough to allow me to think about something other than Petriv. My thoughts drifted to my mother. Wonderful. It seemed like my head was a veritable minefield of dangerous topics today.

When I was younger, I'd romanticized my parents' tragic

relationship. As I grew older, I still clung to the fantasy I'd created because I had nothing to replace it with. Now I had part of the truth and I couldn't decide if I was angry or scared at the prospect of learning more.

I tapped my c-tex bracelet before I could start brooding. Time to deal with reality. I looked around the flight-limo and peered out the window at the buildings below as the shim sent out the ping to launch a face-chat. The shim connected before finishing its first flicker.

"Felicia, is that you? Where the fuck have you been?"

I braced myself. "Hi, Charlie. Sorry, I haven't been in touch. It's been...crazy."

"Goddamn right you're sorry!" His baritone filled the flight-limo. I hastily detached the earpiece hidden in one of the bracelet's jewels and popped it in. "I'd fire your sorry ass if we weren't business partners. You didn't message. Didn't shim. Hell, you didn't even leave a goddamn note! What the fuck's wrong with you? Natty's been cancelling all your appointments, making up lies to cover your disappearance, and we've lost a goddamn fortune! What happened? Are you okay, kid?"

"Calm down and I'll explain."

"Damn right you'll explain. You've got one minute to tell me what happened before I tear you a new one."

That was Charlie Zero, my business partner. When we first met, he'd terrified me. Now the rants just showed how much he cared. We'd met in Career Design—a program every teenager in the tri-system completed per One Gov decree. To avoid high unemployment, we all went through the two-year stint in Career Design where our aptitudes were tested, our career paths decided, basic training provided, then we were launched into whatever our new future was supposed to be. I'd already had plans to be a Tarot card reader, so Career Design had been a waste of time. Charlie Zero—not his real name—was determined to be his own man and get off the Nairobi streets. We formed a friendship that blossomed into a business. I don't know what drew me to him other than my gut feeling. It had never been romantic, at least not from my side, although I tried for curiosity's sake. When I told him it wasn't working, he'd been angry until he remembered there was money to be made. There was nothing Charlie Zero loved more than money.

I focused on the grainy face-chat image on the c-tex holo-display pop-up and got ready to flat-out lie to my business partner. Like Roy, he hated using such antiquated tech, although he complained less. All I could see was his shock of blond hair standing out in high contrast to his ebony skin. "I have a new client who wants total privacy. He came into the office yesterday morning right before closing and paid ten thousand gold notes for a reading. He's asked for my services for the next two weeks. I agreed."

"You're good, kid, but not ten thousand gold notes good. Did you fuck him too?"

Thank the gods the image was too poor for him to see my blush. "Gods, Charlie! Don't be a pig! I didn't fuck anyone. If you were anyone else, I'd end this shim right now."

"Hey, just asking. I know what you're like, remember? I've never seen anyone flow with the tide as easy as you and still come out ahead. How much is he paying?"

Charlie was coming so close to the truth, it was all I could do not to squirm uncomfortably in my seat. "He says he'll cover all expenses for the next two weeks, shop overhead included."

Charlie whistled. "My kind of client."

"I thought so. Crunch some numbers for the next two weeks, have Natty invoice it and dump it in the CN-net proto-col at the shop. I'll present it to him tomorrow. Tell Natty she gets two weeks paid vacation. She can go on her Arctic cruise while you check out that lunar golf course you're always blath-ering about."

"Nice idea, but I'd have to turn the hell back around by the time I got there. Listen, kid"—he leaned closer to the screen as if that might make his words more significant—"this client's got you worked up. I can see that even through this shitty shim. Don't suppose you'll tell me who it is."

Worked up how, I almost blurted, as if to deny I'd almost had sex in a restaurant less than ten minutes ago. "I have a feeling I should keep quiet on this one."

Charlie nodded. "Suspected as much. If you got someone powerful interested in you and he's moving this fast, be careful. You don't want to end up collateral damage."

Fast was exactly the right word. I shivered, understanding his meaning all too well. And with Petriv, I had no idea how it would all go down. My gut said one thing, but my head said something else entirely. Odd how often the two couldn't agree.

He was silent for a moment, looking off into the distance. People got like that when they were pinged by the CN-net with some kind of hookup or message. He looked back to me, his expression grave. "That was Natty. Told her you were okay. She says thanks for the vacay. Also, two burly dudes came in today looking for you. They asked a few questions then left. Freaked her out."

I frowned. "Did she say if they were Russian?"

"No. Dark suits. Fair skin. Dark hair. Spoke English with odd accents. Clean cut. Could be One Gov. Could be anything. Just looked like muscle." He eyed me shrewdly. "The Russians will mess you up, kid. They'll smile to your face and stab you when you're looking the other way. If your new client is Russian, I'm tempted to tell you to stay away and forget the money."

"Too late. I'm already committed and I have to see this through. Listen, I'm on my way home to get some sleep and pack, then I'm off to Denver tomorrow."

"The auction? I thought you said you couldn't—"

"The client wants me there, so I'm going. All I need to do is bring the cards. Can you ask Natty to grab my deck from the shop and drop it off at my place before she disappears?"

"Last time I checked, your papers weren't in order."

"The client will take care of it."

"You know that means forgeries, right? To get good ones quick enough that'll let you travel tomorrow takes big money. Plus, you mentioned Russians..." He whistled. "Kid, you in with the Tsarist Consortium?"

I'd always admired his cleverness. Now it annoyed me. "Lay off, Charlie. I've had a rough couple of days."

"Don't take it out on me, kid. Who sat by you when everything blasted down shit creek? Who helped when your dad bailed, your great-grandmother died, and that fucker Dante shit all over you and left without a backward look? You know I always got your back."

"I'm sorry. You're right. I'm an ungrateful bitch and don't appreciate you." I sighed and tried to smile. "When this is over, I'll give you every detail I can. And just think how much richer we'll be."

Charlie shook his head. His rueful look translated perfectly despite the terrible connection. "All right, kid. I'll leave it for now. Gold notes are my best friends. But one last thing: Roy's been out of his mind looking for you. I've gotten two dozen pings from him since you vanished. What're you going to say? I know your quirks and I let them go for my own mental health. Plus, it makes us rich. Roy's different. He's got cop-brain. You got a fish on the hook and it's moving fast. I know how much you want to land it, and how far you'll go to do it. It's part of your charm, but watch yourself. Think first, before you get tangled in your own net."

"Too many fishing metaphors, but I get it. Thanks, Charlie. You're a good friend."

"Best you'll ever have. Peace." He broke the connection.

I fought not to sigh again, but Charlie was right. Everything was happening faster than I could think. My decisions were always based on pure feeling and limited common sense. And with Petriv, I suspected I was using less common sense than normal. In Charlie's mind, that was not a good thing. I cared about his opinion, but not enough to let it stop me.

The sensation of descending hit me, sending my stomach fluttering. I looked out the window. Below, or rather rising fast, was my apartment complex. It was a new development in Karen division, all pretty and modern with sleek highrises soaring to incredible heights, surrounded by landscaping, parks, and waterways. It also had easy Y-Line platform access thanks to a series of jump-steps passing by the condo. Better still, no graffiti or gang signs in this part of Nairobi.

The chain-breaker opened my door and I climbed out. I turned to thank him, but he'd already nodded his head and returned to the cockpit. The flight-limo took off the moment I'd cleared enough space. I bet Petriv didn't get dumped like that.

Standing alone on the sidewalk, I could almost believe the past two days hadn't happened—even if the tenderness between my legs said otherwise. I slogged my way up the sidewalk, fishing for the pass codes on my c-tex to show I was a condo resident. Dread hit as each footstep brought me closer to the door. Dread, and guilt enough to drown me. I should have told Roy about the clinic and my plans with Mr. Pennyworth. Hell, I should have told him about my blacklisted status right from the start. Sadly, I was too deep into the lies to stop now.

I trudged by the fountains in front of the apartment and their calming reflection pools, then passed by manicured flowerbeds designed to repel anything the building AI deemed undesirable, be it weed or insect, and trees that only shed their leaves on the last day of autumn. I dialed in my pass codes until I heard the electric lock click and the door opened to admit me. At the end of the lobby was a bank of elevators. I pushed the call button, waiting all of two seconds for the next one; then I was on my way up to the 132nd floor.

The elevator stopped at my floor without interruptions. At the end of the nondescript hall of soothing grays was the unit Roy and I shared. I stood before our door, unsure what to say should Roy be inside. Finally, after I'd stalled long enough, I pressed my access code into the key panel and swung the door wide.

"Hi, honey. I'm home!"

I stopped in the small foyer and waited. Roy's black leather boots lay on their side on the cool blue tile floor and the picture of *Greece Before the Floods* was crooked on the light blue wall. I straightened both while listening for noise. Nothing but quiet. No, wait. I could hear someone snoring. Roy.

The foyer opened up to a living room decorated with plants. I kicked off my own boots, then searched for the source of the snores. I didn't have to go far.

Roy lay sprawled on the cream suede couch in the living room. His chin rested on his chest and his blond hair stuck up in every direction. On the glass table were two bottles of whiskey—the good stuff—and a shot glass. One bottle was empty, the other half full. I frowned. Roy didn't drink. Behind the bottles lay Roy's service blaster, cocked and ready.

Roy stirred and opened his eyes. He looked at me, then threw up all over his shirt. He tried to get up. Fell. Hit the table. Knocked over the bottles. His gun fired, hitting the wall that led down the hall to our bedroom. It took all of five seconds for this to happen. Five seconds, yet more than enough time for me to realize that something significant had shifted in our relationship. Not just shifted—broken. From this moment on, Roy and I would not be the same.

6

Though it was too late to matter, I leaped away from Roy and his firearm. I cast a brief glance at the wall and the scorch mark left behind. If that had hit me... I shuddered. Ironically, part of me actually felt thrilled about it, like it absolved me from the guilt I felt over Petriv. Cheat on your boyfriend and he gets to take a shot at you. Poetic justice and all that.

Roy tried and failed to pull himself upright again. Whiskey was leaking out and staining the pale blue carpet—a color I'd specifically chosen because it matched the shade I'd once seen in a picture from the Old World. That stain made something in me snap.

"Roy, what the fuck are you doing? You don't drink and now you're holed up here, shooting the walls and destroying the carpet! I love this carpet! What's wrong with you?"

He managed to roll himself into a seated position. Vomit streaked his chin and the front of his shirt. His eyes, when he could focus them, centered on me. "Where were you? I've been looking and waiting... I shimmed... I always know where you are, but I couldn't find you... You were gone... Where were you?"

The pitiful tone sounded so unlike him. My disappearance and his inability to find me had reduced him to this: not angry, but defeated, like he'd reached the end of a long race only to lose at the finish line. Guilt flared hot and heavy in my chest.

"I'm sorry, babe," I soothed, crouching beside him. He reeked of alcohol and vomit, and I almost gagged. "I have a new client who wants complete privacy. I thought you were on a long shift and wouldn't notice if I wasn't here."

"No, we were supposed to meet up, remember? It was date night."

Shit! Last night, when I'd been in One Gov's pit. "I know it's no excuse and I always keep you in the loop about where I am and who I'm with, but he threw around so many buckets of gold notes, I just... forgot. Gods, I'm sorry, Roy. I should have..." I was running out of lies. If he'd been angry, I could have been angry in return. But nothing had prepared me to see Roy in such a state. "You need to go to bed and sleep this off."

I reached down to help him stand—awkward given that he had at least fifty pounds on me. I ignored the vomit and the stench, decided they were my penance, and worked to get his arm around my shoulders. He kicked aside the bottles, making more of a mess. With his help, I almost had him up and around the table when I remembered his service blaster. Well, I'd worry about that later.

Roy's head lolled close to mine. "You can't keep doing this. You can't."

"Doing what, babe?" I grunted as we weaved around a floor lamp and staggered down the hall. I spared a glance for the blackened streak on the wall. Would I be able to scrub it off? Maybe a fresh coat of paint?

"You gotta tell me things. Let me know what's happening. I can't... I got scared. Real scared. I gotta know where you are. Always. Don't do that to me."

"It won't happen again. I promise."

"Okay, baby, that's good. Maybe it won't matter. Just don't do it again."

"I said I won't. I'm sorry."

Roy lurched, sending us into the wall. I swerved, righting us enough so Roy took the brunt of it.

"Lights. Dim," I called out once we'd reached the bedroom.

The wall mounts muted themselves to a soft cream, and the window shades darkened to block the afternoon sun. A few more steps and Roy crashed onto the bed, hitting face-first and smearing vomit on the quilted rose-covered duvet. Damn. Granny G had made that for me. Well, maybe I deserved it. Maybe she was reaching from beyond the grave to let me know I'd made a huge mistake today.

"Roy, why was your blaster out? Doesn't the MPLE record unregistered firings? You could get into trouble."

"Worried. I couldn't find you. Things were happening." He rolled over and resettled himself on the duvet. "Impossible to track you. Panicked."

"And your solution was getting drunk, shooting up the condo, and..."

His snores interrupted me. I sighed, then grabbed a blanket from the trunk at the foot of the bed and spread it over him. I set a glass of water on the bedside table along with two red al-effect tablets and a small pail on the floor in case he needed to throw up again. If I'd gotten the al-effects into him first, they would have wiped the alcohol from his system, but it was too late now. We'd both have to suffer through tomorrow's hang-over. I shut off the lights. So much for my homecoming.

Back in the living room, I surveyed the damage and dealt with what I could. The condo's auto-clean AI would handle the menial details, but Roy and I would have to put our own efforts into spot-cleaning the rug and painting over the scorch mark. That definitely fell outside the scope of regular maintenance.

As awful as it was to find Roy in this state, it also meant I didn't have to tell him where I'd been the past two days. We'd have that talk eventually—but not yet. If I could salvage the mess I'd made and still get everything I wanted, it would be worth it. For now, it meant I could start organizing my trip to Denver without a messy relationship fight.

To avoid bothering Roy, I used the guest bathroom instead of the master. It was pretty luxurious considering our general lack of overnight guests. Green and black recon marble graced the walls, floor, and ceiling. In one corner was a sonic-cleanser to slough off grime in a heartbeat—up-and-coming technology from the space transit program was becoming increasingly popu-lar on Earth since it didn't use water. We thought it might help the condo's resale value. In another corner we'd installed a frosted-glass shower/sauna stall with multiple nozzle heads for when you had more time, and frankly, wanted more fun. When we'd been house-hunting, I'd insisted on as many luxuries as we could af-ford. Growing up poor and tech-free could do that to a girl.

I tapped the window, changing its glass to an opaque mirror that hid the outside cityscape. I winced at the dirty, forlorn-looking waif I saw reflected back at me. My clothes showed the ravages of a night in jail and a sexual manhandling, and I looked worn-out and just a little scared. Dark circles ringed my eyes like bruises, and my hair stuck out in all directions. Nice to know I'd looked like ass all day despite my best efforts.

I turned on the water and adjusted the temperature. Then I kicked aside my clothes and removed my c-tex bracelet. Stepping under the hot water was pure bliss. I sighed as I lathered and rinsed, washing away the grime of the past two days. Then I stood under the heated jets and let myself unwind.

How was I going to explain everything to Roy? He'd never understand, as much as I owed him the truth. I mean, I'd essentially cheated on him today, hadn't I? If I told him everything, he'd leave me. Worse, arrest me. Plus, I had another wrinkle to consider—my mother. I needed my cards. After I ran a few spreads, maybe I'd better understand the situation.

I considered Alexei Petriv…again. He was ridiculously good-looking—far beyond the typical genetic upgrades One Gov offered. Sure, a pretty face and a great body were nice, but when the package was too genetically and technologically enhanced, what lay below the surface? How could you be sure that what you were getting was still real? What made someone's reactions genuine? His Tsarist Consortium connections also made him extremely powerful. He was everything I should avoid, yet my gut had reacted the moment he'd appeared in my shop—a reaction stronger than anything I'd experienced in a long time. Hopefully the cards would provide a clue as to what he represented for me.

And because I couldn't help myself, I recalled the width of his shoulders and how my hand felt so small in his. Then how he looked at me during lunch and his voice as he discussed his plans. His slight Russian accent was sexier than it had any right to be. And then after, what he'd done to me. Oh gods, what he'd done. Without thinking, I slipped a hand between my legs, touching myself. As the hot water ran down my body, I imagined Alexei Petriv, not Roy. My fingers quickened along with my breathing as I thought about him finishing what he'd started in the restaurant. With ease, he would lift me and place my legs around his waist. He would pin me to the shower wall with his powerful body and pound me as I screamed his name, my back slick against the wet tiles.

A second later, I came. My legs gave way and I went to my knees. I fought to catch my breath, horrified at my behavior, yet not completely surprised. Long ago, I'd learned never to lie to myself. Still, that didn't stop my disgusted groan. Charlie Zero was right. I wanted Alexei Petriv bad and wouldn't be satisfied until I had all of him.

⭒

Shower finished, I pulled on a bathrobe and wrapped a towel around my hair. Roy was still asleep. The room stank of alcohol and his snores nearly shook the walls. I retreated to the kitchen and made myself a cup of coffee before padding barefoot to my office, which was nothing like the shop on Night Alley.

While the shop was decorated to impress clients, giving them what they thought they wanted—an exotic Tarot card reader who spoke in riddles and unraveled the mysteries of the universe (never mind that my readings were genuine and would be the same wherever I did them)—it didn't reflect the real me. Or rather, it reflected an over-the-top, amplified version of me.

At home, my office walls were set to the muted plum of a sky at dawn, with faint dark mountains far in the distance. Scenes like this existed almost everywhere in Kenya, though not where I presently sat, so I had my walls re-create them. The room was small, containing a metal desk, a nav-look for when I wanted to access the CN-net and didn't want to bother with my bracelet, a comfortable, form-molded chair, and a cupboard for my extra card decks. In the center of the room was my work-memory table. At its most basic, I used it for reheating my coffee. At its most complex, it recorded my readings should I need to recall them later and helped track my star charts and any associated research, its avatar making not-always-useful suggestions when it thought I was stuck. I'd considered disabling the personality mode, but I liked its quirkiness, even if it had moments where it tried to contradict my gut feelings.

I sipped my coffee as I opened my card cabinet and rifled through the decks, afraid of what I was about to do next. For the first time in my life, I was going to do a reading for my mother.

I've never held by the theory that the person you're reading needs to handle the deck. It's a nice theatrical touch if you're putting on a show, but I've found it's unnecessary. Usually I concentrate on the person, what I want to know—or what they want—then lay the spread.

I pulled a deck at random, and believe me, there were a lot to choose from. I collected decks of Tarot cards the way some girls collected shoes—although I collected a lot of those as well. I pulled the Heart and Soul deck. Interesting. It had been a gift from a former lover who'd wanted me to run away with him to Mars. Brody Williams had been fun for a few months and helped me get over the crushing pain of Dante's desertion, but Mars wasn't practical and I had no desire to get emotionally involved with anyone so soon after Dante, even if Brody had brought me back to life when I felt like dying. He'd told me to keep them as a reminder of our time together. Then he disappeared and I didn't hear from him again. Sometimes I still wondered about him and what might have happened if he'd approached me at a different time in my life. I assumed he was living on Mars now, but I'd probably never really know.

I slipped the cards from their case—which was lined with black satin to keep the energies neutral—and idly shuffled, thinking about my mother. It was a small palm-sized deck, so shuffling was easy. The backs were patterned in swirling pastels, beginning with ridges of spikes and ending in curlicues. The cards had a velvety feel and for some reason smelled like cinnamon to me. I always felt comforted when I used them—they felt like a hug from a good friend.

I touched the table and it lit up a clear, warm white; then the reflective surface became opaque. "Good afternoon, Felicia," the table said, its voice warm and feminine. "It has been several days since you were here last. I'm glad you're back."

"Thanks Eleat. Start a new file, please. Call it 'Vaillancourt.' Lock it with the usual password security."

"Yes, Felicia. I will begin recording when you are ready. I see you have selected the Heart and Soul deck. This must be regarding a personal issue?"

See? Quirky table. "I won't know for sure until I'm done. Begin recording."

I took another sip of coffee and cut the cards. "Okay, Mom, let's see what you've been up to while you pretended to be dead."

I laid down a classic ten-card spread. As I suspected, the reading contained many Major Arcana—the High Priestess, the Hermit, and the Wheel of Fortune. Monique Vaillancourt was a focused, driven woman, determined to make her own way in the world, whatever the cost. She was intelligent and looked to herself for answers, knowing that only she had the will to make what she wanted a reality. No surprise there. Of the Minor Arcana, the cards were split between golds and souls. Finance and career. I found no evidence of any strong personal relationships influencing her. Nothing whatsoever about a love interest—not even my father as a love from the past. She made decisions solely on how they influenced her career. She felt no regret about the choices she'd made or the things she'd left behind, including me. I shivered. My mother was a frightening woman.

I dictated a few notes to Eleat on my general feelings and impressions, made sure the layout had been recorded, and gathered up the cards. Next, I opened a new file and laid another spread, focusing on the man who worked for my mother—the one Petriv wanted me to discredit. Maybe the cards would give me something I could twist to my advantage.

This time, the deck gave me all Minor Arcana—daggers, hearts, and golds. This man led a double life and had an unfaithful heart. He was a liar and a cheat. I saw the Queen of Daggers—definitely my mother—controlling his actions, but he didn't mind, because it paid well as shown by the Four of Daggers, reversed. A greedy bastard. Oddly, it showed love lost as well. Interesting. That would give me something to work with once Petriv introduced us. I squelched any feelings of guilt. This was for my future with Roy. If I couldn't do this, I should just quit now.

I scooped up the deck, gazing thoughtfully into the distance. My coffee had gone cold by the time I sipped it again, so I tapped the table for more heat. With my interaction, Eleat woke from suspend mode.

"You have been quiet, Felicia. Shall I shut down?"

"No, let's try one more. Open a new file. Call it 'Petriv.'"

"Yes, Felicia. Begin recording when ready."

To my shame, I ran the cards no less than eight times—Eleat was kind enough to keep track. I ran spreads on the success of his venture, his past, his future, his work relationships, his love life, his relationship with me. I wanted to understand him and what he and the Tsarist Consortium hoped to gain by controlling the Earth-to-Mars transit link. What did he mean when he said he wanted to bring down One Gov?

By the time I'd finished, my head spun, but I'd learned something about Petriv. Unfortunately, it scared me. His readings contained too many daggers—strategy and conflict. They were also rife with Major Arcana, meaning his struggles were internalized. He acted on his surroundings, not the other way round. Most troubling, again and again in every reading, I drew the Lovers and Death. Symbolic? Maybe. Something to be wary of? Most definitely. I looked at the Lovers again, my mind flashing back to Petriv's lips on mine and one of the last things he'd said to me before I left the restaurant: *"There is very little standing in my way."* I trembled at those words and wondered what he'd really meant by them.

A glance out the window showed the sky had faded to black. The sun typically set around six thirty in Nairobi, meaning I'd worked the whole afternoon. Four solid hours of readings. No wonder I felt drained. My hair had dried into a frizzy mess and my feet and legs were cold. Hell, I was still wearing my bathrobe. My stomach rumbled too. Plus, that meant Roy was still out cold in the bedroom. I needed to check on him.

I glanced at my c-tex messages. One from Natty, invoicing our expenses for the next two weeks. My eyebrows rose at the total—I suspected Charlie Zero had padded the numbers with some magic math. Still, I left it. Who knew what situations I'd run into over the next two weeks? I deserved some danger pay. I moved the invoice to the CN-net protocol at the shop. Once I saw Petriv, I would transfer it to him.

I got up from the desk and stretched. A soft knock sounded on the door. "Can I come in?" Roy stepped inside before I could speak, looking rumpled and greenish, eyes bloodshot.

"I have to go in to work tonight. Just got a ping from the CN-net."

My mouth opened in surprise. "That's kind of last minute."

He shrugged. "I was expecting it, actually. There's a shipment coming in from Mars with a couple of perps that need tailing. It could make or break my case. I have to be at Spencer Lift Station in two hours. I'll be pulling at least three twenty-four-hour shifts back-to-back."

Spencer Lift Station was the terminal point for the Indian Ocean space elevator. If Roy left now, MPLE transport would have him there just in time. For everyone else, the trip meant a Y-Line shoot to Jomo Kenyatta International, a twenty-minute speed-burst flight to Moi International in Mombasa, another pod ride to Kilindini Harbor, and finally a hovercraft jaunt out to the terminal point proper. The whole journey could take most of the day. That MPLE could do it in two hours was impressive.

"Will you be okay?" I asked. "You had a lot to drink."

"I woke up earlier and took the al-effects. They helped. Doesn't matter anyway. MPLE wants me there."

I knew it was wrong, but the relief I felt at the change in plans left me weak-kneed. I'd be gone and back from Denver with Roy none the wiser.

"When you get home, we need to talk."

"I know." He ducked his head, looked sheepish, and ran his fingers through his short blond hair. It stood up in various places. "I overreacted. I'm not sure what got into me. When I couldn't locate you, I got scared."

"So you decided to drink? That doesn't seem like the logical thing to do."

"I never said it was logical. I just got scared."

"About what? You could have contacted the police or..." I caught myself mid-sentence. I didn't want to discuss this now that I was off the hook.

He stepped farther into the office, shrugging into his jacket at the same time. "I just want to know you're safe and sticking close to home until I get back."

"I'll be here. No big plans for the next few days," I said, shoving down the guilt.

I stood, offering my cheek for a perfunctory good-bye kiss. Petriv's words came back to me like a blow, along with the realization that if I truly loved Roy, I never would have let him touch me. Fucker.

When Roy's kiss came, it was in the form of lips pressed against my hairline. No passion whatsoever. "I'll see you in four days. We'll do something special when I get back."

"Okay. I'll try to think of something," I made myself say.

He grinned, pulling me closer. I molded myself to him. I'd show Petriv how much I loved my boyfriend! "That's my girl. Maybe we could try that—"

My bracelet fluttered against my wrist. "Felicia, you have received a face-chat shim. I have it in suspend. Contact and location are unrecognizable and unhackable. I cannot identify this link. Would you like me to reroute and dump?" the ever-helpful Eleat asked.

Weird. I only received face-chat shims from friends and family. You needed an old c-tex for that and hardly anyone outside my circle of contacts owned one. If Eleat couldn't identify them, this wasn't a shim I needed to deal with.

"Yes," I said, keeping my eyes on Roy, whose smile became a frown.

"What's that about?" he asked.

"I've no idea. What were you saying?"

My bracelet fluttered again. Again, Eleat intercepted. "Felicia, you have another shim. Same contact and location as previously. Would you like me to reroute and dump?"

"They seem persistent," Roy mused.

"It's probably nothing. Eleat, disconnect." Back to Roy: "I just want to know everything's okay."

"We're okay." His arm tightened around me. "Everything is fine, and like I said, we'll do something special—"

My bracelet fluttered. "Felicia, you have another shim. Same contact and location. Shall I reroute and dump?"

Roy pulled back and gave me a level look. "I think you should answer it."

I frowned, not liking the expression on his face. I tapped the jewels, releasing the shim. Up popped the holo face-chat. "Yes?"

"Felicia Sevigny?" asked a high-pitched nasal voice, words heavily accented. In the display, I could see a sandy-haired male. He wore a dark suit with a glittery collar fastened just below his Adam's apple. "Why do you use such ancient, primitive tech? I must begin an immediate download and have no local CN-net protocol to latch against. Without your CNP, how do I know this is even a secure link? Your flat-file avatar is atrocious. No download, no travel documentation, and no immunity."

"Who the hell is that?" Roy asked, brows drawn in a frown to match his mouth. "Why is he talking about your travel permits?" He fixed me with his cop stare and my whole world began to slide sideways.

He couldn't know! He just couldn't or it would all be for nothing! He wouldn't understand, much less approve. So I panicked and did the only thing I could think of: I cut the link.

7

ood one, Felicia, I berated myself. *Way to be a confident woman in charge of your own destiny.*

"Did you just disconnect so I couldn't see?" Roy looked at me in disbelief. "Are you five years old or something?"

"No. I mean, yes. I didn't want you to see," I said, stalling. "I mean, he works for a new client who's asked for complete privacy. I didn't realize he'd contact me so quickly or I'd have reprogrammed Eleat to accept the message. He wants me to run the cards on the success of his racing picks for the Nairobi regatta this weekend, and that's all I'm saying. Everything else is confidential." *Good save,* I congratulated myself.

"Must be one hell of a client if you gave him your direct shim link."

"The race starts in two days. There isn't a lot of time. And he's paying well."

His frown eased a little. "Fair enough. Word of advice though: Russians are vicious. Avoid them if you can. If not, get your money and get out as fast as possible. Based on his flunky, this one seems like a piece of work. Be careful about what you're getting yourself into."

"Felicia, you have another shim. Shall I—?"

"Put it on hold, Eleat! I'll deal with it in a minute."

"Yes, Felicia. Timer commencing now."

Roy laughed. "Looks like we're both on a countdown. I need to get going. Love you."

"Love you back," I answered, and received another kiss on the forehead. Then he headed down the hall and out the door. I heard it slam behind him. Crisis averted.

"One minute is up. Recommencing shim," Eleat announced.

"Wait. No. I'm not ready!"

Unconcerned with my state of readiness, Eleat launched the shim and I faced a pissed-off, irate-looking Russian. "Does *Gospodin* Petriv allow you to treat him so rudely?"

Wonderful. Maybe I needed to rethink the Russian language lessons. "I don't know what that means. *Gospodin*?"

"It's a title of respect. Something you know little about."

"I apologize," I ground out in my best "aim to please" voice. "You called at an inconvenient time."

"I plan on making a full report of this arrogance," he ranted. "It is a mistake, involving someone so ignorant. A Tarot card reader. *Vy durak*. Not even chipped! I can't even do the most basic workup on you! I've never been party to something so ill-advised and ridiculous."

More insults rained down in both English and Russian. He may have also spat on the ground. Gods, who was this officious twerp?

"May I speak with Mr. Petriv?" I interrupted. "I'm sure we can clear this up."

The look on his face suggested I'd asked him to hand me a golden apple directly from the sun. I wasn't sure if it was his disgust in me or his need to protect Petriv that had him so horrified, but I didn't wait around to find out. Two could play this game.

"Please give my regards to Mr. Petriv, and be sure to tell him it was your fault I couldn't attend the auction in Denver. However, I still expect to be paid for my time. Good evening."

Take that, asshole! I disconnected and went to see what was for supper. I needed to think about getting dressed too, or at least getting out of my robe and dealing with however much of the day I had left.

I padded down the hall, averting my eyes from the scorch mark, which would just have made me angry all over again. At the end of the hall was the extra bedroom we'd converted into a closet. This was another condo upgrade, installing a dummy-closet AI with limited intelligence that could handle sorting, cleaning, and clothing repair and maintenance if needed. We described what clothing we wanted, and the closet would present it. It did everything but dress us. I loved it more than I loved the shower.

I stood at the closet interface just outside the door, facing an array of clothing and shoes lined up on rod after rod, shelf after shelf. I had so much more stuff than Roy—almost like he didn't even live here. Then again, I had a look to maintain for the shop, while Roy spent his time undercover or in uniform. It made sense the closet held fewer of his belongings. Plus, I might have a *tiny* weakness when it comes to shopping.

"Loungewear," I instructed.

The display flashed its selections, I tapped the screen, and the rods rotated along the track until soft black cotton pants and a tunic appeared. I slipped them on, threw my robe into the laundry basket, and went to the kitchen.

My bracelet fluttered against my forearm again. I grinned; it took all of fifteen minutes for the Consortium to get back to me. I sat in an armchair, put my feet up, and tapped the jewels on my bracelet. Flunky was back. His expression looked chastened, and unlike the previous state of his immaculate clothing, it appeared there might be blood on his collar. Note to self: Don't get on Petriv's bad side.

"Ms. Sevigny, I apologize for my earlier behavior. I spoke without thinking and should not have let my irritation with your lack of tech get the better of me. I've been set to rights and have come up with a way around this situation."

"I'm so glad we can come to an understanding, Mr.... I'm sorry, what did you say your name was?"

"Dr. Karol Rogov. You may call me Karol."

"That's wonderful, Karol." I sounded like a bitch even to myself. "And will we be working together on an ongoing basis?"

"I work as *Gospodin* Petriv sees fit. I have your documentation ready to enter the United Confederation of the West, which I will transfer to your c-tex bracelet. I also have your itinerary and resource allocation. Without a neural connection to the CN-net, you won't be able to upload directly to memory and will need time to glean the basics. You will also find the information you requested regarding Monique Vaillancourt, which you may examine at your leisure."

"Perfect. Begin the transfer to my shop's CNP. I'm linked through there. Also, I've had my assistant prepare an invoice for my services for two weeks. You'll find that on the CNP. Please deliver it to Mr. Petriv."

"As you wish. The transfer will begin once I disconnect. Your transportation will arrive at your home sharply at ten-thirty a.m. local time." His eyes darted off to the side before he returned to neutral face. "And, Ms. Sevigny, I have been asked to wish you a good night's rest."

I sat up. Was Petriv out of sight feeding Karol his lines? A ridiculous warmth spread through me. It was wrong and I should have been doing everything in my power to prevent myself from feeling it, and yet the kick in my gut said otherwise. Still, I did swallow the grin that threatened to make an appearance.

"Thank you, Karol. Tell Mr. Petriv I wish him a good night as well."

———⟡———

I didn't have a good night's rest at all. Karol was right—if I'd had the t-mods, I could have dumped the files into my head and absorbed the information in a nanosecond. Now I had to rely on my fallible human memory. Not for the first time I cursed my family and their aversion to the technological modifications the rest of the world embraced.

I focused on my mother first. I had to hand it to Petriv; his data was thorough. It detailed her childhood, her impressive education, her Career Design path, her initial research projects, then her employment with TransWorld. Petriv's data also included a One Gov–issued certificate of marriage, as well as photos of the actual event. Hell, it even contained one of my baby pictures. After that, everything career-related stopped, presumably because TransWorld owned her research.

The material showed that she was a native Brazilian of Old

World descent. Her family resided in Rio and seemed to be extremely wealthy. There was a vague One Gov connection, though the file didn't elaborate on its exact nature. They were a sharp contrast to the unorthodox world in which I'd grown up. Raised by my great-grandmother and grandmother on my father's side, and surrounded by dozens of cousins and family friends, I'd been happy but poor. It wasn't until I grew older that I realized that without t-mods or any sort of MH Factor, we were second-class citizens. I frowned. What would my life have been like if I'd been a part of my mother's family? I wondered if they knew about my existence or if I would ever get a chance to meet them. Or maybe it would be better to remain ignorant. After all, you couldn't miss something you didn't know existed. Except now that I knew they existed, part of me *did* want to know.

The file also didn't contain much information on my mother's assistant either. If I was supposed to discredit him, shouldn't I know something about him? Yet there was no picture and not much in the way of a write-up. I'd have to ask about that the next time I saw Petriv. Either that, or just wing it.

Otherwise, everything seemed in order and I sifted through the remaining data while gobbling my dinner—a handful of crackers and cheese—then spent several hours throwing everything I thought I'd need into two suitcases. Natty stopped by with Granny G's Tarot cards. If I wanted to look impressive at the auction, they were what I needed. Stunningly ornate, they were large enough that shuffling posed a challenge. I'd practiced a long time to manage the feat. If I ever dropped them in front of a client, I suspected Granny G would find a way to reach from beyond the grave and smack me. Their backs were a rich ebony showing a cross-section of the Milky Way and displaying a spinning void known to hypnotize the unaware. The faces were hand-painted with an assortment of knights, princesses, and wizards from a time when courtly love influenced the known world. The colors were as vibrant and rich as if they'd been painted yesterday. Tech did that: I renewed the pigments with a nano-dip every year. It also prevented them from getting moldy and worn.

When Natty dropped off the cards, she hovered in the doorway, wringing her hands. Typically fresh-faced and bright-eyed, she looked frazzled. Though she had the thin build and dark skin of a native Kenyan, I could see the Middle Eastern features of her mixed heritage. When I first met her, she'd been eighteen and floundering through the first year of her mandatory Career Design program. Based on One Gov's assessment criteria, it was determined that her path lay in drafting arts—meaning she'd work in a government subsidized position at the local engineering institute. Unfortunately, she wanted to cook. She even brought her efforts into the shop at least once a week. It was probably lucky we'd found each other as I'm not sure what might have happened to her otherwise.

She came to my shop one day asking for a reading. Apparently she'd been placed on academic probation for manipulating her test results, hoping to be rerouted to cooking arts instead. When she couldn't pay my reading fee, I told her to come back with a tray of home-baked brownies instead. Her desire to buck the system echoed my own situation, and I couldn't help but empathize. To be honest, I fully expected to never see her again. Instead, she brought me brownies the next day. With minimal prodding from my gut, I hired her on the spot. I needed someone to file paperwork and she needed somewhere to test her creations: a perfect fit.

"Did Mr. Zero tell you about the pegs that came by the office?" she asked. "Both big, scary guys. Skin like yours, but darker…like coffee with cream, maybe. They had accents. English wasn't their first language, but neither was Swahili or Sheng. It sounded all pretty and flowery, with lots of rolling *r*'s."

"Yes, Charlie mentioned it. He said they worried you." Rolling *r*'s? I thought of my long-lost mom, living in Brazil. Maybe they spoke Portuguese. Also, what were the chances of two men from Brazil looking for me on the same day I learned my mother was alive? I didn't need cards to figure that one out. "What did they want?"

"They asked questions about you. Where you were. When I saw you last. If you were with anyone. I got nervous. They were hella big. I told them to contact Mr. Zero if they wanted to know more."

"Smart idea. Charlie can talk circles around all of us. Don't worry about it. Take two weeks off and I'll see you after your cruise."

Her eyes went wide. "You were really serious? Mr. Zero said you had a big client, but I didn't know how big."

Then she was off, describing the cruise in detail. As she rambled, I had a thought. Did Roy know about my Brazilian admirers? Maybe they'd paid him a visit as well. It would explain his erratic behavior. If so, why hadn't he said anything? I sighed, knowing I'd have to save those questions until I saw him again. In the meantime, maybe Petriv had information that could clear up the mystery. Natty hugged me good-bye, and I resumed packing and learning my itinerary.

Ten thirty found me at the best I could manage with next-to-no sleep. I'd taken extra care getting ready, determined to make up for how grubby I'd looked the last time I saw Petriv. I wasn't the sort of a woman who wore the same clothes days at a time or spent my nights in jail. Though, who was I kidding, really? I wanted to look good for Petriv, end of story. I wore a red tailored suit with a skirt slit that cut nearly to my hip, and spike-heeled knee boots. My makeup was perfect, and I'd even coaxed my mass of hair into a slicked-back low ponytail. Not the most comfortable traveling outfit, but I knew I looked hot. Petriv wasn't going to catch me unprepared and vulnerable today. I always felt invincible in my red suit, and I was certainly a far cry from the mess Petriv bailed out of the pit. Unfortunately, the prep work left me no time to offer a formal prayer of safety and deliverance. I made due with lighting an incense stick, whispering a few prayers, and crossing my fingers. After the Dark Times, religion of all kinds had gone on the upswing, and it didn't hurt to cover all my bases.

The building AI pinged my bracelet at exactly ten thirty. I couldn't stop the shiver of both anticipation and near dread as I let them in. A light knock sounded against the door. I fought to keep my breathing even. I wasn't going to fall at Petriv's feet. Sure, I wanted him and yesterday had blown my mind, but there was no way in hell I was going to repeat it.

Opening the door wide, I got an eyeful of chain-breaker. Four to be exact, overly muscled and neck-kinkingly tall. They were so identical in dress, features, and coloring, I couldn't tell one from the other. Standing in their midst, not quite as tall but certainly as impressively built, was Alexei Petriv. He wore a dark suit that seemed to blend into his black hair, and an ice-blue shirt that matched his eyes. He looked good. Too good. When he smiled and hit me with those startling blue eyes, I suspected I was in for trouble.

"I could have met you in the lobby. Still, I'm glad you're here," I said with a wave to my suitcases. "I could use a hand."

"I wanted to see where you live," Petriv answered, stepping inside. The chain-breakers flowed around him, enveloping me in the same human shield as he approached. A quick exchange of Russian, then, "My men have asked permission to scan you for weapons. It's their job and they're paid well to do so. I try not to get in their way if I can help it. I promise it will be non-invasive."

So we were back to business then. Good. I could handle that. "Go ahead."

One of the chain-breakers, the brown-haired one, removed a tiny gray marble from his suit jacket. It emitted a high-pitched hum. He held it a few inches above my body, my suitcases, and then the small travel case I used for my Tarot cards. The marble hummed and pinged as it read both me and the luggage.

"*Nyet*," he said.

Even I knew what that meant. I arched an eyebrow at Petriv. He shrugged. "In some respects, my life is not my own." Then he brushed by me, chain-breakers following in his wake. I caught the musky scent of his cologne, and while I didn't swoon, part of me wanted to.

"Um...what do you think you're doing?"

"As I said, I want to see your home."

He looked around the condo, taking in the decor as he moved from room to room. I trailed behind as if he were giving me a tour of his home, not the other way round. It was...odd.

The scorch mark on the wall was noticed, without comment. When he entered the bedroom he spent a long moment looking at the bed. I could feel myself blush, more so when he cast an inscrutable glance at me before exiting. I wanted to ask the reason for it, but he'd moved on and I lost the opportunity. Besides, I wasn't sure I truly wanted to know what he was thinking.

"Very different from your shop," he said eventually. "You live here with your boyfriend?"

"Yes. It will be a year together this June." It came out more defensively than intended. "Shouldn't we get going? Don't we have to catch a flight or something?"

Petriv looked down at my suitcases. "You truly need all this?"

"Unless you plan to keep me rolling in clean underwear, shoes, and hair products, yes."

He laughed, then directed one of the chain-breakers to take my bags before claiming my arm. "The flight-limo is waiting downstairs."

There is nothing remotely sexy about riding in an elevator when it's full of armed security and luggage. Or, there shouldn't be. Instead, I found myself pressed shoulder to shoulder with Petriv. He looked down at me, his eyes on my breasts first before moving to my face. I boldly returned the stare, daring him to say something, try something. Instead, I got a big fat nothing. What a letdown.

"Must be interesting always traveling with your own posse," I said finally. "I bet they're lots of fun at parties."

"They're excellent at determining and reacting to potential threats. Conversation is not their primary function."

The ride ended and we were escorted to two waiting flight-limos. I kept my travel case containing my cards beside me. The chain-breakers took up positions around the first vehicle as Petriv and I slid inside. One of the chain-breakers slid in with us, forcing me to sit on the bench seat next to Petriv rather than the one facing him. The two men exchanged words in Russian, the conversation ending with an annoyed look from Petriv and an impassive one from the chain-breaker. So, no alone time with Petriv then. Oddly, I couldn't tell if I was relieved or upset.

Moments later, I watched with interest as we ascended to low street orbit. I swallowed to unplug my ears as we climbed, then momentarily closed my eyes when the buildings were too small to see and I felt the weight of acceleration press me back. I breathed a quiet sigh once it eased. As rough as I found the initial takeoff, it kicked the crap out of the Y-Line commute.

I studied Petriv. He was staring off into the distance, probably linked to the CN-net. I'd never met anyone who so exceeded One Gov's genetic specification guidelines. It almost seemed as if he'd been crafted as a means of showing off. Whoever whipped up his MH Factor had captured perfection. It made me curious since my own genetic makeup was so lacking. Any genetic manipulation would have come through my mother's side, with limited adjustments while in the womb.

I cleared my throat and Petriv turned to me. Gods, how would I keep from shivering under his gaze? "When my assistant dropped off my cards, she said two men came to the shop looking for me. They had accents she didn't recognize. You show up, tell me my mother is still alive, and suddenly I have strangers interested in my whereabouts. That's too much coincidence. I suspect that the language was Portuguese, which would make them Brazilian. Is there anything you'd like to share?"

Petriv looked thoughtful. "Since our meeting, I've had you followed for your own protection, as I'm sure you noticed." I hadn't, but nodded like I'd realized it all along. My eyes slid to the chain-breaker across from us. "However, I hadn't considered that TransWorld's people might approach those closest to you."

"Are you saying someone might hurt my friends? My family? Roy?" Gods, so I'd been right about Roy's off behavior! They *had* gotten to him!

"Nothing so extreme. However, just because you believed your mother was dead doesn't mean they were unaware of you. The Tsarist Consortium is TransWorld's primary competition in the transit bid. They would certainly be interested to learn of our association."

"How did they know we'd met?"

"I wasn't subtle in my efforts to remove you from One Gov's clutches."

"If that asshole Mr. Pennyworth hadn't hung me out to dry none of this would have happened."

Petriv laughed. "Despite what you may think, Pennyworth has his uses."

"You'll have to forgive me if I disagree. If TransWorld suspects we're working together, what does that mean for the auction? How will I get through their security?"

"You are an invited participant. You just chose to accept at the last minute. Furthermore, it's a private event. The same checks won't apply, even though the guest list indicates many of their employees will be there. I'm not saying it's entirely risk-free, but we have the element of surprise on our side."

"And at some point, I'll be meeting my mother?" I asked with no less than a little fear.

"I would say it's inevitable."

I turned to gaze out the window, not wanting to continue the conversation. What would I say to her? After the card readings last night, I had an inkling of what she might be like and suspected any meeting would be civil, but cold. I pushed the depressing thought aside to focus on what was right in front of me.

Which, to my amazement, was Spencer Lift Point. We were coming in to land at the terminal point of the space elevator itself! No flight from Jomo to Moi. No shuttle to the harbor. I glanced at my bracelet for a time check. All of twenty minutes had passed.

I looked at Petriv, whistling in admiration. "Must be nice bypassing the crowds."

"What's the English expression? 'Go big or go home,' I believe." He looked just this side of smug. Most men couldn't do smug well—not without me wanting to kick them in the gonads, at any rate. Petriv's smug expression made my heartbeat kick up a notch.

"You could have warned me we'd be taking a high-orbit, low-g flight instead of regular commercial. I'd have done something different with my hair. Karol left that out of his itinerary."

"It could be because I asked him to. I hate to lose the opportunity to impress a beautiful woman," he said, taking another sweeping glance of my hair and the rest of me. Yes, heart rate increasing. I'd scoffed before when he'd called me beautiful. But after the incident at the Kremlin, I was starting to buy the bullshit. Damn it, I needed to get away from Petriv. I repeated my new mantra: *Roy, Roy, Roy. Focus on the end goal.* "We're taking the Consortium's jet. It's already docked at the JLA station. Your hair will be fine."

That did it. Without waiting for the chain-breaker, I slid open the flight-limo door and climbed out. The smell of salt air was strong as the wind caught my hair, tossing it in my face.

I stood at the terminal point proper. Soaring to heights unimaginable was Tsiolkovsky Tower Two, or TT2—a mass of carbon nanotube cabling that ran up to the JLA Space Station and was named after the Russian scientist who'd first conceptualized the idea of a space elevator and how it might work. At the base of the cable was the spiderlike climber known as the Daddy Longlegs. It waited to ferry passengers to JLA Station. The station itself was the counterweight that kept the cable in a geosynchronous orbit around Earth. There, some would catch speedy high-orbit, low-g commercial flights to TT1, located in the Pacific and connected to the GLC Space Station. Then from there, one could continue on to Mars or to other points on that side of the Earth. Anyone else at TT2 would be a colonist en route to Venus.

Of course, those were all facts I knew about the space elevator. None reflected the reality I saw in front of me. I had to hold on to the flight-limo door to steady myself as I looked up. Roy used it all the time because of work, but I'd never had the opportunity. Now I stood on the platform itself, where only an authorized few, or the rich and powerful like Petriv, were allowed to be. Everyone else would be in a protected pod or on the catwalk leading from the hovercraft to the DLL.

I looked up. The cable, deceptively thin given the job it did, reached into the clear blue sky. I couldn't see the end of it. It just went up and up until it disappeared into a blue-white expanse of nothing. Clouds drifted around it. Seagulls dipped by, flying around a cable arcing into infinity.

"It's so high," I whispered, voice trailing off.

Vertigo hit as I tried to follow its length with my eyes. I couldn't breathe. It was so massive, so mind-boggling. It was one thing to read about it or see images on the CN-net, but quite another to be this close and so exposed. I felt like I was standing at the beginning of infinity.

Hands caught me, holding me upright. Then strong arms lifted me off my feet. I was swung around so that the cable was behind me and blessedly out of sight.

"Don't look at it," said a voice in my ear. "Just breathe and close your eyes. Let the sea air calm you. It's refreshing, isn't it? You can hear the waves."

Petriv carried me. He had me pressed against his chest. He seemed like the most solid thing in a world gone crazy. I clung to him, my face to his throat and my arms around his neck, fighting to keep from throwing up. When I could raise my head, we were no longer on the platform. We were inside, away from the elements, and about to be lifted to the DLL.

My eyes met his. He smiled. "Better?"

"Yes. Thank you."

"You're welcome. It happens to everyone the first time they see the elevator. The scale is so colossal few can wrap their minds around it."

"What about you?"

He shrugged, a difficult move he made look easy considering he had his hands full.

"You can put me down. I think the danger of me fainting is over."

He grinned. "Far be it from me to go against a lady's wishes."

As soon as I was on my feet, I smoothed my skirt, hair,

and whatever else I could find that needed smoothing. Petriv had caught me in a vulnerable state, and I didn't want to seem weak. I also didn't want to encourage whatever the hell was happening between us. This would destroy everything I had with Roy. I wasn't stupid, despite evidence to the contrary. Even if he never learned about Petriv, guilt would consume me until I ruined it myself.

My eyes darted to the floor-to-ceiling windows. Through them I could see the Indian Ocean and make out the shadowy line of the Kenyan coastline. The elevator pod rose slowly. I found if I concentrated on the shoreline, my panic hovered at a minimum. I shot a quick glance around the elevator and found that myself, Petriv, and the four chain-breakers were the pod's only occupants. It could have held dozens more.

"Security concerns. We've booked the DLL as well," Petriv said. "The entire climb takes an hour and a half. Once we board the Consortium's jet, we'll reach Tsiolkovsky Tower One in the Pacific in three hours; then it's a quick flight to Denver. There's a nine-hour time delay between Nairobi and Denver, so it will be three in the morning local time when we arrive."

"So we left before we started," I offered, doing my best to play along like all of this was completely normal. "I should have plenty of time to overcome any jet lag before the auction."

"If you had t-mods, you could reset your internal clock. But there are zone acclimatization meds I can provide to help your body adapt."

"I don't have t-mods and I'd prefer to avoid the drugs unless it's absolutely necessary."

"That could pose a difficulty. You've no idea what could be required of you in the next few weeks."

I shot him a look. Was he smirking? "I'll take my chances," I said drily.

Eventually, the pod stopped and we entered the DLL. I kept my eyes straight ahead, worried I'd have another fainting episode. I expected the DLL to look like the elevator pod, but it was an actual room—rectangle shaped, long and thin, with a low ceiling. Tiny windows of thick pressurized glass lined each wall. Seats were arranged in rows of four across, an aisle down the middle, with fifty or so rows in total. Gray and utilitarian looking, their cushions were emblazoned with One Gov's tri-system symbol of a yellow sun and three white dots.

I picked a seat near the back, close to the exit. Petriv sat beside me. The security detail took up position around us, but not close enough to feel like they were intruding.

"All these seats to choose from and this is where you decide to sit?"

"A man has to sit somewhere. May as well be here," he reasoned.

I sensed he wanted to say more, but an automated voice came over the speaker system, instructing us to secure our shoulder and lap harnesses and detailing what we should expect during the climb. At first, I listened with interest, but as the voice continued in a dull monotone, I got bored.

With a jolt, we began to move. I looked out the window, seeing only the expanse of the Indian Ocean. As we ascended with increasing speed, the ocean grew farther away and I had to crane my neck to see it.

"If you like, we can move closer to the window," Petriv said. I heard a trace of laughter in his voice.

"Nope. Here is fine."

We were passing through clouds now. Then there was nothing to see but blue sky. Blue faded to white as we rose even higher. The motion was remarkably smooth given that I knew the DLL slid along the cable the way a spider crept along its web.

I resettled in my seat and fiddled with my bracelet, considering linking to the CN-net just to give myself something to do. I picked at the jeweled buttons. I wasn't sure why, but I felt fidgety and anxious. *Nerves*, I told myself. *It's just nerves.* Plus guilt. I must never let myself forget the power of guilt.

Except, it wasn't either one. I had a feeling in my gut and the longer I sat locked in my harness, the greater the feeling became. I needed to do something. I had to get up and...And what? Leave. Yes, I had to leave. Get out of the DLL. Now.

I jerked toward Petriv. "How much longer until we dock?"

"A few minutes according to the system AI."

"How many minutes?"

He frowned, brows coming together over laser-like blue eyes. "The AI says fifteen minutes before we link with the space station. Are you all right, Ms. Sevigny?"

"No, I'm not. I can't explain it, but I need to get off this thing."

"Is it a repeat of your earlier experience?"

"I feel agitated." I rubbed a hand over my face. "Like I might jump out of my own skin."

My gut said I had to move. Run. Hide. Move to a safer location. I'd never been in a situation where my gut told me to do something I physically couldn't do, and definitely not for such a long period of time. The feeling grew to unbearable pressure. It hurt, and I whimpered with pain. I tried to focus on

117

the seat in front of me but couldn't. Finally the DLL stopped. The impact was jarring as the braking and locking mechanisms engaged in a series of loud clicks. I tore off my harness with frenzied hands and leaped from my seat.

"Ms. Sevigny, what are you doing?" Petriv barked, unbuckling to follow.

His no-nonsense tone should have had me quaking in my designer boots. I ignored him, concentrating on yanking my two suitcases from the storage locker. Petriv grabbed my arms, jerking me away with brutal strength and whirling me to face him.

"Tell me what's happening," he ordered, shaking me a little. Chain-breakers flanked us. I could sense them behind me, felt their hands on me. I tried to shake them off, but couldn't.

The gut feeling turned to screaming panic. I cried and could barely catch my breath to speak. "I need my things. I have to get out of here!"

"Why? What's going through your head?"

"I feel caged." I took a breath, trying to stop the tears long enough to be more coherent. "It's not vertigo or claustrophobia. Just if I don't get out of here, I'm going to die."

There, I said it. Aloud, it sounded stupid, but it wasn't any less true. A second later, the electronic doors unlocked. I shouldered my travel case with my cards, decided the suitcases were a lost cause, and tried to leave the DLL, but I couldn't because Petriv had me in a death grip. He raised me up until I stood on tiptoe, my eyes locked with his.

"You're sure of this? You truly believe you're going to die here?"

"Yes!"

He scooped me up, shouted commands in a fury of guttural Russian, and plunged out the door.

We were on the launch dock. Windows surrounded us, offering a panoramic view of a horizon caught between black and white. The area around us was clear and free of people. Outside the windows were numerous high-orbit planes lined up in their bays, ready for launch.

"There's our transport," Petriv said, directing my attention to a sleek private jet in Bay E, three bays away. "We climb aboard, and we're gone."

I nodded, but my gut feeling hadn't ebbed. Instead, it grew sharper and I fought Petriv as he strode us toward it.

"Stop! Put me down!"

He ignored me and continued toward the jet. As we moved closer—two bays, then one—the panic arced to a fever pitch that had me punching him in the shoulder, fighting to break his hold. He dropped me. I went reeling and staggered to stay upright.

"What now, Ms. Sevigny? We stay? We leave?" He sounded both exasperated and frustrated, his face a dark scowl. He grabbed my left arm, righting me with another shake. "What is it you want?"

I threw my arms in the air. "I don't know! I just feel . . . I don't know what to do!"

"The jet? Do we get on it?" he tried, moving in its direction.

The fear spiked again and I yanked away. "No! I can't. Leave me here. I'll take a commercial flight and catch up with you. I'll even pay for it myself, but I am *not* getting on that fucking jet!"

Which was a good thing too, since the jet exploded.

8

Later I learned "exploded" wasn't the technical term for what happened, though for simplicity's sake, that was what everyone called it. Fire crews reported to the scene, extinguished what remained since fires didn't burn well without oxygen, conducted a preliminary investigation, and determined the cause. One of the engines had a mechanical short the AI hadn't caught during its preflight check, which would have become a problem sooner or later. However, later would have had us flying over the Pacific Ocean, where we would have crashed and died. Three cheers for me and my gut.

Once security determined it wasn't a terrorist attack, and the panicked crowds had been appeased, flights resumed. Petriv decided to cut his losses, denied any connection to the ruined jet, and booked tickets on a commercial flight under false identities. I wasn't sure how he did since it meant scamming One Gov's queenmind, and I would have said that was impossible, but I let it go. Soon we were winging our way to Tsiolkovsky Tower One on the other side of the world.

"I'm sorry I freaked out earlier," I said to Petriv.

It was the first normal thing I'd said in what seemed like hours. Petriv had secured two private cabins in first class. He and I were in one, the four chain-breakers in the other. That had produced some heated debate in Russian. Though I hadn't understood it, I still caught the gist.

At first I'd amused myself by braiding my hair so it wouldn't float every which way during the low-g flight. Then I'd examined the minibar, the CN-net shopping display, and checked my bracelet for shims. Not much there other than a reminder about my grandmother's birthday from my cousin Rainy—well over a month away. He wanted me to bring my cards, which annoyed me. The whole damn family wanted to get their hands on my deck and I had to bring it to every function to prove I hadn't lost or destroyed the thing. If they'd been on Petriv's jet...I laughed at the idea even as it horrified me. There were also several shims from Roy, reassuring me of his love. I squirmed with guilt, deleting them after tapping back that yes, I loved him too and couldn't wait for him to get home.

"Did you hear me?" I asked, leaning closer. "I said I was sorry about earlier."

"I heard. Don't trouble yourself. The situation called for it," he said absently.

Guess he wasn't in a chatty mood. I looked out the window and tried to settle, but after the morning's events, I just wanted someone to talk to. "It's not every day I slug a crime lord," I pressed on. "I'd hate to have a contract put out on me because I'd breached some sort of etiquette."

Petriv wore a pensive expression. "Do you really think now is the time for humor?"

Ouch. "Laughter is a good stress release."

"I'm aware of that."

"So, I'm trying to laugh about what happened because I'm stressed. Maybe this is an everyday occurrence in your world, but not in mine. I suppose you're making plans, consulting your network of mysterious contacts, wondering which heads have to roll and how this affects the bottom line."

His look turned incredulous. I suspected the expression didn't cross his face often. "You don't seem concerned with the fact that someone may have tried to kill you."

"Of course I'm concerned. I've just decided to be happy I'm alive rather than terrified over what could have happened. Give me time. I'm sure I'll be as upset as the next person."

"I see. That's a…unique worldview."

"It comes with being a card reader. I see future events coming at me all the time. It helps me appreciate the near misses," I said, unable to hold back a grin.

He shook his head and returned the grin. It made him look boyish, changing him instantly into a person I felt like I could talk to rather than the leader of a crime syndicate. I caught myself leaning into him, stopped, then decided what the hell—I was still alive, wasn't I?

"Do you have any suspects yet?" I asked. "The Brazilians? A rival for the Mars contract? Someone in your organization with an ax to grind? All of the above?"

The grin turned into laughter. "I have my theories. You'll be the first to know when there's a working hypothesis." He leaned in as well until our shoulders touched. "May I ask you something?"

"What?" I felt like a coconspirator and giddy nervousness bubbled up inside me.

"You wanted off the DLL. You seemed adamant something terrible would happen. Why?"

I leaned back, the spell broken. Ironically, as I moved away, he leaned closer. I stopped, afraid I'd look ridiculous if I smacked into the wall. Should I tell him about my gut feelings, the ones I couldn't describe because they didn't make sense to anyone who wasn't family? What about the readings I'd done about him where the Death card kept appearing? Both made me sound insane.

"Given your limited CN-net immersion and the fact that you believed your mother dead all this time, you haven't had much opportunity to investigate her," he said when I didn't answer. The random statement didn't fit into our discussion, but I bet Petriv rarely said anything that wasn't on point.

"Not much other than the files you sent."

"As a researcher, she had to publish her findings in order to gain recognition in the field. Once TransWorld hired her, her research became company property. It's been several years since she's published anything, but one of her last papers dealt with the potential existence of a luck gene in the human DNA sequence."

I stared at him, sure I'd misheard. "My mother was looking for luck?"

"She was working toward isolating it."

"That's crazy. There's no such thing as a . . . a luck gene. Genes determine eye color, sex, and quantifiable things like that— things you can tweak or boost to some predetermined MH Factor. Luck is intangible. You can't manipulate it. Most people don't even believe it's real."

"Whatever the case, your mother was looking for it."

"If that's true, why didn't you mention it earlier?" I demanded, feeling betrayed. What other nonsense was he holding back?

"Because until I met you, I didn't believe it existed."

I think my jaw may have dropped. "You're saying I have this gene she's looking for because I didn't want to get on the jet? Lots of people have a flying phobia."

He merely looked at me, saying nothing. His silence made me feel even more uncomfortable so I turned away. I would have gotten up from my seat, but the low gravity made stomping off dramatically too difficult.

"I'm just asking you to weigh the options," he said several minutes later. "Consider the accuracy of your card readings. What is it that makes you so skilled? Or think about the times in your life when unusual things have happened. When did you last have a feeling like you did today?"

I was quiet for a long time, then in a small voice I said, "I've never had a feeling like that. The need to get away was so intense, I could barely think."

"It may be more than luck working in your favor. Luck happens. It's random. In your case, you appear to possess a type of self-directed luck. It's almost premonitory, if I had to label it. You have a feeling and the choice is yours as to whether or not you act on it. What happened today is a perfect example."

I shot him a look from the corner of my eye. "That seems far-fetched. I was nervous. I've never been on a high-orbit flight before."

"Then what about a time not so far-fetched?"

I knew what he meant, and it scared me to think about it. I could weave all the elaborate scenarios my mind wanted to, but

I refused to lie to myself when confronted with a reality that I couldn't ignore.

"When you came into my office for the first time. I felt it then," I whispered.

"What did it feel like?" he asked, just as softly.

I closed my eyes and took a steadying breath. "That if I let you walk away, I would regret it for the rest of my life."

"Ah, well. That's something I can at least work with, isn't it?"

The tone of his voice suggested things I shouldn't be hearing. It made me think of the restaurant all over again, the feel of his body against mine, and how he'd brought me to a toe-curling orgasm in minutes.

"Don't," I murmured, fighting back the memory my body so badly wanted to relive.

"You shouldn't deny yourself something you really want," he concluded logically, his tone reasonable. "If everything in you is telling you to accept what's in front of you, perhaps you should."

"What I want isn't always what's good for me."

Petriv's fingers came up under my chin, and he turned my face to his. "In this case, I beg to differ." His other hand came to rest on my throat, his thumb idly stroking my collarbone. "I think it could be very good for you."

"Please don't," I whispered, feeling ridiculously close to tears. I ducked my head, afraid to meet his eyes. "I can't. Don't make this more confusing for me than it already is."

For a few long moments, he said nothing. I could feel the weight of his gaze on me. I swallowed convulsively. So much for my invincible red suit. I felt like I'd failed miserably. I heard him resettle in his seat. Had I made a mistake? My gut seemed to think so, and that made me feel even worse.

Taking a long, shaky breath, I sat back. Right then, what I wanted more than anything was to pull out my Tarot cards. Unfortunately, in low gravity I couldn't count on them remaining where I laid them. Plus, I felt like they'd betrayed me—like they'd known all these things I'd never suspected and had withheld information from me.

Great. Now I'd made things hellishly uncomfortable between us in a small cabin. How could I turn off this crazy reality? By ignoring it, I decided. Besides, I had questions that needed answers, and I refused to let my gnawing hunger for him get the best of me.

"So." I drew the word out, trying to organize my thoughts. "Back to my mother. You say she wants to find a future-predicting luck gene."

"Premonitory luck," he corrected.

"Same difference. If I have it, wouldn't it make sense that she'd want to observe me and take notes?"

He tapped my c-tex bracelet. His hand didn't come into contact with mine, which was no doubt intentional. "For all we know, this transmits a steady stream of information about you at all times."

I looked in horror at the bracelet I'd worn almost every day of my life. "You can't be serious. How would she even gain access to it?"

Petriv shrugged. "I'll have my people examine it when we land. It could be your mother decided it was better to observe you from afar rather than become emotionally attached."

I let that go. I didn't want to let my brain wander down that road because I suspected it would hurt too much. "What would she do if she found this luck gene?"

"In theory, the possibilities are endless."

"What do you mean, 'in theory'? You make it sound like it's a bad thing."

"Not bad, but unpredictable. What may be considered an advantage for one person may not be for another."

I frowned at him. "So I'm being protected at other people's expense? I'm getting things someone else might deserve because I have this luck gene?"

"No, but perhaps..." He sighed, then unbuckled his seat-belt and rose carefully from his seat. In the lower gravity, it was possible to bounce out of control if you didn't pay attention. When he stood, it seemed he took up all the remaining space in the cabin. I felt tiny in comparison and had an awful moment where I wanted him to wrap himself around me.

"Where are you going?" I asked. Gods, had I completely driven him away with my erratic behavior?

Instead he reached down, smoothed back the loose strands of my hair that were floating every which way thanks to the low gravity, and said, "It will be some time before we reach TT1. Try to get some rest. In the meantime, I need to stretch my legs. Rest well, *dorogaya moya*." He kissed the top of my head, a gesture which seemed more fatherly than romantic. Then he ducked out of the cabin and into the hall.

—=◆=—

The delay cost us several hours, but thanks to the time difference, a second jet waiting at TT1, and a flight-limo waiting to take us to our accommodations in Denver, we arrived in plenty of time. With my newly forged documentation indicating my eligibility to enter the United Confederation of the West, I sailed through customs and immigration. The UCW had the tightest security protocols on Earth. That Petriv's people could whip up something so flawless that quickly was nothing short of magic. Too bad I didn't have time to enjoy the sights in Denver. Given what Petriv had crammed into the itinerary, I wondered if I'd even have time to pee.

There were four of us in the flight-limo—myself, Petriv, and two chain-breakers. Petriv was reserved and withdrawn. He could have been deep in conversation with his people on the CN-net for all I knew, but I suspected it had more to do with me rejecting him on the jet. I felt terrible and sick to my stomach, wondering if I'd screwed everything up. I'd ignored my gut and now I was paying the price. It made our trip to the hotel a silent one. At least I got a lengthy shim from Natty, telling me all about her upcoming cruise. I also answered Rainy's shim about Grandmother's birthday party, letting him know I'd be there with the cards.

It was dusk when we reached the hotel—a massive affair of white marble polished to a high gloss. The work involved in maintaining the hotel's pristine façade had to be backbreaking, and I guessed nano-bugs kept things in order. No person had the patience or the dexterity to maintain something like that. With the white and green up-lighting, UCW flags draped over the balconies, and row upon row of tropical flowers and trees planted in enviro-sealed terrariums, it was impressive. Unfortunately, I couldn't admire it because the chain-breakers whisked us inside.

The lobby looked no less majestic. The white marble floor was shot through with green and gold. Columns reached to a high vaulted ceiling, which was a mirrored star surface. It reflected the birth of a black hole. The scene played out in time-elapsed high speed, but even still it took a day to show the entire recording. I wondered if they had it on a loop or if it switched to something else when the show ended, then realized I wouldn't be there long enough to find out.

Before we reached the front desk, we were approached by four men and a woman. Only two of the men, chain-breakers, had true youth. I dismissed them from my mind the only way you could when you saw two overgrown gorillas capable of tearing your head off one-handed—just averted my eyes and pretended they couldn't see me.

As for the other three, their eyes gave it away. All were older, anywhere between fifty and sixty if I had to guess. One was Karol, my pain in the ass from Nairobi. He met my scowl with a neutral expression. As for the other man, both he and the woman beside him had blond hair, his cut short against his skull while hers flowed down her back in long golden waves. Green eyes, perfect white teeth, chiseled profiles, and peaches-and-cream complexions made them a matching set.

An exchange of Russian followed, along with lots of cheek-kissing and embracing.

Petriv turned to me. "Ms. Sevigny, allow me to introduce you to my colleagues: Vadim and Oksana Ivchenko. You already know Dr. Karol Rogov, the Consortium's tech-med."

"We've met," I said, eyeing him warily. At least now I understood his disgust with my bracelet. Tech-meds diagnosed and resolved AI issues, be it a simple wiring problem or an entire personality overhaul. Essentially, they were doctors of technology with varying degrees of specialization.

"A misunderstanding, I assure you." Karol's eyes darted between me and Petriv as if to convince us of his sincerity.

I caught Petriv's frown and remembered the blood I had seen on Karol's collar. I dredged up a smile and played nice. "Of course. Nothing to worry about."

Petriv nodded. "Good. Karol will examine your bracelet and determine if it's free of TransWorld spyware. In the meantime, Oksana will prepare you for tonight's auction."

"What will you be doing?" I wanted to know as I placed my c-tex bracelet in Karol's palm. "Rolling heads?"

He smiled but it felt remote, like it didn't quite reach his eyes. "Don't worry, you're in capable hands."

I was summarily dismissed as Petriv fell into a rapid and heated conversation with Vadim and they walked away. Was this what it would be like now? Was I nothing to him? If so, it hurt more than I could have imagined. I wanted to call after him, say I was sorry, and tell him...What? I swore under my breath. I was the one who pushed him away. Besides, it wasn't like we were compatible anyway—him with whatever modifications he had and me with essentially nothing. And Roy...I had to think about Roy. Unfortunately, that didn't make me feel any better as I watched him go.

My attention was drawn back to Karol as he slunk off with my bracelet, muttering to himself. The chain-breakers carried my bags toward the elevators at the far end of the lobby, presumably taking them to my room. That left me with the blonde goddess Oksana, who smiled but eyed me like livestock at a Martian colonial fair.

"It's a shame the original outfit the Consortium chose for you for the auction was destroyed in the explosion," she said.

"Still, who doesn't like an excuse to go shopping? This hotel has an excellent selection of boutiques. I've already contacted them and had several gowns set aside for you. With hair and makeup to consider, we must hurry. And shoes! We mustn't forget the importance of shoes."

And suddenly I'd just found my new best friend in the entire tri-system.

It was impossible not to rally from my funk with Oksana for company. It was like I'd met the sister I never had. The next several hours were a whirlwind of expensive shops and clothing beyond my wildest dreams. As Oksana took me to each boutique and I tried on gown after gown, I felt like I was living the fashionista fairy tale I'd always dreamed of. Long, short, full, skintight, strapless, backless, and in every color I could possibly envision. And if I wasn't sure of a gown, Oksana had the offending garment whisked away and out of sight.

Eventually we both decided on a strapless floor-length gown of deep teal. The material was soft chiffon that floated about my legs as I moved. I didn't even bother looking at the price. It was so beyond my reach, it was laughable.

"I always look best in blue-green," I said, as we each studied the dress critically in the mirror, taking in the view at all angles.

"This shade is perfect," she agreed. "You have fabulous eyes, and this will show them to their best advantage."

"I'm not really here to draw attention to myself," I said regretfully, running my hands along the dress. The fabric felt like a dream. I think I may have even sighed.

"Ah, but it would be a greater shame to go unnoticed, wouldn't you agree?" Oksana asked, winking at me. "I know Alexei would think so."

"To be honest, I don't know what that man thinks."

She met my eyes in the mirror. "Well, yes, I suppose he can be an enigma at times. However, I have known him for years and can say with certainty he is driven to succeed like no man I've ever known. When he wants something, nothing gets in his way." She broke the stare and turned away. "Now then, let's see about finding you some shoes."

Before I could pursue the subject further, Oksana disappeared and returned with a selection of shoes. I spent the next hour trying on shoes I could never afford. We settled on a pair of matching sandals with sapphire and emerald-encrusted heels. Ridiculous, yet I was instantly in love. Also added to the "could never afford" list were earrings, a necklace, and a bracelet of blue-green sapphires and white diamonds which Oksana said I could wear "on loan" for the evening. Hair and makeup were done in the hotel salon. My hair was left down to preserve mystery, and my makeup was done dramatically to reflect my Romani heritage. Intrigued, I asked the stylist to record her steps and the colors she used and send me a copy. She had an interesting brush technique I wanted to try myself once I returned home and life got back to normal. And there *would* be a "back to normal," I promised myself. All this shopping may have been fun, but I couldn't let it go to my head.

While I was in the salon, Karol made an appearance to return my c-tex bracelet, reporting he'd found no bugs, tracers, or anything suspicious. I checked it myself but it seemed the same as before. Then again, it wasn't like spyware would be obvious—hence the term "spy."

Three hours later as I managed a quick bite of food, Oksana finally declared me ready. I stood in a lavishly appointed bedroom before a large framed mirror and considered the finished product—dress, hair, makeup, shoes, jewelry. I'd never felt more beautiful and glamorous in my life, and more than anything, I wanted Petriv to see me. See me and...and damn it, what did I want? I'd told him no, and he'd backed off. I knew I shouldn't let my thoughts wander in that direction. Roy. I needed to focus on what I loved about him. What had originally attracted me? His appearance? Kindness? Sense of humor? Hell, what if I was with him only because he'd been available when I'd needed someone? No, that was too awful to consider. But what did it say about me that I couldn't remember?

I heard a knock at the door, then Oksana's lilting voice. My heart leaped into my throat in anticipation, imagining Petriv in the other room. Several deep breaths and a few prayers later— I stepped into the drawing room.

Except it wasn't Petriv. Not by a longshot. My heart dropped and my stomach did a somersault. My apprehension was replaced with boiling, searing rage.

"You!" I screeched, pointing a turquoise-holoed fingernail. "You goddamn piece of shit! What the hell are you doing here? Get the fuck away from me or I'll kill you!"

It was Mr. Pennyworth.

9

I launched myself at Pennyworth, striding across the carpeted floor to scratch out his eyes even if it ruined my three-hundred-gold-note manicure and shorted the temporary nail holos. I'd almost reached him when hands restrained me. Two chain-breakers held me effortlessly. I struggled to get free, which was kind of like wrestling a fish underwater—utterly impossible. Only when I went limp did they set me down. By then, I'd exhausted the best of my profanity and worst heat of my anger.

"What's he doing here?" I demanded, swinging to Oksana in the loose chain-breaker grip.

"We contract out to him on occasion," she said, a concerned look on her face. "He comes highly recommended and is quite skilled."

"Skilled at what? Setting people up and leaving them for dead?" I turned to Pennyworth. "I spent a night in a One Gov pit thanks to you!"

"It appears you made it out unscathed," he answered in the voice that sounded neither male nor female.

"It doesn't matter if I'm unscathed! What matters is you left me to take the heat for your shitty plan! The clinic had sensors that picked up your worthless smart-matter gas. I paid you to..." My voice trailed off as several things clicked into place. I turned to Oksana. "Where's Mr. Petriv?" I was surprised at how calm I sounded. "I'd like to speak with him."

"I'm afraid he's unavailable." She looked sorry too.

"I see." I held myself as still as possible.

Mr. Pennyworth worked for Petriv, though I hadn't known it at the time and wouldn't have cared if I did. But his plan's failure landed me in Petriv's clutches. Perhaps that explained why Petriv had paid so much for my initial Tarot card reading—he already knew the plan would fail and I would be out all my savings. I supposed there was honor in that if I chose to see it that way. I didn't.

"I want to see Mr. Petriv or the deal is off. He can find someone else to do his dirty work." I shook my arms again and glared at Oksana. "Tell these assholes to let me go!"

"Yes, of course, I'm sorry." She spoke some Russian, and the chain-breakers released me. I rubbed my arms, wincing. I'd have bruises tomorrow.

"Ms. Sevigny, I'm sorry you feel this way. Mr. Petriv would have been here, but after the incident at the space elevator, others within the Tsarist Consortium felt it was better that he not be exposed to such risk and he's been recalled. It wouldn't be appropriate to put the Consortium's heir-apparent in jeopardy," Mr. Pennyworth said, as if the logic in this should be obvious to someone as dense as me. "You do look lovely in your dress, by the way."

I rolled my eyes. "Fuck off, Pennyworth." Heir-apparent, my

ass. I paced the room, rubbing my arms. I felt like a caged animal. "I'm not doing this. I want to go home." No one moved and I stomped around some more to no purpose. "Fine. We can wait here all night. The auction will be over in a few hours anyway."

"And you'll return to your shop and your boyfriend, your life having moved no further ahead and all your hopes broken. You'll be no closer to lifting your blacklisted status, or unraveling the mystery of your mother," Mr. Pennyworth said, advancing toward me.

"That's fine."

"Is it?" he asked, tone merciless, moving until he stood right in front of me. "Tonight everything could change, and yet you stand here pouting like a child. I never thought you were an idiot, Ms. Sevigny. However, I believe you're behaving like one now."

I slapped him hard. He didn't even flinch although I winced as a sharp, stinging pain went through my hand. Was his jaw made of steel?

"Did that satisfy you? Would you like to hit me again? I assure you, it will hurt you more than it does me."

"I'm not going anywhere with you!"

"But you would go with Mr. Petriv, I presume?"

"That has nothing to do with this."

"So then you wouldn't go even if he were here? Is that correct?"

I stalked away without answering. He was right: I was pouting. But damn it, how was I supposed to react? I'd just had the rug pulled out from under me, in a situation where I wasn't sure who I could trust. I was attracted to a man with a laundry list of ulterior motives, and worst of all, my gut wasn't telling me anything useful. So I did the only thing I could think to do: I turned to my Tarot cards.

On a nearby desk was the elegant silk evening bag that matched my dress. I fumbled with the clasp, opened it, and dumped out my cards. Then I sat and shuffled. The room grew so silent, I may as well have been alone. Good. That, and the simple act of shuffling, helped calm me.

A one-card spread is the easiest reading in the world. It gives a yes or no answer depending on whether the card is upright or reversed. Deeper analysis can give more information as to the nature of the question, the influencing factors, or how things might be resolved. But in this case, I needed simple: go with Pennyworth or not? I finished shuffling, then cut the deck: Wheel of Fortune, upright. Destiny, success, and an unexpected turn of events. All I could do was hold on and enjoy the ride. I sighed. I'd gotten my answer and then some.

I scooped the cards back into the evening bag. Then I turned to Oksana, the chain-breakers, and Mr. Pennyworth, who stood much too close, having watched everything over my shoulder.

"Show's over, people," I said with resignation. "Let's go."

———◆———

"Ms. Sevigny! What a surprise! We didn't know you were coming until the last minute. We're so pleased you could join us."

Mick Doucette reached for my hands as he met me at the side entrance of the Grand Meridian Hotel, shaking them both vigorously and making my nail holos shimmer with little stars. He had a short mop of curling brown hair that bounced around his face, a thin build, and was of medium height. Cute, but not outstandingly good-looking, with ruddy cheeks that gave him the appearance of having been out in the sun too long without protection. From everything I knew of Mick that was probably true, since he was too busy saving the world to notice. I'd always been impressed with his charity work, but knowing he was connected to TransWorld changed my opinion.

Though he looked no older than twenty-five, the last press release I'd caught put him at 172. Money got him access to up-grades far beyond the basic Renew program package, opening up opportunities I'd never have. It irritated me a little, though if I saved my money and kept up normal routine maintenance with a few tweaks, I could hit a hundred and fifty if I was lucky. Which, I reflected drily, I clearly was.

"Your charity is supporting such a worthwhile cause, I fought like hell to clear my calendar," I answered. "I'm thrilled you could accommodate me and I apologize again for not giv-ing your staff adequate notice."

"Not a problem. My assistant Mitsuki will see you sorted." He waved at a regal-looking woman behind him. With glossy straight black hair and pale porcelain skin, her Asian heritage was obvious. Japanese, I guessed, though Japan itself had been washed from Earth centuries ago. Those who'd escaped the ris-ing waters had taken great pains to preserve their heritage. "Once the guests see your skills, I suspect bids will go through the roof."

Did I mention Mick was also an accomplished bullshit artist? I laughed. "That's lovely of you to say, but let's wait for the auction results first."

"Of course." He'd already dropped my hands and moved on, getting back to the party and his many guests. So many people to glad-hand, so many butts to kiss, so many gold notes to collect. "Mitsuki will take care of you and your assistant. Let her know what you need and she'll ensure you have it."

"Wonderful. Thank you for being so gracious."

"Think nothing of it."

Then he left, leaving me and my assistant—Mr. Pennyworth, damn him—with the unsmiling and frosty Mitsuki.

She bowed formally. "If you will follow me, I will show you where the other parties are arranged."

"I don't need a staging area," I answered, as I'd rehearsed with Mr. Pennyworth. "It's easier to just add me to the bidding list and let me mingle with the crowd instead. I plan on doing one display reading with someone my assistant selects for me. Based on that, people can decide if they want to bid on my services or not."

Mitsuki frowned. "This is highly irregular," she said in perfect, unaccented English.

"Perhaps, but we know from experience that it works," Mr. Pennyworth replied, which made me want to roll my eyes. He wouldn't know what worked if it kicked him in the face.

"Follow me." Her frown vanished as she turned back to the party. "I'll direct you to the Grand Meridian ballroom where the guests are located."

She glided rather than walked down the service hall with its concrete floor, light-duty fiber walls, and poor lighting. Mr. Pennyworth had insisted we use the side entrance to conceal our identities until the last minute. Even worse, as he tried to alert Doucette of our arrival via the CN-net, I'd had to spend twenty minutes shivering outside in the cold. A March evening in Denver was a far cry from Nairobi's heat.

As we walked behind Mitsuki, I had the oddest feeling of déjà vu. I remembered the Mayfair Fertility Clinic, when we'd walked behind the One Gov employee Pennyworth had referred to as third generation MH Factor. I shot him a look from the corner of my eye and found him watching me. Of course he remembered.

"Don't try any bullshit," I whispered.

"A shame you aren't as amenable as our dear Mitsuki."

"Bite me." I stomped ahead, heels clicking angrily.

At the end of the hall, we stepped through a gunmetal gray door. This brought us into the kitchen where we waded through a barrage of chefs and servers yelling orders and jostling for space. The smells were delicious and I longed to reach out and grab a handful of whatever looked good. People gawked at us, but with Mitsuki leading the charge, we passed by without question.

We hustled through an empty dining room with a high vaulted ceiling. Large canvases lined the walls, showing holographic displays of vintage circuses before the Dark Times. Clowns, jugglers, even elephants—extinct for centuries—were depicted in loving detail. The ceiling itself looked like a giant white-and-red-striped tent, and in the center of the dozens of tables were magnificent centerpieces resembling sugary pink puffs of air blown into artistic whims of fancy.

"Is that real candy floss?" I asked Mitsuki. I wondered if it would count toward the calorie consumption index.

"No." Her tone indicated that my obvious idiocy and lack of social grace were an affront to everything she stood for. Lovely.

"You know, I've never met anyone of actual Japanese descent before," I continued. "You must be very proud of your heritage."

"We go to great lengths to maintain our identity," she agreed in the same tone, which translated roughly into: "You're not worthy to speak to me, mongrel dog."

"That's wonderful. My family is the same. We're Romani. We also lost our home during the floods."

"That's sad." Translation: "Silence, cur. You are an inbred mutt."

"One thing we love is curses. Never get on the bad side of a gypsy who can lay a decent curse! I could show you sometime. I inherited my great-grandmother's skills. One of the best."

She threw me a look over her shoulder. "Curses aren't real. Such belief stems from ignorance and superstition." No translation needed there.

"Oh, but that's not true!" I continued blithely. "It takes less than a second to cast even the most innocuous curse. Say like cursing someone to trip over a chair."

At that, she tripped over a chair. Honestly, it was only because she looked at me at that moment and I'd noticed a chair blocking her way. I didn't know the first thing about curses, but the horrified look on her face was so wonderful, I knew I'd enjoy reimagining it for years to come. Mr. Pennyworth helped her rise—such a gentleman—and asked if she was hurt. He shot me an unreadable look to which I couldn't help but smirk. After that, Mitsuki rushed us to the ballroom with no further comment.

Like the dining room, it was also done up in vintage circus theme. Performers worked the crowd—juggling, swallowing swords, and breathing fire. It was all very impressive, though I suspected the performers had some sort of MH Factor that elevated their pain thresholds.

"The other parties with auction items are through there." Mitsuki gestured to a side room where guests wandered in and out. She refused to meet my gaze. I smiled. "I will add your name to the bid list. Please come find me when you wish to perform your reading. Until then, enjoy yourselves."

She scurried off, thank the gods! Around us, beautiful people laughed, talked, and ate. I turned to Mr. Pennyworth, my last choice in the world of a date to an event like this. He hovered like a shadow in the background, unseen and unheard. I had the uncanny feeling that if I took my eyes off him, I'd never find him again.

"Are most of the people here TransWorld employees?" I asked.

"A few. The majority are upper echelon One Gov leaders, or those with political or financial influence that TransWorld hopes to gain. This is a type of luxury very few enjoy under One Gov's rule."

"It sounds like you have a personal problem with that."

"Not at all. Their mandate is unity and equality for all. Thanks to them every citizen is offered basic t-mods and MH Factor boosts, as well as access to the Renew program."

"And what's wrong with that? We're probably better off than any generation before us. Without One Gov, the human race would have fallen apart. We never would have survived the Dark Times without strong leadership. Okay, I'll admit they may be bloated with bureaucracy and we've strayed a little from the path of equality for all, but...well...what government in history has been perfect? No one ever gets it a hundred percent

right. It's not like we live in some horrible dystopia where people disappear in the night."

That earned me a long blink. "Their rule includes a policy
of strict control and monitoring through the CN-net, and they
use those same gifts as means of punishing dissenters. People's
rights are guaranteed, to a point. We are the children and they
are the parents looking out for our welfare. What few realize is
that we're prisoners, not children. Where is the innovation and
the growth? What if there was a way to stretch our reach as humans and become more as a species, but One Gov is holding
us back? Do we really need that sort of leadership anymore?"

"And you think the Consortium will give us more freedom?
Freedom to do what?" I fought back a shiver, suddenly nervous
about whatever he might be implying. What did I really know
about Alexei Petriv? Not much, and what I didn't know might
be terrifying. "Does Petriv have some scheme up his sleeve
that's going to change the world? No, that's going to
change...humans?"

"I assume you disapprove and things are fine as they are.
One Gov should remain in control of humanity's destiny forever as far as you're concerned."

Wow, I needed to tone this down quickly. This attitude was
so not what I'd expected from him. "Look, I'm not here to fight
you or debate the destiny of the human race. I can see we're just
going to have to disagree on this. However you feel about One
Gov, it probably isn't the smartest idea to bash them in their
own home. MH Factor for improved hearing isn't popular, but
you can bet the security here have it," I warned, then eyed him
speculatively. "Not to get you all riled up again, but I wouldn't
have pegged you as a reformist."

"And I wouldn't have imagined you dabbled in curses. My compliments, by the way."

I laughed. Much as I loathed the man, I couldn't help but offer up a bow. "She asked for it. How could I resist?" Then I sobered as I glanced around. "This is a pretty posh event for a lowly assistant to attend. You sure my mother isn't here?"

"The intel gathered from the guest list doesn't show her as attending. Furthermore, her research keeps her at the head office in Curitiba. I don't believe she leaves Brazil often. My understanding is her assistant spends a great deal of time traveling and submits biweekly progress reports."

"If he's here, you'd better find him while I work the crowd. I don't know anything about him, not even what he looks like, so it's all up to you."

That seemed to bring Mr. Pennyworth up short, like I'd cut him off mid-thought. "By all means. Let's get started."

I arched an eyebrow. "That almost sounds like sarcasm. This is your rodeo. I suggest you get busy."

I'd planned on saying more, if only to get my digs in, when something snagged my attention. From the corner of my eye I caught a flash of something familiar. I heard a laugh I'd heard a thousand times before. I turned and stopped and stared.

Less than twenty feet away was a dark-haired woman, heavily pregnant. She stood at a roulette table, clapping and laughing. Presumably she'd won. I didn't know nor did it matter. What *did* matter was who stood beside her, arm around her with easy grace. Looking so in love, it was a wonder they didn't produce enough energy between them to solve the Earth's potential HE-3 shortage.

Roy.

"There's the assistant," I heard Mr. Pennyworth say, his voice sounding as if it came from thousands of miles away. "By the roulette table. I believe he's with his wife."

With calmness I didn't feel, I turned to Pennyworth. We stared at each other for what seemed an eternity. I received several long blinks in return.

"I don't understand." I said, because for that split second, I didn't. My brain couldn't make the images fall into a pattern that made sense.

"That's the assistant," Mr. Pennyworth repeated. "He's the man you must discredit."

My gut didn't kick me, and yet everything abruptly clicked like a jigsaw falling into place. Roy, his wife, his baby on the way. Roy, who already lived the perfect life, without me. Roy, who was supposed to be on duty right now as a member of Mars Planetary Law Enforcement.

"Roy is my mother's assistant," I said aloud, just to make sure I had it right.

"Yes."

"The woman with him is his wife. She's having his baby." In my mind's eye, I could see the spinning Wheel of Fortune.

Again, the same answer: "Yes."

That was when I snapped. Not out loud, of course. Inside, I felt something shatter. Everything I'd felt for Roy. Everything we'd done together. The plans we made. The possibility of a baby that didn't even exist yet. That I'd even gone to jail because of it...Our whole relationship from our first meeting nearly a year ago to our last kiss—was it yesterday?—was all lies. Every second of every day for all that time...Lies. To Roy, I had been nothing. Meant nothing. Gods, I was just a *job*! I was a nine-to-five, punch out at the end of the day, job. And when he wasn't with me, which was often because he was supposedly working undercover with the MPLE, was he with her? With his goddamn pregnant *wife*?

"Ms. Sevigny?" Mr. Pennyworth's voice broke into my thoughts. When I looked at him, my eyes felt overly bright, like they were full of tears that refused to fall because that would mean everything I saw before me was true. "I've been calling you for some time. Are you well? Would you like to sit?"

"No. I don't want to sit. I want to..." I shook my head harder than I intended. I didn't know what I wanted. Tears went flying off in all directions. "Did he know? Gods, did Petriv know about this?"

Several long blinks followed. "Yes. But if he had told you and you hadn't witnessed the proof yourself, would you have believed him?"

"No. I'd have said he was lying." Then I flinched, thinking about the guilt I'd felt over being with Petriv, believing I'd betrayed Roy when now it turned out that Roy had been the one betraying me all along.

"He wanted you to see firsthand the levels of manipulation around you, orchestrated both by TransWorld and your mother."

In the background I could hear the woman's laughter. Then Roy's. I swiped at my eyes, scrubbing the wetness from my cheeks. No more crying. Not where the world could see how much it hurt me.

"I can't fault his logic, but he's a fucking bastard," I whispered. Another tear fell and I swore under my breath. No. No more tears. Not now.

"You've seen what he intended. We should leave," he suggested.

Fuck no. Not yet. I shook my head and instead asked, "How does my makeup look?"

"I don't understand your question."

"How does my makeup look?" I repeated, the first spark of anger beginning to flare. Gods, was he stupid? "Does it look like I was crying?"

He frowned and I received several long blinks. "You look adequate."

"Adequate? What the hell does that even mean? Who tells a woman she looks adequate?"

"Ms. Sevigny, I don't understand your line of questioning. It doesn't seem relevant to this situation."

I blew out a hard puff of air. "Oh, believe me. It's *very* relevant."

"You're angry," he prodded.

"Not quite yet, but give me time and I'll be fucking furious."

I turned from Mr. Pennyworth and took a halting step forward. Then two. A few more and I'd crossed to the roulette table. It didn't take long for Roy to notice me. After all, who could miss a woman standing on the other side of the table, watching with an unblinking stare?

Roy met my gaze and froze, his face a rictus of horror. He was so stunned he couldn't even speak. The woman looked up as well. She looked startled, then alarmed.

I smiled and knew it wasn't pleasant. I didn't yell, put on a show, scream, cry, or do any of the things a hysterical woman would do. Maybe because I'd lived this moment before with Dante and had used up all my hysterics. Maybe you were only allowed to lose your mind because of a man once in a lifetime. I wasn't that girl anymore, cutting her teeth on her first real relationship. I'd cried too much over one man already. Maybe deep down I'd been expecting this all along. Or maybe I'd gone into shock. Whatever the case, it didn't matter. I leaned in as close as the table would allow.

"Hello, Roy."

"Felicia! What are you doing here?" Roy cried, spilling his drink all over his hand and jacket. Water beaded on the material and dripped off. His hand shook. "I thought you weren't going to the auction. I would never...You said..."

His voice faded to nothing. My presence had stolen all words.

"And this is your wife," I continued, not making it a question. "Does she know about our relationship? Does she know what you do for my mother?"

Roy had gone so pale, even his lips were drained of color. He set his glass down with a thud, spilling the remaining liquid. "Felicia—"

"He tracks your movements and reports back to TransWorld." The woman's chin tipped up in defiance. "He's been doing it for months. He said in all the time you worked together, you never suspected him of being anything more than a friend."

Gods, he'd lied to both of us! "Friend? Is that what he told you I was? His *friend*? Like a work buddy or something? Wow. No, I never suspected anything—probably because I thought he was my boyfriend and we've been living together the past few months. You tend to overlook the discrepancies in a man's story when there's mind-blowing sex involved," I added just so I could enjoy the look of horror on her face.

There were so many other things I could have said, but I didn't. Mostly because my stunted thoughts wouldn't let me ad-

148

equately express everything I wanted to spew forth. Instead, I faced Roy and kept it simple. "Be sure to let my mother know I'm done with the games and the lies."

"Felicia, let me explain!"

"I really don't think there's any explanation in existence that covers what this is. I will destroy you for this, even if it takes the rest of my life. You are dead to me."

Then I turned and walked away from the life I'd always believed I wanted.

⊰◈⊱

Mr. Pennyworth reached me first, taking my arm in a firm grip. "Did you say all you needed to?"

I looked from his hand to his face, confused more than anything. "I think so."

"Was the sex as mind-blowing as you claim?"

Gods, had I said that? "No. I did all the work until it wasn't even fun anymore."

That earned me a brisk nod. "We need to leave. TransWorld security is moving to intercept."

I looked around, noting sudden motion around us. Several large men wended toward us, the crowd parting for them as they drew closer. Their build and sheer size reminded me of Petriv's chain-breakers, but these men were dressed to blend with the crowd. One approached from the right. One from the left. One in front. Mr. Pennyworth began a casual but purposeful stroll in the other direction.

"Why would they do that?" I asked, both stumped and startled by the whole thing.

"The stakes are high and you are a piece in the game that has made an unexpected move. The first act would be to put you back in play: you would be captured, your memories modified, then shipped back to Nairobi, none the wiser."

I gasped, horrified. "You're kidding."

"No, I'm not. I know how TransWorld does business. You don't stay on top without a certain amount of ruthlessness. If they can't modify your behavior, they may kill you. It depends on your perceived value."

"Why would I be valuable?"

"Your luck," he said, as if it should be obvious to any idiot. "Step lively, Ms. Sevigny. I've sniped into the mainline CN-net here and a mass transit pod will be waiting at the front entrance. Mrs. Ivchenko will meet you at the hotel."

Mr. Pennyworth rushed us through the crowd. Those who didn't step aside were sent sprawling. I stumbled after him, his hand on my arm the only thing holding me upright. Panic blossomed in my chest. These people would kill me. Or worse—alter my memories. A few days ago, I'd known nothing about this world. Now I was drowning in chaos while running for my life. I wanted to scream at Pennyworth to make it all stop, but could only follow where he led. I cast a look back. The security detail was gaining ground.

"I encourage you to hurry, Ms. Sevigny, not enjoy the sights."

"Don't be an asshole! I am hurrying!"

A hand reached out and caught the trailing fabric of my dress. I heard material tear as an outer layer of chiffon ripped away. Pennyworth hauled me down a flight of stairs—I missed at least three and lost a shoe—and ran us through the main lobby. We skidded across the marble floor, barely missing the reflecting pool and the cascading series of waterfalls positioned in the center of the lobby.

The main doors were already open as new guests flowed into the auction. Pennyworth dove through and pulled me into the chilly night air. Then with unexpected strength, he scooped me off the ground and pushed me into a waiting pod. The pod door shut with a gentle *whoosh* of suctioned air, and I whirled around the second I got my balance.

I was alone. Pennyworth remained outside on the sidewalk, hands raised in a fighting stance.

I pounded on the window. "What the hell are you doing? Get in here!"

No response other than a single glance back. Three men advanced. Two lunged for him, while the third moved to intercept the pod. Pennyworth dodged the first two and reached for the man racing for my pod. He caught him easily, grabbing the man's left wrist the way you might pluck a lazy bug out of the air. Even from inside the pod, I heard bone crunch. The man grunted and went down. When he tried to get up, Mr. Pennyworth delivered a kick to his knee. I heard another sickening crunch and the man didn't rise again. Then Pennyworth engaged the remaining two men. The first was tossed aside. The other leaped onto his back, taking him down. Then his partner recovered and hauled himself upright and they both proceeded to beat Pennyworth to a bloody pulp.

The pod pulled away from the hotel and its momentum knocked me into one of its seats. I tried to get up. Couldn't. My legs wouldn't lift me. Instead, I could do little more than remain in my seat as the pod carried me away from the fighting, and presumably, to safety.

10

I cried all the way back to the hotel. When Oksana found me huddled in the pod, I tried to tell her about Pennyworth. She said she already knew, and Petriv's instructions were to get me out of the country on the next commercial flight. To her knowledge, Pennyworth reported that the TransWorld *golovorez*—"thugs" in Russian—had been dealt with and he'd gone to ground. As for where Petriv was, I had no idea. Which really hurt. He'd orchestrated this whole thing, and I wanted him to clean up the mess he'd made of my life.

As for Roy, I wasn't sure what devastated me most: that he'd probably never loved me, or that he'd been a plant and reported my every move back to my mother. I'm sure he liked me well enough, or he couldn't have played at being my boyfriend as well as he had. Maybe he'd found it exciting to fuck two different women at the same time. Whatever the case, I felt violated and sick to my stomach. It made me feel dirty. It hurt, but in a different way from what Petriv had done, even though I was still mad at him too. At least Petriv wanted to wake me up from the lies. Still, how was I supposed to trust anyone now? This...this was just too much for anyone to live through.

The great surprise in all of this was Oksana. She sat by my side, held my hand, wiped my tears, made sure I ate and slept, and got me on the right plane home. She didn't offer any mood-altering medications. I'm not sure I would have accepted if she had, but was glad I didn't have the option.

The worst moment of all came when she escorted me back to the condo I shared with Roy and we stood at the door, about to go in.

"This is an unwise decision," Oksana said, not for the first time. "We could be playing directly into TransWorld's hands. If Alexei knew about this, he would never allow it."

"This is my home and I can't run away from my life. I just want a few things from the condo."

"There's nothing here you can't purchase elsewhere. What's more, you lived here with that dog who played on your emotions. Stay in a hotel. Come back when you're certain it's safe," she said.

"I know you're right, but I'm afraid I'll never come back if I wait too long."

I punched in my access code and unlocked the door. It swung open without resistance. I stepped inside, looked around, and my jaw dropped. Everything, I mean *everything*, was gone. The furniture. Wall hangings and pictures. Even the scorch mark. The carpet had changed. The flooring was different. The cupboards in the kitchen looked as if they'd never been used. I ran to the bedroom. Nothing. My closet. Nothing. All my clothes were gone. My office. My cupboard filled with cards. Oh gods, *my cards!* My quirky table, Eleat. Gone. The only deck I had was the one I'd taken to Denver.

I swayed on my feet, clutching my chest. This was worse than the auction. Worse than Roy's betrayal. This was my whole life gone. Me, erased. As if I'd never existed!

"Tell me Petriv had nothing to do with this! *Tell me!*"

"Nothing! I swear it," Oksana replied, hands up in surrender, looking as horrified as I felt.

"I want him to tell me that to my face." I looked at my bracelet in frustration, realizing I had no way to actually get in touch with him. How was that possible when the man seemed to have complete control over my life? "How do I shim him? I want to talk to him, *now*."

"Right now, our priority is to leave. If whoever did this left you access to the condo, it means they still expect you to return here. Your being here may have triggered an alarm. We could have unwanted guests any minute."

"TransWorld?"

"It seems likely. I've contacted Alexei. He will send a team. If any clues remain, they will find them. In the meantime, we must leave here immediately."

"Why would they do this to me? Why would they take all my things?"

"To make you believe you can't fight back. They want you to think that turning yourself over to them is the only option."

I looked wide-eyed at Oksana.

"I swear to you Alexei will not let that happen."

"How? How can he do anything against people who can do this?" I gestured to my empty condo. "What if he can't find my things? My cards? My whole life was here! What if—?"

"I swear to you, he will."

"But what if he can't—?"

Oksana grabbed my shoulders and shook me a little. "I promise you, he will move heaven and earth to find who did this and restore everything you lost."

An involuntary tear leaked out. I dashed it away with an angry swipe. "What happens now? Where do I go?"

"Oh, dear girl," Oksana murmured, embracing me. I let her because it just felt nice to have someone care. "You're part of the Tsarist Consortium now. We always look after our own."

⊰⋅⊱

A flight-limo had already arrived to pick us up. During the ride, I focused on my bracelet, tapping in a list of things I needed to do: find somewhere to live, get clothes, destroy TransWorld—though not necessarily in that order. I could always crash with family. However, the news of my breakup with Roy would sweep through the clan like wildfire and I'd have to endure their questions. I couldn't handle scrutiny and judgment now. Worse, what if TransWorld came looking for me and someone got hurt? I'd have to stay away until this nightmare was over.

As for my things, once I calmed down a little, I realized I didn't care about most of them. The furniture and the paintings—I may have selected them with care at the time, but it really didn't matter if I ever saw them again. I certainly didn't want to see anything that reminded me of Roy. I suppose I didn't even care that much about my clothes or my shoes; everything was replaceable with enough money. Plus, the shop hadn't been touched and I still had some things there. What really mattered to me were my cards, Eleat, and family memen-

155

tos like Granny G's quilt—personal things that could never be replaced, the things that told the story of who I was. Those I wanted back desperately.

A tug in my stomach announced the flight-limo's descent. I looked out the window, unfamiliar with the scenery. In fact, I doubted the Y-Line, for all its claims of public transit for all, even reached this part of the world.

I couldn't see any highways—just huge tracts of lush forest, grass, and flowers, all impeccably manicured. Against the blue sky and its puffy white clouds, the landscape was a sea of emerald. As we dropped lower, I saw a multitude of sidewalks. These linked shops and cafés hidden among gardens. Beyond that were the houses. My breath caught. They were massive affairs sprawling over thousands of square feet. In the city, we lived on top of each other in condos piled high enough to brush the clouds. Outside the Kibera slum and any government-sanctioned parks, every space imaginable contained at least some sort of high-rise. What I saw now didn't exist anymore, at least not in the world I lived. No one I knew could afford something like this when space was at a premium.

I threw a look over my shoulder at Oksana. "Is this still Nairobi?" I asked as the flight-limo set down on a paved landing pad in a field of rolling greenery. One of the massive homes I'd admired earlier sat a short distance away. Up close, it looked even more impressive.

"For tax purposes, I suppose it is. The locals call it the Glade, though I'm not sure the name's appropriate since it's all manmade and none of the plants are native."

Ah, the Glade. Where the richest of the rich lived. Unsurprising. I should have guessed, but then again, I wasn't at my brightest.

"Whose house is that?"

"Oh, I'm sorry. Without the direct CN-net access, I some-times forget you don't connect things as the rest of us do...I apologize—that sounds rude. Blame it on my no-nonsense Russian upbringing. It's Alexei's home. It's where he lives when-ever he's in this part of the world."

"Okay..." I pressed, "but why am I here?"

"Again, I apologize. He's invited you to live here until you've sorted yourself out."

It was as bad as I feared. "Pardon me for saying so, but that's a terrible idea. I can't possibly live here. It's dozens of miles from the city. How will I get to my shop? What if I need...I don't know...milk or something?"

"You will have a flight-limo on standby at all times. How-ever, it might be best to not worry about work until we've sorted some things out."

"I don't think living in his house is really appropriate."

She waved a hand, dismissing my protests. "Bah! The house is so large you'll never see each other. And he's here so rarely. Anyway, you are with the Consortium now, so it's all irrele-vant."

"I'm not even Russian. Isn't that a requirement?"

Oksana laughed. "If Alexei has offered you employment, you're one of us for as long as the relationship is mutually bene-ficial."

Part of me wondered if something was lost in translation, so I tried again. "That's great, but this is only temporary. After I've finished with this...project...I'll be going back to my old life." Ugh. My old life didn't exist anymore. "Well, I mean...I can't stay here forever."

Oksana smiled and patted my hand. "That's not what's intended. What happened to you is awful. You need help and we are offering. Nothing more, nothing less. If you have another plan, we will not stand in your way."

I didn't say what I thought, which was I wouldn't have needed their help if not for them. But all they'd done was remove the blindfold and reveal the truth. How could I blame them? I sighed. "When you put it like that, how can I refuse? Thank you."

"Here comes the man himself," Oksana replied with a nod toward the tinted window behind me. "You can thank him personally."

A chain-breaker slid my door open. With no little fear and trepidation, I crawled out, blinking in the sunlight like some creature who'd emerged from under a rock. A sidewalk of smooth, irregularly shaped gray stones about ten feet wide led from the landing pad to the house. Gardens lined either side. Petriv came down the sidewalk, and my stomach gave a lurch.

He looked like he'd been caught relaxing, taking a walk, or doing whatever crime lords did on their days off. His dark hair was slicked back from his face and he wore a lightweight white sweater and gray pants. Despite the horror of the last twelve hours, I found myself wanting him. I suspected I probably shouldn't be having such thoughts, yet there they were. Maybe I'd temporarily gone into shock and wasn't thinking properly. Or maybe it was because I no longer had boyfriend guilt to worry about. The only person I had to worry about hurting was me.

Petriv stopped in front of me, put his hands along my neck, and tilted my face up to his with his thumbs. His hands were warm as he moved my head back and forth, examining me as if he were a doctor and could read all my problems from my face. The proprietary gesture and the closeness unnerved me, but he wouldn't let me pull away.

"How are you?" he asked, his expression severe and assessing as he studied me. "Have you even slept? When did you eat last?"

There were so many unresolved issues, it didn't surprise me in the least when I started in with: "Why didn't you tell me I'd have Pennyworth riding shotgun?"

Without missing a beat, he said, "He had unique skills for the job we required. I knew he could get you in and out of the auction without issue, as well as contain the situation should things go awry."

"You knew seeing him would be a problem for me."

"Regardless, he could do what I needed. He accepted our retainer and fulfilled our contract's terms."

I frowned. "What exactly does that mean?"

"It means he kept you safe to the best of his abilities. Would you like to know specifics?"

No I wouldn't, but decided I couldn't afford to be a coward about it. "Tell me."

"Three TransWorld agents tried to detain you as you left the auction, which you witnessed. Pennyworth killed them and disposed of the bodies. Another two attempted to capture you at TT1. Mr. Pennyworth intercepted those as well."

Wow. That was *not* what I had expected. I would have slumped a little if Petriv hadn't held me up.

"You're shocked?"

"Of course I'm shocked! He killed five people! How did you think I'd react?" I bit my tongue, fighting to hold back the rest of what threatened to come out of my mouth. Finally I managed to ask, "Is Pennyworth is still alive?"

Petriv looked amused. "He's more difficult to kill than one might expect."

I swallowed and tried not to hyperventilate. "Is this how the Tsarist Consortium handles everything? With murder? Is this what the tri-system can expect if you win the transit link contract?"

"We aren't the monsters the CN-net news outlets portray. Everyone knows One Gov fears what it can't control. It's time for change, and the Consortium is the only group with the vision and the resources to bring it about. One Gov's utopia has cracks and you would know that if you chose to see beyond the propaganda." Petriv's hands tightened around my neck. Not in a frightening way, but enough that I grabbed his wrists as if I could somehow hold him still.

"What I've seen so far doesn't look all that great. Will more people die before this is over?"

He leaned close and pulled me nearer until our faces were inches apart. I couldn't fight him without hurting myself. Oddly, I didn't want to fight anymore. Instead, a curious weakness swept over me and I felt my insides tighten with want. After everything I'd been through, how could I still feel like this for him? I should have been angrier or having a meltdown of epic proportions, screaming at him for using me and putting me in this awful situation. I shouldn't have wanted to be closer to him. Damn me and my stupid gut feeling.

"I prefer it not to be the case, but it may be unavoidable. Mr. Pennyworth did as ordered. He kept you safe and intact. Or would you rather have had your memory wiped clean and been sent back to your existence of lies? I'm sure all your things are set up in another condo somewhere, sitting just as you remember them, waiting for you to return none the wiser. Perhaps Roy is waiting there for you as well, ready to act as if none of this happened."

My stomach twisted into a knot and I felt sick. I shuddered. "I *can't* go back to that life. I'd rather die first."

"And I would very much prefer it if you stayed alive, regardless of how many other lives get in the way."

"My life isn't more important than anyone else's."

"Not true. In my estimation, you are too valuable to lose and I won't waste what you represent."

"And what do I represent to you? Is it just luck and easy access to my mother, or something more?" I asked, my voice a breathy whisper.

"Stay around long enough and find out."

I swallowed again and fought the shiver at the promise in those words. "Oksana says you'll be able to find the things they took. I know they can all be replaced—even my Tarot decks, but... but it's me. They're trying to mess with what it means to be me. I'm not just a shell that they can wipe free of memories and fill with whatever personality they want."

His expression softened and his hands grew gentle, his touch becoming a caress. "I will get it all back for you."

"Thank you." Despite everything, I believed him. Even if I didn't trust him, I knew he would do this for me. The realization that he now held so much of my life in his hands made me shiver again. "You should probably let me go."

He smiled, but there was nothing gentle in it anymore. He'd felt my shiver, all right. Whatever distance that had sprung up between us since the flight to Denver was now gone. "What if I say no?"

I had no response to that. In that moment, part of me just

wanted someone to look after everything and take away the chaos. I knew he could do that, and much more. After the past few days, it would be a blessing not to think, to know I could take what was in front of me without worrying about the rest of the world.

Behind us, Oksana cleared her throat. "Perhaps we should go inside," she suggested. "Felicia needs to rest. She's refused the zone acclimatization meds and has been running too many hours without sleep. You can continue your discussion once she's refreshed."

"Take the zone meds," Petriv advised, pulling back. Apparently the interrogation was over. "Without them, you won't make it through the next two weeks."

"More traveling?" I asked, fighting back sudden exhaustion. I'd been gearing up for this confrontation and now that it was done, so were the last of my reserves.

"That, and potentially other things," he said, then let me go. Without his hands on me, I felt adrift. "I'd planned a debriefing for later today to discuss your next task, but I'll reschedule."

Now I knew fatigue was getting the best of me—Petriv hinted at the next step in his master plan and I hadn't even blinked. In fact, I couldn't even seem to work up the proper fear or worry I knew was required.

"And what's next?" I ventured.

"We're going to Brazil. It's time you met your mother."

⇒◆⇐

I'm not sure how long I slept. Hours, or maybe minutes. Though the bed was beyond comfortable and I couldn't hear any sound from outside, I couldn't seem to settle. I felt terror mixed with rage and regret every time I closed my eyes. I was angry with Roy, my mother, Petriv, Pennyworth—everyone associated with this mess. I felt stupid and lied to, and not sure who I could trust. I could see the horror on Roy's wife's face every time I closed my eyes. And the jealousy I felt ate at me like some awful, consuming beast. She had the life I was supposed to have.

I gave up on sleep as sunlight crept around the drawn window shades. I sighed and considered my surroundings. The sheets and one of my pillows were on the floor. I must have kicked them off in the night. A quick check of my c-tex bracelet showed it wasn't even seven yet. Having my shop on Night Alley meant I worked most nights and rarely saw anything resembling morning. What did one do with oneself so early in the day?

I got out of bed and threw on a robe over my nightgown. Actually, a blue-green silk negligee was a better description. I wasn't sure why I'd even packed it. Sometimes I could be such an idiot. Still, at least it was mine, which counted for something. Right now, all I owned in the world was stashed in the two suitcases I'd originally brought from home. Did that make me lucky or just foresighted?

"It makes me fucking brilliant," I muttered as I dragged both to the bed and surveyed their contents. A few outfits, plus toiletries. That wouldn't get me far unless I planned on washing my clothes every other day. I swore in frustration and scrubbed a hand over my face. The thought of TransWorld breaking into my condo, rifling through my belongings, and taking my things left me feeling violated and helpless all over again. I alternated between knowing rationally they were just things that could be replaced and freaking out because I wanted my favorite lounge pants. What was I to my mother and TransWorld? A pawn in their scheme? A science experiment that needed monitoring? Had Roy constantly looked for examples of my supposed "luckiness" and reported back to them?

I took a breath, then two, counted to a hundred, and didn't feel better. I needed to talk this over with...well, *someone* before I lost what remained of my sanity. Besides, I was starving. When had I last eaten?

After a quick shower in a sunken tub with numerous hoses and nozzles I didn't have time for, I slapped myself together with whatever I had on hand. My luggage contained items selected for Denver's colder weather, not the warmer temperatures of Nairobi, so I threw on the coolest outfit I could manage—a cream microfiber skirt and cami with breast-molding enhancements that held everything wonderfully in place. Both were stain-repellant, thank the gods, or the cream would have never stayed cream. They also had temperature controls built in so if I got too hot or cold, they regulated as needed. I put on a pair of sandals, and that was the best I could do.

Opening the shades, I discovered a balcony overlooking the yard. The weather was perfection, the sky without a hint of rain. That would change soon enough when the rainy season hit in a few weeks. I cast a glance up at the sun. Its rays felt like nothing on my skin and I whistled in amazement. A nano-sunshade must have covered the balcony, or I'd already be feeling a slight burn.

From my balcony I could see the entire back of the house. I counted six other balconies in addition to mine. How many guest rooms did Petriv have? In the distance, trees ensured maximum privacy; I couldn't see another house and had no idea how far away one might be. I could hear the drone of a helicon overhead. Was it security, or just more richie-riches heading into the city?

Far to the left was a large swimming pool where someone was swimming laps. I could also see an extensive patio where people were eating. Gods, was this what rich people did in the morning? Ate breakfast at ridiculous hours and swam insane numbers of laps over bodies of water the size of small lakes? Apparently, or at least in Alexei Petriv's world.

I left my bedroom, stepping into the hall. It was long and narrow, marked with lots of closed doors, sedate lighting, and many small tables with vases of fresh flowers. I wondered if those were replaced daily, then decided I needed to concentrate on finding the pool.

I found a promising-looking staircase leading down to an open foyer on the main floor. It looked familiar; I was sure I'd used it earlier. Overhead was an enormous chandelier I also recognized. At the bottom of the marble staircase, I turned left on my gut's advice and headed down another hall. I heard voices. I didn't recognize them, but maybe I could ask for directions to the pool, or better yet, the kitchen.

The first door on the left was a living room. Strike that—a hotel lobby, given its sheer size, tasteful furniture, high ceiling, and art hanging on the walls. Inside were two men. With them were four chain-breakers, taking up various positions around the room.

"Sorry to interrupt. I was just..." A quick look told me I was in the wrong place at the wrong time. The scowls on both men's faces said as much, and I backpedaled with more speed than I normally mustered.

Two chain-breakers caught me in a firm grip and I shrieked. Damn it! I was so sick of being molested by these vat-grown, musclebound apes! I tried to jerk free. No good, but I did get more bruises to add to the ones I'd already collected.

"If you just let me go, I'll be heading to the pool," I snapped.

One of the men fixed me with a wintery gaze. Older, he looked to be in his late forties, which meant he was clearly *old*. He had dark hair graying at the temples and blue eyes that could cut you to the quick. They weren't as impressive as Petriv's, but I suspected few were. Broad-shouldered, with ramrod-straight posture despite sitting in an oversized armchair, he looked like some medieval king of old. Tattoos covered the backs of his hands and his knuckles, but I was too far away to see them clearly.

"So you're Alexei's latest project," he said, the words reflecting a subtle hint of Russian accent. His tone was not kind.

He turned to the other man, who was even older. That was a shock all on its own. Nearly everyone began One Gov's sponsored Renew treatments the month of their twenty-fifth birthday, with upgrades done annually. Not even Grandmother at eighty-one looked as old as this second man did. His hair was a thick, flowing mane of white that reached his stooping shoulders. Deep lines were etched in his tanned face and milky green eyes regarded me with nothing short of armed hostility.

"This is what he believes will bring us an empire?" continued the younger man, gesturing at me.

"There seems to be a mistake. I just want to know where the pool is." I tugged again. Maybe I could talk my way out of this. Maybe—

"Bring her here," he ordered the chain-breakers. "Let's have a closer examination of the savior of Mother Russia."

With that, I was frog-marched inside. I wasn't getting out of anything.

II

My gut, I decided as I was forced into a wingback leather chair, meant for me to be there since it had indirectly led me to this room. Maybe I needed to learn about my role in the Tsarist Consortium's little scheme. After all, I couldn't keep wandering around in blithe ignorance, mooning after Petriv and letting him decide my future. Maybe these were the true power players. Or maybe they were just thugs. Time to find out. Behind me, I heard the doors lock. I didn't like the finality of that sound.

"Well, this is pleasant," I said, offering a glare around the room. "Last time I checked, I was a guest, not a prisoner."

The younger man laughed. In a way, I was glad Petriv wasn't here. When he was around, somehow the full force of my anger was blunted by my confused lust.

"He would say that to a pretty girl," he said, looking to the older man. "Sometimes I can't help but wish to be that young again, enjoying the excitement of the chase. He'll get it out of his system in time, I suppose."

The older man said nothing.

I took a breath, thinking before I spoke. Anger wouldn't get me far, and gods only knew what was really happening here. "I assure you, it isn't my goal to be the most popular girl at the party, and I think you know I'm not here for anyone's entertainment—my own included." I looked from one man to the other, meeting their eyes and using every skill I'd gained in years of reading both the Tarot and people. "You seem to know who I am, but I can't claim the same. I assume you are Mr. Petriv's associates in the TransWorld bid."

Both men startled at that. "So Alexei has told you our business? He must be quite taken with your abilities then," the younger man said.

"If you mean my ability to read the Tarot cards, then yes." I leaned forward and smiled with a confidence I didn't feel. "Mr. Petriv wants me to ensure the Consortium wins the bid. We have an arrangement beneficial to both of us. If you want to know more, you'll have to ask him. If you don't know the details, I suppose that's because he doesn't want you to."

The older man fixed me with a steady gaze, his faded green eyes boring into me. "You've no doubt never met anyone as old as I," he said in a deep, gravelly voice, no trace of Russian in his accent. "To me, you are but a gnat on an elephant's ass. Or rather, a baby wailing fresh from her mother's womb. It is an act of kindness on my part to even suppose you have relevant thoughts. For me to believe you are the key to resolving our past wrongs and reconciling the future of the tri-system is beyond laughable. Alexei believes it to be true, so we will work with him so long as good sense allows. My only concern is, given the time and resources we've put into his training, that we reap the rewards of that investment. He will guide the Tsarist Consortium to its rightful place. If you are a tool that will help him succeed, so be it. But you will never be more than that and I am too old to see you as anything other."

Wow. I narrowed my eyes and returned his stare. "May I ask your name, sir?"

"Konstantin Belikov," he answered, giving the name such a regal quality, I wondered if I should kiss his ring.

"Mr. Belikov, I appreciate your honesty. It appears we have something of a gap between us, which neither of us is able to properly cross. However, I'd like to assure you I never go back on my word. I have an arrangement with Mr. Petriv and I will see it through to the end, whatever that end might be. By the same token, I'm working on good faith that the Consortium will do the same. And though I may seem like an…ass gnat to you, my life is as worthwhile to me as yours is to you. To you, I'm a child. To me, you're an old man grasping for control that's slipped from your fingers." I stood up, and eyed them both. My knees shook a little, but I rose smoothly enough. I don't think they caught my falter. "Now, if you'll excuse me, I'm heading to the pool. Again, I'm a guest here, and I was going to rustle up some breakfast."

I was halfway to the door on my unsteady legs when Belikov called out to me.

"Girl!"

"My name is Felicia Sevigny," I answered without turning. "You may call me Felicia or Ms. Sevigny, but I don't answer to 'girl.'"

"Felicia, then." The tone sounded exasperated. I turned and found the man half in, half out of his chair. He sat in a huff, the chair groaning under him.

"Yes?" I asked sweetly. "Did you have something to add?"

"I am two years shy of five hundred years old. I remember the world before One Gov crushed it under its heel. Few of us do, but I do. Grigori does."

"Konstantin!" the other man protested—Grigori apparently. "This is not how we agreed to handle this!"

Belikov waved a dismissive hand. "Clearly she believes what she says. Not even pawns can afford to be alienated."

Thanks a lot, my brain screamed. Outwardly, I gave nothing away. "You were born before the Dark Times."

"That's a pretty way of saying we thought the Earth was finished, but yes, that's correct. Oceans rose. Earthquakes. Anomalies in the planet's tilt. All these things conspired to destroy civilization. Then, One Gov was necessary. No one would have survived without strong central leadership. It was harsh because it was needed, but they were greedy bastards. They took what they could and stole what they couldn't. The Tsarist Consortium was one group of many who suffered under their rule. The Renew treatments were ours, and they took them from us. They said they needed a more robust version of humanity to survive the dangerous conditions throughout the tri-system. We understood, but the time has come to reclaim what is ours."

"And Mr. Petriv is who you believe can do that," I said, getting it, though it didn't make me less irritated. "Well, I am the person he believes can crack TransWorld. If you can't accept that, it doesn't speak well for your confidence in him."

"You misunderstand, Felicia," Grigori, the younger man, said. He cast a look at Belikov, who nodded. "We are the ones endorsing Alexei. There are many in the Consortium who believe him too young, and that he is bringing too much change, too quickly. The TransWorld bid is where he will make his name among us and begin his true ascent to leadership. We are here to ensure that happens. There is much riding on his success with this project. It will usher in plans for a potential future we would like to make a reality. We also report to the other *vory v zakone* should there be cause for concern. Others would prefer to see him fail."

"What's *vory v zakone*?" I asked, mangling the Russian.

"It belongs to a time when we were the only law in a land full of corruption. 'Thieves in Law,'" Belikov answered. "Despite what you think, we follow a code of honor, though time and history have distorted it. Of course, your thoughts on the matter are irrelevant to me."

I frowned. "Why are you telling me this?

"Because Alexei is the best hope we have for unity within the Tsarist Consortium. We will not allow him to be led astray, not by you, or by anyone. Alexei was crafted to be the leader we need. He thinks you are relevant. We do not. We felt you should know where you stand and that we will act if any issues arise," Grigori finished.

"I see. Well then, now that we've all laid our cards on the table, I'm starving and would like to get some breakfast."

I had to get the hell out of there before I ran screaming. I headed for the doors, doing my best not to hurry, when they burst open. The lock securing them shattered as if it was nothing. I was far enough away to miss the brunt of the entry, but not so far to avoid coming face-to-face with an enraged, dripping-wet Alexei Petriv. Or rather face-to-chest, since the top of my head didn't clear his shoulders. Well, at least now I knew who'd been in the pool.

Chain-breakers leaped into action, taking up defensive positions around the seated men. Through the open door, I glimpsed a frightened-looking woman in a gray maid's outfit. Her mouth was a frozen *O* of horror while she blessed herself with the sign of the cross.

The room quieted. Everyone looked at everyone else. I took a step away from the barely winded Petriv. Part of it was shock. One of the doors had torn clean off its hinges and lay on the floor. The sheer strength something like that took was mind-boggling. The violence behind it was staggering as well, even if being rescued was nice. The rest of my retreat was so I could admire the partially clad Petriv.

He was still soaking wet, hair slicked back from the pool, and my eyes couldn't help but follow the water as it dripped down his chest to dampen the floor. Tiny black swim trunks left little to my imagination. I suspected there wasn't an extra pound of fat anywhere on his body. His shoulders, arms, chest, abs—all looked sculpted, chiseled, and cut to perfection, as if he'd been carved from marble.

However, what held my eyes were the tattoos covering his body. Not head to toe, but an extensive array of old-school blue-black ink was spread over the canvas of his skin. Stars on his shoulders and knees. A crucifix in the center of his chest. A serpent, or perhaps a dragon, coiled around his waist and down his left leg. A small Madonna and child over his heart. A spider near his right collarbone. I blinked, but couldn't see more as he stalked nearer, his hands on my shoulders giving me a little shake to break my stare.

"Did they hurt you?" he asked, blue eyes darting over me. His hands were still wet, but the water trickling down my skin was warm.

"No. I'm fine." I pulled my gaze away from the star on his left shoulder. Eight points. In the Tarot, it meant power. "I was looking for breakfast when I met your...associates. We talked."

"About?" His voice dipped dangerously low, making me glad the anger wasn't focused my way.

"They had some questions, but I think we've come to an understanding."

"She's right, Alexei. There's no need for such dramatics," Belikov said from where he remained seated behind me. "We are done and satisfied with her answers."

Petriv gazed over my head at the men. His face was calm, but his grip on my shoulders told a different story. "I told you not to interfere. I have things well in hand."

"So well you were almost killed in an explosion two days ago," Grigori chided like a scolding parent.

"The situation was contained. There was no need for your ridiculous recall."

Was that why he'd left me in Denver—not because of anything I'd said or done but because they'd thought the situation was too dangerous? Obviously there were things going on I didn't completely understand, but I hadn't been *that* blind, had I? It seemed Petriv didn't have as much control over the situation as I'd first imagined. I thawed a little at that. I couldn't hold on to my earlier anger if his leaving me in Denver wasn't entirely his fault.

"But it was a situation nonetheless. You are gambling with the balance of power in the Consortium. You were not groomed for this position to put everything at risk."

"Without risk, nothing changes. Isn't that what you always say, Konstantin? Isn't that why I'm here?" Petriv challenged. He let go of me and I fought not to rub the circulation back into my arms. "The Consortium wants the Earth-Mars transit link. As I've explained before, Ms. Sevigny is vital to our success."

"Yes, but we've yet to see results," Grigori continued. "All we have is a girl to whom you've developed an unhealthy attachment, if the evidence we just witnessed is any indication."

"We're leaving for Curitiba this afternoon. You will see the expected results," came the reply, offered with all the confidence in the world.

We were? But we'd just gotten back from Denver! He'd mentioned Brazil but I never imagined we'd go so soon. I looked up at Petriv, wanting answers but not sure if we were supposed to present a united front against the old guard. Or was I merely Petriv's puppet? Did I have any say in what happened next or what route my life took? Go to Curitiba this afternoon? Sure. What next? Destroy my mother? Absolutely.

Belikov rubbed his hands together with glee as if he were some cartoon villain from an Old World melodrama, about to tie the heroine to the railway tracks. "Perfect. With you there in Trans-World's nest of snakes, I look forward to seeing the ripple in the CN-net. However, I advise you not to let what happened at the space elevator reoccur. Contract Pennyworth. He's reliable in a pinch."

"I think you'll be pleased with what I have in mind. I plan to remove TransWorld entirely from the field."

"*Zamechatel'nyy.* That is wonderful news. *Udacha*, though I suppose saying good luck is redundant." Belikov laughed at his own terrible joke. "I look forward to the end results."

I fought not to roll my eyes before stepping around Petriv to leave the whole sordid scene behind me. We'd been dismissed, or at least I had. Funny how I no longer cared about breakfast.

Not sure what to do with myself, I passed the maid still covering her mouth and decided to continue in my original direction. I'd gone a handful of steps, my sandals clicking on the floor tiles, when I heard a smattering of Russian and footsteps, and a hand reached out to stop me.

I whirled. Petriv, naturally. We were alone in the hall, the maid having disappeared.

"Allow me to escort you. The dining room is this way," he said, tucking my hand around his arm. It was ludicrous given the situation, but he seemed intent on it.

"I'm not hungry." I tried, and failed, to tug my hand away. I stopped walking and got better results since it forced him to stop with me.

"You need to eat. You also need to take the zone acclimatization meds if we're leaving this afternoon. You've gone two nights without sleep. You'll make yourself ill."

It unnerved me that he knew how much sleep I'd gotten. "What if I don't feel like going anywhere?"

"I believe I indicated the terms of our agreement were up to my discretion, Ms. Sevigny. Are you saying you want to change that?"

I didn't like what I heard in his voice. It added another layer to my fear. "No, it isn't that," I said, resuming my tugging and actually placing a hand on his chest to brace myself. No good, though I noted touching him was like touching warm rock. What sort of workout regimen did the man have? "Those men in there... What happened in Denver... Being in this house... You... I think I'm finally understanding the scope of what's going on and... I'm scared. No. More than that, I'm angry."

"I didn't realize Konstantin and Grigori would question you.

They're looking after their interests as any businessmen would. Still, it was unexpected."

"Which naturally explains why you kicked in the door earlier."

"I hadn't anticipated they would approach you—not in my home. They come from an older school of thought when it comes to gathering information, so I was concerned."

"Why? Would they have tortured me?" I asked.

A shrug. "I should have assigned you a security detail to protect you from their curiosity."

"Who? Mr. Pennyworth?"

"If I thought he was up to the job, yes."

"Then think again. All I wanted was my blacklisted status revoked. Instead, I'm getting dragged deeper into this than I want, seeing things I don't want to see, and now I've come face-to-face with people who actually want to change the world as we know it. Three worlds, actually. Gods, Belikov admitted to being almost five hundred years old! Five hundred! I didn't even think that was possible! The thought of living in a world where people like them call the shots scares me more than the government that's already in place."

Petriv put a silencing hand over my mouth. Then he moved me bodily down the hall into an empty room. It looked like it might be an office. I saw very little, and even less so when Petriv shut the door behind us and towered over me. I looked up at him, wide-eyed and bewildered.

"Before you shriek in outrage let me warn you that for your own safety, it would be best if you lowered your voice. You've yet to prove your value to them, and I can only do so much." His voice dropped to little more than a whisper. "I thought you were smarter than that."

Ouch. That hurt. I did know better. Or, I did most of the time. I caught his wrist in my hand, tugging it away from my mouth, though I'm sure he moved only because he wanted to.

"I said I was scared and angry, not a rocket scientist," I replied in the same low voice. "You brought me into this, using Pennyworth to trap me. Thanks for the setup and making me indebted to you, by the way. Pennyworth is a complete asshole and I'd fire him if I were you. He's creepy as hell."

That earned me a half smile. "I'll take it under advisement."

"Don't patronize me! I've seen enough to know there are games within games, and players behind the scenes that I'll never know and don't *want* to know about. My own boyfriend spied on me and reported back to my supposedly dead mother for fuck's sake! Do you even know how that makes me feel? Now I'm suspicious of everyone. All my past relationships. All my friends. I don't know who to trust anymore."

"You can trust me."

"Bullshit. How? You knew about Roy, yet you let me walk into that situation in Denver. Logically I understand what you were trying to do, but it doesn't mean you had to do what you did. It hurt me and it was humiliating. Does it mean that every task I do for you is going reveal some deeper level of horror you already knew about but needed to 'show' me? Is my blacklisted status even going to be lifted at the end of this? Will I even be alive when it's all done? It seems like you're the golden boy, leading the charge and pulling everyone's strings. What makes you so special everyone's deferring to you? Who are you?"

He took a deep breath then let it out slowly, running fingers through his damp hair and leaving it a disheveled mess. Muscles rippled in his arms and chest, and I noted the wilder and more distracted he became, the hotter he seemed to get.

"I am not getting into this with you now, Ms. Sevigny."

"Were you ever?"

He stepped in so close, I stumbled into the door. Yes, it was meant to intimidate me, but it was all I could do not to reach out and touch him. My thoughts immediately flew back to the restaurant and the first time he kissed me. I swallowed audibly. Was I about to experience a repeat performance? Did I want to? I knew I should be focusing on the Consortium's plans, worrying about what could happen in Brazil, or sweating over a host of other problems. Instead as Petriv looked down at me, all I wanted was his hands on me more than I wanted my next breath.

His head dipped in close, lips gliding along my throat. I fought back a shiver. When he spoke, his voice was a soft purr in my ear. "This discussion is finished. We leave for Brazil this afternoon. I suggest you get some breakfast and take the zone meds. Oksana is seeing to your belongings and will ensure you have everything you need."

I looked up at the ceiling, all but holding my breath. My heart beat fast and my nipples hardened as his lips brushed my throat. My mind and my body were so confused about what they each wanted, I couldn't think. "What if I say no?"

"As I've stated previously, you will do what I want, when I want it. You don't strike me as someone who goes back on her word."

"Not true. I lie all the time. It's one of my favorite things to do." Damn, my voice came out breathier than intended.

He laughed softly, his lips now on the crook of my neck

where my pulse beat wildly. "I don't think so. I suspect you were always the girl who grew up doing what she was told, playing by the rules, and never getting into trouble. Whereas I am nothing but."

"Nothing but what?"

"Trouble."

He tucked a strand of hair behind my ear, then braced his hand on the wall near my head, caging me with his body.

"What if that's what I'm looking for now?" I whispered, my stomach quivering in a way that matched my pulse—excited, eager, afraid of what I was asking for.

He pulled back enough so he could see my face. The look he gave me was intense, primal. I could feel the heat of his body as he loomed over me, and the effect made me both dizzy and tense. With one of his hands—the one not on the wall—he cupped my left breast. He stroked my nipple with the pad of his thumb, and the sensation rocked my entire body. I moaned and pushed myself further into his hand. His lips quirked into a smile.

"If that's what you want, I am more than happy to give it to you."

"I want."

A heartbeat later, his lips were on mine. My mouth opened under his, my head tipped back. I felt my body liquefy against his as the kiss deepened. I thought he would rush like at the restaurant. He didn't, kissing with deep licks that felt like a slow, sensual dance of his mouth against mine. I couldn't help but moan as I leaned into him. How long had it been since I'd been kissed like this? Like I was the most important, sexiest woman in the tri-system? Never, I reflected dimly. Absolutely never.

He sucked on my lower lip as his other hand went to my other breast. I'd thought my nipples were hard before. I was wrong. With his thumbs pressing firmly, they became stiff little pebbles of want, demanding that I get them out of clothes and into his bare hands.

"You're so soft," he whispered against my lips. "So damned soft."

His hands then slid into the top of my cami and pushed the fabric down until it was under my breasts, which lifted them up toward him. With a satisfied grunt, he bent his head down and took one nipple in his mouth. I cried out in sheer, blissful ecstasy, my hands behind his head now, bringing him closer. His hands migrated to my back, forcing me to arch against him as his mouth pulled hard on my breast, biting my nipple in a way that sent ripples of arousal straight to my groin.

"More," I murmured helplessly as I clung to him. "I need more."

Suddenly I found myself on my back, lying on a couch in the office. Petriv was poised over me, lips still on my breast, his sucking becoming greedy and insistent. His hands were at the edge of my skirt; then he lifted the hem and pushed it out of his way. With ease, he parted my legs and slid a finger inside my panties. I shamelessly arched up to meet his hand.

"You're wet." His words were a fierce growl of pleasure. He parted me with his fingers, caressing my slick folds with an expert touch. "Do you know how good you feel? How much I've wanted to touch you?"

I was so aroused, I could barely think. He was *not* someone I should want. Everything about him screamed he wasn't good or right for me. Yet even knowing that, I didn't care. My breathing was ragged and hitched as I looked up at him. Shadows played across his skin, making him look both dark and dangerous, and so hot I thought I might spontaneously combust just looking at him. His expression was one of ferocious hunger as he gazed down at me, like I was a thing he'd craved for an eternity. It was frightening, but also heady. All that power, concentration, and desire focused on me. Wanting me. I had never been so turned on by anything in my life.

He tore away my panties. I gasped in surprise. A heartbeat later, he slid another finger inside me. My eyes fluttered closed, stunned that a man I'd met only a few days ago could make me feel like this, or that I was even letting him touch me this way. His breath came out in a hiss and he swore softly in Russian.

"You feel like a dream. God, you're so tight," he whispered, inserting another finger, then rubbing his thumb on my clitoris. I moaned as my hips played into his hand, circling and grinding as pleasure spiraled within me.

"I'm close," I murmured, arching against him. "So close…"

"How close?" I heard a teasing note to the words.

My eyes flew open. "Don't you dare stop! I will strangle you if you stop!"

He bent over me, lips brushing mine, then nipped at my throat. When he spoke, the words were punctuated with kisses. "Wouldn't dream of it. I want to feel you come in my hand as I fuck you with my fingers. I want you to know I can make you feel this way whenever I see fit, and how much it pleases me to do this to you." He took one of my hands from his chest and used it to release his erection. I felt him naked in my hand, like satin and steel. I could barely close my fingers around him. I was rewarded with a deep, guttural groan, and then he removed

181

my hand. "That's how much I want you. I could tear you apart with how much I want to be inside you."

His crude words pushed me over the edge. That, and his skilled, thrusting fingers. A searing orgasm pulsed through me and I screamed. Or tried to. His lips were on mine, muffling my sounds as he pushed my body to its breaking point, blood roaring in my ears. I bucked against the feeling of him on top of me. I would have done anything he wanted then. I would have bent to any demand.

When I finally stopped quivering, to my surprise, his hand hadn't moved. Instead, it was still between my legs, pressing mercilessly inside me. He circled his thumb again and I moaned. I was so sensitive and swollen, and yet I felt him expertly building desire again, thrusting into me with shallow digs.

"I could do this to you for hours," he whispered into my ear. "Your body responds to me in ways it would for no one else. Already I can feel it purring for me."

I struggled against him, feeling deliciously helpless. His arrogant words were true, even if the logical part of my brain rebelled against such caveman-like manhandling.

"You're pretty sure of yourself, aren't you?" I couldn't help but challenge him.

"I would say the evidence speaks for itself." Another smooth glide of his hand made me gasp. "I would also say I'm about to have more evidence supporting my case in a moment. That the pile is mounting very quickly in my favor."

Maybe he was right, but I'd be damned if I'd let him know it. "Hardly. This isn't my first rodeo, you know. It isn't like I'm going to just lie back and let you get away with anything your imagination comes up with."

"I think you'll find my imagination is *very* creative."

I snorted back a laugh. I just bet it was. Still... "I can be pretty creative too. In fact, let me show you."

I wriggled beneath him, pressing up against his erection, marveling at its throbbing heat against my hip. I ran my hands over his shoulders and down his chest and abs until my fingers grazed the edge of his swim trunks. My fingers slipped inside, reaching lower, and...

Against my wrist, my c-tex bracelet fluttered. Shit, I had an incoming shim *now*? Petriv felt it too and pulled back, cursing at the interruption.

"Ignore it," he said, reaching to remove the offending piece of technology.

Gods I wanted to, but I didn't want him to know how into this I was. Yes I worked for him, and he was running most of my life right now, but he didn't control everything... I hoped. "What if it's important?"

He rolled his hips skillfully into mine. "More important than this?"

I whimpered beneath him, wanting to rise up to meet his thrust. The c-tex fluttered again. And again. Whoever it was had no intention of giving up and the tickle at my wrist became an annoying distraction. I needed it to stop. Fumbling awkwardly, I tried to pull off the bracelet. Instead, I hit the release button and launched the shim.

"Hello? Felicia? What the fuck? I can't see anything."

A face-chat shim? *Now*? At that point, I swore too. It was my cousin, Rainy. Shit. Abruptly I sat up and pulled away from Petriv. Damn, damn, damn. I hardly ever spoke to him. Well, that wasn't quite true, but why now of all times?

"Felicia? Are you there? Damn it, I need to talk to you!" He sounded urgent, like he was in some kind of trouble. My heart jumped a little in response and my arousal died a quick death. Even if I wasn't that close to Rainy, family was family. If they were in trouble, that trumped everything—including sexy crime lords tearing off my panties.

I held my wrist aloft in the air so he wouldn't catch sight of his cousin with her breasts out on display and a nearly naked man lying on top of her. "Yes, just give me a second. You...you woke me up," I said as I fought to put myself back together. Petriv scowled as he watched me struggle, barely giving me room to get organized.

Once I decided I was presentable, I tapped the screen and Rainy's face filled the holo that popped up. He had the same coloring as the rest of the Sevigny clan—straight, nearly black hair which he wore long and tied back along his neck, and blue-green eyes, though his were even more green than mine. However, while I resembled my mother with her more rigidly defined, classic One Gov features, Rainy's nose was sloped, his chin more pointed, his lips thinner. Still attractive, but not up to the ridiculous code.

"Felicia. Good, I caught you."

"Yes, you did," I said. Petriv arched an eyebrow.

"You sound strange. Are you in the middle of something?"

"Like I said, you woke me up. What do you want?"

"Right. I always forget the odd hours you keep. Listen, I wanted to make sure you'd be at Gran's birthday and that you're bringing the family deck."

I'd been interrupted from another orgasm for this? "I got your messages—all half dozen of them. Yes, I'll be there with *my* cards. I haven't lost them if that's what everyone is so damned concerned about."

"No, it's not that. I need a reading. Don't tell Gran I said that though. She's still pissed over the whole inheritance thing."

"It's been years since Granny G died." I studied his expression, difficult in the grainy holo. "If that's it, can I shim you back later? I'm kind of—"

"Are you alone right now? I need to talk to you about something," he said, looking disconsolate.

I shot another look at Petriv, who made no move to leave. I sighed and tried to turn away. Yet another problem with the c-tex bracelet—lack of privacy. Without the earplug in, anyone could overhear my conversation.

"Not really. I can shim you back if—"

"I just found out I've been blacklisted."

I froze. Any thought of getting back to more orgasms faded immediately. "*What?*"

Rainy stumbled on, speaking as if he couldn't stop now that he'd broken the seal. "Zita and I applied to have a baby. We did the paperwork, jumped through all the hoops, did everything we were expected to, but we were rejected. I had some people I know look into it. That's when I found out I've been blacklisted. Felicia, we can't have a baby. Zita's devastated. She wants to leave me. I can't let that happen. I love her too much. I thought maybe you could do a reading and convince her everything's okay. Maybe tell her it's a glitch in One Gov's AI. Something. Anything to make her stay. I'm not concerned about the baby, but I can't lose her. You have to help me."

Rainy was so close to breaking. My heart hurt and I found

my eyes welling with tears. Along with the pain came fury. It wasn't just my life my mother had manipulated.

"Rainy, I'm so sorry. Of course I'll help. I'm not sure how yet, but you know I'll do whatever I can," I promised. "Let me think about this for a bit and see what answers I can come up with. I have to go now, but I'll see you at the party."

"Okay. Thanks, Felicia. See you in a few weeks."

The face-chat shim ended and the pop-up vanished. I sat back on the couch, my breath coming out in a shocked whoosh. This wasn't just about me anymore. It was more than feeling betrayed by Roy, or missing my personal belongings. We'd all been played by TransWorld and my mother without even realizing it. Every person I loved was affected.

It took a moment for me to calm down enough to speak. I looked up at Petriv. "Did you know about this? Did you know it wasn't just me who was blacklisted?"

"I suspected, but didn't investigate. It's the connection to your mother that interests me, not the rest of your family."

Though I couldn't really fault his logic, his answer left me cold. Didn't he have people in his life he would do anything to protect? Was there no one he would willingly die for to keep them safe? "You don't touch family. Family is sacred."

"Of course. I'll have someone look into their status."

That answer wasn't good enough. "Not just look into it. I want their blacklisted status revoked too." I thought quickly, making a decision. "I want to change our agreement. I'll work for you and get you access to my mother, and the Consortium fixes this for my family."

He gave me a level look. "No. That's not what we agreed to, Ms. Sevigny. This isn't how these things work."

"I don't care how they work. This is my entire family I'm talking about! You can't just fix my status and leave the rest unchanged. That's inhuman! If you can change mine, how hard can it be to change the rest?"

"This isn't up for negotiation. The answer is still no."

I shot up off the couch, pissed. "Then you can just forget all this!" I waved vaguely in the air, gesturing at everything and nothing. "Get your own damn access to my mother. Oh, that's right! You can't. You need me. Well, I need this fixed."

Petriv rose as well, his expression surprised. "Are you actually threatening me?"

Gods, was I? What the hell was I thinking? But I also knew I couldn't let this go. My gut agreed.

"I'm just modifying our original agreement. All I know is that I can't leave things like this if there's a way to fix them. What kind of person would I be if I did nothing to help them when I could make this right? If you can't do anything, that's fine. But if you *won't* do anything, then...I'm not sure I can do what you want either. I can't have my blacklisted status revoked and leave the rest of my family to rot. I just can't."

He gave me a long, piercing look, his blue eyes narrowing. I returned it with one of my own until I began to wonder if what I wanted was impossible and I'd have to back down.

"I'll consider it," he said finally. All signs of the man who'd just been between my legs had disappeared. It was as if he were a different person now, all business and logic with desire packed away in an untouchable box.

"Thank you." I guess that was as good as I was going to get for now. Still, I pressed on with "Why would my mother do that? What would she gain by blacklisting my whole family?"

"There's a simple way to answer that," he reminded me, his tone bland.

I sighed. "I know. We're going to Brazil."

"Exactly." He held out an arm to me. Confused, I took it and let him walk us to the hall. He pointed me in the direction of the dining room. "I suggest you get some breakfast and take the zone meds. We're leaving this afternoon. Please be ready by noon, Ms. Sevigny."

Startled, I watched him walk off in the other direction until he vanished around the corner. What. The. Fuck. The whole thing was so bizarre I wasn't even sure what had happened. Obviously he was annoyed I'd answered Rainy's shim, and maybe I shouldn't have done it given how close he'd been to being inside me. The timing had truly been horrible. Still, after hearing from Rainy, how could I react any differently? How could I not try to change things? If Petriv had a problem with how I worked, he could take it up with me later.

I went in the direction he'd pointed me, though no longer interested in eating. Instead, I wanted to run my cards. Sometimes they were the only things in the world that could calm me—my own special brand of therapy. Even if I didn't like their answers, they at least made me feel like I was doing something.

It was only once I reached the dining room that I realized I'd completely lost track of my panties. Petriv had destroyed them, and I had no idea where they'd ended up. Mortified someone might find them, I raced back to the study to look. And look I did. I spent fifteen minutes crawling all over the room, looking under furniture, flipping cushions. They weren't there, and there was no way anyone could have entered the room in the short time I'd been gone. That meant one thing—Petriv had them. That sneaky bastard had walked off with them like they were some sort of trophy. Maybe he planned on tossing them, but my gut said otherwise. In fact, a ridiculous warm glow spread through me that I couldn't shut off. I mean, gods, the man had stolen my underwear even after I'd threatened him. How kinky was that? It was also annoying and made me angry. What kind of messed up relationship was this becoming? What else did he want from me and how far was this going to go? Maybe he wasn't as remote or controlled as I thought and I had more power here than I realized. I just had to dig a little deeper to find out what made him tick. Not a problem. He was one puzzle I was most definitely interested in solving. Of course, once I solved it, was I going to like what I found?

12

The journey to Brazil passed in a blur thanks to the combination of zone meds and lack of sleep. As Petriv had disturbingly noted, I'd barely slept in the past two days. I took the two dissolving mint-flavored pills as instructed by Karol, but either I'd been too exhausted or the dosage was too high because they knocked me for a loop. I was so far gone, I wasn't even sure if we flew regular commercial or took another fast high-orbit flight.

As far as I could tell, Petriv, Oksana, her husband, Vadim, whom I vaguely remembered from Denver, and more chainbreakers traveled with us. Karol also could have been there, plus a few others for all I knew. The last thing I remembered was Petriv crouching before my seat, smoothing my hair and saying something to Oksana. After that, I was well and truly out cold.

When I woke, I was fully clothed on a strange bed in the dark. I sat up with a start and swore. "Lights," I said, my voice hoarse from lack of use. Instantly the room was ablaze, as if every fixture had been programmed to turn on at the sound of my voice. I blinked and shielded my eyes with my hand.

Once they'd adjusted to the brightness, I found myself alone in a standard-issue hotel room, though far better than anything I could afford. The bed itself was massive and it took some work to climb off the thing.

Checking my bracelet, I found a message from Oksana. It indicated the details of the hotel, my room number, that my belongings were unpacked, and that I should make myself comfortable. Everyone else was "out" and would return by noon, local time. That gave me four hours to amuse myself. I frowned; I'd slept for almost twenty-four hours.

I ordered room service, took a bath, checked out the balcony and the view overlooking the pool, caught up with shims I'd saved for later, and ran a few Tarot spreads while I cooled my heels. Soon, I'd meet my mother. What would she be like? I'd seen the pictures and read the cards so I knew what to expect, but who was she really? Nerves twisted my stomach. Worse, I couldn't concentrate on the reading, which made me wish I could access Eleat. That in turn reminded me of my missing cards, TransWorld's violation of my home, and Roy's lies, and all that stirred up a fresh serving of anger and nerves.

By the sixth or seventh spread, I gave up. I'd focused on my mother and her environment, but the cards kept showing children around her. Was it my family's children I saw—the ones she and TransWorld denied us? Or did she have other children besides me—even though that was illegal? She was a geneticist, Petriv said. Maybe she experimented on them, although the idea was too awful to contemplate. Besides, the cards weren't giving me that vibe. She cared about the children, yet didn't. I couldn't figure it out and the more I poked at the idea, the less the cards told me.

I had decided to try one last spread as I sprawled on the massive bed when I heard a knock at the door. High noon. The mobsters were back. My exile was over.

"Felicia, hello? Are you in there?"

Oksana. I swept my cards into a bedside drawer, then jumped down from the bed—yes, jumped—and trotted to the door. I was only slightly winded by the time I got there. Seriously, how big a room did a person need?

A quick scan of the hall using the AI access screen beside the door showed four people. None were Petriv, to which my stomach offered a jolt of anxiety. Not my gut—my stomach. This was nerves talking, not luck. Nerves meant I looked forward to seeing him, even after yesterday's exchange. Like chasing the dragon, I *wanted* to re-experience the dangerous feelings I had whenever he was around. Not good. Those feelings made things complicated. How could it be otherwise given what he could do to me and whatever he represented? I shook my head and opened the door.

I found Oksana and three bodyguards. Two were holding various packages. The third had his hands free to do whatever... Guard bodies, I supposed. As usual, I couldn't tell them apart. I wondered if I kept seeing the same group over and over again or if they were being switched around. I guess it didn't matter. It wasn't my job to keep them sorted.

Oksana swept into the room, a golden vision with her blond hair in flowing waves, wearing a gold fabric tube-mini that molded to her body, skimmed the top of her breasts and along her butt, and fastened in front with three buttons. She pulled me into a hug that ended with kisses on both cheeks.

"Ah, Felicia, finally you're awake! You slept a long time, but you needed it. Rest can do wonderful things for the mind and body. The zone meds are working as they should and you're regulated to local time." She tilted my head critically, holding my face up to the light, studying it. "Very good. And with no modifications whatsoever, I'm told. Lucky girl."

This seemed like high praise from the golden goddess. "I just started the Renew therapy this year."

"Ah, what I wouldn't give to be twenty-five and do it all over again! Bah. Not worth dwelling on." She waved a hand at the air. Then she turned to the chain-breakers, ordering them about in Russian. They jumped into action, dumping their packages on the room's two settees and the floor. That got Oksana yelling and waving her arms wildly. She gave me a disparaging look. "These galoots are so useless and stupid sometimes. Terrible for shopping. I often wonder what might happen if they had to deal with real danger."

"Maybe just don't take them shopping?" I suggested, watching as one big chain-breaker fought to juggle several pairs of shoes and boots at once. Part of me was disappointed I hadn't been able to go with her. Another part of me wanted to clap my hands like an overexcited child, thrilled to see what she'd brought me.

"Alexei insisted." Oksana plucked up a pair of sandals. "He doesn't like Brazil. Actually, 'doesn't like' is too mild. He loathes this part of the world."

"Why? What's not to love?"

"You've no doubt noticed how much Alexei likes control. When the world governments collapsed and One Gov moved to consolidate, they scouted locations relatively free of natural disasters with a homogeneous population who wouldn't revert to homegrown terrorism. At that point, Brazil was such a country. To Alexei, it's too much power in one place that's not Russia or anywhere he holds influence." She turned to face me, grinning. "He asked me to sort out your wardrobe. Hopefully you'll like what I selected."

There, I did clap my hands and bounced a little on my feet. Even if it was frivolous of me, it was nice to be in a moment where I could just enjoy myself. "Show me everything!"

Her grin widened as she straightened various articles of clothing on the settees for my consideration. So many little dresses and in so many different colors; it seemed like everything glittered and stretched and revealed much more skin than it hid.

"We don't dress like this back in Kenya," I remarked as I held up a tube-shaped dress that I wasn't sure would cover both my breasts and butt at the same time, no matter how stretchy the material.

"This is Brazil," Oksana said knowingly. "It is one of my favorite things about this country. There is so much freedom here to be exactly who you want to be." In her next breath, she said something in Russian to the chain-breakers standing at attention and flung a hand toward the door. All three exited, the door slamming behind them.

"There's no need for their services now. Alexei would be quite angry if he learned they witnessed this."

I frowned. "You make it sound like he's trying to shield me from male attention."

Oksana put down the glittering shoes she'd been holding and looked at me. "Yes, I suppose there is an element of that involved. He can be…possessive. My understanding is you have an arrangement with him, do you not?"

"A business arrangement that seems to keep sliding into something else," I muttered, feeling my face burn. "Regardless, it ends when the TransWorld bid is awarded."

"I see." Her voice drifted off thoughtfully; then she added, "There are many women who would be envious of your position in his life right now."

I started at the sharp stab of jealousy I felt at the thought of other women. "Frankly, I'm not sure what that position actually is."

"Well, I can tell you he's asked me to do everything in my power to see that you're comfortable. That he is investing more of his personal time in this project than usual. That he's rarely so hands-on once a plan has been set in motion. Depending on its complexities, he typically leaves the job to Vadim, myself, and those we deem appropriate. His involvement now is highly unusual. I assumed you were the reason."

I felt my stomach twist in a nosediving rush of excitement and nerves. "I know he wants me, and of course it's impossible not to be attracted to him. I mean, look at him. How could I not want him? He's..." I sighed, not sure what I wanted to say. Telling her he was *too* perfect wouldn't cut it. "I know I'm just here to unravel TransWorld for the Consortium. Without me, there's no plan. Beyond that, I'm not sure I'm comfortable with the Consortium's agenda. I don't think the two of us would really be compatible in the end."

She tapped her lips, then smiled. "Perhaps it's as you say. However if I may offer a word of advice, I do suggest that you open yourself up a little. There are very few men like Alexei in this world, and I would hate for you to regret a missed opportunity." Then she brushed the whole situation away with a wave of her hand and held up a dress. "Come. Try this on. Alexei wants you ready on the hour and we've already wasted twenty minutes."

I knew nothing about Petriv's plans for the afternoon other than the fact that I needed to wear comfortable clothing. Aside from shoes without heels, Oksana and I had very dissimilar ideas when it came to what to wear. In this case—a strapless green tube-mini and hair swept into an elaborate uptwist.

Precisely at one, two chain-breakers escorted me to the elevator and down to the hotel lobby. The elevator was encased in a thick glass tube on the outside of the building, allowing passengers a bird's-eye view of Curitiba. I looked out at the sprawling megacity with its massive towers housing thousands. Brazil was one of the most populated countries in the world and it seemed its city planners were intent on building straight up. Much of its eastern coast had been decimated by the rising global floodwaters during the Dark Times. Some cities had been abandoned while others retreated inland. In theory, the idea was that in building up, green space would still be available rather than overrun with housing. But looking out the elevator glass, all I could see was urban sprawl.

The elevator doors opened into an impressive lobby. I'd studied the hotel floor plans earlier on the CN-net—I was big on knowing where emergency exists were located—but to see it firsthand was something else. It looked the way I imagined a hotel might have looked in colonial times. Not when Mars was first colonized—older, back when the Old World discovered they weren't the center of the universe and set about exploiting everything they could. Dark fab-wood furniture. A marble floor with alternating tiles of black and white. Murals of exotic animals on the walls. Ornamental palm trees in the corners. Chandeliers dripping with crystals and lighting up the mosaic-patterned ceilings high above. The air was cool and dry and smelled faintly of woodsy musk. Hotel guests sat in clusters of intimately arranged wicker furniture scattered around the massive room.

Tucked into a separate room of its own was the hotel bar. Aside from the bartender who wiped glasses in a way suggesting he had nothing else better to do, I saw only one person there.

Alexei Petriv leaned a forearm on the bar, holding a half-finished drink. One foot rested on a barstool and he had a vacant look on his face, suggesting he was browsing the CN-net. As we approached, I noticed female guests whispering to each other and shooting glances in his direction. I completely understood. If I'd been them, I'd be whispering to my girl-friends about Petriv too.

We were halfway to him when he switched on again. He turned and I caught the full force of his gaze. If not for the chain-breakers with me, I think I might have stopped walking altogether. He wore a lightweight gray suit, white shirt open to mid-chest, leaving some of his tattoos partially visible. Black hair fell into his eyes and he pushed it away with an absent swipe of his hand, and there was about a day's growth of dark stubble on his face. He looked predatory and dangerous. Watching him watching me, I knew something had changed. I wasn't sure what or why, but I felt our relationship had shifted. Was this the real Petriv, come out to play? Gods help me if it was.

He finished his drink, set down the glass, and offered up the sexiest smile I'd ever seen. Hell. His eyes took me in from head to toe, as if considering all of Oksana's careful work and deciding it was more than adequate. When he reached out to me, part of me wanted to slap his hand away, while the other part of me simply went to him, unable to refuse.

His hand took mine, engulfing it. This close, I could smell subtle cologne that nearly had me falling into his arms. I also caught a faint odor of alcohol, which made me wonder how long he'd waited there. Over my head, he spoke in Russian to the bodyguards, who peeled off and disappeared. My tension rose a notch. Did I think I needed protection from him?

"Have a seat," he said, and before I could protest, he picked me up by the waist and set me on the barstool beside him as if I weighed nothing.

My eyes narrowed. "Are you drunk?" I didn't care if I sounded critical and disapproving. It was the only defense I had against him.

"Unfortunately, no. I metabolize alcohol too quickly. It would take a significant amount of time, effort, and alcohol to work me up into a proper stupor."

"Then why bother?"

He stared into his empty glass. "I like the taste and it reminds me of home."

"Isn't it a bit stereotypical to be Russian and drink vodka?"

He laughed. "I never imagined I might one day be considered a stereotypical Russian."

We were moving dangerously close to flirting so I tried to rein myself in. "So what's the plan?"

"Today is the feast of *Nossa Senhora das águas*," he said, signaling the bartender for another drink. I contemplated getting one myself but declined when he looked expectantly at me. He might not get drunk, but I would. With Petriv, I needed all my wits about me.

His drink came with relative speed. I noted the clear liquid served straight up, three fingers in the glass.

"Our Lady of the Waters," I translated from the Portuguese. "I've never heard of it."

"It's a local religious holiday commemorating two days more than three hundred years ago when the Blessed Virgin saved the city from the rising oceans. The story goes that people prayed continuously as the ocean rose and threatened to swamp the countryside. On the third day, the moon eclipsed the sun, the sun swept down across the land, the Blessed Virgin spoke and told the citizens they needed to overthrow false gods, revealed three secrets, and the waters receded. Every year, the city shuts down for two days in commemoration and celebration of the miracle."

I nodded. Who was I to judge miracles and faith? After the terror of the Dark Times, people swung back to religion with fanatical furor. My family held a wide range of beliefs. I burned incense to any number of deities, Christian included—I liked to cover all my bases.

"How does that relate to my mother and TransWorld?"

"It doesn't," he said, offering up a grin before taking a sip of his drink.

"I'm not following. If we're not going to confront her, why are we here?"

Another sip of vodka. "Because I don't yet have the evidence I need. I've nothing to work with."

I wanted to bang my head on the bar in frustration. "Then maybe I should be drinking too. I thought you told your Tsarist friends they could expect results."

"Telling them what they want to hear makes things much simpler."

"What happens if you can't deliver? Do they break your legs? Or mine, for that matter?"

Petriv cast a look at my legs, left bare thanks to the butt-brushing tube-mini. He spent a long moment considering—so long, I felt myself flush. "I would say there's no danger of anything happening to your legs or other parts of your anatomy. Not from them, at least."

Yup, that did it. The flush grew, even as I tried to fight it. Petriv went back to his drink.

"I'm not without ideas," he continued. "Just nothing concrete to present. As I was saying, the city shuts down for two days for the feast of *Nossa Senhora das águas*. TransWorld is a large employer here, so they host a companywide picnic at the botanical gardens. The entire city is invited. Based on research, we know your mother usually attends. My hope is to intercept her and use your presence to force a reaction."

"Sounds like wishful thinking," I offered. "After what happened at the auction, she may even be expecting me."

"Well, it's not without its flaws, but the timing is perfect. If I get what I need to spoil the bid now, so much the better. If not, we try again. We have two weeks, after all."

"What happens if you fail? What will the Consortium do?"

He drained his drink in a long swallow, then set the glass down with deliberate care, as if uncertain whether or not he might smash it. "I won't fail."

"But what if you do?" I pressed because I couldn't seem to stop myself. "What makes you so confident?"

He turned to me, his gaze appraising where before it was playful. Then he stepped in close, one leg finding its way between my knees, a hand coming to rest on the back of my barstool. He placed his other hand on my thigh, his long fingers brushing just under the hemline of my dress. His thumb rested close to my left hip bone and began to circle gently. The overall effect left me both aroused and confused. I fought not to move, feeling like I might startle a wild animal if I did. "Have you seen something of interest in your cards, my little Tarot card reader?"

I thought of the countless readings I'd done on him, Death and the Lovers appearing over and over again, and my throat went dry. "Nothing I can recall."

Petriv cocked an eyebrow. "Should that change, please mention it. What I'm paying you should entitle me to at least one reading. In answer to your question, I'm confident because I was born for this. One day I will lead the Consortium. Failure in this, or in anything, is not an option. TransWorld is only a stepping stone. Beyond lies true power."

"You're aware you sound like a megalomaniac, right?" The words were out before I could stop them. It was all I could do not to clamp a hand over my mouth.

"Perhaps. I've been called worse." He barked a laugh, but it sounded bitter. The rubbing on my hip stopped and he removed his hand. When he stepped out from between my knees I felt a mixture of both relief and disappointment. "Time to go, Ms. Sevigny. We have a picnic to attend."

He reached out and eased me from the barstool. My inner thigh accidentally brushed his. Our eyes met and again I saw the heat in his gaze.

"Careful, Ms. Sevigny," he whispered, his lips at my ear. "I believe we still have some unresolved business."

Oh yes, Petriv had definitely come out to play. "And if we had the time, maybe I'd let you resolve it. But as you said, we have a picnic to attend."

He laughed, deep and throaty without any trace of the earlier bitterness. Then he stepped back and held out an arm for me to take, grinning at me, clearly amused. Odd, but knowing I could make him laugh somehow took the pressure off. I felt less like I was in the middle of a sexual powder keg.

Unfortunately, I realized that by not being so focused on Petriv, I had a host of other problems with which to concern myself. I had plenty of room left in my brain to worry about my mother. Today may or may not be the day I met her after years of thinking she was dead. What would I say to her? How would I react? What emotions was I supposed to feel? Hell, was I even emotionally ready to see her? I didn't know, but with Petriv dragging me inexorably after him, I was certainly going to find out.

13

A flight-limo dropped us off a block from the picnic. With the streets closed and filled with foot traffic, it was as near as we could get. The weather was hot, the sky cloudless, and the sun beat down mercilessly. Petriv's suit and Tru-Tan meant he was better protected against its damaging rays, but we both applied UV protection spray to any exposed skin. In ten minutes, the intense Brazilian sun could cause terrible burns.

The streets were lined with palm trees. Urns filled with exotic flowers I didn't recognize were spaced every few meters, though I could scan them with my bracelet if I was curious. There were also open-air shops and cafés. The atmosphere was one of general celebration as people waded around us. I watched through my sunshades—couples and families of three, laughing and enjoying the holiday without a care. A week ago, I'd been one of them.

All at once, it hit me again. Sharp, piercing rage filled me and I felt like my heart would beat its way through my chest. I thought of Roy and his stupid, pregnant wife and wanted to lash out with a vengeance that staggered me. How could anyone do that to a person? How had he rationalized our relationship to himself? I had to stop walking, both hands clutching my chest as if that would hold me together.

"Ms. Sevigny? Are you ill?"

"I'm fine. Give me a second," I said, the words a grunt. Better that than crying.

Petriv steered me away from the crowd until we were shaded by a line of palm trees. I let him. Easier to do that than resist. Besides, I didn't feel like resisting. Not when the rage turned to a gnawing sadness. Even if it had been all lies, I'd still loved my easy life with Roy with its lack of complications. *Or passion*, I reminded myself. Maybe that's why it had been so simple—he fit into the fantasy of what I thought my life should be. After Dante, it was so much easier not to care too much. That way, things hurt less when they all went wrong and you ended up disappointed. Perhaps I could have inserted any man. No, not true. For a second, I tried to imagine what a life with Alexei Petriv might be like, and couldn't. It was beyond anything I could envision.

"You're not fine," Petriv said, bringing my attention to him as he tipped my face to his. He'd already removed his sunshades and tucked them into a jacket pocket before he plucked mine from my face to study me. "You're anything but."

I sniffed and fought back tears. "I'm just having a moment. That's what I do. I cry and have dramatic moments all the time."

He smiled. "So far, you haven't struck me as the type unless the situation calls for it. What's wrong? Nerves?"

"No. Not yet, anyway," I said, shaking my head in his loose

hold. "It just hit me that this wasn't the life I ordered. I'm nowhere near where I thought I'd be." I gestured vaguely to the people around us. "I thought I'd have... *that* by now."

"Few get exactly what they want in life." He smoothed a piece of hair back from my face, one Oksana had left free to be artfully wispy. His smile faded. "If you want, I will kill Roy for you."

My eyes went wide. I could see it in his face. He would kill Roy if I asked him. My heart dropped into my stomach as I again realized the world I'd fallen into. *Hello, Alice. Fall through the looking glass much?*

"No, don't. He's going to be a father and I don't want that on my conscience." I thought a moment longer. "I don't think I care about him enough to want him dead."

"As you wish," he said, inclining his head in a small nod.

I pulled away, or tried to. It unnerved me to have him touch me so intimately as we stood beneath the palm trees and discussed murder while the rest of the world strolled around us. I needed our relationship to get back to normal—whatever qualified as normal.

After a few seconds, he let me go and handed back my sunshades. Our fingers touched and he murmured, "What I said is a standing offer. Say the word, and I will do it."

I swallowed, breathless. "Okay."

He put his own glasses back on and held out his arm. "Shall we continue? My people on the ground have sighted your mother at the picnic. However, we can try again tomorrow if you're not ready."

A few more seconds of my bumbling as I put on the sunshades. "But she won't be there tomorrow, will she?"

"There is that," he conceded.

The prospect of running was tantalizing, but that was fear talking. I had to keep going if I wanted my life back. My gut agreed. It pushed me forward with an intensity I rarely felt. In fact since meeting Petriv, the kick in my gut feeling seemed to have increased a thousandfold.

I took his arm and squared my shoulders. "We're here. Let's do this."

A short time later, we waited in line for the botanical gardens. From where I stood, I saw the main greenhouse. I also caught the telltale shimmer of the nano-sunshade over the entire affair. It filtered out the worst of the sun's damaging rays while letting in the rest of the elements. I closed myself off to the laughing children and the chatter of families around us, and concentrated on the task at hand. Unfortunately, I couldn't block out the scents as the perfumes of hundreds of flowers filled the air. They even managed to drown out Petriv's cologne—a good thing, I decided.

At the entry gate, all attendees were allocated five extra calorie consumption points. I saw them pop up in the calorie monitor on my bracelet with a giddy thrill, then realized I had to use them at the festival or they'd be deducted within the next three hours. Then we were directed to pass through a weapons scanner. I went first and made it without so much as a beep. Petriv followed while I watched with interest. He came out clean as well.

I arched an eyebrow when he took my arm again. "I didn't expect it to be so easy."

"I'm offended, Ms. Sevigny. Did you think I would shut down the whole event with a secret weapons cache?"

"I think you'd do whatever you needed to get what you wanted."

"Well, to your point, I wouldn't carry it with me. It would already be onsite."

"Nice to know I wasn't completely wrong."

He grinned down at me. "No, not completely."

He stopped then, looking around the picnic. I followed his gaze, but also tried to determine in which direction my gut wanted me to go. We were standing in a courtyard, with plants and trees arranged to create pathways leading off in numerous directions. Though I saw no overt signage, a check of the CN-net showed the grounds' layout. The smell of food wafted around me from the food pavilions ahead. In another direction, I heard playful screams and laughter, which must have been where the rides were located. Costumed performers danced to piped-in music, juggled, and worked magic tricks. This was one hell of a picnic; TransWorld certainly went all out when it came to keeping everyone entertained.

"If you win the bid, does all this stop?" I asked Petriv.

"People still need their bread and circuses, Ms. Sevigny," he answered as he scanned the crowds. "Just because one thing changes doesn't mean the world changes with it."

I noticed a group of young women eyeing Petriv: five in total, in their early twenties. They were no more than babies, really, not even old enough to begin the Renew treatments. All wore open-back, tailbone-skimming dresses that displayed their tats—sequined butterflies with holographic wings that actually flapped—as well as the latest fad in color-cycling filament braids, linked to their t-mods and changing color depending on their mood. I felt a spurt of envy. Stupid, yet I couldn't help it. To them, I was a lesser being: an unmodified human, a spook. They were the future. Yet as different as each tried to be, they still looked the same—tall, thin, busty, long straight hair—all striving to reflect One Gov's predetermined ideal based on gene decisions their parents had made before conception.

The girls stood by a pair of massive stone urns filled to overflowing with colorful hydrangeas. I thought of Belikov and hoped he didn't cast me in the same light as these bauble-heads as they giggled and shot glances at Petriv. The most brazen of the girls gave me a pointed look, presumably hoping I would drop dead or go away. Part of me nearly laughed aloud at the idea of her trying to handle Petriv.

"You have admirers," I couldn't help but point out.

In return, his arm settled around my waist and he drew me closer until my hip brushed his thigh. "No need to be jealous," he said, mouth close to my ear. "I'm flattered by the attention, but I don't have patience for giggling females."

"What do you have the patience for?" The words were out before I could stop them.

He hit me with the smile I'd caught back at the hotel. "I am constantly surprised by the ever-expanding list of things I want." His smile faded and his expression grew vacant until a beat later, he frowned at me. "It seems TransWorld is aware of our presence and is moving to intercept. We need to leave."

I recalled the mess in Denver and what could have happened if not for Pennyworth. Petriv was right; we had to leave. Except…my gut said otherwise. I looked around as if I could figure out what to do based on sight alone. Useless, as usual. I couldn't see what I wanted. I had to feel it.

"No," I said, a hand on his chest to steady myself. "Not yet. If we leave now, we'll lose...well, we'll lose whatever opportunity you hoped to gain. I can't explain it, but I can't go."

"Then what do you suggest, Ms. Sevigny?" I heard both frustration and amusement in his voice. "No secret weapons cache, remember?"

"Just...follow me."

I walked farther into the gardens to where the rides were located. The crowds grew dense, the noises louder. I pushed through it, keeping a hand on Petriv's wrist, afraid I'd lose him if I let go. Or rather, he'd lose me. The smell of manure wafted through the air, strong and pungent. A minute later I saw the reason: we'd stumbled across a petting zoo with real, live animals.

I entered the gated enclosure, unconcerned about those waiting their turn or the gatekeeper who barked in protest as we passed. Straw crunched and snapped underfoot. I stepped around small children, overturned food bowls, and a parade of tiny chicks. I led Petriv by the pigpen, past several cows, and around the goat stall. Something was there. So close. Only a little farther now. My gut was so insistent I would have started running if not for the fact that it would have been impossible given the crowds.

Past the sheep, I saw what my gut wanted me to. I stopped in my tracks, staring, trying to make sense of it. Pony rides. There were seven ponies in all, each a dull brown-and-white color, indistinguishable from one another. They walked a predetermined circle, moving with docile gentility. On each sat a child. The youngest was three or four, the oldest no more than ten—all girls. Beside each was an adult, either male or female, ensuring their charges remained in their saddles. It made sense for the youngest children, but not the ten-year-old. Looking closer, I noticed that none of the children laughed or smiled. Gods knew I'd wished for a pony often enough, and the fact that they didn't seem to care struck me as odd. Some had contented looks on their face, but for the most part, they were blank slates without emotion. There was something... *off* with these girls, something that didn't add up.

Petriv was speaking. Words came out of his mouth, but I couldn't grasp their full meaning. I tore my eyes from the girls.

"They seem to have a form of neurological impairment, though I don't have enough information to judge what the cause might be. That would require neural scans and testing to determine the full extent," he said. I looked at him blankly. "The development of their brains and central nervous systems has been tampered with, causing a host of mental and emotional disorders. There are no other known cases of such neurological damage in the world at present. Genetics therapy would have eliminated it."

"And yet here they are," I whispered. "But there's something else. Those things... You wouldn't know this... I mean... how could you? How thorough could your background research be?"

"Say it, Ms. Sevigny. We're rapidly running out of time."

"They look like me." I glanced up at him. "Back when I was a little girl. All of them. They are... identical to me when I was growing up. Honestly, I'd say they could *be* me."

He swore under his breath. I followed his gaze and froze. Standing beside the pony circuit, arms crossed, overseeing the entire production, was my mother. Blond hair was pulled back from her flawless face; she was as gorgeous as she'd been in the picture Petriv had shown me days ago. She watched over the ponies, nodding at the girls when they deigned to look at her. These were the children my cards had seen. I wasn't the only child my mother had produced. She'd gotten around the Shared Hope program regulations... Or had she?

"Clones," I breathed in horror. "Those are clones of me."

A beat of silence from Petriv, then, "You're sure of this?"

"Wish I wasn't, but yes, I'm sure."

I didn't know what to do next. Confront my mother? Pull the clones off their ponies and take them with me? But it didn't matter. In that moment, as if she'd sensed me, my mother's eyes met mine. A touch of shock crossed her face before it smoothed over. Then she nodded, small and precise as if greeting an old friend. Or an enemy. She knew me. Yes, she knew exactly who I was.

Petriv grabbed my arm. "We've got company. Time to go."

Like at the auction, TransWorld security had found us. I counted four beefy guards closing in. Petriv backpedaled us through the crowd. Animals and people dashed out of the way as we charged by. I threw a backward glance at our pursuers. They were closing in.

"What now?"

"We run."

<hr />

Our escape from the botanical gardens wasn't as dramatic as it seemed. Petriv's people quickly stepped in and dealt with the TransWorld goons. We left unscathed with relative haste, jumping into the waiting flight-limo just outside the gardens. I wasn't sure what fancy maneuvering had been required to have a getaway vehicle in place given the trouble we'd had on the way in, but we made it out with little fuss.

I stared out the flight-limo's window, reliving what I'd just witnessed. I couldn't think what it meant; my mind refused to process the details. My mother was making illegal full-body clones. Not just clones, but ones with impaired neural development. How did this relate to my blacklisted status? No, my whole family's status? I drummed my fingers on my lap. I needed my cards. My palms practically itched with the need to consult the Tarot.

Abruptly Petriv placed his hand on mine. "I realize you're anxious, but please stop."

"Sorry. Nervous habit. Just thinking about running my cards," I explained, feeling sheepish he'd caught me struggling with myself.

"You believe they will provide some insight?"

"I know they will. I ran them this morning and saw the children. I just didn't know what it meant. Sometimes the readings don't make sense because they defy my own logic. Now that I know what I'm looking for, I can refocus."

"I know what she's looking for." He glanced out the window and ran a distracted hand through his hair. "In fact, I suspect she's found it and is researching how best to exploit it."

I watched his profile and bit my lip. "The luck gene. Did you know she wanted to manipulate luck this the whole time?"

When he swung back to face me, he looked so serious, I swallowed my questions.

"No, not at first," he said, settling back in his seat. "I surmised it based on the research I'd uncovered, but I couldn't fathom the expected outcome. First, luck is a fickle thing. How do you quantify it? What's lucky for one isn't necessarily lucky for all. Second, if she could mass-produce luck, no one would truly be lucky—each person would cancel out the other. No one would hold the advantage. There's no far-reaching financial gain for any multinational if only a select few benefit in the short-term. Yet somehow TransWorld has found a way to profit from it. Perhaps not as they intended, but certainly in some way. It's obviously through the children, but I don't understand how."

"Did you know about them?" I pressed. "Did you know about the clones? Did you ever suspect I was just a science experiment to her? That all she wanted from me was my luck gene?"

"No, I didn't." He said it gently, as if I were some wounded animal he might spook into fleeing. Maybe it would have been better if he'd told me some fabulous lie. But no, I refused to live in a cocoon anymore. "It could be there's more going on we don't yet know."

"Neither of us believes that. I was a means to an end." I sighed and looked at my hands. "I'm not going to whine about my life being awful because I grew up without a mother. It wasn't. But it still hurts. She was there all along and I didn't matter because she already got what she needed from me. It pisses me off knowing how thoroughly she manipulated my life." I shot him a look from the corner of my eye. "You're right, by the way. Part of me does want to kill her."

"For making you her experiment," he clarified.

"Not just that. She cloned me! Was the real thing not good

enough for her? We only saw seven. Who knows what else she's done? Full-body cloning is illegal, though she's obviously not concerned by the fact that they're not legally human."

"So you're not opposed to the clones. Just their treatment."

"Everyone grows partials to replace failed organs; hell, it's part of the Renew program. It's that she's taken some essential element of me and twisted it to suit her needs. The fact that I'm a person with feelings and wants doesn't matter. In her eyes, the clones hold more value than the original. I'm a second-class citizen to . . . to myself. And what is she doing with them? Why would she make these . . . things and purposely take away their wills and thoughts so they're mindless slaves? What kind of lives do they have? What does it say about her as a person that she could do this?"

"I would venture to say people have done worse with better intentions," he answered. He sounded both unhappy and thoughtful, or maybe I was just projecting my feelings onto him.

"Funny, but that doesn't make me feel better."

We both resumed looking out our respective windows until we reached the hotel. Petriv climbed out before turning back to help me from my seat. Chain-breakers closed around us, escorting us through the lobby.

"Now what?" I asked after we stepped into the first available elevator. Three chain-breakers followed us inside, making for close quarters. My shoulder bumped Petriv's chest. His hand went to the small of my back, steadying me. The move felt possessive and I turned my body into his.

"Now I firm the specifics for the next phase in the plan."

Ah yes, the plan. For Petriv, I was also a means to an end.

The elevator stopped at my floor. From what Oksana had told me, Petriv occupied the penthouse one floor up. I wasn't sure why we weren't all staying nearer to one another or in a suite of rooms, but I wasn't footing the bill.

"I'll run the cards. I'll see if I can come up with anything useful and let you know what I find. See you tomorrow," I said, trying to edge toward the open elevator door. Hopefully I didn't sound as pathetic as I felt.

Petriv had yet to move his hand from my waist. "I'd like to watch, if that won't disturb you."

The door started to close. One of the chain-breakers had to catch it with his hand. Sudden heat shot through me at the thought of Petriv in my room, and my stomach lurched, but in a way not remotely comparable to a rough flight-limo landing.

"But if you prefer to be alone after today, that's perfectly understandable."

"No, it's fine," I managed after a ridiculous length of silence. "Sometimes it helps to have another person to trade ideas with."

He smiled. "Good, though I'm not sure how useful I'll be. I'm more interested in seeing how you work."

"You saw in Nairobi," I countered.

"Then, you were humoring me in an attempt to rush me out the door. This is different."

Yes, it was. Then, I'd had another set of priorities and thought I knew how events would play out. Now I was at loose ends, attracted to a very dangerous and powerful man from whom my gut and the Tarot cards wouldn't let me stay away. Frankly, it scared me.

"Just try not to get in my way," I said, fighting to keep the tone light.

215

I stepped out of the elevator, waiting as Petriv murmured to his security detail in Russian. They didn't sound pleased, but he ignored their complaints and followed me to my room. The door opened when my bracelet touched the handle, the lock keyed to the citizen chip in my c-tex. Thankfully, the door opened on the first try rather than the twentieth. The curtains were open and sunlight streamed through the sitting room's filtered windows. Normally, I would have kicked off my shoes and flopped on the bed. Petriv's presence left me at a loss as to what to do next.

When I looked back at him, he'd removed his jacket and proceeded to roll up the sleeves of his white shirt. He'd also undone another button on his shirt to expose more of his chest. There wasn't anything sexy about it, I decided. It just seemed like he wanted to get more comfortable. It wasn't his fault if it made me drool.

"The cards are in the bedroom. I'll be right back," I called, then dashed into the other room.

I caught myself in the mirror. I looked flushed and overexcited, and the green dress, while flattering, was *too* flattering. I needed to tone down this whole scene. After today, Petriv was right: I didn't think my nerves could take any more stimulation. Diving into the closet, I found sedate flannel shorts and a cami, both in blue. I changed quickly, though I left my hair alone since Oksana had worked so hard to style it.

When I returned, Petriv was sitting on one of the settees, a low table in front of him. He'd closed the window shades and turned on a lamp. It made the space seem more intimate and my heartbeat picked up a notch. I had nowhere to sit but beside him unless I wanted to make a fool of myself and rearrange the furniture.

"Room service will be here shortly," he said as I sat on his right. "I don't know about you, but I'm starving. We did miss the picnic, after all. Plus I would hate for you to miss out on the extra consumption points before they disappeared."

"True," I agreed, shuffling the cards without thinking, their feel and texture as familiar as my own skin.

He watched me shuffle. "What happens next?"

"I think about what I want to know and how complete an answer I want, and lay the spread. Then I interpret what the cards tell me."

"Are you always accurate in your predictions?"

"Usually, but it depends on how you slant the interpretation. For example, the Death card doesn't necessarily mean death. It could refer to a change in your life, like the death of a bad habit or a new job, although not necessarily a good one. Or, it can mean exactly what it seems like it means. It depends on the cards around it, influencing events." I started to lay a ten-card spread, concentrating on keeping my hands from shaking.

"Has the Death card appeared in any readings you've done about me?" he asked. I stilled and looked at him, uncertain how to answer. "Come now, Ms. Sevigny. I know how much you rely on your cards. I suspect your accuracy is a manifestation of your luck gene. I also think you've done several readings on how this venture ends, as well as on the key players. I just want to know what you've discovered."

"Maybe there are things you're better off not knowing."

"So yes to the Death card." He shook his head and laughed softly as if I confirmed what he'd always suspected. "Anything else?"

"I don't feel comfortable discussing this."

He arched an eyebrow. "Why is that?"

"Because I don't want to plant ideas that aren't necessarily true," I said, hedging.

He leaned toward me, eliminating the space between us. "Is there another card in your readings about me that bothers you?"

"The Lovers." I bowed my head, feeling my cheeks flush. "It appears in all the readings."

"Well, that's not unexpected. You already know what I want," he said. "Although I'm sure you would say I shouldn't take it as a literal interpretation of future events."

"It's your future. You can interpret it however you want."

"Yes, I suppose I can."

Silence descended as I laid the remainder of the spread. It was all I could do to hold back a sigh as the reading charted the course of my relationship with Petriv. The eighth card, representing outside influences, was Death. And there, in the hopes-and-fears slot as Card Nine, was the Lovers.

"I assume that's the answer for whatever it is you asked," he said, instead tapping the final card in the spread. "What does it mean?"

"Two of Cups, reversed. It means there are problems getting in the way of this." I tapped the Lovers, my hand next to his, and forced myself to fall into the patter I used when reading for customers. "This is the beginning of a partnership. Based on the Lovers, I'd say it's a romantic relationship with immense potential. However, there are obstacles in its path that could be possible showstoppers because of this." I touched the Death card. "It represents the people around you, reacting to you. Sudden change is coming and you could lose everything you hoped to gain." I also touched the card in the seventh position:

the Hermit, reversed. It had also come up in many of the readings I'd done. "There's also a problem here. This shows your attitude toward what's happening. You're concealing the truth, or spreading misinformation. There's something you're holding back, and until that secret comes out or you change how you react to the world, you're not going to get your happy ending."

I bent to gather up the cards in one swoop. Petriv's hand on my wrist stopped me. I looked up at him and my breath caught; he watched me with an intensity that made me shiver. I swallowed and left the cards, holding his gaze.

"It's your future too," he said simply. "What do you want?"

I blinked. I'd never thought about it that way—that this future could be mine as well and that if I wanted it, if I wanted *him*... The truth was sitting right there on the table in front of us, for both of us to see... Maybe with Alexei Petriv, even if he was a man I had no business being with, I could somehow have something more.

So, what did I want? "I don't want to ever wonder where I stand with someone. I don't want lies or secrets, or to have to hide who I am. I don't want anything like the disastrous relationships I've had in the past."

"A tall order, considering."

"You asked what I wanted. That's what I want."

A resigned look flitted across his face and he sighed. "We both know that whatever might happen between us will never be anything but complicated."

I thought my heart would beat its way out of my chest with both fear and anticipation. "True, but I think we both knew that right from the beginning."

"Unfortunately, I have never wanted complicated. I would

have you on your back or your knees in less time than it takes you to draw breath, but this... The thing you want is impossible for me." He took a deep breath, let it out, and ran both hands through his hair, creating a sexy mess. It was a gesture I noticed he made whenever he was agitated with me.

Then to my absolute horror, he stood and grabbed his jacket from the back of the chair where he'd left it. I watched open-mouthed as he slipped it over his shoulders.

"You're leaving?" I think I actually shrieked the words. "I do one Tarot reading for you and *this* is what happens? You run away? Because this is too *complicated*? What about the restaurant, or the day before when you said you wanted nothing more than to touch me? I thought you... wanted me." My voice hitched and I found myself dangerously close to tears. How could I have been so wrong about him? "Why did you say all those things to me if you didn't mean them?"

"Because sometimes a man will say anything in order to have a woman under him. I would still very much like to fuck you, but I see now it would mean very different things to each of us. Two of Cups reversed, after all. One of us will ruin this. I suspect it will be me. It would be better to end this before it starts."

I sat there shocked, watching his back and broad shoulders, his posture stiff with resolve. Gods, was this actually happening? A tear leaked out before I could blink it back. How many damned times would I pick the wrong man? I claimed to never lie to myself, and yet here I was, letting myself believe that this mattered, that he might actually want me after the fiasco with Roy and the crushing heartbreak of Dante. How could I be so stupid all over again?

I looked down at the cards on the table. They'd always held the truth even if I still lacked some of the details. Was I willing to let that go yet? "But what if it's already started?"

"If it has, it will not go further. I will not go down this road with you." He strode across the room, his hand on the door handle. "Once I determine the best way to approach your mother, I'll be in touch. Until then, *do svidaniya*, Ms. Sevigny."

And before I could think of a retort or jump to my feet to stop him, he was gone.

14

I don't care what anyone says—cold showers are useless.

Even still, I spent the next half hour standing in the shower stall, alternating the water temperature between freezing and tepid as if that might somehow calm me down. The room also contained a deluxe sonic-cleaner. Seeing that made me cry a little, reminding me of the condo I'd shared with Roy and my shattered dreams for the future—a future I wasn't even sure I wanted anymore. Petriv's rejection was the finishing touch to one of the most horrific weeks of my entire life.

When I could no longer stay in the shower, I paced the room like the cage it was. From one end of the suite to the other, to the balcony and the cool evening air, then back again—I ran the circuit until I exhausted myself, alternating between tears and vicious bouts of profanity. I was angry at myself for getting into this situation. At Petriv for making me want him, then tossing me aside. At Roy for his lies. At my mother for making me little more than a research project. At TransWorld and their manipulation designed to exploit and capitalize on my alleged luck gene. I sure as shit didn't feel lucky now.

My c-tex fluttered against my wrist, indicating room service had arrived with whatever Petriv had ordered earlier. I ignored it, hoping it would explode his calorie consumption index through the roof, though I knew he wasn't affected by such things. I continued pacing instead, unable to get a grip on my feelings. I couldn't even imagine eating now.

Sometime later, I heard a knock at the door. Startled, I answered without having the AI scan the hall, illogically hoping it was Petriv. My face fell when I found his tech-med standing on the threshold.

"Karol. Hi. What are you doing here?"

I knew I looked terrible. My eyes were red and blotchy, and my nose ran like a broken faucet. I was distraught over something I'd created in my own head and Petriv wasn't interested in pursuing—or at least not in the way I wanted. Maybe he'd even told Karol to deal with me because he thought me too unstable.

If Karol noticed my state of disarray, he said nothing. Instead, he entered looking as ill at ease as I did, displaying none of the arrogance of our first shim communication.

"Good evening, Ms. Sevigny. I have some good news," he said in that nasally, accented voice. "The team *Gospodin* Petriv assigned to locate the contents of your condo was successful earlier today. Everything was found in a storage facility outside Nairobi. As we speak, your belongings are being returned to their original location."

I blinked. I'd forgotten all about that in light of my current Petriv-induced drama. I tried to dredge up a spurt of excitement and failed miserably. "So I can go back to my condo?"

"It's unadvisable given TransWorld's interest in you, but yes. *Gospodin* Petriv bought the condo from the holding company and transferred sole ownership to your name. You'll find a shim with the new building access codes, which should prevent future break-ins."

Wow. He'd bought the condo for me. What a lovely parting gift. Should I be amazed and grateful or pissed and irritated? Pissed and irritated won, hands down. "What if I don't want to live there anymore? It's not like it's chock-full of good memories now."

Karol looked at a loss for words, as if I'd said something outside whatever script he usually followed. "You could always sell it back to the Consortium, I suppose," he tried. "It's yours, so you can do whatever you wish with it."

"What would Mr. Petriv do if I said I didn't want it?"

"I'm not certain he would mind one way or the other. He rarely comments to me on such matters."

The man looked uncomfortable—probably wondering if Petriv would smack him around again because of a minor slight toward me—so I gave up tormenting him. The joke was on him anyway. Petriv had cock-blocked himself; there was no need to cozy up to me. "It's fine. I appreciate the condo."

I don't think my thanks were effusive enough, or maybe Karol wanted more. He blinked and cleared his throat, then made a few "ahms" and "well thens" before resettling himself.

"Do you like the new updates to your c-tex bracelet?" he tried. "I gave you mainline AI access for whatever region you happen to be in, bumped your CN-net space to unlimited storage, and upgraded the holo pop-up capacity. I would have done more but I'm restricted by the technology. You should consider external t-mod adapters. They may not have the same abilities as internal, but they're an improvement over your c-tex."

"Did Mr. Petriv tell you to do that?"

"He asked me earlier to improve your tech situation. I thought these were useful additions."

As infuriated as I was with Petriv, I couldn't help being interested. "I didn't know external t-mods were possible."

"It's something the Tsarist Consortium perfected years ago, but One Gov wasn't interested. They believed the population segment that might benefit was too small. However, the product does quite well in the underground markets on Mars and Venus."

Black markets on Mars and Venus—I filed that information for later. In the meantime I considered the benefits of a tech boost, though it would drive my family insane. "What other projects are you working on?"

"Quantum teleporting of solid matter. Lightspeed propulsion drives. Remote asteroid mining via AI drones, cellular reconstruction to allow for more rapid healing and potential shape-shifting abilities," he rattled off immediately. I blinked. No wonder the man had scoffed at my antiquated c-tex bracelet.

"People could actually change their shape to whatever they wanted?"

"Possibly. We're also exploring the potential to upgrade MH Factors after birth rather than in the womb. Most of the projects are still in the planning and hypothetical phases, though we've made good progress on the teleporting. Some testing, but nothing concrete we're ready to present. A foothold on Mars would be a significant step to furthering our research."

"I thought teleporting was illegal."

"Not precisely. One Gov hasn't decreed it yet, at any rate."

"Probably because no one thinks it can be done. Listen, are you sure you should tell me this? Isn't it confidential Consortium information?" I asked, deciding I couldn't hear any more. The less I knew about their business, the better, even if secrets were spilled to me at every turn.

"*Gospodin* Petriv obviously values you. Otherwise, why all this?" He made a vague gesture that could encompass anything from my being in the hotel, to buying my condo, to my recent globetrotting. To Karol, I was Petriv's newest toy. *A toy he didn't want to play with anymore*, I reminded myself.

"This has all been very interesting, and thank you for the...news. I think I'll turn in for the evening," I said. Time to get him out of the room so I could continue my freak-out.

"Yes, I understand. I believe I heard Oksana suggest asking you to join them for a night out in the city, but there was some concern that you needed your rest. *Gospodin* Petriv felt it best you not be disturbed, though I was sure he would have wanted you to know about the condo findings as soon as they became available."

I frowned. "He's not here?"

"Correct. He's never cared for Brazil, so I found it strange that he accepted Oksana's invitation, but..." He shrugged. "I'm the only one on-site at the moment. I've some AI issues to address."

"I see." No, I didn't see. Petriv was out while I paced my hotel room, driving myself insane because all I could think of was him. That...asshole!

Oblivious to my turmoil, Karol nodded. "Have a pleasant

evening and sleep well, Ms. Sevigny." He bowed a little and showed himself out.

Once again, I was alone. Yet instead of being sexually frustrated and confused, I also had the pleasure of being angrier than I'd ever been in my life. Before I even knew what I was doing, I threw on one of the outfits in the closet—a trendy metallic shimmer dress in dark turquoise. I fought to wriggle it into place. It was strapless and skintight, with terrific support in the bust. I spent some time fiddling with front and rear coverage. When I felt comfortable, I pulled on matching knee boots, ran a heat-brush through my hair with the setting on "sleek," and applied makeup with gusto. I didn't know my ultimate objective—only that I felt unfocused, unsteady, and needed to go out. That attitude usually got me into trouble but I didn't care.

I headed straight to the hotel bar. Now that it was evening, there was a good deal more activity. The music was loud, all the tables were occupied, and three bartenders were on duty. Perfect.

I found an empty stool and ordered a Venusian Blush. It was delivered promptly and set before me in a glass that glittered as if it contained diamonds. Removing the cherry, I sipped the shimmering pink liquid. Gods, it was strong and sweet enough to rot my teeth. I took a bigger sip before I put it down and considered my options.

I locked eyes with a man on the other side of the bar. The dim lighting made it difficult to see him clearly but I noted brown hair a little too long and just this side of shaggy, and possibly brown eyes. He was clean shaven, with even and regular features, and nice shoulders—well within One Gov specifications. Unfortunately, after spending time with Petriv, my view of men had become skewed in the wrong direction. A man I once considered perfectly acceptable seemed unremarkable and bland. That revelation made me even angrier.

It looked like he'd been attempting eye contact for some time because he smiled and raised his glass when I met his gaze. I returned the gesture. No doubt he'd already perused my CN-net avatar. Good luck, considering I didn't have one—at least not in the traditional sense.

Everyone had a presence on the CN-net, some more elaborate than others depending on their t-mods' complexity. When you wanted to hook up, your avatar contacted whomever you found interesting and exchanged information. If you liked what you saw, you could initiate physical contact—although I knew people who maintained intimate relationships through their avatars alone. Mind-fuck was the slang for it. If you didn't like what the avatar offered, you moved on. According to Natty, this saved heaps of time when it came to dating. You knew in a nanosecond if your avatars meshed. In my case, my avatar was a non-interactive flat-file placeholder stating I existed in One Gov's AI queenmind but little else. If a man wanted to get to know me, he had to do it the old-fashioned way—which apparently made me too complicated for some men. Fuck that stupid Russian crime lord anyway.

I took another sip of my drink, except it was empty now. Shit. When had that happened? The man got up and moved in my direction. Uh-oh. Being here was probably a mistake, yet I honestly didn't know what else to do with myself. I felt uncomfortable in my own skin and, deep down, had a petty and vindictive need to punish Petriv—even though I knew what I did tonight wouldn't matter to him in the least. Even if I regretted it later, I was too angry to care. I wouldn't be the first woman in the world who slept with another man in order to forget someone else. So I turned in the stranger's direction even though I had no interest, crossed my legs to their best advantage, and smiled.

"Hello, Felicia," said a voice behind me, slightly accented. "I'd hoped to find you alone. I think it's time we talked."

I whirled in my stool so quickly, I nearly fell off. On the formerly empty stool beside me sat a willowy blonde, hair cascading over her shoulders.

Monique Vaillancourt. My mother.

Poised on the edge of her stool, she wore a lavender dress-suit that hit mid-thigh and managed to look remarkably crisp given the late hour. There were large diamond studs in her ears and an enormous emerald ring on the middle finger of her right hand. When she smiled, I caught gleaming white teeth. Her face was perfect—unlined and flawless—but her green eyes looked hardened by time and experience. I couldn't believe this extravagantly gorgeous creature was my mother.

"What are you doing here?"

"I could ask you the same, but neither of us would reveal the whole answer," she said in that accented voice. Portuguese, I guessed. She met the bartender's eye and a moment later had a drink identical to what I'd downed earlier. She sipped and looked surprised. "Sweet. I wouldn't have expected that."

"Maybe Roy didn't include that in his reports."

"I'm sure he did, but not everything the man recorded was interesting or relevant."

"Where is he now?" I made myself ask.

Monique frowned, though it didn't mar her perfect face. "Reassigned after Denver. He failed so spectacularly, he may have been fired. He may even be dead. I'm not certain."

Her cold disregard made me shiver. The man who'd been my world for almost a year was simply a data collection tool to her, and not a very good one.

She set down the glass and looked at me. Or rather, studied me. Her green eyes, so like my own, took in every detail from head to toe, examining me as I did her. At last, she gestured at me in a dismissive sweep. "I've seen this countless times, in variations not worth mentioning and some that far surpass anything you might become. I know every aspect of who you are and there is nothing you could do that would surprise me. And yet, here you sit—the original. You are the child I actually birthed, yet didn't have a single hand in shaping. Part of me can't help but be amazed at what I created and set free into the world."

"With my father," I reminded her, in case she thought she'd made me all on her own.

"I understand he's unwell. Nerves, the reports said. That's unfortunate. Such a handsome man, and charming as sin. When we met..." She smiled at a memory. "I don't think I could help but fall a little bit in love with him."

I stared at her, stunned by her callousness—first toward me, then my father. "He still loves you."

"Despite the fact I'm legally dead? Such a romantic fool."

I fought the urge to slap her. How could she be so tactless? I debated what to say next, afraid any misstep would uncork my own anger and send her running. "Why fake your own death?" I asked finally.

She shrugged. "It was necessary. I had a hypothesis to prove. Funding was lined up and the stakes were high. If the university grant committee suspected a link between us, my research would be compromised and my breakthroughs invalidated. I couldn't afford to contaminate the control group." There she shook her head, as if the story of her research struggles was too sad to continue.

"Which I assume was me and my family?"

"Naturally. How is Granny G, by the way? Such an amazing woman. I don't think she likes me though."

The desire to slap Monique grew. Granny G had raised me when it seemed like the world wanted to do nothing more than take away the people I loved. My great-grandmother had shown me more love and kindness than anyone. Not my father. Not my grandmother. Not cousins. Not friends. No one. And the fact that Monique spoke so casually about her, like she had any right at all to say her name, made me livid.

"She died five years ago."

"A shame. I suppose science doesn't have all the answers yet, even with the Renew treatments." She leaned an elbow on the bar and looked thoughtful. "It's sad to think all my hopes to avoid contamination were for nothing. The Tsarist Consortium found you despite my best efforts—the perceived weak link in TransWorld's armor. In a way, they're right. Then again, you're a weak link to whatever side owns you. They just haven't discovered that yet. Now Alexei Petriv... That's a specimen I'd love to get my hands on. When I saw you together at the picnic, I realized the irresistible force had finally met the immovable object. That's when I knew I had to break my silence and speak with you."

I signaled for another drink, got it, and took a sip that turned into a gulp. What kind of game was she playing? Was she trying to warn me away from Petriv? From the Consortium? From her project and TransWorld? The whole thing annoyed me, but nothing more so than her casual cruelty in treating me as nothing more than a random acquaintance. And thanks to that, mixed with the horror of the past few days, Petriv's rejection, and my too-strong drink, I was ready to explode.

"Gee, that's mighty nice of you, *Mom*. It's so great you're taking an interest in my life. This newfound concern is *so* touching. We can completely overlook that you faked your own death, had me and my family blacklisted from the Shared Hope program, and are creating clones of me in Brazil! Did you find the luck gene you were after? Did you figure out how to use it for TransWorld's benefit?"

She smiled, unfazed. "You have no idea of the work I'm doing or the value of what I've harnessed. There were reasons I had to separate myself from you. Sacrifices had to be made. Your mere presence would have contaminated my research. If you saw the variables as I did and understood the levels of interconnectedness in seemingly random acts, you wouldn't have hesitated in making the same choices I did."

"Then show me. Take me to your lab," I challenged. Thanks to the alcohol, the feeling in my gut had grown to reckless proportions. Every word she spoke was another dig I wanted to challenge. "I want to see everything you've done for the past twenty-five years."

"Why do you think I'm here? If you're willing, we'll go right now. The facility is closed because of the festival so most of the staff are off. There's no better time to show you."

The feeling in my gut kicked me so hard, it was a wonder I didn't fall off my stool. "That's lucky," I said, with irony.

She arched an eyebrow and climbed down from her stool. "Isn't it? Follow me. I have transportation waiting."

"I need to let Mr. Petriv know first." I paused, realizing I had absolutely no way to get in touch with him, and that pissed me off even more. However, I could reach Oksana. That would have to be good enough. I tapped my bracelet, sending a quick shim, pleased I could still manage a logical thought despite myself. *Monique's here. Leaving with her now. Let Petriv know.*

"Not on a first-name basis yet?"

"I'm not sure what you're implying," I said icily. "We have a business arrangement, with details I don't need to discuss with you."

The bracelet fluttered against my wrist. No picture. No name. Nothing to identify who it was until I read the actual message. *Wait. I'll be there in ten minutes.* Petriv. I could almost hear his voice in my head, demanding I not move until he arrived. Alcohol-fueled anger flared again.

"He wants to go with us. He says he'll be here shortly," I relayed, fighting to keep the annoyance out of my voice.

She shook her head emphatically. "No. Absolutely not. Alexei Petriv cannot set foot on TransWorld property."

I couldn't blame her. At the same time, my ass was on the line even if my gut didn't care about practicality. "I seem to recall several instances where TransWorld tried to kill me. It would be stupid to go by myself."

"I told the Director he was behaving foolishly." Monique sounded rueful. "They tried to recover you in Nairobi after your handler lost initial contact. And again at the auction.

They'd hoped you could be reprogrammed and returned to the field control group."

I didn't think it was possible for me to get any madder. I was wrong. Seething, I had a moment where I actually imagined choking her. Instead I settled on saying, "My *handler*? And here I was stupidly thinking he was my boyfriend. You do realize you're talking about me like I'm some sort of lab animal running a maze, right?"

She gave me a puzzled look. "No one was controlling you, Felicia. Your life has been entirely your own—until you crossed paths with the Tsarist Consortium, that is. Then it was felt that precautions needed to be taken to protect our investments."

"Such as the bomb in the Consortium's jet? Was that TransWorld too?"

"Well, I certainly hope you don't think *I* was behind it. The Director thought he could remove Alexei Petriv from the equation even when I told him that with the two of you together, his probability of success was less than zero. If he'd asked, I could have told him it wouldn't work."

I blinked. This woman was unbelievable! "So...you *want* to kill me?"

"Of course not. Your existence is vital to the acceptance of my research."

"What happens when I relay all this to Mr. Petriv?"

She shrugged. "What you tell him is irrelevant. One Gov's bid is all but awarded. There's nothing you can do to change its outcome, and little you could influence after the fact. What I'm willing to show you is a one-time offer. The Director doesn't know I'm here. But you're my daughter, and after seeing you today..." Her voice trailed off and she shrugged again. "If you choose to wait for Mr. Petriv, I'm afraid I'll have to leave you now."

That was no choice at all. "All right then, let's go." I tapped a reply to Petriv's shim. Gods only knew if he'd receive it or not. *Can't wait. Have to go now or not at all. I'll find out what I can.*

We left the bar. I noted we were nearly the same height. I was a little taller, presumably from my father's side. It was an odd thing to realize, and yet something I'd always wondered. Just like I wondered about the sound of her voice. How she smelled. If her hands moved when she spoke. A thousand things I now had the potential to learn—if I didn't throttle her first.

A hand touched my arm. "Leaving so soon?"

I glanced back. Ah...Average-looking guy with the so-so shoulders. I'd forgotten about him.

"I thought we could get a drink? Maybe all three of us," he said, looking to my mother. "I'm Marshall, by the way. And you ladies are?"

"Leaving." I extricated myself from the hand he tried to sweep down my back and walked away with Monique in tow. "Sorry, but you're about ten minutes too late for the best night of your life. We could have had some incredible revenge sex."

We clicked across the lobby to the main doors and outside into the humid Brazilian night. A breeze teased my hair away from my face.

Monique shot me a quizzical look. "My research didn't indicate your casual attitude toward sexuality. I will need to note that in my records."

She didn't see my jaw drop since she'd walked on ahead, but it did. I wanted to defend myself and let her know I wasn't like that, that I was just confused. Then I realized I owed her nothing. She didn't deserve an explanation and could think whatever she liked, even if her tone sounded more curious than judgmental.

I followed her to the waiting flight-limo. Unlike Petriv's non-descript black vehicle, this had a TransWorld logo on the side.

She turned to me before climbing into the open door. "A last request. I would ask that you turn off your c-tex bracelet. The tech is antiquated, but it can still be traced through the CN-net."

"Another deal breaker?" I asked.

"I'm afraid so."

With reluctance, I powered down the bracelet and cut myself off from my only link to the CN-net. I was now a spook in every sense of the word, invisible from the tech world. Funny how despite the fact that my gut wanted me to all but dive into the flight-limo, I'd never been more terrified.

15

The ride to TransWorld headquarters was uneventful and blessedly short. I didn't know how to speak to this stranger beside me. I felt like I'd lost all the small-talk skills I'd mastered over the years. There was so much I wanted to ask, yet anger crippled me into silence.

We set down in front of the TransWorld tower. It stood out as a beacon of light in an already light-saturated city, so tall I couldn't see the corporate logo on top. Monique took my arm and led me up the front steps. The doors opened at our approach and I found myself in a dimly lit lobby. With only the automated security system to greet us, I found the setup creepy. Monique led me to the bank of elevators at the other side.

"What's to stop a stranger from wandering in?" I asked.

"The system scans all visitors. If you don't match preprogrammed protocol, you can't enter the building. Right now, it's on holiday setting so it only lets in authorized personnel."

"Meaning you?"

"And you." When I looked puzzled, she clarified. "Your

DNA is the same as the clones. Also, your lack of tech. The system scans for t-mod signatures, which are absent from your profile."

The elevator doors opened and we stepped inside. It was illuminated from both the floor and ceiling, and after the darkened lobby, I had to shield my eyes a little. I watched Monique tap another light display on the wall—we were going to the two hundreth floor. I watched her, so cool and remote, and wondered what was going through her head. Maybe it was time I asked.

"You know I don't understand you, right?" I began. "I don't understand the lies, why I'm blacklisted, or why you did what you did to my family. I don't even know if I believe this luck gene exists."

"Oh, it exists," she said, turning toward me. "I've found it."

"But what can you do with it? What advantages has it given you? What made you go to these insane lengths to set yourself up like this and—" I broke off, afraid I'd cry and look weak.

"I'm sorry." To her credit, she sounded contrite. "I can only tell you my side and I'm sure it will be nothing you can sympathize with. I discovered empirical evidence of the luck gene while in graduate school. There was no proven research, just anecdotal stories. Other researchers dismissed it, but every legend holds some grain of truth. I knew if I could put real science behind the stories, my career would be made. Offers would pour in and every door in the scientific community would open for me. Success is important to me. If I could do this thing...well, I *had* to do it.

"My research took me around the world. I followed the clues, spoke to hundreds of people to gather firsthand accounts, dug up research to verify the sources myself...I exhausted every avenue I found in literature and ultimately, I found your family. There are others like you—those with a higher probability of success in everything they do, regardless of what it is. In your case, your family decided to turn their luck to crime. The discovery fascinated me. You come from a long line of thieves, grifters, and con artists despite your present circumstances. I was also intrigued by your family's tech aversion. While the world relied on t-mods and MH Factors, your family shunned them. I arranged to meet your father. Or perhaps luck had its way, and the arrangement happened without my intervention. Whatever the case, he was single, handsome, and I was still girlish enough to be swept away. I ran a DNA analysis from a strand of his hair and found the genetic anomalies I was looking for. The next step was to have a baby."

"You just met the man and decided to have his baby?"

The elevator stopped, and doors opened into an empty corridor. White walls, floor, and ceiling stretched out before us. There was a white door several yards away that broke up the monotony, but little else.

"It was a calculated risk. Your father had many admirers. I couldn't chance him turning to someone else so I worked quickly to gain his affection. Plus, I needed genetic material for the experiments to prove my research. A baby would cement everything, although for a time, I worried the luck gene may not strike true and I'd have gone through all that misery for nothing. I've since learned luck isn't as elusive as I'd thought. It seeks to create circumstances to ensure its success—reproduction included."

"I don't understand," I said, the understatement of the day. "Everyone can have luck?"

"What I mean is luck creates circumstances where it can thrive and flourish. Odds change in its favor. Probabilities are skewed. The impossible happens. Long series of event-chains that seem innocuous at first, when studied as whole, show patterns of increased success. Even a thing that appears horrible on the surface, such as the death of a loved one, may be good if it leads to more money, more success, or something the luck gene needs to increase its odds of survival."

For some reason, I thought of Granny G's Tarot cards. She'd died as Charlie Zero and I were about to open the shop on Night Alley. Her heart just stopped, even though she kept up religiously with her Renew treatments. Everyone said she was too young, that it had been too sudden. Now I wondered if there was more to it. I'd inherited her cards exactly when I needed them most. That would mean…No. Impossible. I refused to contemplate anything so horrific.

"I'm not the universe's puppet, changing direction depending on how the wind blows!"

"You're not far off, although I don't think things are quite so arbitrary," she said, completely missing my disgust. "I've discovered there are 'rules,' as it were, which I can explain later. Suffice it to say I worried needlessly about having a baby who carried the luck gene. Ironically, I also felt pressure from my family to have a child. A baby satisfied everyone—giving me the material I needed, and my family the child they wanted. Even better, as the baby grew older, I had a control sample I could use to compare against my findings in the lab."

She stopped talking and moved to the single white door. It opened at her approach. "That's handy. Do all the doors open for you?" I had to ask, barely keeping the scorn from my voice.

"The building is state of the art. The AI knows who to let in and who to keep out. With the clones' impaired mental faculties, it knows to keep them inside for their own safety. The rest of us have access, depending on the set protocols." Monique stepped inside while I hesitated in the hallway, afraid. I did not want to see what waited in that room. She looked back to me. "Come, Felicia. Come meet your sisters."

Sisters? Were we all the same to her? I bit my lip. I couldn't make myself cross that threshold.

In the end, the choice was made for me. A little dark-haired specter launched itself from the room's muted darkness. It threw itself around Monique's waist with an almost animalistic squeal.

"Momma! Missed you!" said the creature. No, not creature. A little clone about five years old with long dark hair in twin braids down its back, waif-thin in a pink nightie. It looked up, eyes unfocused, face fighting to find its smile. Drool crusted around its mouth and I saw a bruise at its left temple.

"What are you doing up, sweetie? You should be asleep."

Monique rubbed at the clone's mouth with the back of her hand, attempting to wipe away the stain. The clone flinched, then ambled back into the room, squealing the whole way. As Monique stepped farther into the darkened room, more lights came on, creating a path to follow.

I hovered in the doorway, afraid to fully commit. The room looked like a playroom, large and airy, yet windowless. I saw workstations, child-sized desks, toys stacked on shelving units, and brightly colored interactive displays on the walls.

"What is this place?" I called out. Monique had disappeared down one of the hallways branching off the playroom.

"The nursery," she said once back in view.

"And the . . . girls live here?"

"Live. Learn. Play. Train. Everything. It's a wonderful setup and TransWorld provides everything we need. I wouldn't be where I am without their generosity. They've been tremendously supportive of my research. It's one of the best-funded programs in the corporation."

"I hear a 'but' coming," I offered. There was something in her voice. I had a sense she wanted, no *needed*, to unburden herself to someone.

"Sometimes they're shortsighted. The results I've uncovered . . . They could do so much more with the luck gene if they looked beyond the obvious. Further, my findings are their property so I'm unable to publish. No one knows about the work I'm doing. If they did, there would be no limit to the offers, the money, the opportunities. Sometimes it's stifling here."

She sat in one of the small chairs and stretched her legs. Feeling like I had no choice but to join her, I hunkered down in my skintight, shimmering minidress and tried not to feel self-conscious. I had bigger things to worry about.

"I approached the Tsarist Consortium first, years ago. They've done things with gene modification that shook the world, so I thought they would be interested in my research. They were, but not as I'd hoped. They said there was no practical application for luck. In fact, they felt it best to remove luck from the equation. It was too random and unpredictable. But I knew if I could determine the rules and an element of predictability, I could ensure its reliability in any scenario."

"And did you?"

Monique smiled. "I did. Luck will always work to preserve itself, forever putting itself in a situation to its best advantage. After all, look at you."

My eyes narrowed. "Look at me how?"

She laughed softly, as if I were an idiot. In this case, I suspected I was. "You've fallen in with the Tsarist Consortium, under the watchful eye of Alexei Petriv."

"How is that an advantage?"

"I'm sure it hasn't escaped your notice that he's one of the finest specimens on the planet. Genetically, he's perfect. I suspect he's never been sick a day in his life."

"You make it sound like you want to dissect him."

"Do I?" She laughed at that as if I'd said something particularly amusing. "Yes, in some ways, I suppose I do. My point is you alone have his attention. There is no better place for you to feel secure. He's handsome, rich, powerful, and has no women of significance in his life. If he isn't enamored of you already, he will be, and vice versa. The luck gene will see to it."

"You make it sound like we're trapped," I answered, appalled.

"You're not looking at it properly. If you remove religious bias from the equation, everyone is brought together through random chance and coincidence—except you. In your case, events work in your favor. Things may not go as you want, but they will always be in your best interest. You have an advantage over everyone. Or rather, anyone with the luck gene has the advantage."

I shook my head. I couldn't focus on this right now. "What about the other rules?"

"If you believe the cause is just or sincerely believe what

you're doing is in another's best interest, you can short-circuit your own luck on another's behalf, even at the cost of your own life."

"So I can give away my luck?"

"Yes, though it can require some indoctrination," she agreed. "This is the element TransWorld has focused on. The clones believe they're doing valuable work on the corporation's behalf. They can be difficult to train, but I've discovered how to dull their egos and superimpose TransWorld's agenda. It was one of the most significant challenges I faced since finding the initial gene, but it appears to be working."

"Let me guess: the impaired mental development?"

"Correct, although it's more complex than that. The clones' personalities are subverted and their mental capacity limited with a few modest DNA tweaks. Then, we begin service training, making them understand the value of their own lives and the need to protect all things TransWorld. We've found that subjects aged five to ten have the highest rates of success. Older, and their personalities begin to express themselves, leading to violence and self-destruction. Too young, and the training hasn't taken a firm hold."

"How does TransWorld use the luck?" I asked. This was the crux of what Petriv wanted to know. If I could uncover that detail, I could end my association with the Consortium and be free of Petriv forever.

"The clones attend all business meetings. They watch the proceedings, but are kept out of sight. They also fly on all shuttles between Earth and Mars, ensuring the flight's safety. In fact, I believe two of them are on the round-trip back from Mars due to launch in the next few days. No flight will have any life-threatening incident if they're onboard, thinking good thoughts about its success. It's a genius way around the paradox of luck, even if it isn't what I originally intended. I just wish I could do more."

"What happens to subjects older than ten? How did you discover the optimal age?"

For the first time since she'd appeared beside me, Monique looked uncomfortable. She got up and began to pace. "No research is without setbacks. You can't expect everything to go as planned or every hypothesis to be proven correct. With the Tsarist Consortium, this would never have happened. They'd already made the genetic leaps I had to discover on my own. I made mistakes and there were some...abominations."

"Abominations? What does that mean?"

"I know now what I did wrong and how to correct that," she said instead, ignoring me.

"Tell me about the—"

"If you could just talk to Mr. Petriv and make him understand my work, that's all I ask."

Okay, then. So apparently I wasn't allowed to discuss the abominations. "You expect me to put you in touch with him to see if he's interested in the clones?"

"No, of course not. They're TransWorld's property. I can't touch them. But I could start again and rebuild."

"With what?" I asked in growing horror.

She looked at me as if it should have been obvious. "With the two of you. Why do you think the two of you came together in the first place? As I said, luck is seeking to preserve and replicate itself. With your luck and his genetic perfection, I could create gods." She breathed a sigh and a look of radiant happiness touched her face, making her appear both beautiful and insane. Her earlier irritation disappeared. "Of course, I would have to be allowed to publish. The world needs to know. Publish or perish, after all. I can't even begin to imagine the resulting benefits to the human race. This"—she waved her hand around the room in a dismissive gesture—"is nothing. I don't care what happens to this. When I saw you today, I realized the potential I'd missed. You are my daughter. All this effort spent creating what was in front of me the whole time, worried about keeping myself separate from you, or how you might contaminate the lab results...Such a waste of time."

"Is that why we've been blacklisted?"

"Naturally," she said. "I have One Gov connections who worked on my behalf. We wanted a control group. Without those checks on your family, the whole experiment would have been out of balance."

I stood up abruptly, knocking over my tiny chair in the process. My mother was a monster and I had to get away before I snapped. "I...I need to go. You've given me a lot to consider. I'll have to...think...about how to present this to Mr. Petriv."

"So you will tell him? Thank you." She reached out and for an awkward moment, I thought she might hug me. Instead, she offered a hand. "This is the best thing for all involved—you, me, and the Consortium. You're making the smartest decision of your life."

I shook the hand she extended. It was much easier to extricate myself from that than a hug—a fact I found gratifying since I didn't want to touch her. My gut screamed at me to leave. I agreed. Any longer in her presence and I wasn't sure what I might do.

"I have to go," I said again.

Monique looked vaguely off into space, getting that look of CN-net contact. Then she shot me a hard look and almost laughed. "I'm not certain why, but the Director's on his way up. What an odd coincidence. You're right; it's best you leave. We'll talk later. There's another elevator around the corner on the other side of this corridor. Use it instead."

She waved me toward the door. It slid open at my approach; then she all but threw me out into the white hallway. "That way," she mouthed, pointing right.

In front of me was the elevator we'd used earlier. The overhead readout displayed the ascending floors: 186, 187, 188...I pivoted on my heel and sprinted down the hall. Behind me, I could hear the door to the clones' room close. I paid it no attention; I had to concentrate on my own escape.

Another long hall of white greeted me. I raced its length, my heart pounding in my chest, my gut pushing me to get the hell out as adrenaline flooded my body. I rounded the next corner and found the second elevator. I pressed the call button, horrified to find the overhead display showed it on the ground floor.

I pressed myself against the wall and tried to control my breathing, fighting to keep from taking huge gasping breaths of panic. On the other side of the corridor, I heard the ding of the elevator. Then footsteps: two distinct sets. Then, chatting. Two men, but too far away for me to make out what they said.

My elevator's overhead display showed it had just cleared the 152nd floor. A few more seconds and it would be there, dinging its arrival and announcing itself. The men continued to talk. Fuck! What was I going to do? The elevator cleared 170. Why didn't they go in? Why hadn't Monique done something to distract them? What was she waiting for? Why were they taking so long? Was she testing my luck? Bitch! A look to the elevator. 189. I closed my eyes and prayed to all the deities I knew. Gods, what would happen if I was found out? Would I have my memories wiped and be placed back in my old life in Nairobi with Roy—my *handler*? Would I even remember Petriv? Or would they hand me over to my mother after she convinced them I was vital raw material for some new experiment?

Just when I'd given up hope, the voices stopped. They were gone, whisked away by Monique. A second later, the elevator dinged its arrival. The door opened, revealing an empty interior. I hurled myself inside, pressing the ground floor, breathing a sigh of relief only when the doors closed behind me.

I'd escaped. Was it the luck gene? How could I even tell? The things Monique had told me were so outrageous, I couldn't get my head around them. The clones. My mother's careless cruelty and warped dreams of success. And Petriv... What had I learned about him? Genetic perfection. Had he been created in a genetic stew like the Consortium's chain-breakers? Did I even want to know? Monique implied we were helplessly drawn to each other. Maybe, but given what had happened today, luck had obviously missed its mark. I ran my fingers through my hair and rubbed my face. It was too much. I needed time to absorb it all.

Ground floor. The elevator doors opened and I raced to the exit, my boot heels clicking on the floor and echoing in the cavernous void. Finally, I swung through the front door, free. I filled my lungs with cool night air, trying not to sob my relief. Monique hadn't lied. I could come and go from TransWorld with impunity.

It appeared I was in the city's business district, given the neon corporate logos overhead, but with so many massive towers, I couldn't get my bearings. The streets were quiet, but that didn't mean I couldn't get into trouble. I knew nothing about Curitiba—where I was, if I was safe, or where I needed to be.

I ducked into the closest building alcove—a dimly lit side entrance of a tiny restaurant, now closed. A single overhead light stood between me and the darkness. I powered up my c-tex. It would reactivate my nav-look and with any luck—no pun intended—Petriv could track me. Presumably, he was already looking. I scrolled through my messages. Yup, there were numerous shims from him, all with increasing urgency and mounting rage if their curtness was any indication.

I hit Reply on the last one, tapping a quick message that I'd finished with Monique, I needed a ride, and he had to come find me because I had no idea where I was. Then I waited for a reply. And waited. Seconds lengthened until a good five minutes passed. Maybe he was too angry to answer? I'd have to save myself.

I stepped from my alcove and scanned the sidewalk. If they had a Y-line like Nairobi, I could call a pod to the nearest launchpad. That seemed my best option, provided both were close. I scrolled through the local transportation system choices, searching for anything reminiscent of the Y-line. As I scrolled, I heard the scrape of a footstep along the sidewalk. I looked up and saw a figure approach. I tensed, prepared to run. Why hadn't my gut warned me? Things didn't jump out at me! I always knew when something bad was on the way. Except...

Mr. Pennyworth. I swore out loud as he strolled toward me with that irritating, unhurried gait. He stopped a few feet away, regarding me with frustrating inscrutability. The over-head lights were not kind to his features.

"I've been searching for you for several hours," he said. "You couldn't be traced until you used your c-tex."

I checked the time: almost midnight. I'd been offline over three hours. "I had no choice. Monique refused to meet otherwise," I answered as if we were having a reasonable conversation about mundane things. "I decided it was in everyone's best interest to give her what she wanted."

"It seems she wanted a large number of things."

I looked back to the TransWorld tower and shivered, feeling hollowed out and haunted. I hugged myself, realizing how terrified I'd been now that I was safe. I let out a shuddering breath and swiped at tears I hadn't known I'd shed. "She does. She wants more than I can give."

"I've been sent to retrieve you. You can discuss the details when we return to the hotel."

I nodded, continuing the ruse this was a civilized conversation. "Is he angry?"

We both knew who I meant. "Livid. That's why I'm here. He didn't trust himself with you. He doesn't like when those working for him defy his orders."

His orders? Well, Mr. Pennyworth was right; I worked for the man. But still...His orders? "Must be my night for unpleasant chats." I squared my shoulders and tried to prepare myself for whatever came next. I shot Mr. Pennyworth a look. "Your boss is a fickle bastard. He doesn't make it easy to know where you stand with him."

"Perhaps you bring out the worst in him."

I cast another glance up at the TransWorld tower. "And

maybe I'm just a pawn everyone wants to manipulate until they win the game. Maybe I don't really matter to anyone at all." I sighed and shook myself. "Let's go back to the hotel and get the firing squad over with."

I spent the ride staring moodily out the window. Beside me, Mr. Pennyworth was as still and silent as death. Once at the hotel, he took my arm in a firm grip, yanked me from the limo, and handed me over to two chain-breakers.

"My contract here is finished. They will escort you upstairs."

"Hanging out with me must be very lucrative." I couldn't help getting in a dig. "I hope Petriv pays you well to keep hauling my ass in and out of trouble."

Not even so much as an eye twitch from him. "You have no idea. Good luck, Ms. Sevigny."

I smirked. I couldn't help it, even if it was false bravado. "Didn't you know? All my luck's good. I'll have Petriv eating out of my hand in no time."

"That is something I would enjoy seeing." He sauntered down the street, out of sight.

As for me, I was escorted into the hotel to face Alexei Petriv's displeasure.

16

The elevator took us to the penthouse. It required specific AI permission, meaning I couldn't have come up even if I'd wanted to. With a chain-breaker on either side, I felt like a prisoner. Did they think after one visit with my mother I'd flipped over to TransWorld? Was that the reason for the heavy-handed treatment? Or was it a reflection of Petriv's anger?

The elevator doors opened and we stepped into a massive foyer the likes of which I'd never seen in a hotel room. I took in the checkerboard-tiled floor, the massive chandelier, the gold-leaf walls, and the ornate marble table in the center of it all with an arrangement of white lilies and tulips so large, I couldn't see around it. Apparently this was what endless gold notes got you.

One of the security guards took my arm and ushered me inside. My anxiety kicked up another notch and my heart beat with enough force to feel like it might actually leave my chest. I tried to calm down. I wasn't a prisoner. I had valuable information Petriv would find useful. I knew the real problem: I didn't want to face him. He'd left me an unstable mess. I wanted—

and didn't want—to see him. Further, given what Monique had said, was it even safe for us to be around each other?

We entered a sitting room. My suite had the same, but not on such an intimidating scale. This room had a lush cream carpet, floor-to-ceiling windows, several chandeliers to match the one in the foyer, and endless arrangements of furniture. People were scattered about, talking quietly. Oksana. Her husband, Vadim. Other security detail given the suits and uniformity of their appearance. Also, possibly other Tsarist Consortium members—three people I'd never seen before. Interestingly, no Petriv. I looked at the newcomers. Each appeared to be in their mid-twenties to early thirties, but I caught that hard look around the eyes and knew some weren't as young as they appeared. Again, I recalled Monique's words—the Tsarist Consortium had perfected genetic manipulation long ago. I thought of Konstantin and Grigori and knew she was right. I also knew how badly she must want to be where I stood right now.

I felt all eyes on me. Wonderful. "Don't stop the party on my account." Gods, where had that come from? "I'm just glad to be invited."

Oksana rushed to my side. She threw her arms around me in a dramatic hug, pulling me away from the chain-breakers. "I'm so glad you're all right! I was so worried."

"Thanks for the concern," I answered, returning it. Then I pulled away to look at her. "Where is he?"

She nodded slightly, indicating behind me. Shit. I went rigid, not sure what to do next, then decided just to whirl and face him. Oksana's grip held me in place, stopping me. "Tread lightly. I've never seen him this angry. Stop him from doing something reckless," she whispered.

"How?" I whispered back.

"By being what he needs."

"I'm not even sure I know what the hell that is."

"You both need to stop lying to yourselves and denying the truth of what you want. You're the only one who can fix him." And before I could say another word, Oksana spun me around.

Petriv leaned against the doorframe to what I assumed was a bedroom. The room behind him was in partial shadow so I couldn't be sure. Had he been resting? It seemed odd all things considered, but I let it go. He had a drink in his hand which he finished as soon as I turned, letting the empty glass dangle from his fingers. He wore a white shirt, hanging open to reveal the tattoos I'd seen days before. He had yet to shave and his dark hair was a tousled mess. My throat went dry just looking at him.

His blue eyes caught and pinned me. The weight of that gaze was too much. I wanted to sink into a chair, look away, close my eyes—anything to avoid it. He barked something in Russian. I didn't know what it meant, but it was definitely an order. Someone spoke up, in protest I think. Without taking his eyes from me, he repeated himself. The room cleared. I heard chairs scraping, the sound of feet, and doors closing until only the two of us remained.

"What did you tell them?" I whispered.

"If they didn't leave within two minutes, they would not live to see morning."

"Oh." Yup, I needed to sit and think about what I wanted to say next. I had the feeling if I said the wrong thing, something scary would happen. Unfortunately, there were no nearby chairs and I felt too rooted to the spot to move. *Fix him*, Oksana had said. How the hell did I do that? And what truth was I supposed to stop denying? "Do you want to know what I found out tonight?"

Silence. Instead, he went to the wet bar on the other side of the room, poured another drink, and downed it in one long swallow.

"Seems like a waste of a glass if that's how you plan on taking care of business," I observed, because I just couldn't seem to hold back the smart-ass answers. Then I plowed on with, "Monique took me to TransWorld's headquarters. Sorry I couldn't wait for you but she called the shots. On the plus side, I found out how they're using the luck gene."

Petriv poured yet another drink and drained it as quickly as he had the previous two. Earlier he'd said it was nearly impossible for him to get drunk, but it looked like he was putting a solid effort into it now. I frowned, uncertain how to continue.

"Why don't I come back later when you're feeling more like yourself?" I tried.

"You will stay exactly where you are," he said without turning.

Okay, then. I blew out a sigh, though I would have preferred to scream. "Gods, I am so *sick* of taking this bullshit from everyone! I'm not a slave for you to order around. I did what I thought you wanted, so give it a rest. I found out about Monique and TransWorld tonight. I also have an idea how to derail the bid, if you're interested. Let me tell you what happened and you can decide how to handle it. Then...the Consortium will have what it wants, you can remove my black-listed status, and it'll be like none of this ever happened."

"But it did happen, Ms. Sevigny." He walked toward me as

he spoke, empty glass in hand. Every move both terrified and aroused me whether I wanted to feel that way or not. "Isn't that what you said earlier? That it's already started?"

"And you were very clear that things weren't going any further," I replied, reasonably, I thought. My voice didn't waver in the least.

"Which I assume is why you were in the hotel bar this evening, soliciting 'revenge sex.'"

I'm not sure what my expression was. Horror, maybe. "I wasn't…I mean…I might have said something like that…" Shit, this wasn't coming out right. "How do you even know that?"

"Your last c-tex location was the hotel bar. I accessed the memory blocks of the hotel guests and found the data stored in the CN-net."

I stared at him. Memory blocks on the CN-net had the best encryption in the tri-system and he'd cracked it? Not just for one person, but for everyone in the entire hotel. How was that even possible?

"That's illegal!" I sputtered, trying to cover my surprise. Petriv merely shrugged a shoulder with disdain. "Some guy just wanted to buy me a drink."

"*Just?*"

"Okay, maybe not 'just,' but it meant nothing."

"But presumably it would have become something had you not been interrupted."

"I don't know. Maybe. I don't have to defend myself to you."

Petriv prowled around me. I stood in place, refusing to let him intimidate me. "What matters is, had it happened, I would have hated to have to kill him. He's now on his way home and will be barred from all air travel for the rest of his life. You will not be seeing him again. Ever."

"What? That's crazy! You have no say in what I do with my personal life!"

He stood behind me, so close I could feel his body heat and smell alcohol on his breath. I fought to hold myself still; if I moved so much as an inch, we would be touching. I closed my eyes, trying not to let his nearness scatter my thoughts.

"I don't share what's mine, Ms. Sevigny," he murmured in my ear, his voice a soft growl. "Not with anyone."

"I'm not yours. We have a business arrangement. In a few days, we'll go back to our regular lives and can forget we ever met."

"Is that what you think will happen?"

His left hand brushed my shoulder and I could feel his lips move lightly over my hair. It took everything in me not to run from the room. I shivered instead. How could he talk so causally about killing a man just because I spoke to him? This was jealousy and possessiveness amped to a level I'd never experienced before. It felt like we'd gone so far beyond normal, I needed to get away from him just for my own sanity.

"That's what you said you wanted this afternoon and after listening to Monique and seeing you like this, I think you were right. It's obvious we're not good together. It's best if I leave for Nairobi and we get away from each other as soon as possible."

With a violence that didn't surprise me, he hurled his glass and it shattered against the far wall. He whirled me around, fingers digging hard into my shoulders, and drew me in until we were inches apart, his expression wild.

"What did that bitch say to you?"

"Does it matter? You're the one who doesn't want complicated, remember? You're the one who thinks *relationship* is a dirty word. Did you ever think maybe I don't want a relationship either? After all, look at how spectacularly my last one ended. Maybe...maybe I just want to know what you're like in bed and then I'll be on my way!"

That seemed to enrage him more. He shook me then, not hard, but enough to shut my mouth. "Do you truly believe it would only be one night together and we would both walk away? That it all stops because you want it to?"

"Yes. That's exactly what's going to happen. It's just sex, after all. Uncomplicated sex!" I shouted, trying to get free of his hands. His fingers tightened, illustrating how impossible that was. "That's what you want, isn't it? So let's just do it and get it over with. You want me one minute, you don't the next, so fine! Let's pick a time when you do and then be done with it, because right now, I don't know what the hell you want from me!"

For a moment, it looked like he might do just that—throw me over a table and fuck me, putting us both out of our misery. I watched him visibly fight for calm until he asked, "Did your mother explain the luck gene to you?"

The question was so out of left field, it surprised me into silence. I ignored my aching shoulders and focused on my answer. "She said it warps everything so it always goes in my favor. She said it would warp...you." Realization hit me. "You already knew."

"I've always known. From the moment I learned you existed, I knew I would be drawn into the paradox surrounding you. It was inevitable. Luck would find a way to twist us both into whatever the other needed."

I frowned. "And you're trying to fight it, is that it? Is this some sick test of your willpower to see if you can resist me?" I started struggling again, more pissed than ever. "Do you have any idea how much this is messing with my head? I don't want to be this...force that makes people afraid to be around me because they're scared I'll change how they really feel. If that's what you believe about me, why bother coming into my shop at all? You could have walked away and never laid eyes on me."

He smiled ruefully and something in it tugged at my heart. "Because I didn't want to avoid it. You were the challenge I couldn't help but accept and the prize I became obsessed with winning. Would I be ensnared in luck's web, or would I survive unscathed? The more I considered the puzzle you represented, the more consumed I became with the answer. I wanted to know how I would feel once we met. Would things be any different?"

I looked at him incredulously. "And how did that work out for you?"

"What do you think? One minute I was idly wondering about the mechanics of luck. The next, I was leaving your shop, knowing I would go insane if I couldn't have you."

My heart suddenly took off at a gallop. "Have me how?" I asked, faintly.

"Have you in every way possible," he murmured. "I knew I would never want to let you go, and nothing else would matter to me but this."

I stopped fighting altogether and sagged in his arms. I felt an amazed sort of awe as he spoke, stunned he could feel something this overwhelming for me or that he would even admit it. "You make it sound like it's a bad thing."

"Because it is. I can't be consumed by this and be what the Consortium needs. I wasn't made to feel like this. I'm rational. Logical. Precise. That is who I am. Instead, since I met you, I have no control. No logic. I would destroy everything the Consortium has worked for, everything I am, just to have you. I would burn it all to the ground for this one moment, and that knowledge terrifies me."

As he spoke, his hands swept over my shoulders, down my back, and to the base of my spine in a caress that left me breathless. I brought my hands between us, pushing against his bare chest if only to keep a semblance of distance. His intensity mesmerized me. I could feel his heart racing beneath my palms and his skin felt hot to the touch. I hadn't realized I was so cold.

"You're scaring me," I whispered, eyes on his chest. I let my fingers trace the elaborate crucifix tattoo there. "I've never wanted anything as much as I want you and I'm afraid of that. These past few days with you—I feel like I've gone crazy because I can't get you out of my head. Even when I thought it was wrong to be with you, I still couldn't stop myself. But after what Monique said about the luck gene, I'm scared I'll wake up one day and want someone else because luck has decided something better has come along. What if it makes what seems so real right now just disappear? I'm so afraid that this, and you, will mean nothing to me, and I don't want that to happen. What would you do then?"

"That will *never* happen."

"Monique said luck always seeks to preserve itself and find the best advantage. How can you be sure?"

"Because it won't." His tone was stubborn and resolute. "I will see to it."

I finally looked up at him. "What are we supposed to do now? How can you prove this even matters?"

He leaned down and kissed me then, crushing me to him. I returned the kiss, my body straining against his, my arms reaching to pull his head down closer to mine, not caring that his stubble scratched my face. Even with my boots on, I still went up on tiptoe to press closer. My mouth opened under his and I could taste the alcohol he'd been drinking. His hands slid down the backs of my thighs and he simply lifted me and wrapped my legs around his waist, molding my body to fit against his. As he carried me, his fingers slipped between my legs and pushed aside the material in his way, which wasn't much. He stroked me and I cried out and writhed against him.

We moved into the semi-darkened room. I had a sense of a bed behind me. He lowered me and I found myself on the edge of the mattress as he went to his knees on the floor. With swift movements, he removed my boots, then his hands drifted up my thighs, eyes on mine.

"Do you want this, Felicia?" he asked, his voice a hoarse whisper. His hands rested on my hips under my dress, thumbs moving in lazy circles on my lower abdomen. It seemed his body vibrated with both desire and restraint as he waited for my answer.

"Using my name, I see," I said instead, suddenly nervous. This was the plunge I'd been hoping for, yet fearing. After this, everything between us would change.

"You wanted this arrangement kept strictly professional. However..." He leaned in closer, his hands more insistent, the pressure on my hips increasing and making my body ache for his. "I don't believe it's professional any longer."

"I don't think it was professional for more than five minutes."

"Maybe not." He offered a brief smile that faded quickly. The intensity returned. His eyes were on mine and refused to let go. "Are you certain you want this, because once this begins, I will not stop. No interruptions, no distractions. Even if the world falls down around us, nothing will stop this. I need to have you—all of you. You have no idea how much I want this."

I nodded and swallowed, shivering at his words. "I want it too."

"Good."

He rocked me back until I lay stretched out on the bed with my legs dangling over the edge. He lay beside me, bracing himself on his forearm so that he hovered over me. Then he leaned in, his lips on mine again, opening my mouth with his tongue. Gods, the man knew how to kiss. Just his mouth on mine was enough to leave me senseless and oblivious to everything but him.

A hand strayed down my side, to my hip, then drifted between my legs. A finger slipped inside me, caressing gently. He made a pleased noise deep in his throat at finding me already soaked as I writhed against his hand, lifting my hips, desperate for more of his touch.

"Not yet," he teased gruffly, sounding amused. "Do you know how long I've been thinking about what I'm going to do to you? We're not in a restaurant now, Felicia. Do you really believe I'd let it end so quickly again?"

I pushed my hips insistently against his hand. I was ready to explode *now*. "How long do you think you'll need?" I panted against his mouth.

"Difficult to say. Dawn is in a few hours. Check back with me then."

He resumed the kiss, cutting me off in mid-thought. Not

that I was really thinking anymore. Everything was focused on him and his body over mine. I ran my hands over his chest and shoulders, truly feeling those hard, formidable muscles for the first time. I tried to pull him closer, but he pulled back, his lips sliding to my throat and leaving a trail of hot kisses as he made his way lower. I felt his teeth on my shoulder, biting gently while he kneaded my breasts, first one then the other, with his hand. My fingers were in his hair, urging him on impatiently as I squirmed, wanting his touch everywhere he could reach. When he moved on, I protested with a moan and tried to bring him back up to my lips. He resisted. Instead, he got up from the mattress and moved between my legs.

"We are doing this my way," he murmured, his voice a soft purr as he stood over me.

"Let me touch you," I begged. "Please, I need to feel you."

"You will," he promised. "But right now...."

His voice trailed off as his hands skimmed the hem of the dress. A moment later, I heard material rip as he tore it away. My panties followed just as quickly—perhaps even quicker—leaving me naked. I'd barely had time to brace myself.

I looked up at him, wide-eyed. "You're going to be hell on my wardrobe if you keep that up."

His smile was wickedly sinful. "I'll buy you a dozen like it when we get home. But right now I need to see you. Need to feel you in my hands."

The last was said as his lips found my breasts—he sucked and licked until both nipples were taut peaks and my laughter turned to gasps. His fingers easily coaxed my legs open until they were splayed wide and he kneeled on the floor. He caught my wrists one-handed, holding them captive against my hip, and used his other hand to drag my hips closer to the edge of the mattress. Then he looked up the length of me, the wicked smile on his lips turning my bones to liquid.

"As I said before, I've been thinking about this for too long, so you'll have to indulge me."

Before I could protest, his lips were gliding along my inner thigh. Then his mouth and tongue swept between my legs, moving with a skill no other man had ever managed. He placed my legs over his shoulders then held me firmly in place—one hand still holding my wrists, the other, my hip. His tongue teased me, licking deeply, and then circling my clit in rhythmic movements that would have driven my hips off the bed if not for his hand holding me still. And even that drove me with delicious need—my helplessness, his powerful control over my body, his skill as his mouth sucked greedily. I couldn't get away, couldn't touch him, and could only take what he allowed me to feel. It seemed I would explode or lose my mind from the assault of sensation, and a heartbeat later as his tongue speared into me with faster strokes, an orgasm tore through me. I shrieked with violent relief, bucking against him. The pressure between my legs continued, his tongue darting in again. I fought him, trying to get away. It was too much. I needed space. Instead, he let go of my wrists and lifted my hips in both hands to better position me. His tongue drove in again and sucked with tireless effort until I had a second, shattering orgasm that left me limp, panting, and unable to focus.

"Stop!" I begged. "I've never...I can't take any more."

"Yes, you can," was the answer, the words a growl against my thigh.

He was right. I could, and did several more times.

When he'd decided it was enough, all I could do was look up at the ceiling with unseeing eyes, legs hanging over the edge of the bed, arms dead at my sides. I couldn't catch my breath and my heart beat wildly. I heard a deep, masculine chuckle and the rustle of fabric. A moment later, he loomed over me, hands braced on the bed by my shoulders.

I couldn't raise my head. In fact, I may have been delirious from too many orgasms if such a thing were possible. "You're finished already?"

He bent down, lips nuzzling my throat. "Actually, I've barely started."

I raised a hand to trace his jaw, bringing his gaze to mine. "I want to feel you inside of me. Please."

He held my eyes for a long moment. Then said, "What the lady wants, she gets."

He gathered me up to lay me more fully on the bed. I rose up on my knees, my hands skimming along his chest to push his shirt off his shoulders. I leaned in to kiss him; he dipped his head to accommodate me, and I could taste myself on his lips. Knowing what he could do with his mouth was unbearably erotic, and I felt a new surge of heat at the thought.

When his hands moved to his pants, I stopped him.

"Let me," I whispered, my fingers brushing his erection, which was clearly straining against the fabric. "I want to undress you."

He stilled and his hands dropped to his sides, his breathing growing shallow as he waited. I made quick work of it, pushing them down over his hips. In the room's dim light, I was finally granted a view of Alexei Petriv in all his naked magnificence. I gasped softly. He was like some exquisite work of art. The tattoos did nothing to take away from the sculpted musculature, enhancing it instead. My hands drifted over his chest, his shoulders, down his arms, then to his abs and lower. All of him was hard, lean muscle, the opposite of my softness. Just feeling his body, feeling that strength and knowing how powerful he was, aroused me unbearably. I could feel my own wetness drip down my inner thigh; I wanted him so badly.

My hands drifted to his penis and cupped him, feeling the heavy weight. I couldn't help but make an interested hum as I explored, the hum both appreciative and a little daunted by the sheer size. It was impressive to say the least, throbbing in my hands as if it had a life of its own. I closed my fingers around him, barely able to hold that demanding thickness as he twitched. His breath came out in a hiss and his eyes drifted closed.

"Do you know how much it turns me on just to look at you?" I told him. "Do you know how badly I've wanted to feel you inside me? I wanted it from the first moment you walked into my shop," I whispered, stroking him with one hand while kissing along the column of his throat. "When we were at your house and you had your hands on me, I thought I would go insane if I couldn't have this. Then you walked away and I wanted to die because all I wanted was the feeling of you, pushing inside me."

He jerked in my hand and I felt a bead of pre-cum on my fingers. I grinned into his neck, feeling triumphant that finally I had power over him too. The feeling continued when he warned, "I'm not going to last if you do that."

I gave his chest a long, slow lick of my own followed by a series of sharp, biting kisses. "I think that's the point."

He grabbed my wrists, pinning them against my back as if intending to slow the pace. I was having none of that. I pressed myself to him until my naked body brushed fully against his for the first time. I moaned, feeling his erection against my stomach, then lower where it settled between my thighs. The promise of all that power shafting up inside me left me whimpering and desperate to clutch at his body, to feel all of him pressed against me.

"I need you. Please, just take me," I whispered.

"I think," he said pointedly, "that we should get down to business."

My breath came out in a sigh as he pushed me back onto the mattress with unsteady hands and followed me down. "I completely agree."

Then he stopped, poised over me, and looked at me so long I began to feel self-conscious. "Stop that."

"Just admiring the view," he said, before sinking down beside me.

"I'm sure you've admired plenty," I replied drily.

"No." His voice grew husky. "Not like this. Not like you."

When he kissed me again, it started slowly, sweetly. It wasn't enough. We'd moved long past sweet and I needed more. As if he could sense it, he took my hands in his, lacing our fingers together, and stretched my arms over my head. At the same time, he kicked my legs wide and settled his hips between them, pinning me to the mattress. I shifted restlessly under his weight, unbelievably aroused to feel him there poised against my opening, hard and ready to tear me apart as he'd promised earlier. I met his eyes in the semidarkness.

"You are so beautiful," he whispered. "You have no idea what you do to me."

The sentiment was so raw, so unexpectedly passionate, I felt tears rise. "Now," I demanded instead, challenging him and lifting my hips. "I need you inside me now."

That was all it took. In one solid thrust, he rammed into me as deep as he could go. I cried out as my body worked to accommodate his, filled almost to the point of discomfort. He went still, his body rigid over mine, both of us gasping, waiting, wanting. He was so big, so deep. I'd never felt so full before. Had never been so possessed by another man, or been claimed so completely.

"Open your eyes," he ordered. I hadn't even realized they'd been closed and they flew open. His hips ground against mine and my body clenched around him. "I want to watch you. I need to see you come."

I felt the strain in his entire body as he carefully pulled out. A second later, he slammed into me again, his width making me whimper. It felt so good, so raw, my body couldn't help but arch to meet his, my hips rising. Another thrust, just as hard and fierce as the first. Then another that left me breathless. His hips swiveled into me, melting me with every deep, shattering plunge. Another thrust. Another, and I lost all sense of time or place as his body rode mine, owning me, hungrily demanding it meet his needs and work for his pleasure alone.

"Come for me, Felicia. *Now*," was the command.

Helplessly I did, my body clutching his as I shuddered around him. The orgasm was so powerful, it left me wanting to bite him, claw at his back, anything that would give me an outlet for all that heat burning through me. But with my hands trapped in his, I could only take what his body gave. He threw his head back then, my orgasm finally bringing his. I felt him jerk inside me, his hips crashing into mine. His entire body went rigid after a final thrust so deep, I lost my breath as he shouted my name.

Finally he released my hands as he collapsed on top of me, the bulk of his weight falling to my left. My arms were numb, but I clutched him to me, afraid to let him go, desperate to make the moment last. He pressed his lips to my shoulder, and his hands held my hips so that when he moved, he wouldn't dislodge himself. I could feel his heart hammering against my chest, mine keeping pace. His breath came in ragged pants and sweat coated us both.

An eternity later, he raised a hand to my hair. The caress was gentle, almost tentative, given his earlier domination. Then he pressed a kiss to my throat. When he finally raised his head until his face hovered above mine, I saw a look of fierce determination.

"Fuck your cards. I am never letting you go."

I swallowed at his intensity, not expecting it. "They didn't say you had to let me go. Just that things could get in the way. We'll figure it out."

He nodded and gathered me in his arms, tucking me against him. When he pulled the blankets over us, I snuggled into him and pressed my face to his throat. His vehemence both scared and thrilled me. He threw a leg over mine, still semi-hard inside me, and kissed the top of my head.

"It's late. You need to rest," he whispered, lips at my ear.

"Oh? You mean that's all you've got? I thought you said to check back with you at dawn."

He thrust his hips subtly and I spasmed around him, the aftershock taking me off guard. My breath caught as I felt him begin to swell inside me. He chuckled. "Not quite. We'll be busy shortly and it would be a crime on my part to leave you so exhausted that you miss something."

"Very thoughtful of you."

Another shallow thrust made me gasp, then a third. "I try to be."

He was right. Not long after, we were very busy, and I didn't miss a moment.

———◆◆◆———

"Tell me what happened with Monique," Petriv said, hours later.

I'd been dozing on my side, half asleep yet always aware of him beside me. Now he lay propped on his right elbow, looking down at me. His free hand brushed strands of hair from my face. As tired and sore as I was, I also wanted to push him back onto the mattress and start all over again.

"I could have told you ages ago if you hadn't been so intent on other things."

"Things I'll be intent on again," he promised, making me shiver. "What did she say?"

I sighed and rolled onto my back. Beside me, Petriv moved his hand to continue stroking my hair. Sorting my thoughts, I told him everything: how TransWorld used the clones to manipulate circumstances in their favor, the rules of luck my mother had uncovered, how she'd found my family and why we'd been blacklisted, the Consortium's rejection of her research which drove her to TransWorld, and lastly her growing frustration at her inability to receive the global acclaim she felt she deserved. Everything, except her obsession with him. I couldn't go there because it scared me. I didn't want to see below the surface of who or what he might be.

"There's no kindness in her," I said at last. "Not that I expected any, given what I read in the cards, but I guess I thought she might care about the clones. She doesn't. They're disposable to her. It's *all* disposable, like she's bored and it no longer entertains her. That's when I knew she was a monster. TransWorld keeps her in check, if you can believe it."

"And you said you have a plan to discredit TransWorld?"

"More like a thought with lots of holes in it. We kidnap a clone, run a comparison against my DNA, and present it to some CN-net news outlet. Once One Gov realizes TransWorld is producing illegal full-body clones, they'll have to bow out of the bid."

"How would you explain why they're creating a clone army? Do you propose telling them about the luck gene as well?"

I lightly swatted his chest. "Okay, I already admitted it wasn't a great plan. Obviously, I'd rather people didn't know about the luck gene. I'd like to understand it myself, and maybe tell my family. I don't want to be studied like a lab rat. Let's just focus on getting a clone first and worry about the rest later."

He caught my hand and kissed along the knuckles. "In theory, it could work," he conceded, lips moving to my wrist. "However, breaking into TransWorld will be a problem. By the time we acquire the security specs to their AI, the bid will be awarded."

"Weeeell," I began, drawing out the word. "Not if we break in tomorrow. And not if it's me."

He stilled. "How?"

"I'm a spook. No t-mods. Plus, I'm a genetic match to the clones. The building security won't tag me." I held up the hand he'd been kissing. "This unlocks all the doors. If we do it tomorrow night—or I guess it's tonight now—while they're still celebrating the holiday, I can enter the building, grab a clone while she's asleep, and walk out. Simple."

"Absolutely not."

"Why not? It's a good plan." I consulted my gut. Nothing. I had no feeling one way or the other about the plan's success. "Well it's better than what you currently have."

"No. I will not endanger you again in such a situation. You're not prepared for fieldwork. Further, we don't have the building schematics so we've no idea where the clones actually reside. We also can't guarantee whether or not their handlers might be present, or what sort of deterrents they could use against you. And suppose you do get in? You and the clone both have luck working for you. Who would win such a contest? And now, after this"—he gestured to the two of us in bed—"even if we had years to devise the perfect plan, you are not going." With urgent hands, he parted my thighs and resettled himself between my legs as if he'd never left. His lips were feverish on mine. "You are not going."

I turned my head from his kiss and pushed against his chest. I couldn't stop him nor did I want to, but he needed to know I was serious. Even as my traitorous body happily responded to his hands and lips, I smacked his shoulder to make him listen.

"I'm the only one who can do this." My words became moans as I arched with him.

His erection pushed against me, on the verge of sliding home. "No. I'm *not* risking you."

272

In he went with the same urgent speed as before, moving with ruthless intent. Again, my body struggled to accommodate him, overwhelmed by both his size and the speed with which he took me. In the end, I couldn't resist him. My body clenched around him as if I'd been made solely for him to use as he saw fit. And use me he did. Dimly I was aware of the headboard striking the wall until it seemed the whole room shook. All I could do was cry out and cling to him as the force of his powerful thrusts rammed me up the bed and into a blinding burst of orgasms that didn't seem to end. My brain wanted to protest, but my body cheerfully overrode all logic and reveled in everything he did with it.

I'm not sure how much time passed before I came to my senses. In the end, I lay sprawled across his chest, trying to catch my breath while listening to his heart's frantic rhythm.

"That's cheating," I said, eventually.

"I don't care. I need you safe and will do everything in my power to keep you that way."

I turned my face to his, looking at him through the fall of my hair. "Deep down, you know it has to be me. No one else can do it and you'll never have this opportunity again. If I don't stop her now, I'm terrified of what she'll do in the future."

Petriv looked at me. For a long time, he did nothing other than toy with my hair. I tried to gauge his expression. It wasn't the look of someone checking in with the CN-net or running through all his options to determine the best course of action. Rather, it was a man who suspected he was losing everything he cared about and could do nothing to prevent it.

"You may think it's too dangerous or the situation isn't ideal, but it doesn't matter. She's creating distorted versions of me and turning them into slaves. I know the TransWorld bid is your priority, but the way she uses those clones and the things she's done to justify herself . . . I don't think I could live with myself if I stood by and did nothing," I said, realizing in my gut it was true. "And I don't think I could forgive you if you tried to stop me from doing something to help."

"All right then." He tilted my head so he could kiss me again. Funny how it felt so final as his lips brushed mine. "It will be tonight."

17

I woke to sunlight streaming through the windows. I was also alone in the largest bed I'd ever seen. Definitely orgy sized. As I rolled over and contemplated the ceiling, my body announced a series of aches in places I didn't think it capable of aching. Happily, they were the kinds of aches I could live with and would like to repeat in the future.

Sometime during the night, he had removed my c-tex bracelet. I grabbed it from the bedside table, saw it was almost noon, and checked my messages. I had one from Petriv saying he'd gone to make preparations for tonight and would return soon. How soon was soon? Should I stay in bed and wait for him? While the idea had definite appeal, my body decided it was hungry and needed to pee, so I reluctantly got up. I noticed bruises on my thighs but ignored them, knowing they'd been for the greater good.

Next came several brilliant realizations. Firstly, I had nothing to wear since Petriv had destroyed everything except for my boots. Secondly, I had no idea where anything was in this enormous suite. With a bit of investigating, I found the bathroom, then the closet, where I asked the AI for a standard hotel robe. I considered ordering room service, but it seemed presumptuous given this wasn't my room. Besides, I wanted my cards. My hands practically itched with the need to touch them. There were so many things to verify: tonight, Monique, and naturally Petriv and any fallout from last night.

Last night. I shivered. He'd been brutal and demanding, although that hadn't shocked me. He was the sort who got his own way in everything—almost a stereotypical trait for someone in his position. You didn't get to the top without some level of ruthlessness. What surprised me was the desperation I'd sensed, as if he needed to connect with someone. Whether he intended it or not, I had probably seen emotions he never exposed to the rest of the world. It made me realize I needed to stop trying to distance myself by thinking of him as Mr. Petriv or just Petriv. It wasn't like that between us anymore. I didn't know what it was going to be in the future, but it couldn't go back to what it had been. Being with Alexei would be unlike anything I'd ever experienced before. Part of me wondered if I was ready for this level of consuming intensity. Would he regret opening up to me? Maybe that was why he wasn't with me now. Or maybe I was borrowing trouble. Whatever the case, I wanted to be on more equal footing next time I saw him, and lounging naked in his bed wasn't how to go about it.

Still in my bathrobe, I tugged on my green boots, cast a longing look at the bed, and pressed my ear to the door. I couldn't hear anyone, so hopefully the room was deserted. In fact, I hoped the whole damned route was deserted. Maybe it was prudish, but I didn't want anyone seeing my walk of shame—even if I didn't feel particularly shameful at the moment.

I made it all the way to the front foyer before I heard the voices. They were muffled and distant, coming from the far end of a hallway across from the elevator. Good. I could still get away without being noticed. I pushed the call button and waited, refraining from tapping my toe. Time passed. Gods, how long did the damned thing take? I'd never had to wait more than a few seconds before, yet when I needed it most, it took days!

I found myself listening to the voices. It sounded like two men, chatting back and forth. I recognized one of them as Karol. Why did all these people have access to Alexei's rooms anyway? Did they come and go as they pleased?

The longer I waited, the more curious I became. Why was Karol there? Who was he talking to? What were they discussing? I wandered toward the voices, cinching my robe tighter as I eavesdropped. I had no business listening in. This had nothing to do with me and I should get the hell out of there. Gods, I wasn't even dressed! Boots and a bathrobe? What would they think? *Walk of shame, remember?* I scolded myself. Yet, I couldn't seem to stop. Hell, I couldn't even rationalize it. I just went.

There were several doors along the way, some open, some not. The voices came from the closed door farthest away. They spoke Russian, which infuriated me. I'd need to learn the language if I wanted to fit in. Great, one more thing to add to my to-do list. Again, I cursed my lack of t-mods. I couldn't download it and speak with fluency the way others could. Like everything else, I'd have to do it the hard way with long hours of study and practice. Presumably Alexei would help. Oksana as well.

It wasn't until my hand stretched out to grasp the door handle that my gut kicked me. Hard. Everything stopped. My breathing. My happy, horny thoughts thanks to last night. My plans to speak Russian. I teetered on the cusp of...something. Opening that door would change everything; I could tell that much from the force of the kick. The desire to run from it was so overpowering, I almost bolted. I fought the fear down with wishes, prayers, and the hard-won knowledge that I had to face whatever waited inside. Avoiding it would only bring me a world of misery.

So, I opened the door and stepped inside.

At first, I couldn't make sense of it. Karol and a blond man stood beside a large, upright rectangular-shaped box. An endless web of cables connected the box to a monitoring device then filtered to a series of outlets in the wall. Was it a generator or maybe an AI superlink? Karol turned dials, possibly taking measurements, then calling out the results. The other man sorted through the cabling and laughed about something as he threw in an occasional comment. I studied the box: clear, about six feet tall and three wide. Something was inside it. No, someone.

Mr. Pennyworth was in the box, eyes closed as if in sleep. His skin had an unusual waxy cast and shimmered as if coated in oil or gel. If I didn't know better, I would have said he was dead, since the glass box resembled an upright coffin. He certainly didn't look asleep, at any rate. In fact, he looked not quite human. I took another step forward. What the hell was going on?

Karol saw me and swore impressively. The blond man looked

up, caught sight of me, and looked like he might faint. Then he started jabbering in Russian at Karol and moved to grab my arm. I dodged away while Karol started yelling. I took advantage of the chaos to examine the box.

Mr. Pennyworth was fully clothed in his all-purpose gray-green suit. I leaned closer. He wasn't breathing. I also saw that the tubes outside the box fed into it and disappeared into his stomach, under his shirt. Were they attached to his body? I had reached out to open the box for a closer look when hands stopped me. Karol grabbed my wrist and yanked me back.

"Don't, Ms. Sevigny. We're running a decontamination program and it's unwise to open the sarcophagus," he warned. "As the nanobots eliminate the toxins, they create a gaseous byproduct that could seriously harm us should it seep into the room."

"Of course," I said, as if that made perfect sense. I couldn't tear my eyes from Mr. Pennyworth's face. "What is he?"

"It's a first generation homunculus," Karol answered at my side.

"Meaning what?"

"It's science's first attempt at creating an artificial human. We're still in the prototype phase, so the design is crude and not without its flaws. Its thoughts need to be guided externally by others rather than working in concert with a host, and it can't be piloted for long periods. The machine mind and human aren't entirely compatible, so we're getting a toxin buildup. Despite that, we're getting wonderful results with you in the field. In melding human and machine, we were seeing the first true post-human. Laying there is humanity's next step toward conquering the universe—the birth of a new god and true eternal life," he said, voice reverent.

I frowned. It seemed a lot of people were interested in creating new gods when I wasn't sure we were finished with the old ones yet.

"You said he...it has a pilot," I prompted.

"*Gospodin* Petriv, naturally. He's been specifically trained to pilot it, but the man is adept at whatever he turns his hand to so I'm unsurprised by the excellent results. And with his unique abilities at manipulating the CN-net and thought replication, is it any wonder?"

"Unique abilities?"

"It's quite astounding actually. He may not be immortal, but he's as close as humanity's come so far. He's also the first success the Consortium's had in transferring consciousness to the CN-net without death or severe physical and mental trauma."

"So..." Words temporarily failed me. "Mr. Petriv can link his mind with...this and pilot it like a puppet?"

"I wouldn't use such a crass comparison, but yes, that's it." Karol turned to me, eyes narrowing. "You're behaving like this is a great surprise. I assumed you'd been told these details since you're involved in the field testing. Otherwise, you couldn't have gotten in without proper clearance. The door was locked."

I couldn't answer Karol's questions because I had better than proper clearance: I had luck, and it wanted me to see what was in the room. As I stood there, drawing conclusions and making connections, horror blossomed in my stomach as the associations weaved together in my head.

What exactly was I involved in? Who, or rather *what*, was Alexei Petriv? Then came the more frightening realization: it had been Alexei manipulating me all along.

From the first moment I'd contacted the mysterious voice and hatched a plan to manipulate my fertility records, he'd guided my every movement, stripping away all choice until I had no options left but to do what he wanted. He made me take the fall at the clinic and spend the night in the pit. Then engineered the so-called rescue where I felt indebted to him and more inclined to listen to what he had to say. Then hooked me by dangling information about my mother and offering to revoke my blacklisted status. Lastly and most disturbing of all was the manipulation of my feelings. He'd taken my vulnerability over Roy's betrayal and my mother's callousness and created a careful seduction that ensured I kept running back to him—pushing me away and drawing me in until I didn't know up from down.

Humiliation gripped me, followed by a rage I'd never imagined myself capable of feeling. I wasn't simply angry. I was livid to the point where I couldn't speak, wasn't sure I could breathe, and if I tried to open my mouth, I would vomit because I couldn't control the fury. With all his tech and his genetic modifications and gods only knew what else, he was everything my family rebelled against when they refused One Gov's t-mods and MH Factor upgrades. To them he was a monster, and now I could finally see what my cards wanted me to know. This was the true Alexei Petriv—and he was horrifying.

I turned on my heel. I had to get out of there. Out of the hotel. Out of Curitiba. Out of Brazil. Hell, off the planet if that was even possible.

"Ms. Sevigny! Please! Wait!" Karol sounded panicked as he called after me. "I'm not sure what I've said to upset you, but if you'll let me explain—"

"I don't need more explanations," I hurled over my shoulder through gritted teeth as I stormed down the hall. "I've seen enough."

He ran after me. "If I've upset you, I apologize. Truly I

do. I just ask you say nothing to *Gospodin* Petriv. Please, if he knew...I mean...It would make my life difficult."

"Don't care. Not my problem."

I hurried to the foyer and frantically pushed the elevator call button. Karol trailed behind me, pleading and plucking at my robe.

"You don't understand! He might kill me. My family might disappear. You don't know what he's capable of. If he learns I upset you—"

I pushed his hand away and landed a solid punch in the stomach that made him stagger back. "If he kills you because you have a big mouth, then he's an asshole. Look for another goddamn job if you're so scared! Now leave me alone because I can't listen to this any longer!"

The elevator doors opened. Alexei was there, naturally. Big fucking surprise. Luck truly wanted to assault me today. With him were Oksana, one of the people from last night, and a few chain-breakers.

With ease, I wended my way through the group. There were too many of them, causing too much confusion as they all tried to exit at once. I found myself in the elevator alone, gazing out at them. A few looked at the babbling Karol. Oksana reached for him, asking what had happened. The chain-breakers were drawing weapons, training them on Karol, then me. I shrugged and pushed the button for my floor. As if they would shoot me. I couldn't imagine luck would pound me so severely just to get me shot while I made my getaway. Then again, maybe it would. Fuck it. I pressed the button again.

Alexei lunged toward me as the doors closed. Security blocked him, no doubt thinking they needed to protect him from some undetermined threat.

"Felicia? What's wrong?" he shouted over the chaos.

I looked at him, then away before I could start crying. Fuck that bastard; I did not want him to see me cry.

He was almost through the chain-breakers, pushing them aside with that scary insane strength I'd seen him use on several occasions. I swiped my eyes with the sleeve of my robe, the tears coming despite my resolve.

"Felicia! Say something!"

"Two of Cups, reversed," I whispered. Then the doors closed and the elevator began its descent.

—◦—◦—◦—

It's impossible to make a getaway when you're wearing a bathrobe, boots, and your room is one floor down from where you just left. I mean honestly, what was I thinking? Even so, I let myself in and looked around as if I could somehow grab my things and go. I had dithered for all of a minute, swiping at tears, when the pounding started.

"Felicia, open the door." Alexei was pounding with a ferocity that shook the walls if not the entire floor. "We need to talk."

I ignored him. In the bedroom I slipped into a form-fitting green tunic top and tights—at this point, anything was better than the hotel robe. The pounding and his shouts continued as I threw my cards into my travel case and returned to the foyer. The door's locking seals seemed to groan in protest under his fists. I paused, knowing I couldn't avoid a confrontation. My insides churned. I didn't want to see him, never mind talk to him. And yet, I also wanted to launch myself into his arms and forget the last few minutes. My hand hovered over the handle.

The pounding stopped. "I can hear you on the other side." His voice sounded raw from yelling and I could hear a panic in it that bordered on anger. "Whether I have the hotel staff open the door or break it down myself, I'm coming in. I would prefer if you opened it, but whatever the case, we are talking."

Arrogant bastard. I blew out a sigh and threw open the door, standing aside to let him in. He looked surprisingly unruffled given he'd had to fight his way free of his own security detail to get down to my room. I hadn't noticed earlier, but he wore a black T-shirt, black denim pants, and black boots. He'd shaved as well. The T-shirt emphasized the breadth of his shoulders and definition of his chest while the denim drew my eyes downward and made me remember exactly what was in them. I'd never seen him dressed so casually, and as betrayed as I felt, I couldn't help but notice.

He eased the door from my hand, gently closed it, and then leaned against it. "Leaving?"

"Seems like the thing to do." My eyes darted from the floor, to the wall, up to the ceiling—anywhere but him. As an afterthought I tossed in, "Did you kill Karol? He seemed concerned. Thought you might have to because he let something slip and ruined your plans."

"Contrary to popular belief, I'm not a monster who indiscriminately kills people when they've irritated me. Karol is stupid and paranoid, but he's also excellent at what he does. What happened was my fault, not his. Felicia, look at me." He sighed when I refused and continued my examination of the room. "Please."

Something in his voice made me glance at him. Probably the way he'd said please, with its undercurrent of desperation. I gritted my teeth, fighting like hell to keep from crying.

284

He wasn't as unruffled as I thought. I'd even venture to say the haunted look on his face was fear. "Felicia, I'm sorry. It was not my intention for you to see that. You were never supposed to know."

A laugh escaped me. "Know what? Know you were lying to me this whole time? Know you created this elaborate charade to get me to work for the Consortium? Or know about that...thing in the other room and what you can do? If I hadn't seen it for myself, were you *ever* going to tell me?"

"There's no right answer I can give, is there?"

"I guess that means no, then, doesn't it? Can you imagine how I feel right now? You came to me to get access to my mother because you couldn't do it on your own. I get that. But you trapped me in this web of lies and manipulated my every move. And apparently you can manipulate the CN-net as well. Maybe *you're* the reason my appeals to the Shared Hope program were always denied. Maybe you suspected it would force me to do something desperate to change my blacklisted status. If I was arrested, of course I'd turn to you. How could I not when you were the only one offering any hope? Maybe the explosion was your doing too, so you could test my luck gene. Or killing the Arbiter? How do I know what's real anymore? I guess you must think I'm some gullible idiot." I took a shaky breath, unable to say more around the lump in my throat.

"Felicia, no. I've never once thought that. The situation was...difficult. You saw the reports on your mother so you'll know the depth of research involved. I've been aware of you for years. I wanted you left untouched, but you were also the most direct route to achieving the Consortium's aims. Yes, I engineered your situations at the clinic and the pit so they worked to my advantage. I regret the Arbiter's death. That wasn't my intention."

"And Mr. Pennyworth? What was that all about?"

He ran a distracted hand through his hair. "I needed distance between us. After our first meeting, I could barely concentrate. Once I'd met you, you became part of every thought and I couldn't have that. The homunculus allowed me to keep my perspective. When I bonded with it, my feelings for you were…nullified."

"I see. So I was an emotional drain to you? You had feelings but didn't want them. Bonding with Mr. Pennyworth made them go away."

He shook his head, growing impatient. "Don't twist what I want with what I need to do for the Consortium."

"And that's what it comes down to, isn't it?" I retorted. "Sounds like I'm just your stepping stone to taking over the entire tri-system."

"No, damn it. You were never like that to me. I meant everything I said last night. Every word," he said fiercely, pushing off the door and advancing toward me. "You know I did."

"Gods, it's like you can't even see what you did wrong! It's the fact that you were behind everything. You played me from both sides, making me believe you cared and this mattered while at the same time tearing my life to pieces regardless of what that did to me. Even if that life was bullshit, you hid behind your mask and tore everything in me apart. *You*, all by yourself. After what I've been through, I deserve better."

"And knowing the truth now isn't enough?"

I shook my head. "It's too late. How could you ever expect me to trust you when you're the biggest liar of all?"

"That's an unfair statement. I told you—"

"I said I didn't want lies, but that's all this is. You twisted the truth to what you needed it to be. And if I can't trust you, nothing else matters. Whatever this thing is between us would mean nothing because I'd always wonder if it was a lie too."

I ran out of words as gasping sobs took over. He put his arms around me and pulled me to him. I tried to push away. Impossible as always. Instead, I cried into his chest, soaking his T-shirt as he stroked my back. My travel case fell to the floor unheeded. We stood like that for a long time, saying nothing until my shoulders stopped shaking and I ran temporarily out of tears.

"It was never all lies," he whispered. "I just couldn't allow you to know what I truly was. I knew you would never fully understand to what extent the Consortium owned me or to what lengths I needed to go because of that ownership."

"What's to understand? Are you even human?" I didn't expect the silence that followed. He might be able to do things I didn't understand, but I'd never fully embraced my family's mistrust and dislike of most things tech. Yet as the silence stretched, I lifted my head to look up at him and felt a little kick in my gut. "Are you human?"

"I don't know." His voice rumbled in his chest when he spoke.

I wasn't sure what I thought he might say, but it wasn't that. Horrified, I backed away and his hands dropped to my hips. I looked at him again. I mean *really* looked at him. The hair. The face. The shoulders, chest...the whole package. Everything about him was flawless. I hadn't given it much thought before, but no one could be that perfect no matter how carefully their parents had followed One Gov's specs when mapping their child.

"Monique said you're genetic perfection. Karol said you're on the verge of becoming post-human. What does that mean?" I made myself ask.

His hands dropped away completely. "It means I'm a stew of this and that, stirred in a dish, created by Consortium geneticists to be the next step in human evolution. The perfect vessel to rule the world, ushering in a reign of peace and logic."

"And how does... Mr. Pennyworth fit into this?"

"The homunculus will be a global physical upgrade. As much as they reengineer the human body, it can't live forever. Once the link between me and the AI host stabilizes, the world will learn they don't have to remain in the prison of their bodies anymore. Eventually, humans will be able to download their minds into their own individual homunculus. For humanity to evolve, they need more. I'm to show them that they can be immortal. Or, at least that's the Consortium's plan."

And there it was: the thing I hadn't really acknowledged but suspected all along. To him, humans were a "they," not an "us." He wasn't even sure if he was human himself. I backed away even farther, more than a little scared.

"Do you think we're all lesser beings compared to you?" I whispered. "That I'm less?"

"I've never thought that about you. Never. To me, you were a dream I wanted to experience while I had the opportunity."

"How can you think I'm a dream when the future you're describing sounds like a nightmare? It's the most terrifying thing I've ever heard. The Consortium wants us to become these homunculi with all of us here forever, never changing or moving on. Never creating anything new. Not even really feeling anything. Can you even... love like that? You have this amazing body that can do things no one else can, yet you would throw that away and don't even think you're human. What happens to the rest of us, then? Will we even still consider ourselves human when the Consortium is finished? Is this how everything ends?" I whispered. "I don't belong in this world you're describing. I can't be part of it. I never will be."

There was a desolate look on his face. "You were always the one element I couldn't reconcile into the equation. I don't know how to make you fit."

He walked back to me and kissed me. Not on the mouth, but on both my eyes and the top of my head. I stiffened, uncertain. If he'd kissed me as he had last night or so much as turned in the direction of the bedroom, would I have relented? Instead, he merely held me. My arms crept around him of their own volition until I clung despite my anger.

"Part of me hates you and will continue to for a long time," I murmured into his chest. "I'll still do this thing for you with TransWorld because I keep my promises, but I can't...I can't be with you. I just can't."

"I know," he whispered. "I think I knew that from the first, but it didn't stop me from wanting to believe otherwise. I hid the truth because I wanted you to see *me* and not the Consortium's creation. I wanted to imagine this could be real and understand how it might feel if we were more." He shook his head. "I see now that it's impossible." He let me go and turned away. "I'll send Oksana to brief you on the specifics for tonight. Until then, good afternoon, Ms. Sevigny."

Then he opened the door, and left.

18

Vadim Ivchenko plucked at the button he'd snapped onto the collar of my black stealth-suit until its positioning satisfied him. I wanted to slap his hand and tell him to stop fussing. Instead I kept my mouth shut. The less I said, the sooner this would be over.

"This records both video and audio, and since it's organic, the building sensors won't detect it. Don't touch it or we could lose your signal. It's temperamental and the best we could get on short notice. Your earpiece is also finicky. We can communicate back and forth, but it's primitive." He stepped back, green eyes narrowing as he studied me and tapped his lips. He cast a look at Oksana. "I would have liked the meta-gauge sensors, but Alexei wouldn't allow it."

"It's fine," Oksana soothed. "This mission has many constraints. Even the stealth-suit may be too much. Still, I've no doubt Felicia will do what needs to be done."

"I just wish Alexei hadn't been so interfering and let me do my job. Using this outdated tech is frustrating," Vadim complained. He reached up to touch the button again. This time, I slapped the hand away. "We can't even be sure it will work when we need it."

Oksana met my eyes, and I shrugged. She looked sad. "I think in this instance Alexei doesn't wish to take chances. There's much at stake for both him and the Consortium."

I ignored the jab, not wanting to set off more tears. "It's going to work," I said instead, though that wasn't necessarily true. My gut was quiet and I hadn't had time to run the cards.

The three of us were in my hotel room. With half an hour until midnight, we ran through the last stages of the plan. The world outside was dark but not quiet as the city celebrated its festival. The streets were filled with revelers and fireworks were scheduled for midnight, the same time I would enter the TransWorld tower. Monique had said staffing would be virtually nonexistent as a result, so I hoped to get in and out with no one the wiser.

The tower had been under surveillance all day with no signs of unusual activity—anyone who'd entered the building had also left. Unfortunately, we had no clear idea if anyone had been inside before we started the surveillance. I would have to get in, take the first clone I thought I could manage, knock her out with chloroform since I couldn't use any sort of smartmatter compound, then get out. It was a horrible plan. Everyone knew it. Yet if we failed, there were no alternatives. TransWorld wouldn't let itself be caught off guard again.

I just had to make it through tonight. After that, my life would be normal again. I'd go back to my shop. Natty would return from her cruise. Charlie Zero would ride my ass about more clients and changes we needed to make. I'd go to Grandmother's birthday and tell everyone about Roy. They'd pretend to be upset, but secretly be glad because they hadn't liked him anyway. And I'd be alone. My blacklisted status would be revoked, though at this point I had as much interest in having a child as I did in digging out my own kidneys with a rusty spoon. After the past few days, my view of the world had shifted significantly.

I brought the stealth-suit hood up to cover my hair. "We're as ready as we can be. Let's go. The fireworks will be starting soon."

Both Oksana and Vadim nodded and we hustled to the private penthouse elevator, then to the underground parking and waiting flight-limo. I sat on the bench seat facing them, rearranging the tubes and bottles in my belt so they wouldn't dig into my back.

"I wish we had helicon support," Vadim complained. "The citywide flight restrictions are a headache we don't need."

"Alexei has people staged on the closest buildings," Oksana replied, not for the first time. Apparently Vadim was a chronic worrier. "We also have ground support and as an absolute last resort, enough fire power to vaporize the entire building."

I frowned at Oksana. My gut woke up with a twinge. Nerves or something more? In my mind's eye, I couldn't help but visualize the Falling Tower from my Tarot deck and all the associations that went with it. "We didn't talk about this."

"Alexei's instructions. He'd prefer to destroy the building rather than put anyone at undue risk. No one will be able to trace it back to the Consortium, should they investigate."

"That's unusually sentimental of him," Vadim mused. "Alexei never worries about the risk ratio."

"Vadim, shut up," Oksana snarled.

"But—"

"Shut up."

He did once Oksana delivered an elbow to his midsection. The ride lapsed into silence. We maneuvered through the streets at a low orbit, taking what seemed to be a complicated and confusing route since many roads were closed due to the celebrations. I saw partygoers wending their ways through the streets, drunk and happy as they walked arm in arm, in groups and in couples. The image stung and I looked away.

A few more turns and we reached the business district with its towering skyscrapers. As if on cue, the fireworks began. Bright bits of color illuminated the night. Shades of gold, red, blue danced in the sky and threw the towers into a kaleidoscope of color. At the same time, the flight-limo touched down. The TransWorld tower was dark, just like the previous evening. I took what I hoped were calming breaths and squared my shoulders.

Oksana grasped my hand. "Be careful," she urged. "We'll be listening and watching, and will do what we can should you run into trouble. Just because he isn't here doesn't mean he isn't paying absolute attention."

I offered a fleeting smile. "I know." I waved a hand up at the sky. "Now let me do this before the show's over."

I jogged up the front steps to the building's doors. There was a moment's hesitation; then the doors opened as they had last night. First hurdle passed. I crossed the foyer to the elevator. Again, it opened with ease when I pressed the call button and stepped inside. I selected the two hundreth floor and within minutes, the elevator door opened and I stood exactly where I'd been the previous evening. Now for the second hurdle.

I pushed on the door handle, heard the automated lock

click, then resistance disappeared and the door opened. Had it made that noise before? I couldn't remember. My heart rate picked up and all I could hear was blood rushing in my ears. Stepping into the darkened room, I made out the small desks and chairs from yesterday. The only lights came from the fireworks outside, visible through what I knew was a one-way mirrored glass ceiling overhead.

I paused by the first desk, listening but hearing nothing. Still, that didn't mean no one was nearby—I couldn't imagine the clones were completely unattended. I glanced toward the darkened hallway. Monique had gone that way when she'd put the little clone to bed.

"You need to investigate the hall," came Vadim's voice in my ear.

"No shit, Sherlock," I whispered under my breath, nerves on edge. "Try to keep the obvious commentary at a minimum."

My feet were soundless, the stealth-suit's noise-canceling fabric muffling all sounds. A few footsteps in and I noticed the hallway was brighter, lit up with muted emergency lighting. I counted six doors, all dark. Monique hadn't lied—no one was on duty. Or maybe they'd return once the fireworks finished. If so, I couldn't afford to waste time.

With careful movements, I opened the first door and held my breath. There were four beds inside, each occupied by a clone. Unfortunately, they were also the bigger, older clones. I wouldn't be able to manage them if things went bad. Hell, I couldn't even lift one now if I gassed her into next week. Rather than risk potential disaster, I moved on to the next door.

"Where are you going?" came Vadim in my ear.

"Relax, I know what I'm doing." Which was a lie, but I didn't need his pestering.

The second door was a utility closet. Ditto for the one across the hall. The fourth had four more beds. Or rather, two beds and two cribs. Perfect. I crept to the cribs. Both had little clones in them, sound asleep. One even sucked her thumb. Something in me startled at that. I'd only ever thought of the clones as extensions of me, not individuals in their own right. These beings were people, modified and brainwashed, but still human at their core. Me, but also not me. Gods, I was sick of this! Sick of how she'd used us—not just me, but *us*—and would continue to do so. To protect all of us, I needed to stop her.

I removed an aerosol canister from my belt. I shook it as Karol had instructed—aerosol was primitive technology the AI would never detect—and sprayed a light chloroform mist over the clone's head, covering my own nose and mouth with my sleeve. Then I tucked the canister back into my belt and eased the girl into my arms. She was unbelievably light, smelling like cookies and talcum powder, and wearing fuzzy pajamas covered with what looked like bunnies.

My heart constricted. This was why I was there: because I believed I wanted a baby. Yet as I held her, I began to doubt myself. Was this really all I'd wanted? Or had I been so obsessed with the thing I couldn't have that I'd thrown myself down this ridiculous road, blinding myself to everything? Or worse, had luck pushed me to this moment so it could destroy what it saw as competition? Maybe it was luck's plan to get me to this point, and my feelings had never been real. I didn't know. Maybe I never would.

Slowly, I retraced my steps. A few more minutes and I'd be finished. I breathed a sigh. Not exactly relief, but my nerves eased a little.

Then my gut gave me a kick so powerful, I doubled over and almost dropped the clone. When I could stand again, I leaned against the wall, breathing in and out as I fought to catch my breath. No, no, no! This couldn't be happening! I had to get out! I resumed my creep down the hall. Again, my gut kicked me and I went to my knees.

"Felicia, what is it!" Vadim shouted in my ear.

I hefted the clone over my shoulder. Then I stood, swearing under my breath. I turned and went back the way I'd come.

"Felicia, you have the clone. Get out!" Vadim again.

"I can't," I whispered. "I have to see what's in the other rooms."

"Take the clone and get out!"

"Sorry, but I'm changing the plan," I murmured. Then I removed the earpiece and trotted down the hall. His yelling gave me more of a headache than I already had. Besides, they were still getting feed from the button on my collar.

The fifth room had more sleeping clones, though two beds were empty. Those must be the two en route from Mars. I closed the door and headed toward the sixth and final door. My gut pulsed with a ferocity that made me wince. Obviously I headed the right way.

I pressed my ear against the door, holding the clone to the side. I pushed back my hood, listening hard. Inside, I heard the hum of machinery. Okay, so no sleeping clones in there. My hand went to the handle, pressing down without even thinking about it. With the fireworks overhead still illuminating the hall, I let that light carry me from muted darkness into a room alive with color and sound.

I stopped, stared, and gasped.

I was in a laboratory, lit overhead with soft, glowing fluorescents. I stood on a platform overlooking row upon row of glass sarcophagi like the one containing Mr. Pennyworth. Some held unborn fetuses in sacs of amniotic fluid. Others contained clones similar to the one I held in my arms. Others still held clones close to my own age and older. It was as if all the stages of my entire life from conception to death were laid out for me to contemplate. All floated in a comalike suspension, tubes running in and out from each of their various bodily openings.

I pressed my free hand against the platform railing, not sure what to do. That grip was the only thing keeping me on my feet. I wanted to run away, cry, cover my eyes, and pretend I hadn't seen it. My gut was having none of that. I turned to the staircase on my right and marched down into the mass of clones.

At the bottom waited Monique.

She watched my progress until I stopped in front of her, still holding the clone. In the harsh lighting, her features looked fiendish, or maybe that was my imagination.

"I see you selected the perfect opportunity to break in. How lucky for you. Is there something I can help you with?" she asked with all the civility in the world.

I suspected my mother was a hell of a lot smarter than me. All I could do was bluff my way through and hope for the best.

"I spoke to Mr. Petriv and told him you were interested in switching sides," I said, hedging.

"Given how late you left last night, it must have been pillow talk," she said, voice cold. "Did you tell him everything? Did the luck gene work as anticipated? Are you lovers now?"

I fought not to react to the goading. She actually sounded

jealous. Did she want to be in my place? That sent the creep factor through the roof.

"I told you our relationship was business only. Obviously if I disappear for several hours and he knows I'm with you, he'll also want a report when I get back."

"Yes, of course." She looked visibly relieved. "What did he say?"

"He's intrigued but wants to see the clones for himself. He wants his people to verify the luck gene is real."

"That makes sense," she agreed, nodding. "You're the original, but with free will, how can what you do be attributed to luck? A series of comparisons between you and the clone would be the perfect experiment. Of course, the fact that you're here stealing a clone is suspect. He could have contacted me directly. There's no need for such cloak-and-dagger nonsense, especially considering you would never have been able to leave the building anyway."

I frowned. "Why not?"

"You'll notice the collar she's wearing." Monique stepped forward and tapped the sleeping clone's neck. Now that she'd drawn my attention to it, I saw a tightfitting strap around her throat. It was finger-width and fit snugly, but not close enough to chafe. "Once she's thirty feet outside the building perimeter, it explodes. The blast radius is small, but powerful enough to destroy the clone and anything nearby. We remove them whenever we leave the tower, such as at the picnic yesterday. I apologize for not mentioning that earlier." Her tone was smug.

At least now I knew why my gut had reacted so strongly. I would have been killed once I'd gotten the clone outside.

"You could have just asked. To appease the Consortium's

curiosity, you could have any number of these. I've plenty to spare. TransWorld has no use for them." She smiled and gestured to the canisters behind her.

I set the clone on the floor at my feet. Holding it, knowing we were all part of some grand experiment, made me feel dirty. Monique watched me, the half smile never leaving her face.

"You're not here for the reasons you claimed, are you? The clones don't hold the interest for him I'd hoped. He doesn't want to exploit the luck gene. He wants to stop it."

"I didn't say that."

"No, but your expression shows nothing but disgust." She sighed and shook her head. "You won't prevent the Mars contract from being awarded to TransWorld. It's too late. The contract's all but signed. It's unfortunate it's come to this. I truly believed my knowledge, added to the Consortium's research pool, would yield results beyond their wildest dreams."

I glanced at the canisters again and couldn't contain my shiver. "Was there ever a moment when I was more than an experiment to you? When you thought, 'I'm going to be a mother. I've just created life'?"

She laughed. "Felicia, I'm not going to participate in this silly discussion. I know what you're going to say even before you say it. It's predictable and I've heard it a thousand times over." A gesture to the canisters. "You want me to feel guilty for abandoning you and being a terrible mother. Or admit to feelings of love and regret. All right, yes. The first time I felt you move in me was one of my life's greatest moments. Did I feel affection? Perhaps, but what I recall most was the sense of satisfaction. I knew I'd completed the first step in a lifelong project. Soon, I would have you and from that, I would have this."

"Which you said you'd abandon to work for the Consortium."

She blinked as if I'd thrown her an unexpected curve. "Well yes, I have no issue with starting over. I told you of Alexei Petriv's genetic potential. Crossbred with your luck, I truly believe the end result would be a significant evolutionary leap. However, it doesn't mean the sample must come from you. After all, I have so much here to choose from."

I couldn't breathe. Not that there was anything wrong with the air, but my head spun with the horror of what lay around me paired with the filth coming out of her mouth. "I'm not sure he'd be into that," I said. It was the best I could manage.

"Perhaps not yet, but I can be very persuasive," she insisted. "You're redundant. He obviously knows you're here. You said yourself it's just business between you, so should you fail to appear with a clone, he'll come looking but he'll hardly be overwrought with grief. And when he's aware of what I've created..." She shrugged and smiled again. "I think the evidence speaks for itself."

"Are you implying you'd actually kill me to get me out of the way?" I don't think my tone could have been any more incredulous.

"It's not my first choice on how this will end, but I've considered it."

I laughed, but it sounded hysterical and unnatural. "I have the luck gene, you know."

"Yes, but it doesn't make you immortal."

She pulled out a laser stun pencil from her desk drawer and pointed it at my heart. The tiny weapon could sever me in half before I could blink. So much for tech restrictions. I think I may have laughed again because Monique looked at me like I'd lost my mind.

"You really are like your father." Her lip curled in distaste. "Cocky and delusional all at once. Would you like to share what you find so hilarious?"

I shook my head, feeling like the universe had played the most colossal joke at my expense. "Just that in all the readings I've done, I assumed the Death card referred to him, not me. Kind of sucks knowing how wrong I was."

"What gibberish are you going on about?"

I didn't have a chance to say more. High-pitched alarms sounded, so loud and shrill we both covered our ears.

"What is that?" I screamed at Monique.

"AI security! There's unauthorized tech in the building!"

A second later, the entire building shook as if with the force of an explosion. I lost my footing and tumbled against the lab stairs, catching the railing at the last minute and hauling myself upright. I scrambled to the platform and back down the hallway, covering my ears. The building shook again. My shoulder hit the wall with a solid thud. This time, I was certain it was an explosion. I had to get out of there! My gut agreed with a hearty "get the fuck out" kick that had me scrambling.

I stumbled by the closed doors. The clones! I hesitated. There was no way I could get them out of the building with the collars they wore. Hell, I couldn't even get myself out. Still, I couldn't leave them. I opened a door and out they came, screaming, running everywhere, arms flailing over their heads as they ran into each other and the wall. I opened another. Out flew more clones.

"You idiot! You've ruined everything!" Monique shrieked as she barreled from the lab.

She shoved me aside with a brutal push and began firing

indiscriminately on the clones, killing two if their lack of movement was any indication, and missing the rest who continued running and screaming. I watched in paralyzed horror as blood spattered the walls and the floor. *Monster* wasn't even the right word to describe this woman as she mowed down her creations with cold precision.

"What are you doing?" I cried, chasing her into the schoolroom.

"Use your brain, you stupid cow! The alarms mean a breech. Do you think I'm going to let anyone take what I've worked so hard to create? These are *mine* and I will do what I see fit with them. No one is taking them from me! Not you. Not the Consortium."

In the open space, chaos reigned. Clones screaming. Monique firing. Alarms sounding. The building swaying. All of it illuminated by the fireworks overhead. For some reason, that made me look up at the glass ceiling. Suddenly I saw a figure up there. Several figures, in fact.

Glass shattered next, raining down in a million crystal sparkles. I stepped back out of range. Monique wasn't so lucky and took the brunt of it, screaming as glass cut her. Blessedly, the shooting stopped. It didn't deter the clones, however, as they continued screaming and running. It also didn't stop the deafening alarm.

I looked up again. The figures on the roof used heavy corded ropes to lower themselves through the hole they'd smashed. I counted three, each dressed in black. I couldn't identify them. Then my brain recognized the stealth-suits and I realized what I saw. The cavalry had arrived.

In fact, not just the cavalry. The first to touch down and

unhook from the harness with brisk, precise movements, as if having done it a thousand times before, was broad-shouldered and tall, the stealth-suit emphasizing his powerful physique. The figure turned, strode a handful of steps toward me, then grabbed me with both hands and hauled me up against him. Alexei.

I sank into his arms, my relief so intense it took my breath away and left me limp. He held me in a death grip, crushing me to his chest and lifting me clear off the ground.

"Did she hurt you?" His mouth was at my ear.

"Not yet. You need to stop her."

"I will. First, I have to get you out of here. I need you safe or I'll lose my mind."

He carried me to the harnesses and secured straps around my waist and under my arms. Then he leaned in close so the alarm wouldn't carry away his words. "The rope is attached to a helicon. It'll lift you out."

"What about the clones?"

"Once we had your visual confirmation, we realized taking a clone wouldn't be enough. We had to catalog all your mother's research. Unfortunately, it's in a closed block of One Gov's queenmind. I'm the only one who can access it, but I need to be on-site to do it."

"That was you with the explosions?"

He nodded, buckling another harness around my legs and hips, and snapping it in place. "You may be able to get around the building's tech restrictions, but I can't. We tried to take out the AI auto-defense, but missed the backup systems."

"The lab. You saw it?"

"I did. TransWorld is finished."

I looked around. With the immediate danger over, I saw the two other black-clad figures subdue the remaining clones and carry them back to the lab.

"What are they going to do with the girls?"

"If they can, they'll try to remove the collars. Monique must have something in the lab to deactivate them."

"What if they can't?"

"Then we salvage what we can from this situation and move on."

A feeling of dread washed over me as I tracked their progress back to the lab. "Why do you make it sound like they're going to kill them?"

"Because if that's what needs to happen, they will." With a hand on my chin, Alexei dragged my gaze back to his. The look on his face was intense and serious.

"I need you to understand this. I'm not a butcher or a tyrant. This is necessary. We can't stop her without proof. If killing the clones so we can remove them from the building is the only way to do it, then so be it."

"But you can't! They're just little girls!" I protested.

"No, that's not what she intended. They're not real to her. None of them are. They're disposable waste she'd cast aside should something better come her way. Not even *you*—her own daughter—are a real person to her. You're another creation to discard once you're no longer useful. That's how twisted her world is. Research without conscience and creating a thing just because you can doesn't mean you should."

"So what are you saying? That the Consortium shouldn't have made you?"

He arched an eyebrow. "Or maybe none of us should be

here. Me. The clones. You. Maybe qualifying as human is more difficult than you think."

I started at him, stunned, taking in the full measure of what he implied. Both of us were experiments, forged in different ways and walking separate paths, but essentially the same at our core. Each of us had been made because someone wanted to "see what would happen," and we'd lived our lives accordingly as best we could. I just hadn't seen it until now.

I wanted to say something then, to let him know that even though he'd hurt me, I still cared—that I would probably always care about him. I just couldn't come up with the words. I, who always knew the right thing to say when I held the Tarot cards in my hand, couldn't figure out how to string together a sentence when it mattered most. I didn't think he was some genetic anomaly the world could do without. If anything, I was the freak. Humanity had moved on and I was the one who was different and would be left behind, not him. The fact he thought I might feel otherwise, and had tried to hide who he was because of it, made me feel sick inside.

He must have seen something in my face because his gloved fingers gently brushed my cheek and he offered a brief smile. "We'll discuss it later when there's time. Right now, I have to deal with Monique." Then he tugged my straps, checking their tension one last time before turning away.

The slack left the rope and I felt myself lifted, slowly at first, then with increasing speed. Grabbing the straps, I fought to both steady myself and keep from vomiting as vertigo overcame me. By the time I'd sorted myself, I was out in the cool night air. Above, a whirling helicon blade whipped my hair in every direction.

I looked back down at the mess and the bodies strewn across the floor. The other two figures with Alexei were back from the lab and securing themselves in their harnesses, preparing to leave. Why? Where were the clones? Couldn't they remove the collars? Something was wrong. I knew it as sure as I knew my own name.

Alexei's cable dangled limply, pooling on the ground. Where was he? Was he still trying to crack One Gov's queenmind? I scanned the scene, searching. At first, I couldn't see him. Then, I did. He was with Monique. It looked like they were arguing. Suddenly, she turned on her heel and darted back to the lab. Alexei followed with determined steps.

The helicon banked sharply left. The engine seemed to stutter before catching again and we swung out wide over the city. I clutched at my harnesses and bit back a scream. Then I felt myself rocketing upward. My shoulder hit the door's edge hard enough to make me shriek, and I was hauled inside with rough hands. Just as briskly, those hands ripped me from my rigging and hurled me into an empty seat.

"What's going on?" I shouted at the winch operator.

"Put on belt," he said in heavily accented English. "Going to be bumpy ride."

"Tell me what's happening!"

"AI backup's firing on us. The deterrent drones will attack next. We move now. Buckle up."

A body landed in the seat beside me, then another in the one facing—the two others with Alexei. Both struggled into their safety harnesses, cursing in Russian as they fought with the straps. At the still-open door of the helicon, the winch operator leaned out, eyes glued to the TransWorld tower. The tower was no longer below us. We hovered higher in the air, a tower away.

I fought my way to the door, tripping over legs and equipment as I went. I caught myself on the winch and looked down. All I could see was Alexei's escape cable listing in the wind, empty.

"We have to go back for him!" I screamed.

"Too much deterrent fire!" came the pilot's snarled reply.

Someone shouted in Russian and I was not imagining it when the tension rose higher.

"What? What did he say?"

"He's activated detonators. The building is set to vaporize."

It felt like I spent an eternity just looking at the pilot before the words actually sank in. "What the fuck are you saying? You're going to vaporize the building?"

"It was precautionary in case things went bad and he couldn't take the queenmind or thought he might be caught. Tsarist Consortium can't be involved."

"But... No, that can't be right. Vaporizing the building? That's insane. He's still down there! We need to go back!"

"We go now or risk pull of vapor-seal when tower goes."

"We can't leave him!"

"Detonation in one minute. We stay, we die."

The helicon banked swiftly, racing from the tower. I tumbled to the other side of the helicon, grabbing what I could to keep steady. The hatch slammed shut and hands hurled me into my seat again. My eyes were glued to the tower. Everything in me stopped. My breathing. My thoughts. My heart. I waited as if in suspended animation, hoping, praying some miracle would happen.

Except, it didn't. One moment the tower stood. The next,

the air sizzled and it seemed like any potential energy in the area was sucked inward, toward the tower. The lights of the buildings around us either dimmed or went out before coming on again seconds later. Then, in one horrendous blast of white light, the tower vanished.

The helicon dipped perilously as the blast wave rocked us. The pilot cursed and wrestled the machine back into position, hitting the instrument panel with each word. The engine sputtered, stalled, restarted again. In those tense moments, no one spoke. Even when we leveled and the pilot's cursing eased, we stayed silent. We banked again, getting one last unobstructed view of what remained of TransWorld.

I gasped. There was nothing but drifting smoke. We were too high up to see the chaos on the ground or how those below had fared. All I could register was how completely it had been vaporized. Everything was gone. Everything.

I sat back in my seat, eyes unseeing, numb and feeling coldness spread through me. I wanted to throw up, but couldn't. I couldn't do anything, not even cry. My body could do nothing but sit there. No, that wasn't true. I could think, but the thoughts kept looping back on themselves, threatening to drown me in a flood of despair: If I had the luck gene, how could it all have gone so wrong? How could I lose everything all at once?

I didn't feel lucky at all, and suspected I wouldn't feel much of anything for a long time.

19

The helicon was abandoned outside Curitiba, and I found my-self back with Oksana and Vadim in the flight-limo. The rest of the people involved presumably had their own means to leave the country and lay low. A terse, silent ride brought the three of us to a private airstrip where a Consortium jet waited. Though I'm sure it was luxurious inside with room enough to fit several people, I was blind to my surroundings.

After I buckled in, Oksana handed me a glass of water and two blue pills. I looked up in question.

"It will make you sleep for the duration of the trip." She sounded tired and drawn. Her lovely face looked pinched. When she took her seat, she knocked back her own handful of pills. "I suggest you take them. You won't have to think for the next several hours."

"I don't understand. There had to be another way. Why did he go back after my mother? Why did he destroy it all?" My voice cracked and I had to clear my throat to get the words out.

"I don't know," she said before turning to gaze out the win-dow. "Just take the pills."

I followed her lead, swallowing, then chasing them with water. Right now, not thinking was a blessing. Soon we were in the air. By the time One Gov closed borders to all traffic, we'd already left Brazil and were en route back to Kenya.

It seemed like only a blink of time passed before we landed in Nairobi. I looked out my window as we began our descent to another private airstrip. The sky was a dark, cloudy gray. The ground looked rain-soaked with evidence of a recent downpour. The roof of the lone shack at the edge of the runway glistened darkly, and stray droplets hit my window. A glance at my bracelet indicated it was midafternoon. The whole trip had taken a little over eight hours.

Without a word, we gathered our gear and exited to the waiting flight-limos. Oksana walked toward one, head down and shoulders hunched. I had moved to follow when Vadim caught my arm and led me to the other. We hurried to avoid the scattering of raindrops.

"This will take you home," he said as the chain-breaker opened the door for me. "Someone will be in touch with the final details regarding the completion of your contract with the Consortium and ensure you are paid in full."

I stared at him.

His expression was very hard and very cold. "Should you decide to speak to any authorities about what happened, your life will be forfeit—though I'm sure you already know that. *Do svidaniya*, Ms. Sevigny. Try to have a nice life."

He strode briskly to where Oksana waited. I watched in mute surprise as they got in, the door slid closed behind them, and the flight-limo engines ignited. Oblivious to the rain on my face, my eyes followed their vapor trail until the clouds obscured it. Their abandonment cut through me like a knife. Did they blame me for what happened? Was it my fault it had all gone so wrong? Had I asked them to come swooping in and put everything at risk? No. Yet they'd done it anyway and the result was more horrible than I could even contemplate. Alexei Petriv was gone. As quickly as he'd come into my life and thrown everything in it into chaos, he'd vanished. It was all over before it had even really begun.

That realization hurt more than I imagined. I felt sliced open and numb, as if everything had been torn out and taken from me. It wasn't like we'd fought, broken up, and would never speak to each other. I was literally never going to see him again. Ever. The way he smelled, how he looked at me, the feeling of his hands on my skin, or his unguarded expression when he came inside me and I saw how much he wanted me—I would never experience any of those things, no matter how much I might want them. It had all been so fleeting and quick, with barely any time to make a proper memory. How would I be able to remember him clearly? How could I hold on to any of this?

The complete and total loss was so staggering, my stomach heaved and I threw up on the ground beside me. I'd barely finished when a hand gripped my arm and hustled me into the waiting flight-limo. Within the hour, I was home. It set down by the curb in front of my condo, and the door slid open. I got out, peering up at the building that had been my home with Roy. Before I'd even gathered the belongings the chain-breaker dumped on the curb, the flight-limo took off.

I had no trouble getting into either the building or the condo with my new access codes. Inside, I found everything placed where it had been before. My precious Tarot decks were all in their cabinet as if they'd never left. My quirky table Eleat was waiting for my input. Even the food I'd had lying around my kitchen was there. The attention to detail shocked me. How had he remembered?

No, that wasn't entirely true. One thing was different: the bed. As soon as I reached the master bedroom, I saw it wasn't the same. This one was more expensive than anything I could have afforded and that shocked me—not the expense, but that he'd been sensitive enough to know this was one thing I'd have wanted to replace. The headboard was one massive piece of carved wood, stained a dark mahogany. I had no doubt in my mind that the wood was real and not a cheap synthetic fab knockoff. The mattress was plush and deep.

I stared at it blindly. Had he thought...that someday he'd be here with me or he'd help me break it in? Perhaps that had been his plan all along, despite everything—that we'd somehow end up together. That I'd look beyond the creature the Consortium had created and see something more, something...human. In our last seconds together, he hadn't wanted me to think of him as a horrific monster grown in a genetics lab, designed to be leader of the Consortium. He'd wanted to be human, for me.

My legs went out from under me and I sank to the edge of the mattress, then crawled to the middle of the bed, inhaling its newness. I pulled the blankets around myself as the horror of everything swept over me at once. I would have liked more blue pills, but Oksana hadn't offered and I'd been too numb to ask. There was nothing I could do but lie there in a fetal position and cry.

I thought of Alexei and how he'd smiled at me the last time, his gentleness as he'd touched my cheek. If everything had gone according to plan, we would have talked after and maybe...maybe, I'd be with him right now. Maybe...No, there were no more maybes. I clutched the blankets tighter as my heart broke. Why hadn't I said something to him? Why hadn't I told him that maybe there could be a future for us? What hadn't my gut warned me sooner? Or let me know that we were never going to have a later?

Terrible, shattering sobs followed. I couldn't control or stop them. I felt like everything in me was broken, leaving me to choke on the pieces. I could have had everything I'd ever wanted. I just hadn't realized it. But wasn't that how it always went—life gives us all a chronic inability to see what is right there in front of us until it's gone? Luck had preserved me, all right; preserved me for a life full of loss, emptiness, and pain. As I lay there on the bed, I realized that luck had a third rule: If you thought you could rely on it to make you happy, you were wrong. It would only smash you apart in the end.

<hr />

That was how Charlie Zero found me many days later. Oh, I'd gotten up to use the bathroom, change out of my stealth-suit, and eat what little food I found in the condo. But beyond that, I'd managed little else. I couldn't bring myself to reply to the endless stream of messages on my c-tex bracelet. What did any of it matter? I ran my cards several times, praying they might offer some sort of hope or an explanation for the disaster in Brazil, or what Alexei had been thinking before he'd vanished. Instead my brain couldn't make sense of the answers and it seemed like all the readings contradicted one another.

When the pounding started on my front door and I heard

Charlie yelling out in the hallway to haul my lazy ass up and answer him, I forced myself out of bed. I'd get complaints from the neighbors otherwise. Plus, dealing with him would let me get back to wallowing in my misery that much quicker.

I shuffled down the hall with a blanket wrapped around me. It was cold in the condo. I hadn't noticed before and made a mental note to adjust the air. In the entranceway, I tripped over the suitcases I'd dumped there days ago. When I finally opened the door, Charlie's pounding had reached a fever pitch.

"Calm down," I said, voice hoarse. "I'm right here."

I'd caught him in mid-pound, his fist raised to offer another blow. Seemed like everyone was interested in breaking down my door. *Not funny*, I told myself, recalling the moment with Alexei when everything had come crashing around me. *Not funny at all.*

Charlie's arm dropped and his dark brown eyes looked me over with a critical gaze. Then it went from harsh to sympathetic, and he made a *tsk*ing sound.

"I told you not to, but you did it anyway. You fucked the Russian."

I sighed. "Hey, Charlie. Want to come in?"

He stepped inside, looked at my mess, and took a none too subtle sniff. Great. Apparently I stank. "I assume Roy no longer lives here?"

"He's an asshole."

"I know more than a few who'd agree with that assessment." He closed the door behind him. In his impeccable black-and-white-striped suit and the shocking blond hair he'd decided to spike today, he looked a damn sight better than I did. "I'd say tell me what happened, but it looks like you may not be ready."

"Thanks, Charlie. I appreciate that."

"Don't appreciate it yet. I'm here because the two weeks are up as of tomorrow and I'm ready to open up shop again. I've been trying to get in touch with you, but you haven't returned my shims, which is frustrating as hell. Plus, the damned Russians haven't paid us. From the look of you, I'm guessing that's a lost cause too. No offense, kid, but I knew those Russian bastards would find a way to fuck us over. So much for my faith in human nature. Two weeks of revenue, all gone. Fucking Russians."

To my surprise, I laughed. It wasn't because I felt better or my life was any less of a mess. I just enjoyed a good Charlie Zero rant, and it was better than crying. He was as dependable as the rainy season and I loved him for it. His anger at the practical and mundane gave me hope things might someday be normal again.

As if my laughter had given it permission, my stomach rumbled to let me know it wanted more than cheese with the mold cut off. I took a whiff inside my oversized sweater. Yup, I stank.

"Let me clean myself up, and move some of this"—I waved at the mess around the front door—"and you can take me out to dinner since I have calories to spare this month. You can tell me how you spent the last two weeks and fill me in on Natty's cooking cruise. I'm sure she bored you with all the details."

He looked at me critically. "You sure you don't need more recovery time, kid? I love money, but I care about you more."

From Charlie Zero, that was high praise. I nodded. My gut seemed to approve with mild hesitancy. Maybe things wouldn't be normal for a long while, but I'd get there. "Yeah, I'm sure."

I threw myself back into work because I had no other choice. We needed to make up for the two weeks of revenue we'd lost, and I needed to keep busy. Worrying about other people's problems was a blessing. Knowing I helped my clients helped me feel better about myself, while giving me less time to dwell on my own pain.

Weeks passed and sometimes, I could almost pretend things were okay. I started taking language classes again since it helped eat up my free time. I reconnected with friends and tried to remember what it was like to have fun. Everyone made sympathetic noises regarding my breakup with Roy—I concocted a simple story about our relationship imploding, which everyone accepted without question. No one had ever understood why I'd even wanted to tie myself down to him in the first place when there were so many other men to choose from.

However there were other times when I relived the whole Brazil nightmare over again. I hadn't seen the initial media coverage of the TransWorld incident, but it dominated the CN-net for weeks afterward. Not only had their main headquarters on Earth vanished, their star cruiser en route from Mars had exploded before takeoff. No passengers were injured, but the ship was damaged beyond repair and the crew had died. There were no suspects, no leads, no terrorist groups stepping forward to take credit. Though I had no proof of it, I suspected it was the Consortium's work and they were cleaning up loose ends. Now nothing stood in the way of them securing a hold on Mars.

The whole TransWorld fiasco was billed as the single greatest assault on humanity since the Dark Times. People were terrified. Worldwide panic almost burned out the CN-net and crashed the markets as information spooled back and forth, uploaded and downloaded in a frenzied sea of chaos. For a while, all flights between Earth, Mars, and Venus were suspended—which caused an uproar. However when there was no follow-up attack, media coverage waned. Flights resumed, and a company called the Burroughs Group—the company the Tsarist Consortium had backed—took over service for TransWorld. Their star cruiser, the *Martian Princess*, launched a few days later. I'd lived with a specter of fear hanging over me, worried I'd be implicated. But as the weeks turned into months and nothing happened, I began to relax.

It would be nice to say my life returned to normal, but it didn't. I occasionally had moments that left me confused and disoriented. I walked around in my own personal fog and didn't know what to do with myself. Restlessness consumed me. I wanted...Well, what I wanted was impossible. I would never see Alexei Petriv again, no matter how much I wished for it or how many sweat-soaked dreams I had about him. I had to find a way to close that chapter of my life whether I wanted to or not.

Along with that came the need to throw away every piece of my old life and start over. Maybe Mars. Maybe Venus, although the settlements weren't as established so there might not be much call for Tarot card readers. All that mattered was getting away from the familiar and trying again. I even avoided Grandmother's birthday party, despite my promise to attend. So much for never going back on my word. It pissed off nearly everyone in the family to the point that even Rainy refused to speak with me. His wife, Zita, ended up leaving him over his blacklisted status—something I hadn't been able to do anything about, yet he held me responsible anyway. Grandmother herself even broke down and shimmed me to give me the tongue-lashing she felt I so richly deserved.

Deep down, I think I was waiting for the other shoe to drop. My past wasn't finished with me yet. The Tarot cards said as much, and my gut knew it too. Vadim's last words had sealed it: "*Someone will be in touch with the final details regarding the completion of your contract with the Consortium and ensure you are paid in full.*" The way he'd said it had been ominous. Some nights—when I wasn't having torrid dreams about Alexei—I'd wake up paralyzed with fear because of those words. Only once I'd dealt with the Consortium would I be free to move on. Unfortunately I was at their mercy, and I suspected they'd come for me when I least expected it.

Another month later, they did.

———◆———

I was sitting in my chaise lounge in the room of decadent mystery Charlie Zero had created for me, where I did all my readings, when Natty ushered in Konstantin Belikov. I'd thought I was ready for anything, but seeing the five-hundred-year-old Tsarist Consortium kingpin was still a shock. I jumped to attention. My first reaction was a relief so intense, it left me boneless. Fear followed, but at least now I could begin to hope that the confused existence I'd been living for the past three months would be over.

With him were two chain-breakers and a pretty blond woman who served as his nursemaid. Pervy old bastard. It took everything in me not to roll my eyes at the cliché. The chain-breakers waited by the door, arms crossed and wearing their ubiquitous shades, despite the fact that they were inside and it was night.

As Belikov shuffled across the carpet, I took a moment to be impressed the old man had come all this way to see me. Then irritation gripped me when I considered how long it had taken him to contact me in the first place. Then fear came again. Why send someone so high-ranking in the Consortium to handle me? What had Belikov called me again? Oh yes, a gnat on an elephant's ass. Also, a baby. Anger was back. Good. I'd rather have that than fear.

"Mr. Belikov." I moved around the table to meet him. "I'm honored you've come to my shop."

He paused halfway to the chaise, a hand resting for support on the nursemaid's arm. "You look well, Felicia," he said in the commanding voice I still remembered. "You seem to have bounced back quite admirably after recent events."

Arrogant son of a bitch. I wasn't going to play that game with him—the game where he wanted to prove his pain and loss were greater than mine, so mine meant nothing. "It's so good to see you too."

"That is a bald-faced lie," he accused, resuming his shuffling walk.

"True enough, but I told it well. Besides, I've been waiting so long for someone to get in touch with me, I suppose it's good to see just about anyone. If that's how your organization works, it's a wonder you get anything done."

He scowled at me, then seated himself in the chaise with the nursemaid's help. She placed herself behind him, her face pleasantly blank. I suspected she didn't speak much English. "The Consortium always honors its agreements."

"And it only took you three months to do it."

"For an organization that's existed nearly a millennium, I would say our record is impeccable," he mused. Then he gave me a hard look. "Consider what you took from us, Felicia. Look at how this arrangement with you has affected the Consortium. Is it any wonder we didn't rush back with payment for services rendered?"

I returned to my chair with as much grace as I could muster, fighting hard not to show he'd scored a direct hit. Pain lanced through my chest—not as sharp or ravaging as it had once been, but still there. I bowed my head and took a moment to collect myself until I could meet his milky green eyes without tears. "I understand. You got what you wanted, but not at the price you expected to pay. I know this doesn't make up for it, but I'm sorrier than you know for what happened. If I could do it over again, I would have done anything I could to stop events from unfolding the way they did."

Belikov cleared his throat and looked uncomfortable. Maybe he hadn't liked the honest sincerity of my answer. "The Consortium will be depositing the agreed upon amount into your shop's account, plus whatever interest would have accrued over the past three months. We have also begun the process of revoking the blacklisted status for both you and your family. Without your mother's pressure and TransWorld's meddling, it should be finalized soon."

A tiny thrill went through me. Not for me, but for my family. I hadn't expected the Consortium to honor that request, so it came as an unexpected gift. "Thank you. This means the world to us."

He made what I could only describe as a gruff, grumpy old man noise and shifted restlessly in his chair. "*Pozhaluysta.* You're welcome."

Awkward silence descended. The meeting felt like it had

come to its end with Belikov making all the motions of a man about to leave. Desperation gripped me. I had a feeling if I let him go, the Consortium would be finished with me forever. "May I ask a question?"

He paused in his fidgeting. "It will have to be quick. I have other appointments to keep."

"Yes, I'm sure you do. It's just that night in Brazil...Why did he go back? I keep racking my brain, going over events until I think I've gone insane. It gives me nightmares and sometimes...Well, never mind. I guess I just can't understand what happened. Everything was finished. We'd won. My mother would have died when the building vaporized. He could have escaped with the rest of us. Instead, he went back. Why? Why not just let her go?"

Belikov looked at me with sudden pity. "We didn't understand it either."

"But you do now," I urged.

"From what our tech-meds pieced together after examining the data, your mother planned to upload all her research to the CN-net. She felt she had nothing to lose so she decided to unleash years of studies and experiments for all the world to see. She'd started her transmission, of which we received a partial sample. We recognized it for what it was only because we knew of you and her research. Few others had that luxury. Alexei stopped the transmission before it went viral."

I frowned. "I don't understand. You said the luck gene is an unpredictable nuisance. What does it matter if people know? The clones didn't need to die. I know the Consortium didn't want to be caught, but there was nothing in that building he had to risk his life over."

"Yes, you're right. Luck is unstable. We've studied the effects and know the results. The rest of the world doesn't. To the average person, it would be wonderful to have a perceived edge over their neighbor. Who wouldn't want luck at their command? The unfortunate thing is, the only way they could have this luck for themselves would be through you or the clones. You are the only person on record with a verified luck gene. If that were made common knowledge, the existence you have now would end and you'd be hounded to death. And if the clones had lived, they would have been bought and sold like cattle. We would have had a race of slaves on our hands—slaves that would have been a source for countless wars throughout the tri-system. That's what Alexei stopped. He went back to stop the upload to protect you."

It took several moments for it to sink in before I started to cry. Silent tears ran down my cheeks that I rushed to wipe away. He'd sacrificed everything, including his chance at immortality, just to save me. Once, I'd wondered if he'd ever cared enough about anyone to die for them. Apparently yes, he had: me. More tears fell. I wiped them away, blew my nose, and tried to pull myself together under Belikov's watchful gaze.

"Thank you for telling me. If anything, I think I feel worse than I did before. It doesn't seem a fair trade—his life for my peace of mind."

"Perhaps, but he chose to view it otherwise." Then he looked at me, puzzled. "Your reaction surprises me. I'd thought you'd moved on. Isn't that what you young people do? No one stays together for long anymore—not as we did before the Dark Times. I thought only sexual conquest and gratification mattered. Without fear of disease or unwanted pregnancies, why stay together? Isn't that how it works?"

"You sound like my friends, but no, that's not how it works. At least, not for me."

"So you're pining for a dead man? Don't tell me you believed yourself in love with him? You've been apart far longer than you were ever together," Belikov said, then laughed with terrible humor.

I winced at the implication. Based on his laughter, he clearly thought me a fool and my feelings, whatever they were, to have no merit. Still, I felt I had to clarify.

"No, I didn't love him," I admitted. "I was attracted to him and I cared about him, but it wasn't love. At least not yet, anyway. I think I may have been on the verge of it or I wouldn't still feel his loss this strongly. We just didn't have enough time. If we'd had more, we could have hashed through all the secrets and lies between us and figured it out. We could have…" I sighed. Two of Cups, reversed yet again. "I guess it doesn't matter now anyway."

"No, I suppose not," he agreed. This time, he did rise from his chair. The nursemaid was beside him and offering assistance, smiling prettily and displaying her cleavage. "I wish you well in your endeavors, Felicia. You may call on the Tsarist Consortium should you require help in the future; however, I would suggest you not abuse the privilege."

He was on his way out when my gut kicked me so hard, it was a wonder I didn't fall out my chair.

"Wait!" I cried, getting up. "There's one thing I'd like. Something I've been thinking about for a while."

Belikov looked irritated, but listened. "Yes? What is it?"

"I'd like to go to Mars."

20

No one was happy with my decision. Hell, even I wasn't happy—not at first. Yet the more I thought about Mars, the more excited I became. I'd have to start over, but it wasn't like I hadn't been at the bottom before. Charlie was upset, as was Natty. Charlie and I had several bitter fights about the partnership and dissolving the assets. I ended up giving him the bulk of the profits just to shut him up. I also gave Natty a healthy severance package which she used to apply to cooking school through the Career Design program as an adult seeking a career change. I ran the cards on her success and the odds came up in her favor, thrilling her. Charlie eventually came around and gave me the name of a friend I could contact on Mars. However, I had to promise I would always shim him regarding any business ventures and not sign anything until I spoke with him first.

My family was furious with me for taking Granny G's cards off-world. One pain in the ass cousin even said the cards wouldn't work in space. Seriously. Sometimes it seemed I was related to morons. I didn't mention the blacklisted business to anyone but Rainy since it affected him directly. The rest of the family hadn't been aware of the issue, so I didn't see a point in upsetting them further. I wouldn't look like a hero and it would just raise questions. Rainy was thrilled, forgave me for being a bitch—his exact words—and reconciled with his wife.

As for my condo, I didn't know if I'd use it again, but didn't want to sell it either. Once you left Earth, you stayed where you went, unless you were ultra-rich. And even then, a move to Mars tended to be permanent. Still, I didn't want to feel like I'd cut ties. Gods only knew what could happen in the future. In the end, I gave the condo back to the Consortium with the understanding I could resume ownership if I so desired.

At the same time, I began the labor-intensive process of filing for permission to immigrate to Mars. It was a nightmare not worth describing, especially given my limited CN-net access. Everything seemed to take twice as long and was three times as difficult. I constantly had to explain my future plans for employment and residency on Mars once the space elevator anchored in the Utopian Ocean spit me out. Apparently the Martian branch of One Gov didn't want freeloaders crashing their party. I had to outline in triplicate my plan to contact Charlie Zero's friend in Elysium City—the largest east coast urban center on Mars and rival to Olympia on the west— and open my shop as a Tarot card reader. Since it was a novel idea, Mars had nothing like it, and I had a modest reputation throughout Kenya, they also gave me a grant to help with relocation expenses. That, of course, meant more forms and more explaining.

I kept an anxious eye on the date, praying the timing worked out. With its revolutionary propulsion system, the *Martian*

Princess could complete the trip between Earth and Mars in forty-two standard Earth days. If all went well, my paperwork and grant applications would be approved the day before the star cruiser docked at the GLC Space Station, the counterweight for Tsiolkovsky Tower One and launchpad to Mars. Otherwise, it would be months before I could catch the next ship.

I needn't have worried. Either it was luck, or the Consortium working behind the scenes to get me off-planet and out of their hair, but everything came through on time. Two months to the day I'd told Belikov I wanted to go to Mars, I sat in the guest lounge on the low-g launch platform, drinking coffee and waiting to board the *Martian Princess*. The coffee tasted awful no matter how much cream and sugar I added.

As I stirred, I couldn't help but remember the time I'd been in this same situation, seated and stirring much like I was now. That had been almost half a year ago on the trip to Denver after the Consortium's private jet had exploded. I'd been a nervous wreck, yet Alexei coolly answered questions from One Gov security until he'd secured our release. I'd been in awe at the ease with which he'd handled the situation—all situations really. He had the world eating out of the palm of his hand. Except me, I suppose. With me, he made a complete and total mess of things. Or had he? It was difficult to remember now. So much time had passed, I couldn't remember all the reasons for my anger. And now, it didn't matter because he was gone and I was starting a new life somewhere else. Even if he had lived, what would we have in common? He would have been head of the Tsarist Consortium, pushing its agenda throughout the tri-system. Where would I have fit in that world? I couldn't imagine us ever having a happy ending. It didn't bear thinking about now.

I took another sip of the horrible coffee and watched the other travelers—people of all ages, some with a child and others without. On Mars, I'd heard the Shared Hope program regulations weren't as strict. Maybe I'd find someone there and...No. Ironically, I wasn't interested in a baby now. With my blacklisted status revoked, the urge that had driven me so recklessly was gone. If it were possible, I would have found my luck gene and kicked its ass for putting me through such misery. Now that it had what it wanted, it was no longer interested.

From my vantage point, I could also see the high-orbit flights leave. These would be people off to TT2 to either catch the star cruiser to Venus or transfer to other commercial high-orbit flights. It made for a busy, congested area. You could easily lose who you were with if you weren't paying attention. Or, find someone you had no interest in seeing...

"Hello, Felicia."

I glanced up at the familiar voice and froze. Roy stood over my table, gazing down at me. He was rough around the edges, his sandy-blond hair unkempt and his cheeks badly in need of shaving. His clothing was threadbare and frayed, and I noted a faded stain on the jacket lapel. A single black duffel sat beside his scuffed boots.

"Mind if I sit?" he asked and sat before I could say anything. "I saw you through the glass and thought I'd stop by for old time's sake. It's a surprise to see you here. You look good."

Maybe I did, but he didn't. "What are you doing here?" I asked, voice cold. It was the first time I'd laid eyes on him since Denver. Long-buried rage bubbled up.

"Just a stopover until my connection leaves for TT2. I'm bound for Venus. What about you? Off to Mars? I remember you always being fascinated by it."

I stared at him. Did he expect us to have a normal conversation? "Where're your wife and baby?" I blurted instead.

"They were denied travel permits. I got a position on Venus with one of the mining companies staking land claims there. After TransWorld, it was all I could get."

Working in the mines on Venus was the next best thing to a death sentence. A Phobos penal cell would be kinder. The pay was phenomenal, but most still considered Venus an uncivilized, stinking hell.

"What do you want me to say? Sorry you're going to Venus. Sorry your family can't join you. Sorry you lost your job at TransWorld pretending to be my loving boyfriend and reporting my every movement to them." I stood up, grabbing my travel case containing my cards. "Excuse me, but I think I'll wait somewhere else. The air's gotten unpleasant here."

I stormed from the lounge, pushing headlong through a crowd fighting its way to different launch platforms. Where was my gate again? Right, at the far end of the terminal, 52F. The cruiser wasn't ready for boarding yet, but maybe if I made a nuisance of myself, they'd get things moving.

"Felicia, wait!" Roy cried, jogging up beside me to catch my arm. "We need to talk."

"Like hell we do! We have nothing to say to each other!" I snarled, fighting to yank myself free. His fingers dug in deeper and I winced. "Let me go!"

"Not until we talk. You may have nothing to say, but I do," he said in a low voice.

That voice terrified me. My gut agreed. I tried to spin away, but he held my left arm in a crushing grip. With a determined jerk, he pulled me after him and hustled me down the first deserted hallway he found. I fought him, but he was too strong and I was too unsteady in my spiky heels. Then we rounded another corner until he stopped in a gray, nondescript, and badly lit corridor—away from all the noise and out of sight. He whipped me against the far wall, hurtling me with all his strength. My right shoulder hit the concrete and I yelped with pain.

"You ruined my life!" he unleashed on me. "Every awful, fucked-up thing that's happened to me is your fault. I lost my job on Earth. Up until a month ago, we were supposed to go to Mars. Then the job dried up and I got transferred to Venus. My family's still on Earth and I'm never going to see them again. I'm going to fucking die on Venus, and that's your fault too. It's all your fucking fault!"

"You're crazy! How the hell could I pull off something like that? I don't have that kind of power." I snarled the words while rubbing my aching shoulder.

He paced in front of me. "I keep remembering what you said in Denver. That if it took the rest of your life, you'd destroy me. That's how I knew it was you. You're connected to the Consortium and they wanted TransWorld to lose the bid. I can't prove it, but I know I'm right."

"You're delusional. You were the one pretending to love me, not the other way round. You were the one who was married with a baby on the way! Gods, a baby! Do you have any idea…?" I stopped. I would never tell him about my failed dreams. *Never.* "I'm the one who gets to be angry, not you! Do you know how messed up I was once I learned the truth? I didn't know who my friends were or if the people who claimed to love me actually cared! You fucked up both our lives!"

I didn't expect the backhanded blow to my face. I really didn't. When my gut warned me, I took a step back, but not enough to avoid it. I stumbled against the wall, hitting my head. Pain blossomed and I crumpled at the impact, falling to the concrete on my knees and tearing my skirt. Sadly, I didn't pass out—which would have been nice, if only to avoid the pain. Instead I tasted blood and saw stars.

"You stupid bitch! You don't get it. I'm a dead man. My life is over. Maybe not today, or tomorrow, but once I'm on Venus, I'm done." Roy crouched over me, his hands reaching for my neck. "I'm just glad I found you in time. Now I can take you with me."

I closed my eyes against both the tightening of his fingers around my throat and the sight of his face distorted by hatred. Vaguely I wondered why he felt his anger should trump my own. Neither of us had gotten what we wanted.

"This is restricted area. Unauthorized personnel not allowed."

The speaker was male, his words mangled by an almost unintelligible Russian accent. I opened my eyes to see two chain-breakers looming over us in identical suits and shades, with only their hair coloring to differentiate them. One blond. One black haired. I wasn't sure which had spoken, though it hardly mattered. The blond tore Roy's hands away from my throat and grabbed him in a similar hold. With easy strength, he hauled Roy up until his feet dangled in midair. Then he proceeded to walk down the hall, holding Roy at arm's length as if he reeked of the foulest stench. The last I heard before they disappeared were Roy's choking whimpers and the clicking of the chain-breaker's shoes as he walked away.

The other chain-breaker helped me stand and gathered my discarded travel case, hoisting it over one massive shoulder. I swayed on my feet, the ground spinning with sickening speed.

"You need to catch flight. Cruiser leaving soon," he said in broken English. You'd think the Consortium would be able to afford better security. Although, maybe language skills weren't a priority. Something to wonder about later, I decided. Right then, I had bigger fish to fry.

"I'm not usually a fainter," I told him, "but I'm having a terrible day."

At which point, I threw up all over his shoes and passed out.

<hr />

When I woke, I was aboard the *Martian Princess*, in my cabin. I also had a ship's medic hovering over me with worried brown eyes.

"You're awake. Glad you've decided to rejoin us. That's quite a bump on the head you have, and your lip is swollen. Nothing a web-compress can't handle. I've applied them to both trauma areas and you should be good as new shortly."

I sat up, taking in my room, my luggage on the floor, the huge bay window showcasing the Earth's blue-green horizon and the edge of black space beyond. The female medic and I were the only ones in the room. She was a pretty redhead, looking crisp and professional in her white uniform. There was a red cross over her right breast and the *Martian Princess* star-and-crown emblem over the left.

I touched my lip, feeling a lump of fabric. The same for the back of my head. "I don't remember what happened. How did I get here?"

The medic's brow wrinkled in confusion and she rose from her perch on the bed. "I'm not sure. I was called up from the infirmary and told to wait in your cabin. Then, a man brought you in. Tall, dark haired. Russian, I think. Scared the bejesus out of me, to be honest. Told me to stay with you until you woke or I'd be fired. Didn't say if he'd be back, but that he had other business to attend to."

"Yeah, they're like that." So Consortium security had kept tabs on me. Nice to know Belikov was so thorough in his hustle to get me off-world. I just wished he'd been on the case sooner. "He didn't say anything else?"

"No, nothing," she said, edging toward the door. "If you're feeling better, I need to get back to the infirmary. We're launching soon and there are always people who panic at the outset. Plus with the two-hour launch delay, there's more concern going round than usual. Nothing to be worried about, but people are still people."

"Two-hour delay? What happened?"

The woman's eyes went wide. "You won't believe it! A man leaped from the station! He was in a restricted area, opened one of the cargo delivery doors, and jumped. Awful. At this height, you don't fall to Earth. You just float away, and in the vacuum of space, you depressurize and well... You explode. It's a gruesome way to go."

I let out the breath I'd been holding, wondering how I felt. Ultimately, I decided I was relieved. Roy was no longer my problem.

"Yes. Gruesome," I agreed.

"Come to the launch festivities when you're feeling up to it," the medic said as she let herself out. "It's always a wonderful party."

"Will do," I said.

I didn't. When she left, I lay back down on the bed and stared up at the dull, gray ceiling, wondering how this event would impact the rest of my new life.

———◆———

Okay, I admit I stayed in my cabin for the next five days. The web-compresses did their job and the bump on my head and cut to my cheek were gone in an hour. The horrible bruising on my arm and neck took longer. Even on the fifth day, the outlines of Roy's fingers still lingered. I could have asked the medic for something to speed up the healing, but in some twisted way, I decided I deserved the bruises. There was a child out there who didn't have a father because of me, albeit indirectly. Despite everything, I couldn't help feeling a little guilty.

I amused myself by watching the programming available on the cruiser's CN-net, reading novels I'd never had time to investigate before, running my cards, or just watching the fading view of Earth. By day five, it was only a speck in the upper corner, a few inches across. The Consortium had set me up well, covering all my shipboard expenses, so I ordered endless room service and had everything I needed—except a shower. That, I missed as I made due with the sonic-cleaners. My understanding was water usage on Mars was fairly restricted, unless you were among the ultra-rich. So no lovely showers for me, although the cards held out hope. Yes, I ran the cards on whether or not I'd have a decent shower in the future. What of it?

I knew why I hid. It wasn't that I was in denial over my situation—Roy, the whole trip to Mars, my uncertain future, or everything that had happened in the past few months. I just needed to gather myself for the next battle. If I wasn't mentally prepared for whatever I might face on Mars, I may as well have stayed on Earth.

Day six, I had the outlines of a plan. I needed to make contacts on this trip and use whatever ounce of charisma and luck I'd gained from my Romani heritage to make these people love me. I would have to lay on the mysterious Tarot card reader persona so thick, they'd be helpless to resist. If things went well, I could use my new cruiser contacts to establish a client base and build from there.

To that end, I booked dinner at the captain's table that night. The Consortium's connections guaranteed me a seat that should get me rubbing shoulders with the most influential people onboard. I spent the rest of the day getting ready. It was as if my entire life of loving clothes, makeup, and accessories had been a dress rehearsal for this one dinner. Hair down, but braided with gemstones I'd sometimes worn in my shop. Makeup just this side of too much with lots of blue-green to bring out my eyes. I'd been playing at being mysterious for years so even if I looked a little tired and gaunt thanks to the past few months, I could pull drama out of my ass with my hands tied behind my back. Lastly, a flowing white dress that fastened at the shoulders, plunged deeply between my breasts at the neckline, hit mid-thigh, and had a gold braided waist. Black would have been better, but I didn't want to look like I peddled sex. Women would hate me and they were the ones I needed to impress. White said innocence, even if everything else didn't.

Dinner was at eight. I was ready half an hour early. I paced my room, nerves eating at me. I knew I looked perfect, but was it enough? I practiced smiles and poses in the mirror and imagined conversations I might have. I made up witty answers, then groaned when I knew I sounded like a dolt in the imaginary conversations I had with imaginary guests. Gods, it wasn't like I'd never made small talk before! But this was important. This night could make or break my future on Mars.

Before I left for dinner, I burned a stick of incense at the makeshift altar in my room, praying for success and good fortune. Then I clapped, bowed, and went out to wow my legion of waiting and, as of yet, unknown fans.

I'd memorized the ship's layout and found the dining room easily. I frowned as I approached, and checked my c-tex bracelet. Yes, I was on time but…Shouldn't there be other people milling about? Dinner was at eight. Why was I the only one there?

The maître d' slipped out from behind the closed door. "Ms. Sevigny, I'm sorry but there's been a change. The dining room is reserved for a private function. Please follow me."

I frowned. "How can the whole room be reserved? Where will everyone else eat?"

"Please, follow me," he said again.

My gut kicked me forward. I knew better than to ignore it despite my misgivings, and followed the maître d'. A glass of something, champagne maybe, found its way into my hand. I walked a handful of paces. Stopped. Looked around the massive room filled with empty tables and chairs, elaborate chandeliers, gorgeous blue up-lighting, windows with a panoramic view of space and winking starlight, and no people. No, that wasn't true. There was one person seated at a table, drinking what was probably vodka, and watching me, watching him.

My gut gave me another hard kick forward, but I couldn't move. Shock had stolen my ability to put one foot in front of the other. Instead, I took a shuddering breath, tried to drink my champagne—which I'd dropped on the floor based on the shattering sound beside me, so that wasn't happening—and said the most ridiculous thing in the world, which I had not spent a single lick of time practicing in front of my mirror.

"You're supposed to be dead. Why aren't you dead?"

Alexei Petriv rose from the table and moved toward me with all the grace of a hunter stalking its prey. My eyes widened, drinking in the details as he advanced. So much time had passed and while he looked the same, he didn't. His dark hair was longer, almost to his shoulders. He also seemed wilder and not so rigidly controlled, if that was possible to judge as he approached. The black suit he wore emphasized the broadness of his shoulders. The gray shirt beneath was open to mid-chest and I could see the tattoos and admire the play of muscles, but he looked thinner. Perhaps a little worn-out—much like how I felt. Even as his blue eyes raked over me, taking me in as I did him, there was a sense of desperation about him he'd never possessed before.

He stopped a few feet away, far enough that I could pretend I was imagining him. Even still, my knees wanted to buckle, making it a fight to stay upright. And my heart knew I wasn't imagining anything since it felt like it might beat its way out of my chest as I stared at him.

"You've been in your room for five days," he said instead.

"I wasn't ready to come out."

He nodded; then his expression hardened. "The bruises."

I self-consciously touched my neck. "It's not as bad as it looks."

"It won't happen again. I've dealt with it personally. You should have let me take care of it when I offered in Brazil."

"I..." Why were we even talking about this? Alexei Petriv was standing in front of me, *alive* after all this time and we were talking about...I suddenly had no idea. I hugged myself because I had absolutely no clue what to do with my arms and I realized my hands were shaking. No, not just my hands. Everything in me was shaking. "You need to explain how it is you're here and why the hell you're still alive because I don't...I can't..." I wanted to rub my eyes, but knew it would destroy my careful makeup. I'd hate to ruin everything for a hallucination. "Is this even real? Are *you* real?"

He took a step closer and I caught the scent of the cologne I'd never forgotten, the one that nearly had me falling at his feet. Oh yes, he was most definitely real.

I held up a hand, halting him. "Don't come any closer until you explain what the hell is going on."

He stopped, lips quirking in a sad smile. "I'm not allowed to touch you?"

"No, you're not. If you do, I won't be able to think. Right now, I need to think."

The smile grew. "That's quite the dilemma you have. By the way, you do realize you look so stunning, I'm not certain *I* can think properly. I would not want another man seeing you in that dress and would kill him if I suspected he had the thoughts I'm currently entertaining."

That shot a bolt of heat through me I didn't expect to feel. I realized it was the first time he'd ever seen me fully dressed in my role as a Tarot card reader—the hair, the clothes, the makeup. I'd always considered it my ultimate disguise to keep the world at bay, but he seemed able to strip me bare with a single look. It was as if he knew me better than I did myself.

"Then close your eyes and quit looking. Start explaining why you're not dead." I sounded angry, and maybe I was. Maybe anger was the only way I could get a grip on all the emotions threatening to swamp me. And why the hell wouldn't my heart calm down? I eyed him warily and blurted, "Are you a clone? Is this Belikov messing with my head for some twisted reason?"

"Konstantin has nothing to do with this." There was that sad, resigned look on his face again. "Would it matter to you if I was a clone?"

Oddly, this was something I'd actually given some thought to over the past few months. After Brazil, my mind had run in odd directions. "It wouldn't if that's who you'd always been and that's who walked into my shop in Nairobi. But if you're just pretending to be him now, then yes, it matters."

The answer seemed to satisfy him because he nodded and his smile didn't seem so broken. "I'm not. It's me. I swear it."

My shivering intensified. "How are you even still alive?"

"Quantum teleporting," he said finally. "I qt'd out of the building before it disappeared."

I frowned. "I didn't think that was possible. Or wait...I guess the Consortium managed to perfect the technique before anyone else, along with all your other...projects?"

"It was still in the experimental stages, not quite ready for a live trial. I hadn't planned on making myself the first test

338

case, but when things took a bad turn in Brazil and I realized I couldn't get out in time...I jumped."

"All this to stop my mother?"

"You couldn't have endured what she planned. Her ambition overruled her common sense. I admire that in some respects, but not in this case. I could not allow her to hurt you."

"Thank you for that. Belikov explained why the clones needed to be destroyed and even if I don't like it, I still understand." This was getting off track. I didn't want to keep owing my life to this man. "So, if you...teleported, where did you go?"

He shrugged, a move I found distracting given the amount of time I'd once spent admiring his shoulders. "That's the thing with experiments—all assumptions and faulty logic. Time isn't linear. Worlds move side by side, traveling at different speeds. You don't know where you may end up, which we hadn't counted on. In my case, I lost time. For me, it all went by in the blink of an eye. To the rest of the world, three months had passed."

I stared at him. "You...time traveled?"

"In a manner of speaking, yes."

I frowned and closed my eyes, pinching the bridge of my nose as I thought hard. It seemed so ridiculous, and yet... "Belikov came into my shop three months after you disappeared. That was the first I'd heard from the Consortium since Brazil and he gave me a pretty speech about fulfilling obligations. Did you make him do that?"

"I was furious when I learned he and Grigori had no intention of honoring our agreement."

"So if you were still alive, why didn't you come to me sooner?

Why the hell did it take six damn months for you to find me? You should have shimmed or done *something* to let me know what had happened!"

"You're right, but I couldn't." He sounded suspiciously closer. When I opened my eyes, only a few hand spans separated us.

I scowled and stepped back. "Couldn't or wouldn't?"

"Couldn't," he said, and closed the distance entirely.

"Stop it." I reached out to block his progress, my hand connecting with his chest. Touching him nearly undid me and I jerked away as if on fire. "You're making this confusing."

"I know. Forgive me." He didn't sound the least bit sorry.

I concentrated on his shirt. Probably not the best place to look since it gave me a distracting view of his broad chest, but he stood too close and there was nowhere else to focus. I didn't want to look up. I would drown in his eyes if I saw them. Plus it would be nearly impossible to hold on to my anger. Instead I merely smelled his cologne, which seemed to be doing funny things to my ability to pretend this wasn't really happening.

"I was disoriented when I first came back," he murmured, the words said close to my ear. "It took time to process what had happened. When Konstantin told me he'd gone to see you and what you said—that you hadn't cared about us and it meant nothing, I began to doubt I was even in the correct world."

"I never said that. He lied!" I retorted, offended.

"I know, but I was confused. The luck gene can be fickle. Perhaps you'd found someone else. I've known Konstantin my whole life. Naturally, I took his words at face value."

"There's no one else! How could I have found anyone—"

Like you, I almost blurted, catching myself. "I'm not that shallow."

He chuckled softly, no doubt hearing what I'd left unsaid. "I think at that point, I went a little insane. I had to be restrained for my own good."

"That must have been awful."

"It was necessary. I would have done things I regretted and would have been unable to recover from. And before you ask, I will never tell you what those things were." He reached up to touch one of my braids. Part of me wanted to jerk away, but couldn't. I had been soundly overruled by the part that wanted him to touch me. "This is pretty. It makes me want..." He sighed and his voice drifted off. Then he tucked a loose strand of hair carefully behind my ear as if afraid he would break me. As I feared, thinking was becoming impossible.

"Konstantin told me you were leaving for Mars, probably thinking I could do nothing to prevent it. He doesn't like the perceived hold you have on me. Nothing personal. Just not good for business. He tried to rush your travel permits. I slowed them. I needed time to consider what I had to do."

His hand moved from my hair to lightly graze my neck and bare shoulder. I shivered.

"Consider what?" I breathed.

"I knew Roy was going to Mars. I transferred him to Venus, which was far better than he deserved. I didn't want him on the same planet as you." The hand on my neck went higher, to my jawline. With light pressure from his thumb, he tilted my head until I looked up at him. His eyes locked with mine. They were as blue as I remembered, maybe even more so. I felt the pull then, like an ocean current drawing me back to him and threatening to drown me, just as I'd known would happen. "Then I sniped the CN-net to discover what you and Konstantin discussed at your shop. I wanted to know if his version of the story was the true one. Plus I wanted to see you again, even if it was through the filter of someone's stored memories."

"Were you successful?"

"What do you think?"

"I don't know. I stopped thinking about five minutes ago."

His laughter was soft and intimate. "It was difficult, given your lack of CN-net presence and Konstantin's t-mod blocks. I couldn't track the actual conversation. Then I realized that ridiculous nursemaid was the key. Doesn't speak any English or hold a thought in her head, but she was there for the entire conversation. I knew it would be in her memory blocks and I could find it on the CN-net somewhere."

He leaned in, lips grazing my throat. I felt his hair brush my ear and cheek, and my breath hitched. His other hand rested at the base of my spine, caressing me gently through my dress. I shivered. His nearness overwhelmed me; there was no escape.

"I said you weren't allowed to touch me."

"I don't follow rules I have no vested interest in, particularly when they're in the way of something I want."

My head swam. "Didn't you once say when you decided to seduce me, you wouldn't need much to get the job done? Seems like you've gone to an awful lot of trouble, considering we're bound for Mars."

"Sometimes, my bluff is called and I need to step up." He pulled back enough to gaze down at me. "You told Konstantin we didn't have enough time. You said we could have worked through the secrets and lies if we'd had more time. We have thirty-six point five standard Earth days until we reach Mars. How much time do you need?"

The man had trapped us together on a star cruiser for over a month just to discuss a relationship? I tried to pull away. The firm hand at the small of my back wouldn't allow it, holding me still with deliberate strength.

"That's a risky move. I'm not the confused woman whose world is falling apart now. I'm starting a new life on Mars and I'm going to make it work."

"Of course you will. I have every faith in you."

"So shouldn't you be on Earth, leading the Consortium's charge across the tri-system? After all, you did what you set out to do. I assume you took over the Consortium's leadership," I said, hearing the bitterness in my voice.

"Yes, it's mine now. All of it." His tone was surprisingly bland.

"Does this mean Mr. Pennyworth will reappear at some point?"

"That project has been shelved for the foreseeable future. The side effects outweigh the benefits so I'm reprioritizing. Mars has issues that require my attention. I'm looking into the asteroid mines between Mars and Jupiter. I've heard there may be a handful of companies for sale. We've already secured the rights to building a base for human settlement on Callisto. Then, we'll see."

Mining companies? Building on one of Jupiter's moons? I tried to imagine the Consortium controlling the tri-system's entire resource base along with access to the outer solar system. What would he do with all that might at his back? Not my problem to worry about. However…

"Then I'm not the real reason you're here."

The pressure in the hand at my back increased until he pressed me flush against him. His other hand stroked my jaw, knuckles grazing my skin in mesmerizing circles. I felt everything then, including how much he wanted me, as he no doubt intended. "You are the *only* reason I'm here. The rest is irrelevant. The things I've spent my life chasing are meaningless—which is the only useful thing I learned in the time we were apart. If I can't make you fit into the world the Consortium wants to build then I have no desire to create it. You know what I am…Who I am…I can't undo that. All I want now is for this to matter. I need you to say you can look beyond what happened before and what I am, and tell me this means something to you."

It was all I could do not to let him sweep me away. Already, my arms rose of their own volition until my hands skimmed along his waist and stomach, tracing the hard muscles there. I raised them so they slid over his chest and went to his shoulders. I pulled myself up onto my toes and tugged him down to me, sighing a little at the feel of his body against mine. I'd missed him, and wanted him in defiance of all common sense. More importantly, I believed him. These past months without him, I thought I'd been living. Instead, I'd barely been existing. I understood now that his fear had always been greater than mine. He may have been the next step in the evolutionary ladder, but what did that mean? Was he still human, and could I want him if he wasn't? And that fear made him very human to me. Maybe this feeling was the luck gene working overtime. Maybe it was real. Maybe I'd know for certain in thirty-six days.

"Does your room have a shower?" I heard myself ask.

"It does." His lips were inches from mine. "Do you have something in mind that requires my assistance?"

"Maybe. We should at least go back to your room now and investigate."

"Yes," he agreed. "We could do that. I've never known a back that could wash itself. There are some things genetic enhancements still can't do."

I arched leisurely against him, starting to melt inside. He molded my body against his; his hands knew exactly where to stroke and his lips placed a line of devout kisses along my throat, as if he were trying to eliminate the bruises there. He'd always known where to touch me right from the beginning, giving me everything I hadn't even known I needed.

"You know, I think I like this business of being seduced," I murmured softly.

He pulled back then, looking down at me with an expression so intense, it took my breath away. I felt the tension sing throughout his body, demanding I answer it.

"Felicia...please." He sounded desperate, as if holding us both back from the edge of a cliff before we tumbled to our deaths. "All this time, I've thought of nothing but you and what I had to do to become the man you needed. But I need to know if I'm what you want and that I matter to you. Or if not now, that someday, I will. Without that, I can't do this. Please, I need to hear the words."

I smiled up at him, my heart feeling like it would burst and explode in my chest as he spoke. "Yes, Alexei, you matter. You matter to me so much I don't even know how I existed before you or how I could go on if you left again. With you here, I feel like I'm finally waking up to the rest of my life." I felt my eyes tear up against my will. "If you make me cry and I ruin my eye makeup, I'll kill you."

"I don't plan on making you cry," he promised solemnly, carefully wiping away the single tear with his thumb before it could fall. "Not now. Not ever."

"Good." I took the hand touching my face and brought it back to my waist, arching an eyebrow at him. A slow, dark grin spread across his face—one that caused all sorts of wicked chain reactions throughout my body and my heart. "Since it looks like I have the evening free, I guess I'm open to other options. Did you plan on talking for the rest of the night, or are you finally going to kiss me? And when do I get my shower?"

"Now," he said softly, pulling me back to him. "It all starts now."

Then he lifted me up until my toes left the floor, and lowered his lips to mine. Tentative at first, the kiss grew deeper and bolder until only feeling remained, and I didn't need my cards to know how events would play out for the rest of the trip. As for what might follow once we reached Mars...Alexei was right. This mattered, and with luck on my side, anything was possible.

The story continues in...

THE CHAOS OF LUCK

BOOK TWO OF THE FELICIA SEVIGNY NOVELS

Keep reading for a sneak peek!

ACKNOWLEDGMENTS

I can honestly say I never thought I'd be writing something like this, so I wish I'd kept better track of things along the way. My husband always tell me I should write myself more notes and I mock him shamelessly for it, but in this case, he would definitely be right.

First, I'd like to thank my family for their love and support even if my mom was disappointed I didn't end up becoming a nurse, and my brother kept stealing my diary, reading it, and critiquing my entries. I'd also like to thank my husband, Steve, who reminds me about the mundane things like when it's tubtime, and maybe I should think about getting ready for bed before I get too caught up in a scene and forget I'm supposed to have a life too. He even built me my own library just so I could write in it. Not every girl gets that kind of lucky.

I'd also like to thank friends and family who read early drafts of this story and were generous with both their praise and their feedback: Dawn Gilbert, Tammy Gunter, Yvonne O'Brien, Tara Lynn Garritano, Shannon Henesey, and Tanja Halloran. Extra thanks to Sandra Lena for her endless inspiration and pointing me in the right direction whenever I was stuck on a particular scene—she knows which ones. Also a special shout-out to Shannon and Tanja who listened to me complain about everything, and when I say everything, I literally mean *everything* (and I am using "literally" in the correct sense of the word). Without them, I would have given up a thousand times over and don't think I could have ever finished this novel.

Many more thanks than I can possibly give go out to my agent, Rena Rossner, who saw something in my manuscript, took a chance on me, and then told me how I could make it better. I can't say enough about her dedication and how she worked to make sure this story saw the light of day. And lastly to my editor, Lindsey Hall, who is always full of genuine excitement and enthusiasm every time I talk to her. She has turned the story into something even *I* didn't envision, and that's saying something.

extras

orbit

meet the author

Photo Credit: Ash Nayler Photography

CATHERINE CERVENY was born in Peterborough, Ontario. She'd always planned to move away to the big city but the small-town life got its hooks in her and that's where she still resides today. Catherine is a huge fan of romance and science fiction and wishes the two genres would cross paths more often. *The Rule of Luck* is her first novel.

interview

When did you first start writing?

I first started writing in kindergarten, just like all the other kids. My printing was terrible. Sometimes the lines on my *d*'s weren't very straight and I'd get in trouble from the teacher. Let's just say, I definitely wasn't earning my weight in gold stars for writing back in those days. As I got older and learned how to read, I soon realized that "seeing Spot run" was really pretty dull because, honestly, who wants to see Spot run? Didn't Spot have better things to do? I started to make up my own stories, although truth be told, they probably weren't much better than seeing Spot run. I was probably around ten or so before I could write a story that had something resembling an actual plot and characters that did things. Then when I was thirteen, I had to complete an independent study project for English class. My topic was dinosaurs, so I handed in a short story about dinosaurs and time travel. I got an A+, although looking back, I'm sure the story was utter crap— not even suitable for lining the bottom of a birdcage. But it made me realize I could write something and people would actually like it. I kept going from there.

extras

Who are some of your biggest influences?

I have a lot of influences. Like, I mean, *a lot*, and it would be impossible to list them all. I'm all over the place when it comes to reading and love many different genres. I love a good hard science fiction story with lots of technical jargon and detailed explanations, but I also love a good weepy romance too. And there was a time when I couldn't get enough of epic fantasies, the more sequels, the better. However, if I have to actually pick someone, I'd have to say my biggest influences in writing are Kim Stanley Robinson, Sylvia Day, Ilona Andrews, Karen Marie Moning, and Hannu Rajaniemi.

Where did the idea for the Felicia Sevigny series come from?

I'm fascinated by the Singularity that's supposed to hit in the next fifteen to twenty years—when scientists predict we'll have real artificial intelligence. Fascinated, but also a little bit horrified about what might become of the human race when computers can think for themselves. I'm also intrigued by the idea of genetic manipulation and what sorts of things can happen when you tinker with DNA. I'm not saying I like everything that's going on in the world right now, but it's out there happening as we speak, and you can't ignore it. At the same time, I also wondered how the human race would fare if all the global disasters that science predicts all suddenly hit. What if the polar ice caps melted? What if the "big one" finally hit and the earthquake was so massive, it changed the face of the earth? I wondered what life would be like if we survived all that. What would the world be like once we came out the other side and managed to rebuild? So I basically took all the worst-case scenarios that could happen to the human race, threw them together into one pot, and set it to boil. What kind of world would we have then, and how would we live in it? And if you could survive all that disaster and still come out with your humanity intact, you must be pretty lucky, which is how Felicia's character sort of came into existence.

The Tarot card elements of the story are so vivid and unique. What made you want to use Tarot in your novels?

It shouldn't come as a surprise to anyone that I like to know how things are going to end up. I'm forever asking "why," "how come," and "what's going to happen next." I want to know how it ends—and when I say "it," I mean *everything*. How does it all end? Where are we going as a species, and how are we ultimately going to get there? I find it upsetting that I'm never going to know. I won't get to see the final curtain fall, so to speak. So I love the idea of using the Tarot as a way to see into the future and get a tiny peek at what's happening and what we might expect.

What, if any, research did you have to do in preparation for writing this series?

I think I did more research than I did actual writing, if you can believe it! I did a lot of research into Tarot cards, and went to more psychic fairs than I care to remember so I could get a sense of the drama and the relationship between the card reader and the client. I also did research into genetics, planet terraforming, geological global disasters, space travel, what living in a post-Singularity society might be like, and the Russian mafia. There was so much world building that had to be done to lay the groundwork for this series, it felt like I was reading a little bit of everything. I wanted to make the world feel real and logical, and as I researched, I realized there was so much I didn't know and had to learn. Obviously, I have absolutely no idea where society will be eight hundred years from now, but it was fun to guess and build it from scratch.

This series has a phenomenal cast of characters. If you had to pick one, who would you say is your favorite? Which character was the most difficult to write?

Aside from Felicia, who I really like but sometimes gets on my nerves, I'd have to say that one of my favorite characters is Lotus. I loved writing her. She's like Felicia, but without the filters or the conscience. She does and says whatever she wants, pushes her boyfriend around, and more or less gets away with everything. I would have loved to expand on her character but there wasn't room with everything else that was going on. A close second was Felicia's mother, Monique. I loved writing from her whacked-out perspective and how she could justify everything she did, no matter how terrible. I found Konstantin Belikov the most difficult to write, mostly because I think writing a good bad guy is tough to do. You don't want to turn him into a cartoon villain, or make him evil for the sake of being evil. It all has to fit into the context of the story and flow logically from that. It's also hard to write about the bad guy's plan and motivations without it sounding like a boring laundry list of evil or turning it into an info dump. If you can create a great villain and write him or her well, you're a rock star as far as I'm concerned.

What's one thing about the series, either the world or the characters, that you loved but couldn't fit into the story?

This story is told from Felicia's point of view, but there were times when I wished I could have shown what Alexei was up to when he and Felicia weren't together. I'm not entirely sure what sort of projects he might have been working on for the Consortium, but I wished there was a way I could have shown them in the story rather than have him describe things to Felicia in passing.

Lastly, we have to ask: If you could have any superpower or futuristic technology, what would it be?

This is going to sound really lazy, but I wish I had a TV that could bring me a snack whenever I'm lying on the couch and there's a commercial break, but I can't be bothered to move. If I had a nickel for every time I wished for that, I would have many, many nickels. Although I guess when the Singularity hits, this might actually become a reality, so maybe computers taking over the world won't be such a bad thing—if they bring me unlimited snacks.

if you enjoyed

THE RULE OF LUCK

look out for

THE CHAOS OF LUCK
A Felicia Sevigny Novel: Book 2

by

Catherine Cerveny

Felicia Sevigny makes her own luck. So it's no surprise that her new life on the Red Planet is off to a good start. She's making a living reading the fortunes of the fabulously wealthy, and making a home with Alexei, the dangerous, handsome love of her life.

Then Alexei is called off-planet unexpectedly, mines in the asteroid belt start collapsing, and an ex-lover walks back into Felicia's life. Felicia's readings predict that there is something bigger going on. Something darker and far more insidious that threatens everything she has come to love.

And as luck would have it, the cards are right for things to go horribly wrong.

I

It used to be that you didn't often see dogs on Mars. With the strict quarantine laws bordering on the ridiculous, and the month-and-a-half-long voyage from Earth, it was easier to clone one from the pet you'd left behind. However, that tended to be expensive when you'd already spent your life savings trying to get to Mars in the first place.

When the Tsarist Consortium took over the transit routes, they'd lobbied hard to abolish the quarantine—a move applauded throughout the tri-system. One Gov relented under general pressure from just about everyone and now all sorts of pets were appearing on the once red planet. The fact that I was seated across from a woman with a teacup Yorkie was actually pretty amazing, given I hadn't known the breed still existed. That the woman wanted me to run my Tarot cards and tell the future of said Yorkie, was not. It took a concerted effort on my part not to sigh out loud or reach over to throttle the woman. Besides, I'd hate to upset the dog, who, though I was loath to admit it, really was a cutie.

"I'm sorry, but I don't do readings for dogs," I said, not for the first time that week. "I know...Sunbeam is a member of your family, but that's not how the cards work."

The woman on the other side of my card reading table, Lila Chandler, was a potential new client. Definitely older, though only her eyes gave it away. They had a hardness to them that came from decades of Renew treatments and a lifestyle that said been there, done that, had the T-shirts to prove it. I would have put her around ninety, or maybe even a hundred. Otherwise, she was flawless with pale porcelain skin, blond hair cascading down her back, and luminous blue eyes—and *luminous* wasn't a word I threw around just for fun. And she was absolutely filthy rich. The kind of rich that got whatever it wanted and could afford to indulge in frivolous things the rest of the world would never think about, like Tarot card readings for dogs apparently. Mars had two social classes—the ultra-rich and everybody else. I was still working out which class I fell into.

About a third of my clients were of this sort—rich, curious women with nothing but time on their hands. In fact, she was the fourth client this week who'd come in requesting a pet reading. I knew exactly who to blame for her presence in my shop and why I was in this situation. If Alexei had been there right then, I would have given him yet another earful.

"I'd heard you'd done a reading for Mrs. Larken's dog, Puddles, and I want the same for Sunbeam," she said instead.

Puddles belonged to Mrs. Larken, whom I'd met onboard the *Martian Princess* on the trip from Earth. She'd been old—like really old, maybe two hundred—and something about her charmed me. Maybe because she reminded me a little of

Granny G, and gods knew I was a sucker for anything that put me in mind of family. Plus, I don't think my head was screwed on straight once I'd reunited with Alexei after having thought him dead for six months. When we'd come up for air, I'd met Mrs. Larken, taken a liking to her, and done a reading. Once on Mars, she'd opened doors for me I'd never dreamed of touching on my own. When she'd imported one of the first dogs allowed on Mars and asked me to do a reading for her mini schnauzer, I couldn't think of a polite way to refuse. The end result was I'd been tagged as some sort of psychic dog whisperer. And although Mrs. Larken had genuinely liked me and vice versa, Lila Chandler was something else entirely.

"Well, then perhaps Mr. Petriv might be here and you could introduce us? I'm told you're acquainted with him and he drops by quite frequently," Ms. Chandler said, meeting my gaze with a level one of her own.

Wonderful. Now the claws were out, along with the real reason for her visit. "I'm sorry, but he isn't here at the moment. Unfortunately, I can't predict when he'll decide to drop in."

"Oh, that is too bad. In that case, perhaps I should rethink this entire appointment. Things don't seem to be going well for either of us today, do they?"

Fuck. And now I was being threatened over a dog card reading.

"Not necessarily. I can run a combined reading for you and Sunbeam," I said brightly, and proceeded to shuffle the Tarot deck, making a mental note to tell Lotus to screen for dogs and their psycho owners beforehand. This would have never happened with Natty back on Earth. Then again, I'd never been in this situation on Earth.

extras

Sorry, Granny G, I thought out to the universe. *A gold note is still a gold note and a girl needs to eat and keep the shoe industry in business. I can't lose business on account of crazy.*

"Oh, how exciting!" Ms. Chandler exclaimed. Then she held her little dog to her face and proceeded to baby talk us to death. "Isn't that right, Sunbeam? Who's a good girl? You are! Mommy loves you. Yes, she does. You're going to get a card reading today! Yes, such a good girl," and on it went until I wanted to put all of us out of our collective misery. At least Sunbeam seemed happy given how quickly she gulped down her doggy treats.

Like my shop back on Earth, I'd used the same décor scheme of exotic Old World meets space-age New World, yet somehow the look hadn't translated well to Mars. And the fact that I now essentially had a day job was a little depressing. On Earth, I'd only worked nights. On Mars, it just hadn't attracted the same clientele, so I had to open during the day instead. The only time evenings were profitable was on weekends during the Witching Time. Then, I could pretty much double my fee. People expected a show extravagant enough to blow their minds, so I gave it to them. A Martian day, or rather a sol, was thirty-seven minutes and twenty-two seconds longer than an Earth day. For some reason people went wild then, as if the extra time meant the rules didn't exist. They partied harder, committed more crimes—even wanted their babies born then. And if it helped my shop's month-end numbers, who was I to argue?

Half an hour later, I walked Ms. Chandler out of my reading room and to the front reception area. I made sure she transferred her three hundred gold notes to the shop's account and reassured her I'd already uploaded the reading transcript to her CN-net memory blocks. Then I got her the hell out the door.

I'd jacked up the price on the spur of the moment, tripling the rate to include an annoyance fee—Sunbeam had passed out in a treat-induced coma after making little tiny doggy poops on my reading table. Besides, we both knew she hadn't come for a reading and wouldn't be a regular client. Nope, all she wanted was a glimpse of the infamous Alexei Petriv, leader of the Tsarist Consortium who was too damn hot for his own good, and to see if she could get the current competition out of her way. Namely, me.

I stood in the middle of my small reception area, taking deep breaths in hopes of avoiding a meltdown. I turned to Lotus, who'd skipped Career Design and looked at me like having me explode might be entertaining to watch. That she was my fourth cousin and had been recommended to me by family back on Earth sometimes made me regret I was such a softy when it came to my relatives.

"No more dogs, Lotus. I don't care how rich the client is, if they have a dog, I don't want to see them."

"Sorry, Felicia." Lotus hung her head, her blunt-edged pixie cut doing nothing to hide her face. She didn't look the slightest bit repentant anyway. Did I mention I come from a family of con artists? "But you have to admit, little Sunbeam was so cute! Did you see her little tiny doggy paws? I've never seen a teacup Yorkie before and I couldn't pass up the chance. Didn't they bring those back from extinction? Maybe you could get one and I could babysit on weekends?"

"Dogs are still too expensive to import from Earth, never mind finding a breeder here. And even if I could afford one, I'm not sure I'd trust you with it."

Lotus rolled her eyes. "Oh, come on, I'm very responsible.

Who practically runs things here? And we both know if you really wanted a dog, *he* would get it for you. The man would try to reterraform the planet if you said you thought Olympus Mons wasn't tall enough."

We both knew exactly who *he* was, and I wasn't going there. "I'm serious, no more dogs. Screen the clients first. If you get the slightest whiff of dog, forget it."

"Fine, whatever. I'll have Buckley sift them on the CN-net and let you know what shakes out," she said, referring to her boyfriend who was fully wired with t-mods, unlike me and Lotus, who relied on antiquated tech like charm-tex bracelets and visual flat-files on the CN-net. I wasn't sure I liked the idea of Buckley going through my potential clients, but my gut hadn't warned me away from him, so I decided to let it slide for now. "I thought you said you needed to increase the shop's revenue. You said—"

"I know what I said, but I changed my mind. I don't need that much money or the headaches that come from dealing with those women," I said, then ran a distracted hand through my hair and froze.

Ah, hell. I'd forgotten I braided a thin chain mesh weave through the nearly black waves that morning. Now my hand was stuck. I sighed as I tried to get free, pulling out a few strands in the process. Lotus watched me struggle before bursting out laughing and coming to rescue me from my own damned hair.

"You really should cut it off. It's so much less work," she said, gesturing to her own short hair.

Hers was just a shade lighter than mine, just like her eyes were more green, her skin a little more olive toned—everything in keeping with the Romani looks she shared with me and most of the Sevigny family. I just happened to look more like my mother, which drove my father crazy. Literally. Me too, actually, though not so literally. I'd gotten off easy in the crazy department, considering my mother had cloned me, then tried to kill me so many months ago. With family like that, it was a wonder I wasn't in therapy.

"I like it long," I said, even as I winced when she tried tugging at my two rings still caught in the mesh weave. "Ouch. Take it easy!"

"Sorry. And does *he* like it too?" she asked with seeming innocence. "I bet he does. I bet he wraps his fists in it and—"

"Just put whatever dirty thoughts you're thinking right out of your mind. We're at work and I'm not discussing this with you now."

"Fine. Don't be any fun. See if I care," Lotus griped. A beat of silence, a little bit of tugging, and my hand was out. "There, you're free, Medusa. You probably shouldn't wear that mesh thing anymore."

"You're probably right," I agreed as I pulled a few long black hairs out of my rings, all of them elaborate costume jewelry I'd brought from Earth. Maybe it was time I did away with all the props. It seemed like everything I used back home wasn't cutting it on Mars. Maybe I needed to rethink the whole business model. "And for the record, yes, he does like it. A lot. Now if you need me, I'll be sanitizing my reading table and spraying air freshener everywhere. Sunbeam shit on it in the middle of the reading."

"Oh, Felicia, I'm sorry!" Lotus laughed behind her hand, green eyes wide. "That's awful. You're right. No more dogs. Let me take care of that since I feel like it's my fault anyway. I'll get the cleaning stuff."

She headed to the supply closet where we kept a few basic cleaning supplies since the shop was professionally cleaned every evening. Then she froze, caught like a baby rabbit in some big bad hunter's trap. I blew out a snort. I knew the exact reason for her reaction. It was written all over her face, plus it wasn't the first time I'd seen this particular behavior from a woman before.

"Good afternoon. Nice to see you," Lotus said in girlish tones. Her cheeks flushed and her tongue darted out to lick her lips as if tasting something sweet.

I turned and my heartbeat seemed to skid to a halt before resuming again, just as I suspected it did for all the women who met him. Except in my case, I knew the look he wore was solely for me.

Alexei Petriv stood in the open doorway of my shop, removed his sunshades, and slid them into the breast pocket of his charcoal gray suit jacket. Tall, broad-shouldered, well-muscled, and built like a rock, he seemed to fill every room he entered with his presence alone. He didn't have to do anything other than just stand there, and he was still overwhelming. His thick black hair fell nearly to his shoulders and his eyes were so intensely blue, sometimes I wondered if they could cut into me if they stared at me long enough. At the very least, they gave the disturbing illusion they could look into your soul. Saying he was gorgeous and sexy as hell was a ridiculous understatement. In fact, words failed me. His MH Factor was off the charts, up in some stratosphere no one could calculate. The same could be said for his t-mods, meaning his mind could manipulate the

Cerebral Neural Net in ways few others could. Looking at him left me breathless and sometimes made me doubt what I saw was real because he was utterly perfect. So perfect, in fact, that he might not actually be human anymore.

I'd secretly been cataloguing the oddities I'd noticed during our time together. So far as I could tell, he never got sick—not even a cold. If he hurt himself, such as when he'd once sliced his palm with a paring knife, the wound healed within a few hours. He needed very little sleep, and some nights I wondered if he even slept at all. He was definitely stronger than average and had no trouble keeping in shape, though he worked out like a fiend and forced me to go to the gym with him, which hadn't thrilled me. He could hold his breath for ridiculously long periods of time, something I'd learned when we'd gone on a day trip to Aeolian Beach. And one thing I'd discovered almost immediately the first time I'd slept with him—he needed almost zero recovery time before he was ready to go again. Sometimes it was thrilling to have that much attention. Other times, it was exhausting and made me wonder how I could ever be enough for him. However, I didn't let myself dwell on it. If I did, I knew I might flee the room screaming, which even I knew wasn't appropriate behavior when your boyfriend came to visit you halfway through the day.

"Hello, Lotus. Glad to see you're doing well," he said in that deep voice of his, a slight hint of a Russian accent present. Sometimes it felt like that voice could slide around your mind, commanding you do to things you weren't entirely sure were a good idea. Or maybe I was the only one he had that effect on?

"I'm fine, Mr. Petriv. Thanks for asking." Lotus continued to stand there gaping, mouth slightly open. I rolled my eyes. Was it *always* going to be like this when other women had his attention?

"Dog shit, Lotus. Remember?" I reminded her, none too subtly.

Lotus shook herself and flushed a brilliant shade of red. "Oh right. Sorry. I forgot. I'll get that cleaned up right away. Excuse me."

In a flash, she was at the supply closet, gathering up some rags and a spray bottle of cleaning solution. Then she disappeared into the backroom, slamming the door so hard behind her, I winced.

"Sorry about that. It's been an interesting day."

"Another dog card reading?" Alexei asked, arching an eyebrow. He left the doorframe and crossed the shop to me, fighting to stop a grin from filling his face. "How many has it been this week? Three? Four?"

I shrugged. "Four, but who's counting?"

"You are."

"Lotus is enamored with dogs lately so she keeps booking pet readings whether I want them or not. She seems to think I should ask you to get me one too."

He laughed. "Do you want a dog?"

"Not if they're going to get excited and shit on everything I own. At least this latest did it on my table, so that's something new." I looked around the shop—a shop that wasn't as successful as I'd hoped it would be. I was doing okay, but not like I had been back home, and I couldn't figure out why. I missed Charlie Zero and his business savvy.

"I assume you were able to convince the owner to stay for a reading of her own?"

"Of course, but you know they're only here because they're hoping to catch a glimpse of you. It's like I have to beat the women away with a stick and it's getting exhausting."

He'd reached me now and his hands were on me, sliding along my neck to tilt my face up. Even in my highest heels, my eyes were barely level with his shoulder. My gaze locked with his and my neck arched under his hands. "You have to stop doing this to yourself, Felicia. You're making yourself crazy and imagining things that don't exist. I have no interest in any other woman."

I swallowed. "I know, but it's hard when I have yet another Martian blueblood in here, judging me. I never cared about any of that before and now...Now it seems to be bothering me all the time."

His expression hardened. "I hate it when you do that, compare yourself to things I have no interest in, because there is no comparison." He looked like he wanted to say more or maybe even yell at me. Instead he stopped and his mouth quirked at the corners. "Besides, you're the only one who can keep me from jumping off the deep end into megalomania—or so you keep reminding me."

"Very funny. Someone needs to keep you humble or you'll think you own the tri-system."

"Actually, I believe I only own half of it, or thereabouts," he said drily. His hands drifted down my body, coming to rest in the small of my back. "Tell me who was here and made you feel this way, and I'll deal with it. Then it's no longer a problem."

It sounded tempting, but I'd noticed that sometimes Alexei's way of dealing with problems tended to be extreme, with no chance for the other party to recover. Depending on what he was after, such as securing ownership of most of the off-world asteroid mines, it ran the gamut from driving his opponents to financial ruin, undercutting prices on business rivals, or pitting family members against each other and taking advantage of the chaos. While none of it was technically illegal, it didn't sit well with me—and those were just the things I knew about. The Tsarist Consortium was considered a legitimate corporate and political entity with plans to revolutionize lives throughout the tri-system, but you could never forget how it started, or where its roots lay. They'd come a long way, but not far enough in some people's minds.

Long before me, I knew that as Alexei worked his way up the Consortium hierarchy, he'd seduced both wives and girlfriends, using his looks and his perfect body to gain whatever secrets they'd offer him regarding the men in their lives. Then he'd use those secrets to either buy or steal whatever it was he was after. I suspected that was why he didn't seem to care about how he looked or the things he was able to do. To him, his body was just another tool to be used.

"I'm a big girl. I'll get over it. It just puts me in a bad mood whenever I have to deal with one of . . . them. Privileged and entitled, with no idea what the rest of us have to deal with. So much for One Gov's unity ideals and all citizens being equal under the law. What are you doing here, anyway? Aren't you supposed to be at your office holding secret closed-door meetings all day?"

"My plans changed and I needed to see you," he said, leaning in to brush a kiss along my throat.

It made me sigh and melt into him, my hands sliding over the ridges of well-muscled abdomen until my arms were around his waist under his jacket. My head dropped to his shoulder and the kiss at my throat turned into something more heated. Soon, he kissed along the line of my jaw and his tongue ran the outer edge of my ear. My hands fisted in his shirt as I wondered how fast I could get to his bare skin. Still, some measure of common sense clamped down on my lust-filled brain.

"This is all really nice, but Lotus is in the other room and I have another appointment in about fifteen minutes." Weird how my voice had gone all breathy and I was barely holding my own weight as I leaned into him. How the hell had he gotten one of my legs hooked around his hip and my dress bunched at my waist so quickly?

He raised his head and the dark look he gave me made my toes curl and had me squirming against him. "We both know I don't need very long to get you exactly where I want you."

No, he didn't. Still… "I don't have time for this right now! It might get awkward when my next client walks in and you have me bent over the reception desk." Which he'd done to me before and I'd totally do again even if it was a bit uncomfortable. "Come to my place tonight. I can have dinner ready for seven if I rush."

Was it weird we didn't live together? Maybe. I wasn't sure. It was another one of those things I didn't think about too much or I'd start doubting myself and let my insecurities eat away at me. I'd never been so on edge in a relationship before. With Alexei Petriv the highs were so high, they could be terrifying, but the lows were equally scary. How could I hold on to someone so frighteningly perfect and fundamentally dark when the only thing I had going for me was luck—another thing I filed under unresolved issues not to be examined too hard.

Alexei let me go, setting me on my feet and letting my dress settle around my hips. His expression became rueful. "That's why I'm here now, and what I wanted to talk to you about. There's been a slight change in plans."

I frowned. "Slight change how, exactly? Does this have anything to do with the big project you've been working on? The one that's supposed to free up more of your time?"

"Or get me out of the Consortium muck, as you so elegantly put it." He grinned a little and I jabbed him lightly in the chest with my finger.

"Hey, that's not what I said! Just that sometimes the Consortium does things that scare me and I don't want to have to pick a side."

"I know what you meant." He caught my hand and kissed the knuckles. "I can't say I was thrilled with the Consortium's approach either, but at least now the mining unions are under unified leadership and we avoided an all-out revolt with the workers. There were issues with some of the mines collapsing, but production yield didn't drop, and no one in the tri-system knew the difference. The troublemakers were handled discretely to avoid publicity, and it showed both the unions and the Consortium in the best possible light. The union leadership would rather deal directly with me than any One Gov agents they send into the field. My being here on Mars has actually made things easier."

I rolled my eyes. "Isn't it lucky you were here, then?"

"Yes, it was." He kissed the inside of my wrist before letting my hand go. "And now that it's done, I'm scaling back. I can focus on things closer to home and spend less time directly on-site. That means more time for us."

My breath caught in a tiny gasp. "Really?"

He grinned. "Yes, really. Unfortunately"—and there the grin faded—"I still need to wrap up this union project and the final timing has been advanced significantly. I'll need to be off-planet for a few weeks to ensure all the key players are in place. Konstantin specifically requested I attend negotiations, so I can't delegate it to someone else."

Konstantin Belikov. The name made me shiver. At nearly five hundred years old, the man had seen things and lived through events that would have sent most people screaming. He'd survived the Dark Times on Earth when the polar ice caps melted, earthquakes ravaged continents, and billions had died. He watched as humanity terraformed Mars and turned it into a paradise, and laughed as they struggled to do the same with Venus, with still less than spectacular results. He knew how to work every angle and drafted plots inside of plots. He was ruthlessness personified and lived his life to ensure the Tsarist Consortium would one day replace One Gov as the ruling power in the tri-system.

He'd all but raised Alexei and ensured Alexei took over as head of the Consortium. He also wasn't pleased I'd lured him away to Mars since wherever Alexei went, so went the Consortium's power. And frankly, I resented the accusations. When I left for Mars, I hadn't even known Alexei was alive. I wasn't in a position to lure him anywhere. I was just glad I was safely here on Mars, and Belikov was hundreds of millions of miles away on Earth. Sometimes though, I wondered if that was far enough.

I ran my hands absently over his chest, enjoying the defined ridges as I looked up at him. "A few weeks? How long is a few?"

"Two, possibly three at most."

"*Three?* You've never been gone that long before! Where are you going? Is it safe? Is it to the mines on Vesta or Pallas? Can't someone else go instead?" It was the only thing that made sense since it wasn't possible to travel to any of the asteroid belt mines and back in a few weeks. Vesta and Pallas both orbited Mars, so a three-week trip was doable. Didn't mean I liked it though.

"I'm afraid not. This is something I need to oversee personally. The union leaders will only work with me and those collapses need to be fully investigated."

"But it's for so long. Will you at least shim me?"

He touched my hair, running his finger through the strands and toying with the mesh. I might have made a joke about how he was more handsy than usual, but right then, I needed the contact. "Konstantin requires a complete blackout on this. Close-looped Consortium access only."

I frowned, not happy with anything I was hearing. A secret mission and that sneaky asshole Belikov was involved. Alexei would be gone for possibly three weeks and I couldn't contact him. It went without saying my gut kicked me hard enough to almost knock the breath out of me. That scared me too. I hadn't had a feeling this intense in months—not since I'd arrived on Mars. I thought everything had settled down. Apparently I was wrong.

"I know it's a long time to be out of contact," he murmured, brushing a hand along my cheek and tilting my face back to his. "I also know you don't trust him, and neither do I to some extent, but he has significant power in the Consortium."

"I don't have a good feeling about it. Are you sure you have to go?"

A kiss on each of my cheeks, then my hairline. "I'm doing it for us," he whispered. "When this is finished and I've secured the Consortium's power base on Mars, we can begin making inroads into One Gov's leadership. That's when I can pull back. I may be the head of the Consortium, but I'm not here to appoint myself king of Mars."

I knew there was something in his words I was missing, but my focus had turned inward, picking at my gut feeling like a tongue wiggling a loose tooth.

"And unfortunately, we're leaving tonight. They're waiting for me outside. I just couldn't go without seeing you first."

That brought me up short and broke through the fog. I pulled back enough to look at him, my roaming hands going still. "Right now? You're leaving me *right now*, for three weeks?"

"I know, I'm sorry, Felicia. I was just informed of the change in plans today. You know I would never tell you like this if I could avoid it." Alexei's hands were on my forearms, his thumbs stroking the inside of my wrists. And he looked genuinely sorry too, sorry enough that I had a moment where I wondered if I could pull him into my card reading room and convince him to stay. But no, Lotus was back there, and my gut was kicking me hard enough that I needed to pay attention to it. Unfortunately the feeling was so vague, I didn't know what to focus on.

So I said what, to me, was the most logical thing in the world: "I need to run my cards."

His hands tightened, stopping me when I would have pulled away. "No."

"Why not? It won't take long."

"No," he said, more firmly this time.

"But…" I looked up into at his face, bewildered. "Something isn't right and I want to check into it."

"No, Felicia. Don't." His voice had gone very soft. "I don't want you to run a spread for me. Not now. Not ever."

Stunned, I'm sure my jaw dropped open. This wasn't anything we'd ever talked about before. Actually now that I thought about it, he'd never really asked me to run the cards for him except for when we'd first met. There was a seriousness in his tone that made me wary. "But it's what I do. I'm good at it. Why wouldn't I run them for you if something feels off?"

"Because I don't ever want you to think I'm with you because your luck gene twisted events in your favor, or I'm using you for some advantage you'll give me over everyone else. I'm with you because I want to be with you. Because you're the only woman I want."

Then he leaned down to kiss me, just a brushing of his lips over mine before he pulled away. It was the kind of kiss he gave me when he was trying hard to be gentle but in reality wanted to throw me down on the nearest flat surface and bury himself inside me for hours. I knew it and he knew it, and I think I may have swooned a little because he reached out to steady me and chuckled softly.

"As you say, there's no time for that, or you know I would," he murmured.

"But…My cards…Fine, I guess. If you don't want a reading, I can't force you," I managed to sputter out.

Behind him, the door to my shop opened and two Consortium bodyguards stepped inside, tall, overly developed muscle with close-cropped hair, the ubiquitous sunshades, and wearing identical black suits so it was impossible to tell one from the other. Though I had my suspicions, I'd never been able to get Alexei to confirm if the Consortium grew all their muscle out of the same vat of genetic goo or what their Modified Human Factor might be.

"Looks like your ride's here," I said, peeking around his shoulder.

He threw a negligent look behind him before refocusing on me. "So it would seem. We'll have to table the rest of this for later." He brushed a thumb over my cheek and across my lips as if memorizing the contours of my face before he kissed my forehead. "I'll be back as soon as I can."

Then he let me go, turned on his heel, and left the shop. The Consortium chain-breakers fell into step behind him. And I was left with nothing but a sharp ache of loneliness that wasn't going away anytime soon, a gut feeling Alexei didn't want me to investigate, and an appointment who tripped through the door staring wide-eyed after Alexei and carrying—gods help me—another dog.

if you enjoyed

THE RULE OF LUCK

look out for

SIX WAKES

by

Mur Lafferty

*A lone ship. A murdered crew. And a clone who must find
her own killer—before they strike again.*

*In the depths of space, it's pretty normal to wake up in a
cloning vat. The streaks of blood, however? Not so normal.*

*Maria Arena has been cloned before. Usually when she
awakens as a new clone, her first memory is of how she died.
This time, she has no idea. Her memories are incomplete.*

And Maria isn't the only one to have died recently.

THIS IS NOT A PIPE

Sound struggled to make its way through the thick synthamneo fluid. Once it reached Maria Arena's ears, it sounded like a chain saw: loud, insistent, and unending. She couldn't make out the words, but it didn't sound like a situation she wanted to be involved in.

Her reluctance at her own rebirth reminded her where she was, and who she was. She grasped for her last backup. The crew had just moved into their quarters on the *Dormire*, and the cloning bay had been the last room they'd visited on their tour. There they had done their first backup on the ship.

Maria must have been in an accident or something soon after, killing her and requiring her next clone to wake. Sloppy use of a life wouldn't make a good impression on the captain, who likely was the source of the angry chain-saw noise.

Maria finally opened her eyes. She tried to make sense of the dark round globules floating in front of her vat, but it was difficult with the freshly cloned brain being put to work for the first time. There were too many things wrong with such a mess.

With the smears on the outside of the vat and the purple color through the bluish fluid Maria floated in, she figured the orbs were blood drops. Blood shouldn't float. That was the first problem. If blood was floating, that meant the grav drive that spun the ship had failed. That was probably another reason someone was yelling. The blood and the grav drive.

Blood in a cloning bay, that was different too. Cloning bays were pristine, clean places, where humans were downloaded into newly cloned bodies when the previous ones had died. It was much cleaner and less painful than human birth, with all its screaming and blood.

Again with the blood.

The cloning bay had six vats in two neat rows, filled with blue-tinted synth-amneo fluid and the waiting clones of the rest of the crew. Blood belonged in the medbay, down the hall. The unlikely occurrence of a drop of blood originating in the medbay, floating down the hall, and entering the cloning bay to float in front of Maria's vat would be extraordinary. But that's not what happened; a body floated above the blood drops. A number of bodies, actually.

Finally, if the grav drive *had* failed, and if someone *had* been injured in the cloning bay, another member of the crew would have cleaned up the blood. Someone was always on call to ensure a new clone made the transition from death into their new body smoothly.

No. A perfect purple sphere of blood shouldn't be floating in front of her face.

Maria had now been awake for a good minute or so. No one worked the computer to drain the synth-amneo fluid to free her.

A small part of her brain began to scream at her that she should be more concerned about the bodies, but only a small part.

She'd never had occasion to use the emergency release valve inside the cloning vats. Scientists had implemented them after some techs had decided to play a prank on a clone, and woke her up only to leave her in the vat alone for hours. When she had gotten free, stories said, the result was messy and violent, resulting in the fresh cloning of some of the techs. After that, engineers added an interior release switch for clones to let themselves out of the tank if they were trapped for whatever reason.

Maria pushed the button and heard a *clunk* as the release triggered, but the synth-amneo fluid stayed where it was.

A drain relied on gravity to help the fluid along its way. Plumbing 101 there. The valve was opened but the fluid remained a stubborn womb around Maria.

She tried to find the source of the yelling. One of the crew floated near the computer bank, naked, with wet hair stuck out in a frightening, spiky corona. Another clone woke. Two of them had died?

Behind her, crewmates floated in four vats. All of their eyes were open, and each was searching for the emergency release. Three *clunk*s sounded, but they remained in the same position Maria was in.

Maria used the other emergency switch to open the vat door. Ideally it would have been used after the fluid had drained away, but there was little ideal about this situation. She and a good quantity of the synth-amneo fluid floated out of her vat, only to collide gently with the orb of blood floating in front of her. The surface tension of both fluids held, and the drop bounced away.

Maria hadn't encountered the problem of how to get out of a liquid prison in zero-grav. She experimented by flailing about, but only made some fluid break off the main bubble and go floating away. In her many lives, she'd been in more than one undignified situation, but this was new.

Action and reaction, she thought, and inhaled as much of the oxygen-rich fluid as she could, then forced everything out of her lungs as if she were sneezing. She didn't go as fast as she would have if it had been air, because she was still inside viscous fluid, but it helped push her backward and out of the bubble. She inhaled air and then coughed and vomited the rest of the fluid in a spray in front of her, banging her head on the computer console as her body's involuntary movements propelled her farther.

Finally out of the fluid, and gasping for air, she looked up. "Oh shit."

Three dead crewmates floated around the room amid the blood and other fluids. Two corpses sprouted a number of gory, tentacles, bloody bubbles that refused to break away from the deadly wounds. A fourth was strapped to a chair at the terminal.

Gallons of synth-amneo fluid joined the gory detritus as the newly cloned crew fought to exit their vats. They looked with as much shock as she felt at their surroundings.

Captain Katrina de la Cruz moved to float beside her, still

focused on the computer. "Maria, stop staring and make yourself useful. Check on the others."

Maria scrambled for a handhold on the wall to pull herself away from the captain's attempt to access the terminal.

Katrina pounded on a keyboard and poked at the console screen. "IAN, what the hell happened?"

"My speech functions are inaccessible," the computer's male, slightly robotic voice said.

"Ceci n'est pas une pipe," muttered a voice above Maria. It broke her shock and reminded her of the captain's order to check on the crew.

The speaker was Akihiro Sato, pilot and navigator. She had met him a few hours ago at the cocktail party before the launch of the *Dormire*.

"Hiro, why are you speaking French?" Maria said, confused. "Are you all right?"

"Someone saying aloud that they can't talk is like that old picture of a pipe that says, 'This is not a pipe.' It's supposed to give art students deep thoughts. Never mind." He waved his hand around the cloning bay. "What happened, anyway?"

"I have no idea," she said. "But—God, what a mess. I have to go check on the others."

"Goddammit, you just spoke," the captain said to the computer, dragging some icons around the screen. "Something's working inside there. Talk to me, IAN."

"My speech functions are inaccessible," the AI said again, and de la Cruz slammed her hand down on the keyboard, grabbing it to keep herself from floating away from it.

Hiro followed Maria as she maneuvered around the room using the handholds on the wall. Maria found herself face-to-face with the gruesome body of Wolfgang, their second in command. She gently pushed him aside, trying not to dislodge the gory, bloody tentacles sprouting from punctures on his body.

She and Hiro floated toward the living Wolfgang, who was doubled over coughing the synth-amneo out of his lungs. "What the hell is going on?" he asked in a ragged voice.

"You know as much as we do," Maria said. "Are you all right?"

He nodded and waved her off. He straightened his back, gaining at least another foot on his tall frame. Wolfgang was born on the moon colony, Luna, several generations of his family developing the long bones of living their whole lives in low gravity. He took a handhold and propelled himself toward the captain.

"What do you remember?" Maria asked Hiro as they approached another crewmember.

"My last backup was right after we boarded the ship. We haven't even left yet," Hiro said.

Maria nodded. "Same for me. We should still be docked, or only a few weeks from Earth."

"I think we have more immediate problems, like our current status," Hiro said.

"True. Our current status is four of us are dead," Maria said, pointing at the bodies. "And I'm guessing the other two are as well."

"What could kill us all?" Hiro asked, looking a bit green as he dodged a bit of bloody skin. "And what happened to me and the captain?"

He referred to the "other two" bodies that were not floating in the cloning bay. Wolfgang, their engineer, Paul Seurat, and

Dr. Joanna Glass all were dead, floating around the room, gently bumping off vats or one another.

Another cough sounded from the last row of vats, then a soft voice. "Something rather violent, I'd say."

"Welcome back, Doctor, you all right?" Maria asked, pulling herself toward the woman.

The new clone of Joanna nodded, her tight curls glistening with the synth-amneo. Her upper body was thin and strong, like all new clones, but her legs were small and twisted. She glanced up at the bodies and pursed her lips. "What happened?" She didn't wait for them to answer, but grasped a handhold and pulled herself toward the ceiling where a body floated.

"Check on Paul," Maria said to Hiro, and followed Joanna.

The doctor turned her own corpse to where she could see it, and her eyes grew wide. She swore quietly. Maria came up behind her and swore much louder.

Her throat had a stab wound, with great waving gouts of blood reaching from her neck. If the doctor's advanced age was any indication, they were well past the beginning of the mission. Maria remembered her as a woman who looked to be in her thirties, with smooth dark skin and black hair. Now wrinkles lined the skin around her eyes and the corners of her mouth, and gray shot through her tightly braided hair. Maria looked at the other bodies; from her vantage point she could now see each also showed his or her age.

"I didn't even notice," she said, breathless. "I—I only noticed the blood and gore. We've been on this ship for *decades*. Do you remember anything?"

"No." Joanna's voice was flat and grim. "We need to tell the captain."